D1617189

THE GOOD SHEPHERD

BOOKS BY THOMAS FLEMING

FICTION

The Sandbox Tree
Romans Countrymen Lovers
A Cry of Whiteness
King of the Hill
The God of Love
All Good Men

NONFICTION

The Forgotten Victory
The Man Who Dared Lightning
The Man from Monticello
West Point
One Small Candle
Beat the Last Drum
Now We Are Enemies

the
good shepherd

A NOVEL BY
THOMAS FLEMING

Doubleday & Company, Inc.
GARDEN CITY, NEW YORK   1974

*All of the characters in this book are fictitious,
and any resemblance to actual persons, living or
dead, is purely coincidental, with the exception
of obvious historical and contemporary public
figures identified by name*

Library of Congress Cataloging in Publication Data

Fleming, Thomas J
 The good shepherd.

    I. Title.
PZ4.F5987Gof [PS3556.L45] 813'.5'4
ISBN 0-385-03746-5
LIBRARY OF CONGRESS CATALOG CARD NUMBER 73–82246

I am come that they may have life and have it more abundantly. I am the good shepherd. The good shepherd giveth his life for his sheep.

—JOHN 10:10–11

As for us, we are philosophers not in word, but in acts; we do not say great things, but we do live them.

—THASCIUS CAECILIANUS CYPRIANUS
BISHOP OF CARTHAGE, 248–258

Roma locuta est, causa finita est.
(Rome has spoken, the matter is closed.)

—ANONYMOUS

THE GOOD SHEPHERD

I

The silver-haired woman walked to the window of her penthouse and gazed down at the city. It was twilight. Faint echoes of the evening traffic's cacophony drifted up to her, muted by her closed windows and the hum of her air conditioners. For a moment Rome was a panorama of magic beauty. The ribbons of streetlights, the headlights of the moving cars, the glow of the illuminated piazzas, were a gigantic festival being staged for her benefit. All because of this piece of paper that she held in her hand, a letter that began: *Your friend will be one of five Americans. The news will be announced tomorrow. . . .*

Beyond the dark hollow of the Tiber, the dome of St. Peter's suddenly rose from the shadows of Trastevere as the floodlights came on. The woman's eyes recoiled from the huge bulbous mass of stone. Not so many years ago the sight of it had soothed and strengthened her. Now it only seemed to arouse enormous sadness in her.

Last night, standing here, she had seen the dome suddenly sprout enormous cracks. Like a huge empty eggshell, it had crumpled before her eyes. Below her the city had become a deadly tempter, the indifferent lights, the mocking sounds whispering: *Come. Come into my meaningless arms.* With sickening panic she had jerked the drapes closed.

Tonight the woman was able to turn her back on St. Peter's dome and walk briskly out of her apartment. She rode to the ground floor in a creaking Eiffel Tower vintage elevator with elaborate black iron scrollwork and walked swiftly through the lobby to the street. She wore a white linen suit and almost no makeup. Her purse, her shoes, were also white. She paused before the wrought-iron doors of the apartment and took a deep breath of the soft air of Roman spring. Past her on the Via Margutta flowed a motley parade of art lovers, some young, dressed in the kinky violently colored clothes that were being sold in several nearby shops, others wearing the more soberly shaped and tinted styles of middle age. She enjoyed the Via Margutta, which doubled as Rome's Carnaby Street and East Village with "now" boutiques beside art galleries and antique stores.

Behind her, unseen and unnoticed, the portiere of the apartment sat at his small narrow window on the street level, swigging beer from a bottle. He was about fifty, a fat little man with bulging, piggish eyes. "There she goes to her lover again," he grunted.

From the kitchen of their tiny apartment, his wife, who resembled him in shape and size, unleashed a stream of vituperation on him and on Italian men in general. The American madonna was beautiful, she swore, but in a spiritual way, a way utterly beyond his animal understanding.

The portiere studied the woman's firm American rump, barely listening to his wife's insults. "I still say she has a lover," he said. "It can be seen by a discerning man. There is something about the way a woman carries herself, once she has awakened a man's desire."

"Perhaps," said his wife, "the desire of a real man. Would that I had had the experience. Perhaps I, too, would have a walk that made men lecherous."

Unaware of the exchange of insults she was generating, the woman in white strode swiftly along the Via Margutta for a few hundred yards and turned down a short silent alley that led to the Via del Babuino. She scarcely glanced at the ravaged Roman statue of Silenus, the drunken old satyr who told King Midas that it was happiest for a man not to be born at all, and failing that to die as soon as possible. Covered with moss and dust, a yellow cigarette butt thrust into his leering mouth, the statue looked more animal than human and gave the Street of the Baboon its name. The woman in white hurried purposively past more antique stores and art galleries. Several times an owner or a staff member rushed to the doorway to call, "Good evening, Signora." She acknowledged the greetings with the smile of an old customer.

In three or four minutes she emerged from the Via del Babuino into the Piazza di Spagna. Guitars twanged through the deepening twilight, and cigarettes glowed up and down the ancient yellow steps, where the embassy of imperial Spain had once sent orders to popes. A half-hundred young people from a dozen nations, most of them wearing clothes and hair that made them sexually indistinguishable, lounged on the steps. Some of them were singing; most stared dully. The woman in white was glad it was too dark to see their faces. The vacuous boredom on so many of them, especially the American faces, always pained her.

She stepped into a small black cab at the head of the taxi rank near the Spanish Steps and said in perfect Italian, "The Church of St. Peter in Chains, please." The driver made a sharp turn into the Via del Babuino while pedestrians fled before his horn. Another swift turn and he was racing down a narrow alley to the Via del Corso, Rome's main street. Here his Italian fondness for physical combat with other drivers flowered. Roaring down the special lane reserved for commercial traffic, he charged between buses and taxis, passed first on the left, then on the right, his horn challenging all comers.

The woman in white sat in the back seat scarcely noticing that her life was in danger. She had survived too many similar rides. Instead, she looked out at the city that was flowing by her window. Halfway down the Corso, she peered into the Piazza Colonna, dominated by the immense column commemorating the victories of the Emperor Marcus Aurelius. Discreetly parked against the buildings of the piazza were gray buses full of riot police. The Palazzo Chigi, home of one of Renaissance Rome's proudest families, was now the office of the Prime Minister of Italy. The Houses of Parliament were also nearby, and this made the Piazza Colonna the favorite arena for Rome's increasingly violent political demonstrations. One day it was the Communists, the next the neo-Fascists, the next the students. At times Rome seemed a city on the brink of chaos.

Another minute or two of reckless driving, and the cab was crawling through the permanent traffic jam of the Piazza Venezia. The woman in white gazed somberly up at the balcony where Mussolini had harangued his Black Shirts and declared his wars. Five minutes later, they were skirting the foot of the Capitol Hill, passing the huge dazzling white marble monument to King Victor Emmanuel II and the unity of Italy, agleam in its nightly bath of floodlights. To Romans it was "the wedding cake," an oblique

3

comment on the mediocrity of both the monument and the Royal family.

Now they were racing down the broad Via dei Fori Imperiali, the Road of the Imperial Forums, where pathetic fragments of ancient Rome's power and glory gleamed in another battery of floodlights. At the head of the street was the Colosseum, with its multiple mouths full of gray darkness, a living monument to ancient Rome's other heritage, her incredible bestiality. Halfway down the Via dei Fori Imperiale, the cabdriver made a heroic left turn which hurtled them past oncoming cars; all their drivers, of course, refused to touch their brakes.

Exultantly shifting gears, the cabdriver headed up the shabby Via Cavour. Already the prostitutes in their net stockings and gold miniskirts and silver lamé blouses were strolling past the dreary pensions and fifth-rate hotels. Opposite the glossily modern Hotel Palatino, which looked like a rich American tourist bravely maintaining his composure among the natives, the cabdriver stopped. The woman in white slipped lire into his hand and got out.

Walking once more with a stride that belied her gray hair, she entered a dark narrow passageway that ran uphill. The tunnel ran beneath the slope of the Borgias. Above it were the grim tower and palace where once lived Vannozza dei Catanei, the mistress of Pope Alexander VI and the mother of Lucrezia and Cesare Borgia and the rest of that murderous clan.

At the end of the passageway the woman in white emerged into a small cobblestone square. On the right were flats with windows aglow. On the left was an old church, built in the fifth century. A man in a white shirt stood in the doorway. The woman took a black veil from her purse and draped it over her carefully molded silver hair. At the doorway, she slipped money into the man's hand and murmured, "Thank you, Mario."

He nodded. "I will wait," he said.

She entered the church and stood in the back for a moment, gazing at the marble statue on the right. It was by Michelangelo, and it depicted Moses not long after he had received the Ten Commandments on Mount Sinai. It was surrounded by a half-dozen other statues, all obviously inferior to this massive masterpiece. Beneath the high altar, candles gleamed on the bronze doors of the reliquary containing the chains that had reputedly bound St. Peter in Jerusalem.

4

The woman in white had not come to worship a relic or admire a statue. Nor had she come to pray. She had come to commune with two men who had brought her to this church ten years ago, two men whom she loved in a way that she herself sometimes found hard to understand, a way that was impossible to explain to anyone else. Especially the love that she felt for the man who was still alive.

He was almost four thousand miles away from her across the dark Mediterranean and darker Africa and the vast shadowy Atlantic. But standing here in this church, she felt his presence, could almost hear his voice, see him smile. She could relive for a brief fierce moment the days and weeks and months when her love for him had been a constant torment. Yet she found strength, even a bittersweet happiness in this memory. Now this man meant something more profound, more immense, than that old lost passionate wish to touch him, to hold him and be held by him. He had acquired a meaning that pervaded her soul.

The woman in white had come here often for this communion during the past five years. More than once it had sustained her when she thought her heart was about to wither like the skin of a gutted tangerine. But tonight she had not come seeking the mysterious strength this man emanated. She had come to commune with his joy, to share with him the joy she felt, too.

For five minutes she stood there, her mind, even her body, radiant. Then she thought of the other man, the one who was dead, and a shadow seemed to fall upon her joy. On the altar the candlelight suddenly flickered weirdly. A frown appeared on Moses' marble brow. She raised her eyes into the darkness beneath the roof of the Church of St. Peter in Chains and whispered: "Watch over us, Don Angelo, watch over us, *please*."

II

At that very moment the man for whom the woman in Rome was praying emerged from his limousine and paused, almost blinded by the bright 11 A.M. American sunshine. With the black seven-passenger Cadillac behind him, he looked like a fan-

5

tasy figure, a man from a time machine or a creature from another planet. On his head he wore a tall elliptical purple and gold miter; in his hand was a bronze shepherd's crosier. He was dressed in purple and gold vestments. A gold cross on a field of purple decorated the chasuble which hung from his shoulders to his knees. A purple and gold cope covered his shoulders and was fastened across his chest by a gold clasp. On his feet were square-toed purple shoes with large silver buckles.

The sun was warm. Only a faint breath of March's often chilly wind stirred the air. Archbishop Matthew Mahan was not in the least disturbed by the humdrum architecture of the church that confronted him. The building was little more than a big slant-roofed red brick rectangle, with a touch of pseudo-Georgian architecture in its white doors and trim. Instead, he noted with silent approval the fresh white paint glistening on the doors. Beside the church the massive rectory, also in red brick, showed the same meticulous maintenance. Across a huge blacktop parking lot, half full of gleaming new station wagons and sleek sedans, the one-story red brick school, built cluster style with walkways between the separate buildings, occupied the entire north side of the block. Up and down the surrounding streets spread the one-acre zoned homes of affluent Catholics which prompted younger priests to call this suburb the Golden Ghetto.

The sarcasm might have disturbed some churchmen in the year of our Lord 1969. But Matthew Mahan prided himself on being a realist. The Church had to serve both the affluent and the poor. If the sight of Holy Angels Church and school stirred any emotion in him, it was pride. His energy, his vision, had planned this center of Catholic life, when the Golden Ghetto was still on the drawing boards of the real estate men. Even more of his energy had raised the money to pay for the nearby Catholic high school, which guaranteed Catholic parents a religious education for their children, from kindergarten through the twelfth grade. It was this kind of foresight, this kind of awareness of the folkways of the modern family, with its seemingly tireless compulsion to flee ever farther from the smoggy city, that had won Matthew Mahan the admiration—and cooperation—of the state's real estate entrepreneurs.

There was also nothing in the least disturbing about the three priests and the crowd of smiling smartly dressed parents who waited for him at the doors of Holy Angels Church. From pug nose and square jaw to bulging belly, Monsignor Paul O'Reilly looked like the personification of the traditional Irish pastor, stern but kind. Flanking him, Fathers Emil Novak and Charles Cannon seemed model curates, earnest, humble, a little timid in the presence of authority. No, Matthew Mahan thought ironically, nothing here to disturb an Archbishop.

But something was disturbing this Archbishop. Beneath his purple and gold vestments, just below the knotted white cincture around his waist, symbol of the whips with which Jesus had been beaten by the thugs of the High Priest, prowled a malevolent pain. It seemed to open and close with every breath he took, like some exotic tropical flower. This morning at 4 A.M., when it had awakened him, another metaphor had suggested itself: a rotating medieval mailed fist with jagged spears on its knuckles. The bread and wine he had consumed at his morning mass, followed by a well-filled plate of bacon and eggs and home-fried potatoes, had temporarily stilled it. But the pain had returned in this more subtle flowering guise as his Cadillac rolled off the expressway and entered the Golden Ghetto.

Since he had recovered from the measles at the age of nine, Matthew Mahan had never had a serious illness. He was not the sort of man who liked to admit that any aspect of his job troubled him. Whatever was happening in his innards, it had nothing to do with the knowledge that behind Monsignor Paul O'Reilly's formal smile of welcome lay inveterate treachery and hatred. Nor was it caused by knowing that behind the timidity on the faces of Fathers Novak and Cannon lay fear and loathing and rebellion. Nor would the Archbishop admit that the pain had anything to do with the weariness that seeped through his body as he paused beside his limousine. Instead, he made the usual promise: Tonight you will go to bed on time, no matter how many letters are undictated or committee or commission reports unread.

He glanced at his wristwatch. They were only ten minutes late—not disastrous if what was to come inside the church and rectory ran on time. With abrupt irritation the Archbishop turned and peered into the dim interior of the limousine. "Come on, Dennis," he said, "we've got a schedule to keep."

The pale freckled face of Father Dennis McLaughlin, made even paler by the round white collar beneath it, responded with a nod.

7

He was frantically clipping notes to pieces of paper scattered on the seat beside him and on the floor. They had gotten through half the day's mail en route from the city.

"I don't want to forget—anything," Dennis said, the hiatus an unspoken apology for the numerous things he had already forgotten in the past ten days.

Dennis McLaughlin emerged into the sunshine and stood beside the Archbishop. He was as wiry, bony, sinewy in build as Matthew Mahan was solid. His shaggy red hair spilled over his ears and rioted around the back edge of his collar. Matthew Mahan consciously suppressed the additional flicker of irritation caused by his new secretary's haircut, or lack of one, and strode up the walk to greet the priests and parishioners of Holy Angels.

Dennis found himself marveling at the broad smile on Matthew Mahan's face as he shook hands with Monsignor Paul O'Reilly and his two curates. Did it prove that the Archbishop was what he liked to consider himself—the thorough politician—or what Dennis suspected: the compleat hypocrite? Fathers Novak and Cannon looked like frightened birds, ready to flutter away at the first gesture of violence. "We're ready whenever you are, Your Excellency," said Monsignor O'Reilly in a superbly neutral tone.

"I'm sorry we're a little behind schedule," Matthew Mahan said, turning as he spoke to smile at the twenty or thirty parents on the steps.

"The children have been very patient," said Monsignor O'Reilly.

"Joe, how are you," the Archbishop was saying to one jowly face he recognized in the generally Irish-American semicircle of watching parents. Joe O'Boyle, the local captain of the annual Archbishop's Fund Drive. Successful insurance man. Father of eight. "One of your gang in here?"

"My daughter Morrin."

"Good. Good."

Matthew Mahan turned back to Monsignor O'Reilly. The pain throbbed ominously in his stomach as he stared into that stolid face. Up close the ravages of age made it look as if it had been chipped from marble by a third-rate sculptor. The whole man was marble—or some cheaper stone. Everything about him—the square jaw, the thick stubby hands folded complacently on the big belly— said *immovable*. Without another word, Monsignor O'Reilly turned and stalked into the church. Fathers Novak and Cannon hurried after him. Matthew Mahan told Dennis to wait for him in the sacristy and followed them.

Going up the aisle, Matthew Mahan found himself wondering why he did not appoint another auxiliary bishop—a young man —to handle these chores. Was it the memory of his own career as auxiliary bishop—the way he had quietly absorbed more and more of the control of the archdiocese from old Hogan? It had not been an easy role to play, especially when the old man had retired within his medieval fortress to brood about Rome's ingratitude. Or was it simply the pleasure that he got out of fulfilling all the rites and duties of his office, especially this one—administering the sacrament of confirmation, conferring the gifts of the Holy Spirit, which only a bishop was empowered to bestow?

It was more than the sacrament, he decided, as he studied Monsignor O'Reilly's thick neck. He enjoyed speaking to the young people as they left childhood. He nodded and smiled at their curious expectant faces in the first ten pews on both sides of the aisle. The girls were all dressed in white; the boys wore blue blazers and gray pants—a minor variation from his day, when they had worn dark blue suits. In the city, where so many of the parishes were now filled with the poor, the nuns had abandoned a strict dress code. It was somehow comforting to see the tradition continued here—although he was sure that Dennis McLaughlin would argue that the youngsters should wear their old clothes and their parents should donate the price of these blazers and dresses to the poor.

Monsignor O'Reilly and his curates entered the sanctuary and took seats to the right of the altar table. Matthew Mahan remained in the center aisle, waiting for the organ music to end. As the last notes died away, he opened his arms and said, "Peace be with you, my dear friends, and especially with you, my dear young people who are going to receive your confirmation today. First though, I'm supposed to find out if you're ready to receive it. Let's see. Do you know why I am here? Why couldn't Monsignor O'Reilly or Father Novak give you this sacrament? Can you tell me?" He pointed to a towhead in the first row. "What's your name, son?"

The boy stood up. "Thomas Maloney, Your Excellency."

"Now, now, don't call me Your Excellency. Just call me Father. The popes don't want us to use all these titles anymore. Pope

John even told me that he would rather be called Don Angelo. Don is an Italian title of respect. But I couldn't manage that one. I called him Santo Padre. That's Italian for Holy Father. Somehow it sounds better. Anyway, I want you to call me Father. I don't stop older people from calling me Excellency, because I'm afraid of hurting their feelings. But I want to start you people off right. You're the ones who will really change the Church. Now, why am I here, Thomas?"

"Because only a bishop can administer the sacrament of confirmation."

"Right. Sit down now, and let me find another victim. Why am I wearing this ridiculous getup?" He gestured to the miter on his head, the cope, and the chasuble on his shoulders, the crosier in his hand, and eyed a boy with a head of blazing red hair, four rows back. "How about you, Red? Don't you think this outfit is pretty ridiculous?"

The boy stood up, his cheeks turning the color of his hair. He shook his head.

"You don't? Come up and take a closer look. Come on. Right up here."

The boy climbed out into the aisle and timidly approached him. Matthew Mahan took off his miter and put it on his head. Everyone roared with laughter. "Now tell me the truth. Wouldn't you feel pretty silly walking around with that thing on your head?"

The boy nodded.

"Then why do you think I'm wearing it? I look like a pretty sensible fellow, don't I?"

"Well, you're wearing it because other bishops wore these things"—he took off the miter and studied it for a moment—"a long time ago."

"Right! I'm wearing these robes, as we call them," Matthew Mahan said, speaking to all the children now, "to remind us that the sacrament of confirmation goes all the way back—almost two thousand years—to the Apostles, who were the first bishops. This getup only looks silly until you understand why I'm wearing it. What does this mean?"

He pointed to the crosier and chose another redhead, a girl this time. Her hair spilled down over her shoulders almost to her waist. "That's to remind us that you're the shepherd of the people."

"Like who?"

"Like Jesus."

"Right. He was the Good Shepherd. I'm only mediocre."

It was amazing, thought Dennis McLaughlin, watching from the sacristy. The total transformation of the man from the moment he began talking to the children. He suddenly seemed to emanate a kind of psychological radiance. Excitement, joy, were visible on his face and audible in his voice. Was he basically an actor? Or was the smooth reserve that you saw most of the time an act, a mask he wore for his own good reasons?

With a pat on the shoulder, Matthew Mahan sent the red-haired boy back to his pew. "You're doing awfully well. If you're as smart as you look and sound, I think I may tell Pope Paul the next time I go to Rome that we all ought to resign and let you people start running the Church when you're eighteen or so. There are just one or two more things I'd like to hear. You, young lady," he said, pointing to a plump dark-haired girl in the first pew. "Tell me who received the first confirmation."

"The Apostles," she said.

"Right. Where?"

"In the same room where Jesus had the Last Supper with them."

"Right again. And how did they receive it? What did they see?"

"Tongues of fire above their heads."

"Right again. Do you think you'll see some tongues of fire today?" Whirling, he pointed to a handsome dark-haired boy sitting on the aisle in the second pew. "What do you think?"

"I—I don't know," he said.

"Well, you won't. The only tongue you'll see is mine. Here it is, wagging away." He stuck his tongue out and walked down the aisle while everyone burst into laughter again. "Just a poor old bishop's tongue," he said as the laughter died away. "Not much good for anything but trying to persuade people to do what they should be doing without being told. Those tongues of fire the Apostles saw—that was to help them *believe* that they were receiving the Holy Spirit. No one had ever received it before, you see, and Jesus knew how hard it was to create *faith* in people, faith that inspires people to *do* things. But when the Apostles went out and started converting people, right in the Temple at Jerusalem

11

before the eyes of the men who had killed Jesus, then people began to see what the Holy Spirit really meant. How many did they convert in the first few days, does anybody know?"

Four or five hands shot up. He picked one in the back row on the boys' side. "Eight thousand," said a deep voice, whose owner did not bother to stand up.

"Eight thousand people. Can you imagine that? And the Apostles laid hands on them, and the Holy Spirit entered into these converts. Then what did they do?" He chose a hand in the back row on the girls' side.

"They went out and converted more people."

"Well, some of them did that. But they *all* did something even more important. What was it? What are Christians supposed to do?"

This time there were no hands. He selected a girl in the pew nearest him. She was tall, bony, and a little stupid-looking. She furrowed her brow and said: "Obey the commandments?"

"That's important. But what's even more important for Christians to do? Come on. Somebody tell me. This is the most important question I've asked yet."

"Love one another," said a clear, sweet voice from the center of the girls' side of the aisle.

"Right. From the very start of the Church, this was what made the Christians stand out. The Romans, the Jews, everyone, used to say: 'See those Christians. How they love one another.' That's how I hope you'll show everyone—your father and mother, your brothers and sisters, your friends, classmates—show them all what it means to receive the Holy Spirit. We don't have time here to discuss what it means to love each other. It's not easy. It's easy to say but not easy to do. I hope you'll discuss it in class this week and write a letter about it. Give me at least one example of how you decided to prove you were a Christian by loving someone and doing something about it."

In the sacristy Dennis McLaughlin almost groaned aloud. He would have to answer all those letters. You are an incurable romantic idiot, he fumed at himself. This man did not talk you into becoming his secretary. You talked yourself into it with your absurd illusions about penetrating to the heart of the power structure. All he wanted and needed was an energetic, reasonably intelligent drudge.

"Now I think we're ready to begin the mass and administer the sacrament of confirmation," Matthew Mahan said. He entered the sanctuary and took the bishop's chair behind the altar. Monsignor O'Reilly said the mass. After the Gospel, Matthew Mahan gave a brief sermon. He talked about his own confirmation, how he had come home convinced that he possessed the Holy Spirit and attempted to convert his younger brother, Charlie. "I didn't think he was a very good Christian," he said. "I told him he had to stop calling me names, that he had to loan me his baseball glove whenever I wanted it, share his candy with me, and give me the last helping of dessert, if there was no more left. That shows what kind of a Christian I was, in those days. I had it all backward. I thought it was my job to start converting everyone else, on the assumption that I was more or less perfect. It took me thirty or forty years to know better.

"Now I know that the most important gift of the Holy Spirit is the *power* to love. That may sound strange to you young people. Of course, you love your fathers and mothers, your brothers and sisters. Love seems easy at your age. But when you grow older, it's much more challenging. Especially the kind of love that Jesus urges us to practice. The love for the lost sheep, for sinners, for people who are in trouble. Read what he says about it. He tells us that it is better to go looking for one lost sheep and let the ninety-nine obedient, faithful sheep stay on the hills. That's risky, hard. Not many Catholics—in fact, not many people of any religion—practice that kind of love. It's the kind I hope you'll practice when you grow up."

He returned to the bishop's chair, and the children streamed up onto the altar in two lines. Matthew Mahan anointed each with the holy chrism and laid his hand against their cheeks. Watching, Dennis McLaughlin remembered the wild rumors that had circulated through the school before his own confirmation. Most were about the blow on the cheek that had no biblical basis whatsoever and was added to the rite to remind the Christians that they must be ready to suffer martyrdom for their faith. There were tales of bishops knocking smaller boys unconscious, especially if they failed to answer correctly a question from the catechism. The whole scene had been projected as melodrama, a personal confrontation between quivering eleven- and twelve-year-olds and the toad-faced old man whose picture glared down from the wall of the principal's office. High Noon in the sanctuary. Instead, they had all been marched to the communion rail and told to stand, not kneel, on the highest step, so His Excellency would not have to bend over so far.

Then the old man, surrounded by altar boys carrying the oil and priests obsequiously holding his robes, had gone down the long line mumbling Latin and daubing on oil and touching an occasional cheek with his hand whenever it occurred to him. Dennis had been one of those touched. He could still remember the scaly coldness of those ancient fingers, the involuntary shudder they had sent through him.

Everyone had gone home bewildered, wondering why they had spent the previous four weeks memorizing dozens of catechism questions which they had never been asked. That night Dennis had lain awake in his bed trying to detect some sign of the Holy Spirit in his body. But he did not feel braver, stronger, or happier. The next day in school the bullies were back tormenting "Brains" McLaughlin, as they called him, Sister was screaming imprecations and whaling away with her ruler, the girls simpered and tattled on the boys and on each other, and the standard topic of male discussion was still Mary McNamara, who would, it was rumored strongly, drop her drawers and hold up her skirts for a nickel. So passed away the light of that world.

After mass, Dennis helped Matthew Mahan take off his vestments. He noticed that the long white undergarment, the alb, was soaked with perspiration. "That's hot work," Matthew Mahan remarked. "I don't know why it is, but whenever I speak in public, I sweat like a steer. It's enough to make me wonder about my vocation sometimes."

"I thought you were having a good time out there," Dennis said.

"I was, I was, and I hope the kids were, too. How do you think it went?"

"I thought you were great," Dennis said.

For a moment Matthew Mahan looked at him with something close to anger on his face. "You're not joking, are you?" he asked.

"No—why—no," Dennis said, totally confused. "I—I mean it."

The pain flowered in Matthew Mahan's stomach. Another misunderstanding. Would you ever be able to talk naturally with this enigmatic young man? "Take these out to the car, will you?" he said, giving the vestments a pat and trying to sound friendly. "And keep Eddie company. I have to pay that little courtesy call on Monsignor O'Reilly."

Dennis was tempted to say good luck. But having collected one rebuke for candor, he decided silence was safer. Miter and crosier in one hand and vestments folded over his other arm, he went out the sacristy door leaving Archbishop Mahan to his fate.

III

Out in the car, rotund Eddie Johnson, the Archbishop's black chauffeur, had a grapefruit-league baseball game on the radio. The home team was getting walloped as usual. Eddie had played semipro baseball in his long-gone youth and considered himself an expert on the national sport. He started monologuing on the home team's deficiencies. All Dennis McLaughlin had to do was nod and murmur yes every other sentence or so. Meanwhile he revised on a pad on his knee a draft of a speech that Matthew Mahan would be making next week to the Knights of Columbus. The subject was the renewal of the Church since Vatican II.

It was, he thought sourly as he neared the end of it, a model of intellectual elegance. Full of "on the one hands" and "on the other hands," like so many statements that emanated from chancery offices and bishops' conferences and the Vatican itself, it had everything in it but passion. It praised the idea of renewal, it committed the archdiocese to it, but there was scarcely a single specific issue discussed—and the last paragraphs were full of cautionary maxims against going too far too fast.

On the radio, another voice was somberly announcing that General Dwight D. Eisenhower had just died in Washington, D.C. "My-my, did you hear that?" Eddie Johnson said. "Poor old Ike." It meant no more to Dennis than the latest score of the baseball game. He finished his revision and took from his coat pocket two letters he had received yesterday morning. One, from his mother, was still unopened. The second, from his friend Andrew Goggin, S.J., in Rome, he had already read twice. He had brought it along to read after Mother's epistle, much as in boy-

hood he had always kept a glass of cherry soda handy when he
was forced to take milk of magnesia.

Dear Dennis:

I thought you had promised to write me a letter once a
week. It's been three weeks now without a word. To my
amazement, your brother Leo has turned out to be a much
more faithful correspondent. I had to find out from him about
your wonderful promotion. I'm not surprised, really. I knew
they would realize they had one of the most brilliant young
priests in America in their employment sooner or later. And I
knew God would not disappoint me twice. You know how
upset I was by your decision to leave the Jesuits.

I can't tell you how pleased I was to hear that you are out
of that dreadful slum neighborhood. I was sure one of those
people was going to stick a knife in you, or hit you on the
head, while you were busy trying to save their souls. That's
the only kind of gratitude they've ever shown for all the
help the government and other Americans have given them,
since the day they freed them from slavery. I guess you'll
be reading this in your office at the Archbishop's residence. I
hope I can get a chance to meet him when I come back home
again. I'm not sure I will come back, except for a visit, however. Living is so much cheaper down here, and I've made a
lot of friends, mostly people from the city who have retired
down here. I can put an air conditioner in the bedroom of
my house and be as comfortable here in the summer as I
ever was in our fair city. It gets almost as hot there as it does in
Florida. We had an awful lot of rain in the last month down
here, and I started getting a lot of pain again. The doctor put
me back on cortisone and it cleared up, thank God. Maybe I
should give you the credit instead of the cortisone. I know you
are remembering me every day in your masses. Now that you
are promoted, I guess you won't be getting a vacation for
a while. That's too bad, because I was hoping you might
spend a week or two down here with me, like you did last
year. Leo sounds like he's working awfully hard, and I can't
see why the editor of the paper won't give him a raise. Can't
you speak to the Archbishop about it?

I hear a horn outside. My neighbor, Mrs. Green, is taking

16

me for a drive down to Miami. It ought to be a nice outing. This is a short letter, and they'll get shorter, until you write me a *good long one.*

Love,
Mother

Good old Mom, Dennis thought, stuffing the letter into his pocket, first a knee in the solar plexus, then a foot in the crotch. The memory of the two weeks he spent with her last year made him shudder for a moment. He had been trying to decide whether to leave the Jesuits or the priesthood or both, ignoring the advice of St. Ignatius that in time of desolation one should never make a change. But then it had never occurred to Ignatius that there could be a fourth reason why a priest was in desolation besides the three he had listed in the Spiritual Exercises. Perhaps because he never tried to cure his desolation by talking it over with his mother.

How strange it was to discover at twenty-nine that this woman who had always seemed to embody everything that was spritely and courageous was also stupid and dull, that her little maxims about praying together and keeping the heart pure, culled from *Grit* and similar magazines, were the fifth-rate philosophy of the world, tag lines for Salada tea bags. Why, why, why hadn't you seen it before, why, Dennis?

Because you had spent ten years of your life in an intellectual balloon, smiling grandly on Mother and the other lilliputians, seeing their shortcomings as no more than mildly amusing. But when the desolation came, when the balloon ran out of hot air and you found yourself in the streets surrounded by leering faces, asking why, why, the intellectual had to go to the roots of his life. He was appalled to discover that his intelligence, which he had always assumed he inherited from Mother, must come from non-existent Father, the man with the smiling face and the pilot's cocky hat, that bodiless being who grinned with such idiotic confidence from Mother's dresser. To see that Mother, once regarded without the ground fog of love in the eyes, was stupid, trite, querulous, there was desolation, St. Ignatius, the desolation of the void. How could a man find sustenance of the sort the intellectual was seeking from a ghost? Perhaps this hunger explained your capitulation to Matthew Mahan. If you were looking for a father there, Dennis, you've found one in the classic mold. A combination slave driver and SOB.

No, he was not *that* bad. Balance, Dennis, what has happened to that beautiful balance, that lovely analytic discrimination that was the intellectual's pride? Has it withered in the glare of burning cities, crunching bombs, bullet-crumpled leaders, the ghastly symbols of the sixties? Was it also, in the classic tradition of Christianity, his curse, the cause of his collapse? Wasn't lack of passion, the very thing for which he taunted the Church, his tragic-comic flaw? Fervor, even the negative brand that poured from so many lips these days, seemed somehow beyond him. He had waited patiently for it to come, had sat through endless discussions of spiritual dryness with his Jesuit superiors, had wondered for a while if the Ph.D. in history he was acquiring from Yale had something to do with his growing sense of inner emptiness, but finally decided the answer was some central flaw in his personality which forced him to see with relentless repetition the fly in every ointment, no matter how secret. By temperament he was a spectator who preferred one of the higher priced seats so he could smile wryly down at both the groundlings and the actors in the modern theater of the absurd.

Ultimately, it was his mounting dread of this fate that had driven him out of the Jesuit order, where he was highly esteemed as one of the province's most promising young intellectuals. His doctoral thesis, published as a book, V*arieties of Eighteenth-Century Humanism,* had been widely praised and sold the expected four thousand copies. His novel, *Infinitedium,* a satire of a group of fuzzy Catholic antiwar activists, had been more chillingly reviewed by a few intellectual magazines, where his hits were tensely recorded as accurate and his motives grimly questioned. It had sold the expected fifteen hundred copies and convinced Dennis that he had no interest in preaching to the elect.

Everywhere he looked, whether at Yale or St. Francis Xavier University, he saw hollow minds, he heard hollow words, he read hollow books, and he felt the same deadly vacuum drying out his insides. He was becoming a papier-mâché priest, withered scraps of questionable wisdom fluttering in his windy emptiness. Only one thing, both idea and feeling, relieved this emptiness while deepening his despair: his lust. Relentlessly, like one of the creatures from the apocalypse, it stalked his body and mind.

Neither prayer nor mortification helped in the least. He toyed for a few months with extremes of penitence, wondering if it was time to fashion a whip of razor blades, favored by some Irish Jesuits in the early years of the century. But the idiocy of the idea made him laugh.

So he resigned from the Jesuits and sought a career in the city's slums, hoping that pity would replace conviction. But there, too, he saw all the wrong things. He was incapable of romanticizing the poor. On the contrary, he was appalled by their stupidity, staggered by their self-hate, their degradation, and anguished by the pitiful formulae he offered them for solace.

When the Archbishop had summoned him to the chancery, Dennis was close to walking out on the whole show. End your sham of a priesthood, he had told himself, give up a role you were never meant to play. Take your Ph.D., pay the Jesuits or the Catholic Church or whomever your conscience selects for your expensive education, and retire to some university faculty where you can devote your life to turning out more students like yourself, dry sophists devoid of moral conviction, wryly amused at the imbecility of contemporary history, and not much more impressed by the banalities of other eras.

"Jee-sus," gasped Eddie Johnson. "You hear that, you hear it? Two out in the ninth inning, two men on, and they pitched to Willie. Right-handed powa hitter like him. Don't even put in a lefty. Leave that poor fella Jones in there to throw against Willie. The first pitch he clears them bases with a triple. Now they hangin' by their finganails. Don't them fools ever hear of the intentional walk?"

"Terrible," Dennis murmured. "Terrible."

Hurriedly he opened Goggin's letter. A few laughs is what you need, Dennis. Old Gog never fails in that department.

Dear Mag,

Your latest depressing letter has been received in my august quarters at the Villa Stritch. It lies on my desk in front of me, while Roman rain patters drearily on the tiles above my head. I don't know how the First Person permits it to rain so much on the very bosom of Mater Ecclesia, but he does. Perhaps it is proof of your dubious speculation that God is a woman, and like all women is instinctively jealous of other females, including her own daughter. Ho-hum.

The Villa Stritch is where the American employees at the Vatican hang their birettas. It is a cold, drafty old barn, but we have a goodly collection of clerical trolls here and we do our best to warm the atmosphere with laughter. God knows it isn't easy, in this the sixth year in the reign of Pontifical Paulus. Never has a pope cried so much in public, nor washed his hands so regularly while the best hopes of the best people are quietly crucified.

As for yours truly, to slightly vary the song from *Pal Joey*,

> My life has no color ever since I left you.
> Oh, what could be duller, the things that I do.

Once a week I wander over to the Jesuit GHQ in the Borgo Santo Spirito, just around the square from the Vatican, and help translate the latest bad news from England, Ireland, Australia, Canada, and the United States into Italian so that Father General's Italian secretary can condense them (no doubt leaving out the cries of despair) for our Maximum Leader. I see nothing but trouble emanating from the idea of moving all of New York's theology students into an apartment building on upper Broadway. What madness! My conservative soul can only wonder that people in authority no longer seem able to exercise it. Men hoary with experience are taking advice from youths even callower than thee and me. We swallowed the advice of the experienced ones and found out it was mostly nonsense. But what is meeting nonsense face to face and gradually recognizing it? I believe that is called maturing. Since the nonsense came from someone else, we have been able to reject it without much guilt. But what will happen to these callow ones, these self-appointed kindergarten charismatics, when they discover that their nostrums are equally—if not more—nonsensical? A catastrophic loss of self-confidence, I fear, and possibly a colossal guilt.

Two days a week I go for a delightful ride in the country behind the wheel of one of our Fiats. Except for the fact that my knees bump against the windshield while I ride and every mile involves at least one duel to the death with an Italian driver, it is a pleasant run. My destination is the Vatican

Radio, not far from beautiful Lake Bracciano. There I broadcast the Divine Line in English to the plebs in South Africa. I can't believe that the good Boers allow my message of racial equality to get across their borders. While I babble, I always have the image of huge electrical ears jamming every word I say. But it no doubt makes good listening for those few who understand English (the elite, naturally) in Black Africa. So maybe Cardinal Rugambwa picks up a few more converts in Tanzania, though I doubt it.

Two more days a week, I go play linguistics at the Biblical Institute, where I listen to a lot of people hint at things that they're afraid to say openly about the Gospels. There won't be much left of the thirteen apparitions on which St. Ignatius dwelt so lovingly, if these boys ever get up the nerve—or get down the permission—to sing out loud and clear. The more I ponder it, the more it becomes for me the Church's only hope—this degodification of Jesus, and the creation of a New Gospel, in which His various sayings are arranged in reasonably chronological order and he himself is placed in the social context of first-century Palestine. If we can see Him as a very intense Jewish boy who broke his skull studying the Scriptures, as many a one has before and since (the voice of experience speaking), tried to persuade the nationalist maniacs of his day, the Pharisees (as power-hungry as any contemporary Communist), to get off the people's backs, and only succeeded in scaring the Pharisees into an alliance with the worst elements in the nation, that bunch of thieves who ran the Temple. In retaliation, J.C. flirted with the lunatic left fringe, the Zealots, giving all concerned a perfect chance to crucify him. Nevertheless, the spiritual miracle still remains—his *acceptance* of the crucifixion, his awareness, gained from studying the sorry fate of most prophets, that only by his death could the spiritual victory which he sought become possible. This to me is so much more poignant, so much more beautiful, than the idea of an all-knowing God condescendingly taking on human form to do the beings he created the favor of redemption—*eeeech*, as Alfred E. Newman would say. What has that kind of thinking produced? Incredible fanatics like Loyola, ecstatic nuts like St. Francis, neurotic nemeses like the Little Flower.

This is burn-at-the-stake thinking, and every one of our grim little band over at the institute knows it. What we need above all is a writer with the power and grace of Teilhard de Chardin and a lot more courage—to wit, you. I curse the day that you blundered into American history in search of your so-called mystery of freedom. The world doesn't want to be free, Mag old boy, and it never did. If we Americans keep riding that horse, we are headed for the historical junk heap. My idea is totally different. The Church is necessary to the stability of mankind. She, and not some cheap, wild-eyed dialectical rationalist, must proclaim the New Gospel, out of the fullness of her wisdom and the depths of her researches into the mystery of God and his dialogue with creation. Instead of Gospels written by first-century ignoramuses who were either trying to make the Jews look bad or the Christians look good, or, in the case of John, smugly saying I told you so after the Romans had reduced Jerusalem to a rubble heap, instead of these four pieces of nonsense, we present the world with a coherent account of one of the greatest acts of love in human history. Wouldn't you want to be remembered as the writer of that book? You could do it, if you could only get your head out of the Declaration of Independence and the sermons of Martin Luther King and get your ass over here to the Vatican Library.

Speaking of that marvelous place, I recently learned that they have now opened the files up to the year 1877. How's that for keeping up with the times? One of my fellow toilers here at the Villa Stritch, a mick named Harrigan from Chicago, is an assistant archivist over there, and he entertains us nightly with the marvelous things that turn up in those dusty corridors. My favorite is Canon Pandolfi Ricasoli, who was confessor of the Convent of Santa Croce in Florence around 1640. He taught the good nuns that if you kept your mind on God while having intercourse, it was an exercise of purity! He said the sexual organs were holy and sacred parts, and he compared the hair around them to veils around holy and precious images. He taught the younger nuns to say the Our Father while he was enjoying them, and on Christmas Eve he slept with two of them "in order to greet the day with greater devotion." The abbess, one Lady Faustina Mainardi, was taught to say, "I renounce you, Satan, and all your iniquities. And I unite myself with you, Jesus Christ," as he entered her. Abbess Faustina was so enthralled she put some of the Canon's semen in a handkerchief and placed it on the altar among the holy relics.

They finally caught up with the old confessor, but his connections were so good in Rome, all they did was excommunicate him for a year or two.

You are not the first to be troubled by a need to express the Life Force, my son. Maybe if you stop being an Irish-American literalist, come to Rome and make some *connessiones* (connections). . . .

Seriously, something has to be done. Or at least begun. I have no intention of spending my life aboard a drifting ship. As for you, all your yakking about lust and emptiness would vanish if you could find a purpose for your priesthood. Come over here and get to work before some swinging nun picks you off and retires you to humdrum domesticity forever.

Penchantly,

Gog

"SWING AND A MISS. MUCCIO STRIKES OUT. THAT RETIRES THE SIDE," cried the announcer.

Dennis stared numbly at Goggin's letter, wondering why he thought it would cure his depression. There was really only one thing that would cure his depression, and he knew it. But where could he find a whole convent as cooperative as the sisters of Santa Croce? Of course, there was another cure. Tearing off this crippling collar, this round white yoke around his neck once and for all, and breathing the sweet air of American freedom. He suddenly found it unbearably close in the Archbishop's limousine. He flung open the door and stood beside it for a few minutes, taking long deep breaths. Yes, out here in the suburbs, the air was still sweet. But in the city? Twenty miles away, over the budding trees, he could see the gray pall of smog. The air of American freedom was anything but sweet these days. Which made Father McLaughlin worse than a man without a country— he was a man without a cause.

IV

Inside Holy Angels' rectory Archbishop Mahan sat at the dining room table with Monsignor Paul O'Reilly at one end and Fathers Emil Novak and Charles Cannon at the other end. "Gentlemen," he said, "I am really very distressed by this situation. Can't I do something to resolve it?"

The two curates stared stonily at him. "Only if you give us a statement in writing that nothing we say will be held against us—either by you or by him," Father Cannon said. Ordained only last year, he was a slight, sandy-haired, freckle-faced young man, who could have passed for a teen-ager. His hair was as finespun as a girl's, and it drifted down over his collar onto the back of his neck.

"Have you ever in your life heard anything that betrays a bad conscience more clearly than that?" Monsignor O'Reilly growled.

"Perhaps it would be better if we discussed the situation separately," Father Novak said. Small and balding, with pug nose that gave his face a boyish look, he was thirty-five. Last year he had been reported to the chancery for paying too much attention to a woman in his previous assignment, St. Brendan's parish. He had denied it vehemently but had accepted a transfer to Holy Angels, at the opposite end of the diocese. Was he making a serious attempt to preserve his priesthood, or was this brawl with his new pastor part of a plan to justify his departure? He was obviously a subtler personality than Father Cannon.

"I hate to do it, but it may be the best way to begin communicating," Matthew Mahan said. "You gentlemen can go back upstairs. I'll talk with Monsignor O'Reilly first."

The two curates stalked from the room. "Would you like something to drink, Your Excellency?" Monsignor O'Reilly said. "Scotch? Bourbon? Sherry?"

"Sherry would be nice," Matthew Mahan said, and in the same moment knew it was futile to pretend friendship with this man, even in its most external forms. They were enemies forever.

O'Reilly arose and opened a door in the mahogany sideboard. It was a French antique and matched the rest of the dining room furniture. Monsignor had obviously inherited the expensive tastes of his mentor, Archbishop Hogan. Into view swung a set of Irish crystal decanters on a hinged bar. O'Reilly selected the one with SHERRY on a silver nameplate and filled two small gold goblets. "Tio Pepe," he said. "I hope you like it. I think the English sherries are vastly overrated."

Archbishop Mahan sipped the sweet tepid wine and fingered his goblet. "You realize that this is a very explosive situation," he said. "We're dealing with a problem that could tear apart the diocese."

"Naturally we each have our own point of view," Monsignor O'Reilly said. "I'm more concerned about the damage to the souls of my parishioners. I was trained by the Jesuits, you know, in Rome. At the Gregorian. That tends to make me much more sensitive to the importance of moral theology."

The old Roman ploy again. Matthew Mahan carefully controlled his temper. How many times had he heard this lofty reminder from Monsignor O'Reilly during the 1950s, when he was summoned to the chancery office to get another rebuke for speaking out of turn—usually on an issue that had nothing whatsoever to do with theology. But to Monsignor O'Reilly, only those who studied in Rome were permitted to think.

"No one is more sensitive to moral theology than I am, Monsignor," Matthew Mahan said softly. He felt the tension rising in his body, the pain stirring. Monsignor O'Reilly had been Archbishop Hogan's vicar-general. At one time he had been considered the probable successor. O'Reilly had taken a very dim view of Matthew Mahan, fund-raiser and public relations monsignor extraordinary, appearing from nowhere to shunt him aside. He could almost see the disdain still visible in those hard, direct eyes, the tough, unsmiling mouth. "But I am also sensitive to what happened in Washington, D.C."

"You mean the firm stand that Cardinal O'Boyle took against those dissident priests who thought they could defy the explicit teaching of the Holy Father?"

"I mean the headlines, the tons of newsprint they consumed, exchanging insults."

"I only followed it at a distance, but I thought Cardinal O'Boyle conducted himself with great dignity. The insults all came from the other side."

"That may be true," Matthew Mahan conceded. "But think of what it did to the faith of the people."

"I suspect it was strengthened in the long run. It helps to know where the Church stands. Isn't that what history tells us? Where would we be today if the popes and councils hadn't struck down heresy every time it arose?"

"I am inclined to agree with Bishop Cronin," said Matthew Mahan. "As you no doubt know, he also studied at the Gregorian. There is nothing very edifying about those early Christian brawls between Arians and Monophysites and popes and patriarchs. Almost all of them were basically political conflicts, with theology and the Church dragged in by ambitious men."

"A rather odd opinion for a bishop—even an auxiliary bishop— to hold. But from what I hear, Bishop Cronin *is* rather odd—"

"Monsignor," said Matthew Mahan abruptly. "I did not come here to debate you. I came to restore peace to this parish, this rectory. Do you have any suggestion about how we should go about it?"

"Only one, Your Excellency," O'Reilly said. "Do your duty. Settle this issue, as other bishops have settled it, by a firm, clear, unequivocal statement."

"If you think you can involve the whole diocese in this personality clash—"

"It is not a personality clash. It is a theological conflict."

"It is both. Do you think it's an accident, Monsignor, that you've had eight assistants in ten years? Why do you think men keep asking for transfers?"

"There are innumerable explanations. Ambition, ideology. The knowledge that I am *persona non grata* at the chancery office."

"That is not true."

"I am hardly *grata*, Your Excellency."

"You are sitting in the rectory of one of the best—and by that I mean wealthiest—parishes in the archdiocese. Who put you here?"

"As far away from the chancery office as geography permits."

"There are other parishes. You might begin thinking about them, Monsignor. Parishes where there are no assistants. And the rectories do not have saunas in the basements."

"Oh. You hear all the latest gossip."

"I hear a good deal, Monsignor. Without trying, I might add."

Monsignor O'Reilly sipped his sherry. "I have only one other suggestion. Direct my curates to acknowledge the Holy Father's teaching—or suspend their faculties. That would satisfy your desire to keep our dispute as secret as possible."

Matthew Mahan shoved aside his half-finished sherry. "Monsignor. I'm going upstairs to find out what Fathers Novak and Cannon have to say. When I come down, I hope you have something more realistic to suggest."

Upstairs in Father Novak's third-floor room Matthew Mahan was appalled by the unmade bed, the pieces of unwashed underwear, the plates with yesterday's supper on them. "He's refused to let the housekeeper come upstairs to clean or even to take the dishes down," Father Novak said. "He said it wasn't safe. Would you put up with that sort of innuendo, that sort of insult, Your Eminence?"

Father Novak lit a cigarette. His hands were trembling. "Sit down, sit down, Emil," said Matthew Mahan. "Tell me how this whole thing started."

For a half hour Matthew Mahan listened while the two curates described in detail the war of petty slights and deprivations Monsignor O'Reilly had waged against them, when he discovered that they did not accept the teaching of *Humanae Vitae*, Pope Paul's encyclical on birth control. "Whether we're right or wrong doctrinally, he hasn't got the authority to tell me to be in by ten o'clock," Father Cannon said, his voice thick with outrage. One night he had been locked out of the rectory and forced to stay at a nearby turnpike motel.

Matthew Mahan accepted a cigarette from Father Novak and assured both priests that the harassment would end, today. "But that won't settle this situation. To do that, you'll have to give a little."

A wary look passed over Father Novak's face. "What do you have in mind, Your Excellency?"

Was Novak taking secret pleasure in this mess? Matthew Mahan wondered. He may still resent the accusation and transfer from his previous assignment. Which in turn suggested that the accusation had probably not been true.

"You will have to agree that under no circumstances will either of you speak publicly against *Humanae Vitae*. This, I might add, is something on which I insist, not Monsignor O'Reilly. He wants a good deal more from you, as you no doubt know."

"How can we be pastors to the people—" Father Cannon began.

"You're free to deal with *individuals* as your conscience sees fit. But when you are up in that pulpit, you are not pastors, you're teachers, and the teaching function is reserved to me—your bishop. You will teach what I tell you to teach."

For a moment Matthew Mahan was appalled by the words he had just spoken. Never had he imagined himself saying such a thing, not since the first vague vision of himself as the man in charge of the archdiocese.

"Let me explain myself. I am trying to keep peace—Christian peace—in this diocese. That is the paramount thing. The peace of this archdiocese. I am ready to do anything—including the suspension of all three of you and putting this parish into the hands of a temporary pastor—to prevent this situation from exploding into a scandal."

Now there was a wary, vaguely resentful look on Father Cannon's face. Plus a little fear. The beginning of wisdom, Matthew Mahan hoped. But Father Novak was the one who needed more delicate handling.

"This must be especially hard for you, Emil. You've already had a taste of injustice at St. Brendan's. Our Lord went through the same thing. He has a devil, they said. Do you remember how furious that made him? There's nothing wrong with being angry about this situation. I'm not telling you to swallow your feelings. Admit they exist, and then ask yourself: All right—but what should we do? What's the best thing for the Church, for the people—all of them?"

Father Novak was silent. He was like most liberals, Matthew Mahan thought. He was not satisfied with an Archbishop who allowed him freedom of conscience on this agonizing issue. He wanted the Archbishop—or the Archbishop's power—on his side. He assumed that his personal opinion should be the official position of the Church. Like the new president of the National Liturgical Conference, who had recently called those who hesitated at the prospect of everything from bongo drums to modern dancers on the altar "stiff-assed honkies."

"Try to see the situation from my point of view. From the

point of view of Catholics who have made tremendous sacrifices to have big families." A voice suddenly howled in Archbishop Mahan's mind, the cry of a lost soul. He could not see his brother's face, only the twisted mouth sneering: *You tell 'em, Bishop.* "Think of how you'll disrupt their faith, disturb their consciences. . . ."

Matthew Mahan sat back in his chair. A pulse throbbed in his forehead. The pain prowled in his stomach. Hard work, he thought, hard work. He looked out the window at the spring sunshine and suddenly wished he was far away, in Florida perhaps, watching a baseball game. Or on that Bahamian cay where Archbishop Hogan used to spend a month each winter.

"What's your personal opinion, Your Excellency?" Father Novak asked. His tone was earnest, his manner suddenly open. Matthew Mahan sensed a trap. Emil was very active in the Archdiocesan Association of Priests, which had rebellious tendencies.

"My opinion isn't the issue here, Emil," Matthew Mahan said. "Let's just say I agree with Cardinal Cushing. You can't put a cop under every bed."

From the sudden pleasure in Father Novak's eyes, Matthew Mahan suspected he had said too much. The mention of Cushing was a mistake. He was a character. He could hold all sorts of far-out opinions without upsetting anyone. In a painful flash Matthew Mahan recalled a morning at the Second Vatican Council, when Cardinals Cushing and Spellman were standing in one of the coffee bars, conversing animatedly. "There they are, the roughie and the smoothie," said an American bishop from Michigan who was standing at Matthew Mahan's elbow. Instantly he had realized that he preferred the smoothie style—without Spellman's conservative politics.

"Well," said Father Cannon, "I'd like to resolve this. It's no way to live. I'll agree to keep silent publicly."

Matthew Mahan suspected that he had been wanting to say this for some time. "Emil?" he asked.

Father Novak was clearly disappointed in Father Cannon. But he was now in the minority. He capitulated with a nod.

"Good," said Matthew Mahan with a heartiness he did not feel. "Let me talk with Monsignor O'Reilly for a few minutes."

Downstairs he found Monsignor O'Reilly had retired to his

study and was watching the home team play down in Florida. "Losing as usual?" Matthew Mahan said, pausing in the doorway.

"As usual." Without getting up, Monsignor O'Reilly turned off the sound with a hand selector but left the color picture on. "No doubt you've heard me thoroughly reviled."

"On the contrary. I got the distinct impression that you had two very contented curates until this business came up. Why shouldn't they admire you? This is one of the two or three best-run parishes in the diocese. Now, have you given this thing a little more thought?"

"Yes," said Monsignor O'Reilly coldly, still looking at the screen, where the home team's best hitter was in the process of striking out. "I can't see any solution that would let me live with my conscience as a pastor other than the one I have proposed."

Rage boiled in Matthew Mahan's brain. Part of it was anger at himself for the conciliatory tone he had just taken. He switched off the television and let O'Reilly have it in a voice that could be heard on the third floor. "I may not have a Roman education, Monsignor. But I am not stupid when it comes to motivation. I consider this entire charade an oblique attack on me. Now, by God, I have never let you arouse my enmity—but you are very close to doing it now. Do you wish to continue as pastor of this parish? Answer me."

For a moment a triumphant hatred—there was no other word for it—gleamed in Monsignor O'Reilly's eyes. In this same moment of the naked display of his power, Matthew Mahan felt a twist of defeat. He had been forced to say what O'Reilly would have said to him if their positions had been reversed. You better get used to saying that sort of thing, he told himself bitterly.

"You know the answer to that question, Your *Excellency.*"

"Then listen to my solution to this mess." He quickly summed up the compromise he had extracted from Fathers Cannon and Novak. "This seems thoroughly fair to me. They have agreed not to make any statement of their views from the pulpit or in any other public forum. You can't ask more than that."

"I say they should interrogate every woman that comes into the confessional on what she is doing and thinking about the Holy Father's encyclical."

Matthew Mahan almost smiled grimly. Monsignor O'Reilly had

overreached himself and given the Archbishop an easy answer. He had been expecting and dreading the issue of the confessional.

"I absolutely disagree, and if I get any evidence that you are doing such a thing, I will revoke your faculties," Matthew Mahan said. "The confessional is not a witness box in a law court, and a priest is not a prosecuting attorney. The care of souls, Monsignor, does not involve forcing them to reveal their guilt."

"Would you put that in writing?"

"No," Matthew Mahan said. "Will you or won't you accept the compromise I have just outlined?"

"If you order me to accept it, I will accept it."

"I order you. I also order you to restore civil discourse to this rectory, to give Fathers Cannon and Novak the housekeeping services they require, and their seats at your dinner table. I must also insist that you give them keys to the front door, so that they can go and come as they please."

"As you say," said Monsignor O'Reilly. "I trust you will also take responsibility for the gross misconduct that may arise from this freedom? Particularly on Father Novak's part."

"Father Novak is thirty-five years old. He will take responsibility for his own actions."

A contemptuous nod. "Is there anything else?"

"Nothing else," said Matthew Mahan, "except a little advice. I think it was Cardinal Mercier who said that the besetting sin of priests was not liquor or women. But jealousy. I urge you to think about that, Monsignor."

Matthew Mahan walked to the door and paused for a moment. Monsignor O'Reilly sat in the chair, his face immobile. He switched on the television set, and the announcer said: "Well, that's all for the home team in the bottom of the sixth. The score—"

Matthew Mahan shut the door and trudged up to the third floor again. There he told Fathers Novak and Cannon what had been decided and urged them to do or say nothing that would further aggravate the situation. He looked hard at Father Novak as he said this. Did he get the message? One could only hope.

As he walked down the rectory steps to the street, Matthew Mahan was again engulfed by a tremendous rage. He saw O'Reilly's face contemptuously staring past him at the television set. Should he go back—? No.

He struggled to calm himself and gradually succeeded. With calm came exhaustion and a severe attack of doubt. Would it have been better to capitulate, to take the hard heartless line that the Pope—apparently without realizing its heartlessness—had laid down? Had *he*—Matthew Mahan—won anything in this compromise? He rubbed his twinging stomach. He had tried to meet them as a fellow priest, a brother in Christ. But how do you maintain that stance when you have to deal with shifty, resentful double-talkers like Novak and sons of bitches like Paul O'Reilly?

V

The tap of the Archbishop's ring on the car window interrupted Dennis McLaughlin in the middle of Goggin's last paragraph. He hastily stuffed the letter into his pocket and opened the door. Matthew Mahan eased himself into the back seat. "God help us, what a mess," he said. "I feel like a member of a United Nations truce team."

"How did it go?"

"It's solved, temporarily."

Dennis, who knew only that it was an argument about birth control, ached to hear some details. But Matthew Mahan obviously had no intention of giving him any.

"Just got a news flash on the radio," Eddie Johnson said. "Ike's dead."

"I'm not surprised," Matthew Mahan said. "When I was in Washington yesterday, several people told me there was no hope."

"You knew him pretty good, didn't ya, Y'Excellency?" Eddie Johnson said as he started the motor.

"No. I just shook hands with him once or twice."

For a moment as they rolled through the quiet streets of the Golden Ghetto, Matthew Mahan had an impulse to tell Dennis McLaughlin everything that had just happened inside Holy Angels' rectory. In fact, it was more than an impulse, it was a need—a need to share with someone the agonizing loneliness of the role he was playing. Perhaps even more important, a need to communicate, really communicate, with the priests of Dennis's generation. He could endure the hostility and contempt of the O'Reillys. He had toughened himself against their cruelty a long time ago. But the subtler, more indirect and impersonal hostility of Dennis's generation disturbed him enormously. The averted eyes, the downturned mouth, of Fathers Novak and Cannon rose before him in memory. To his dismay, as he turned to Dennis, he saw the same patina of negation on his somber face.

Abruptly Matthew Mahan began talking about the death of General Eisenhower. "It makes you feel old," he said. He began telling Dennis where and when he had seen Ike in Europe. This led to one of his favorite World War II stories. "It was right after the Bulge. Everyone was shaky. It was hard to tell what was going to happen next. Suddenly we got word that Ike was inspecting the division in exactly one hour. The general—the division commander —started screaming for his orderly. He wanted his boots polished. The poor guy came running in with the shoe polish and a rag and a cardboard box. The old man forgot he was wearing carpet slippers and put his foot on the box—and the orderly started polishing the slipper. I couldn't repeat what was said next without a papal dispensation."

It was a story that had never failed to draw uproarious laughter from previous listeners. Dennis managed the merest ghost of a smile. Matthew Mahan sighed and rubbed his aching stomach. "It reminds you of the grim fact that we are getting pretty old, all of us World War II types. Is it true what they say, that for people your age and the kids in school it's just a lot of history like the first World War and the Civil War?"

"For a lot of them it is. Then there are some, like me, who'd like to forget the whole thing for personal reasons."

"What are they?"

"My father was killed in it."

"Dennis—I had no idea—"

For a moment the young eyes flashed almost wickedly at him, a penetrating glare that seemed to see as well as hear the hollowness of his automatic sympathy.

"Where—was he killed?"

"I don't know."

"What outfit was he with?"

"He was a pilot. That's all I know. My mother never talked to us about it."

The sad implication of those words was instantly clear to

Matthew Mahan. But now, he sensed, was not the time or place to try to do anything about it. He let Dennis continue talking on about World War II.

"I think it's your enthusiasm that turns the kids off, more than anything else. They just can't understand how you could be enthusiastic about any war, even if Hitler was as much of a monster as everyone says he was."

"I don't think we were enthusiastic," Matthew Mahan said warily. "Not the people I was with, the ones who were getting shot at. The enthusiasm came later, after we won."

"It amounts to the same thing," Dennis McLaughlin said. "Nobody over thirty seems able to understand why we don't have the same attitude toward Vietnam."

"I see," Matthew Mahan said, "I see."

A white lie. He did not see. Everything about the young had been growing more and more opaque for two, perhaps three years now. With a sigh he let the conversation lapse and began worrying about his next appointment, lunch with Monsignor Harold Gargan at Rosewood Seminary. They were a half hour late already. It would not improve Gargan's mournful mood. But it would take a miracle to manage that feat.

"How did things go with the apostolic delegate yesterday?" Dennis McLaughlin asked. "Did Roma locute?"

"I'm afraid not. He spent most of the time telling me to avoid a scandal. They don't want a repetition of Los Angeles, McIntyre's brawl with the Immaculate Hearts."

"It's kind of ridiculous, isn't it? Having to take a problem like that to the A.D. It sort of contradicts what they said in Vatican II about the Pope treating bishops as equals."

This corresponded so closely to what Matthew Mahan thought that he reacted with uneasy caution. "It's the way the system works," he said.

"Have we ever had a decent A.D.? They were all lemons from the very first one. He talked the Pope into condemning the so-called Americanist heresy."

"Oh yes," Matthew Mahan said, although he only had a vague idea what his secretary was talking about. "They gave us an earful of that one at Rosewood in my day."

"Most contemporary theologians consider it a myth. Not that it really matters. All the things that were condemned—freedom of

34

conscience, for instance—were overwhelmingly approved in Vatican II." Dennis McLaughlin hesitated for a moment and then added, "Maybe it's just as well that history is the worst-taught subject in Catholic seminaries."

"I'm not sure I agree with you," Matthew Mahan said. "God knows all the Americans could have used a lot more history at Vatican II. It would have helped us understand why the Germans and the Italians were at each other's throats, for instance. If we had a little more perspective on our own past, we might have had a lot more impact as a group. Most of us just voted with the liberals by instinct. We were the dogfaces, the troops," he added, seeing Dennis did not understand the World War II reference. "It was a pretty unnerving experience, let me tell you. When I came home, I got out a couple of biographies that Davey Cronin out at the seminary recommended. One on Cardinal Gibbons and another on Archbishop John Ireland. I think I learned more from those books than I have from anything I've read since I was ordained."

"Who did you like most?" Dennis McLaughlin asked. It was the first time that Matthew Mahan had seen him genuinely interested in their conversation.

"I admired Ireland's guts, but I have to admit I preferred Gibbons. He had the judgment, the finesse—"

"Yes," Dennis said in the listless automatic tone that Matthew Mahan had learned to read as disagreement. "I suppose you're right."

Irritation flickered through Matthew Mahan's weariness. In the sulky silence he found himself asking tense questions. *I suppose you think finesse is old-fashioned, or, worse, cowardly. Where in God's name did you people get the idea that the Church was supposed to wade into every issue and conduct a running brawl with all comers? You can say what you want about the guidance of the Holy Spirit, common sense is also a very valuable commodity.*

He tried to still this ranting voice by saying something intelligent. "Of course, Gibbons had some guts, too. He did go to Rome and stop the Pope from wrecking the Church by banning labor unions."

"True," Dennis said mildly. "But he had practically unanimous backing for it here in America. That was the way he always oper-

35

ated. He waited for the parade to form and then took charge of it. I prefer that line from Ireland. 'Seek out social evils and lead in movements that tend to rectify them. Laymen need not wait for priest nor priest for bishop nor bishop for Pope.'"

"I wonder if he felt that way when he found his priests or his nuns not waiting for him."

The episcopal tone was growing ominous, Dennis decided. He dropped the subject and was grateful to Eddie Johnson, who filled the next ten minutes with a discussion of their local baseball team's chances in the upcoming season. Archbishop Mahan seemed at least as interested in this subject as he had been in the relative merits of John Ireland and James Gibbons.

A half hour later, Matthew Mahan sat in a booth of the local Red Coach Grill listening to Monsignor Harold Gargan tell him what was wrong with Rosewood Seminary. It was like a visit to the Wailing Wall. The white hair, the veined eyes, the drooping face, dominated by the pendulous nose, seemed to add ten years to Gargan's age. Matthew Mahan had to remind himself that this man had graduated only a year ahead of him. He could not be more than fifty-six or fifty-seven. This was a man who had once confided to Matthew Mahan in his peppery curate days that he had played the piano in a nightclub to pay his way through the seminary. What had happened to him? What was happening to everyone?

According to Rector Gargan, almost everything at Rosewood was bad and getting worse. They had caught another three seminarians saying an unorthodox mass using Gallo wine and Rye Krisp in the locker room of the gymnasium. The class of '69 had dwindled from a paltry thirteen to a pathetic ten. Total enrollment had fallen below a hundred for the first time in twenty-five years. The desperate Gargan could think of only one solution—improve their public relations. A very good man who had handled public relations for the Air Force Academy was available. What did Matthew Mahan think? He wanted a very good $25,000.

"I think we'd both need our heads examined if we hired him. All these kids are antiwar. Can you imagine how they'd react? They'd probably be out on strike in ten minutes. We'd be in every newspaper in the country."

"What about these amateur liturgists?"

"Discipline them—mildly. No weekend privileges, something

like that. I don't want the kind of trouble Krol got into in Philadelphia or worse, what Cushing wound up doing in Boston—throwing out half the senior class."

"But I get this desperate feeling when I wake up in the morning. We've got to do something—to reverse the slide."

"I get the same feeling most mornings, multiplied by ten, Hal. But I don't see what we can do about it except pray. And be patient. Just because some people—or even a lot of people—are losing confidence in the country and the Church doesn't mean we have to do the same thing. The one thing we've got to avoid is public humiliation."

Gargan nodded glumly. He looked very tired.

"I think the best thing you could do is get away from the place for ten days or two weeks. When is the last time you took a vacation?"

"Oh, I got down to the shore last summer for a couple of weeks."

Matthew Mahan took his checkbook out of his briefcase and wrote out a check for a thousand dollars. "Let's see what two weeks in Florida does for you."

"Thanks, Matt," Gargan said, his voice charged with emotion. "I think it might do me a lot of good. I don't think I've slept more than three hours a night for the last month."

"I'm not doing much better," Matthew Mahan said as he laid twenty dollars on the check that the waitress brought him. He peeled another twenty off the roll of cash he had in his pocket and said to her, "This will take care of the young priest who's lunching in the next room with my chauffeur."

All the way back to the seminary in the car, Monsignor Gargan complained about his seminarians' lack of interest in athletics. They had been forced to abandon most of their intramural sports program because so few came out for the teams. "Yet they'll march their legs off down in Washington, or at City Hall, to protest against the war or pollution or eating the wrong kind of lettuce or grapes."

"As long as they act as individuals, Hal, we've got to give them the right to do those things," Matthew Mahan said. "You know what I went through in the forties and fifties every time I opened my mouth."

"I know, I know," said Gargan in a totally unconvinced voice.

For a moment weariness swept over Matthew Mahan again. He felt as tired as Gargan looked.

"Remember what I said, Hal, patience."

Gargan nodded glumly as the car swung through the gate of Rosewood Seminary and swept up the curving path to the administration building. Emotion stirred in Matthew Mahan as he looked across the broad lawn at the drab fieldstone buildings. Here was where his priesthood had begun, where he had spent six of the happiest years of his life. At this time on a Friday afternoon toward the end of March, there would have been at least two softball games going strong on the north and south lawns. Today three seminarians played with a Frisbee on the south lawn. They weren't even doing a good job of catching it.

"They all clear out on weekends these days," Gargan said.

Next year, Matthew Mahan thought, suddenly as morose as Gargan but concealing it, the seminarians will demand the right to live in off-campus apartments. These young people were insatiable. They already had so much more freedom than his generation ever dreamed of achieving, yet they were still morose, sullen, dissatisfied. And what were they doing with their freedom? That was the tormenting question. Mostly thinking up new ways to embarrass, harass, or disturb the Archbishop, so it sometimes seemed. But that was unfair, Matthew Mahan chided himself. Most of his harassment today had come from a hate-filled seventy-two-year-old monsignor.

As Harold Gargan got out in front of the administration building, he turned and with forced humor in his voice said, "Want to see the bishop before you go?"

"No, I haven't got time," Matthew Mahan said hastily. "Give him my best. Tell him I'm going to drag him in for dinner soon."

The door slammed. "Who's the bishop?" Dennis McLaughlin asked as they pulled away.

"My one and only auxiliary," Matthew Mahan said ironically. "Bishop David Cronin. He's eighty-one. One of my sentimental mistakes, I'm afraid. He taught dogmatic theology when I was here. He sort of became—my mentor. To be honest, he got me through this place. I wouldn't have graduated without the tutoring he gave me, and not just in dogmatics. I took him along as one of my experts at Vatican II. That turned out to be another mistake.

The old boy went from moderate to radical overnight. Every time I talk to him now, he scares the life out of me."

"I'd like to meet him," Dennis McLaughlin said, brightening appreciably.

"You will, you will," Matthew Mahan said. "I have him in for a Sunday night supper every so often."

But not so often lately, a nasty voice reminded him. He shook it off and asked, "What's next on the schedule?"

"Seventy-six trombones," Dennis said.

"What?"

"The Fifth Annual Statewide Catholic High School Marching Band Competition."

"Oh yes," Matthew Mahan said. .

"Hopefully it's almost over," Dennis said.

"Now, now," Matthew Mahan said testily, "it won't be that bad. There's a lot to be said for playing in a band. It keeps kids out of trouble. It gives them a sense of community. Everybody can't be an intellectual, Dennis."

Your Excellency is entitled to his opinion, thought Dennis McLaughlin moodily as they took their places in the reviewing stand at Cardinal Beran Regional High School. On the football field in front of them ninety-two green-uniformed members of Our Savior Catholic High School Drum and Bugle Corps, from the southern end of the state, were performing intricate maneuvers while blasting out "Macnamara's Band." Matthew Mahan shook hands with stocky, crew-cut Monsignor Joseph Gumbolton, the forty-year-old principal of Cardinal Beran, and a half-dozen members of the faculty. The crowd in the nearby stands was thin. "Mostly parents," Monsignor Gumbolton explained. He introduced him to Beran's new bandmistress, Sister Margaret Kelly, a tall, thin nun with a perky smile. The nuns' decision to go back to using their baptismal names if they chose constantly threw Matthew Mahan off balance. She took him down on the field and explained the complicated scoring by which the five judges rated the performance of each band.

Dennis McLaughlin followed the Archbishop, persisting in wondering what it all had to do with Catholic education, or any other kind of education. After an hour of deafening brass, the winner was announced: Our Savior for the fifth year in a row. The grinning bandmaster, a popinjay of a man, accompanied by a moon-faced, middle-aged priest who introduced himself as "McGuinnes —the chaplain," rather smugly accepted the gold trophy. Father McGuinnes told Matthew Mahan it was the twenty-sixth trophy that they had won in the last three years. "We almost went to Washington for the inaugural, but our black brothers from Jackson High School in your fair city beat us out."

Archbishop Mahan murmured something vaguely sympathetic and went out on the field to shake hands with the angular drum major. Behind him a half-dozen drum majorettes in net stockings, gold lamé miniskirts, and silvered blouses giggled as Matthew Mahan asked him how he managed to twirl two batons simultaneously.

"Practice, Your Eminence," said the boy, who was surprisingly shy. "I practice four or five hours a day."

The Archbishop congratulated him and the rest of the band and headed for his limousine.

In twenty-five minutes—such was the wonder and variety of the American suburbs—they were beyond the one-acre zoned plots and in the world of the really rich. The houses sat in splendid isolation at the head of oval driveways or on one of the rolling hills surrounded by acres of brownish gold meadow in which saddle horses gamboled. The Archbishop amazed Dennis McLaughlin with his knowledge of each property owner. "There's one of the richest," he said, pointing to an unpretentious-looking white house on an approaching hill. "Old Paul Stapleton. The family ran our city for a long time. They must be worth a hundred million. His wife is a Catholic."

A red brick imitation of Jefferson's Monticello. "The Crowells, they made their money in meat-packing." A Tudor pile a half mile back on an immense lawn. "The Duncans, the carpet company." A cluster of sharp-edged Norman roofs. "The Colemans— electronics."

Finally they swung into the driveway of a combination Spanish-Italian villa. A serving girl with a pugnacious Irish face opened the door. In the huge entrance hall a woman came toward them on a cane. She was a spooky old lady, unusually tall, with a mass of gray hair tied in a sloppy bun at the back of her neck. Her face was gaunt, with deep-socketed intense eyes.

"Miss Childers," said the Archbishop, with a literally beaming smile, "it's so nice to see you."

"Your Excellency," she said in a surprisingly rich girlish voice.

Father McLaughlin was introduced, and they adjourned to tea in a sitting room that was almost Victorian with its profusion of overstuffed chairs and bric-a-brac. But Miss Childers was remarkably contemporary. She wanted to know what the Archbishop thought of the Vietnam War, now that President Nixon seemed committed to fighting on indefinitely. Dennis had trouble concealing a smile as His Excellency did his best to talk out of both sides of his mouth. And the liturgy? What did he think of these floating parishes? Jazzmen and modern dancers performing on the altar? Once more His Excellency tried to sound both with it and against it. Miss Childers startled him by announcing that she had gone to a guitar mass in the city and loved it. His Excellency hastily conceded that there was something to be said for the guitar as a liturgical instrument. And priests marrying? What about that idea? His Excellency temporized. It was an open question. There was nothing inherently wrong with it.

Again, the Archbishop was obviously startled when Miss Childers said: "I see a good deal right with it. Better to marry than burn, as St. Paul said. For me, that word 'burn' has always meant unsatisfied yearning, as much as the fires of hell. Sometimes when I think of the terrible thing my father did to me, I hate him, I really do."

Archbishop Mahan seemed unduly upset by these words. "It's very hard—almost impossible—to judge the previous generation. Especially your father"—he faltered on that word and added only as a murmured afterthought—"your mother."

Miss Childers leaned back in her armchair and belched. Without apologizing she declared, "My father was a selfish old bastard, Your Excellency. I think it's healthier to say that sort of thing, don't you, Father McLaughlin?"

"Yes, yes." Dennis said, hoping there was conviction in his voice. He caught Archbishop Mahan eyeing him and added: "If it's true."

"Oh, it's true, it's true."

The Archbishop was obviously eager to get away. He refused a second cup of tea and spoke vaguely about appointments in the city. "You look terribly tired," Miss Childers said. "Uneasy lies the head and all that, I suppose."

"And all that," Matthew Mahan said, forcing a smile.

41

Out in the car the Archbishop looked uneasily at his secretary. "I suppose that bored you stiff," he said.

"No, not at all," Dennis said. "She's almost a swinger."

"She is an amazing old girl. Her father was governor of the state in the twenties. A ruthless crook. Her mother died when she was quite young, and the old man turned her into his companion. He lived to be eighty-three or so." Matthew Mahan shook his head. "The terrible things people do to each other."

You should know, Your Excellency, whispered a nasty voice.

Suddenly the pain was alive in his body again, ripping at him. While those seemingly innocent words tore his mind from the steel shell of the moving car across thousands of miles of water to a woman's suffering face in Rome.

In counterpoint another voice, which he also did not control, whispered: *Forgive me, Mary, forgive me.*

"I suppose there's a big bequest there," Dennis McLaughlin said.

"What?" Matthew Mahan said dazedly. "Miss Childers? Oh yes, we hope so. She's intimated that it will be around a million."

Again Matthew Mahan glanced uneasily at the impassive yet somehow accusing young face. "I suppose you don't think much of the way a bishop has to hustle around buttering up the rich."

Dennis refused to plead guilty or not guilty to the implied indictment. He decided a simple shrug was the best answer. The Archbishop did not spend all his time chasing bequests. But why say that when he seemed about to make an interesting confession?

"We get twenty per cent of our income—about the same as most dioceses—from bequests. For us that was over two million last year."

A nod this time, Dennis. You may yet emerge unscathed by His Excellency's acerbic tongue. Now a nice neutral question.

"Would you like to do the rest of the mail?"

"Good idea."

They were down to the beggars: requests for help from obscure missionaries in Swaziland, Uganda, Pondicherry. The Indians were the worst. They were indefatigable wailers. "Give them the usual," Matthew Mahan said, which meant a form letter full of blessings and a check for twenty-five dollars.

Next came the problems of the diocesan priests who were serving

42

in Brazil. They were there in response to Pope John's call and their Archbishop's urging. John had asked 10 per cent of the priests from every United States diocese to volunteer for service in South America. But diocesan priests were not enthusiastic about missionary life. Less than one percent had responded. Matthew Mahan had recruited twenty-five—twice as many as any other diocese. Father Tom O'Hara reported the final collapse of his car. What he really needed was a jeep. "Send him thirty-five hundred," Matthew Mahan said. Father Jerome Lang had a bright boy who said he wanted to be a priest but could not afford a university education, which Lang felt he should get first. It would cost three thousand to support him for the first year. "Send it to him," Matthew Mahan said. Father Edward McMullen wanted to build a chapel for an outlying village. "Send him five thousand."

Matthew Mahan could almost hear the groans of protest from his money-manager, iron-jawed Chancellor Terence Malone. He knew he was too generous with these young priests. But it made him feel better—and not many things made him feel that way these days.

There were a half-dozen letters from Washington, D.C., enclosing reports from various committees on which he was serving under the aegis of the National Conference of Bishops. More night work, Matthew Mahan thought glumly. A letter from Father Peter Foley, chaplain of the state prison, introduced one of his model prisoners who was about to be released after serving ten years for armed robbery and felonious assault. The man was totally reformed. Would the Archbishop help get him a job? Matthew Mahan groaned. "Write to Mike Furia. You'll see a dozen previous letters in his file. He manages to hire a lot of these poor guys for his overseas companies."

He twisted his episcopal ring, a habit that Dennis had learned to interpret as a sign of uneasiness. "I wish I could get Foley out of there. He's the only guy in my seminary class I haven't settled in a good parish. He says he *likes* being chaplain."

Dennis found it hard to tell whether the Archbishop was simply baffled by Foley or disapproved of him. "I told him at our last reunion I may not be around forever. My successor may decide he's too old and leave him there for the rest of his life. It didn't seem to bother him. What's next?"

A long letter from the pastor of St. Malachy's parish described the trouble he was in with his parish council, which was in the hands of superconservatives who barely tolerated the use of English in the mass. A sociologist wanted to find out how many priests the diocese had lost in the last five years, with case histories, if possible. Finally there were the usual random letters from various lay men and women, about everything from lack of heat in St. Joseph's parochial school to accusations against two or three priests, alleging they were about to be—or should be—caught *in flagrante delicto* with lady friends.

"Five years ago we could file ninety per cent of those sex letters in the wastebasket," Matthew Mahan said. "But these days every one of them sounds true. Send them to the vicar-general and ask him to make the usual investigation."

Dennis McLaughlin nodded obediently, but there was a droop of disapproval on his sensitive mouth. Suddenly Matthew Mahan found himself wishing he could stop the frantic daily treadmill on which he and Dennis were running. If somehow, somewhere, they had time to sit down and relax for a day or two, to talk about things in a casual honest man-to-man way, he was sure that they would find themselves in substantial agreement. Dennis would be surprised to discover that the Archbishop had been something of a rebel in his youth and understood—or tried to understand—the impatient feelings of young priests and laymen. They would even enjoy a mutual laugh or two, if he managed to explain that he didn't really enjoy always playing the solemn upholder of dignity and authority. But there was no way to turn off the treadmill; there did not even seem to be a way to slow it down.

A batch of letters offered Matthew Mahan a number of supposedly rare seashells and almost as many offers to swap. He was one of the world's foremost collectors of shells, and his letters abounded with references to tritons, conches, turbans, volutes, whelks and miters.

"Tell that guy I've already got an episcopal miter and papal miter. But I wouldn't mind getting a Cardinal miter," he said, flipping the top letter into Dennis's lap.

"Should I send a carbon to the Vatican?" Dennis asked.

"It would be a waste of paper," Matthew Mahan said, smiling.

The rest of the malacologists were swiftly dispatched. Yes, the Archbishop had a Purple Drupe and a Spiral Babylon whelk. But he would like to see an Eye of Judas, from the Galapagos Islands. No, he did not want a Grinning Tun or a Wide-Mouthed *Purpura,* and hence declined to trade his Magnificent Wentletrap from Japan for either of them.

"So many people think I'm a sucker, just because I wear a round collar," the Archbishop growled.

Next came a long memorandum from George MacNamara, the diocesan lawyer, advising Matthew Mahan to settle out of court with a parishioner who had fallen down the front steps of the cathedral last winter and was suing the archdiocese for a million dollars, claiming his back injuries had left him permanently disabled.

"I thought it was a mortal sin or something to sue the Church."

"Them days are gone forever," said Matthew Mahan. "We've had at least one, and sometimes two and three, of these suits every year since I became the ordinary. Everybody thinks we're rich. It's like suing General Motors. Draft a letter making me sound very indignant and swearing by all the angels in heaven that I won't pay a cent more than twenty-five thousand dollars. Then do a covering letter to George MacNamara and tell him to show it to the other lawyer. If it doesn't work, we'll settle for fifty thousand, as he's telling us to do here. After that, draft a memorandum to Monsignor Delaney over at the cathedral, telling him the bad news. It's going to send our insurance premiums out of sight."

Next came invitations to Matthew Mahan, orator. Yes, he would be happy to be the speaker at the annual dinner of the 113th Division; he was sorry but conflicts in his schedule made it impossible for him to address the St. Francis Xavier University alumni dinner. To his even deeper regret, he was unable to give the university any money out of the diocesan treasury this year.

A tough smile played across Matthew Mahan's mouth. "I've been giving those former colleagues of yours a hundred thousand dollars a year for the last few years. What thanks do I get for it? Five of their so-called theologians sign that statement attacking Paul for *Humanae Vitae.* Let's see how they enjoy practicing that vow of poverty for a while, since they don't seem to have much taste for obedience."

"Chastity stock is pretty low out there, too," Dennis said. "I know at least a half-dozen men my age who are dating regularly."

"I can't understand it," Matthew Mahan said. "I thought the Jesuits would be the last ones to fall apart, not the first."

Dennis smiled wryly. "The Jesuits always like to be in the vanguard, even when the line of march leads to the abyss."

Matthew Mahan roared with laughter. "I like that. I'll have to use it the next time I have dinner with President Reagan."

They went swiftly through the rest of the correspondence, with Matthew Mahan roughing out his answers, leaving Dennis the job of putting them into decent English. By the time they finished, Dennis was sitting with at least a pound of papers in his lap. "Well," the Archbishop said, "that takes care of that."

For a moment Dennis was inclined to remind the Archbishop that five or six hours of secretarial labor were still needed before "that" was taken care of. But he found it more satisfying, on second thought, to say nothing. You really prefer your bitterness, don't you? whispered a mocking voice in his mind like the voice of an ironic angel. Yes, he replied. Yes. I do.

VI

They were out on the freeway now. The fading light seemed to soften the landscape on both sides of the road, turning the ugly factories and gas tanks and power grids into inoffensive suggestions of themselves, less grotesque and strangely human, capable of being welcomed in spite of their ugliness. They were part of his city—unchangeably, so it seemed to a man Matthew Mahan's age. Even the acrid odor of cooking ink, the sweetish stench of refinery oil, the stink of rotting flesh from the slaughterhouses' waste pits, did not trouble him. "You probably won't believe this," he said to Dennis McLaughlin, "but even the air smells good to me. I guess you can get used to anything."

"The university Chemistry Department has entered a class action suit against these factories," Dennis said. "There's no reason for them to be releasing those kind of fumes so close to the city."

The city. Yes, there it was ahead of them, looming up on its long narrow hill, most of its ugliness also softened by the deepening dusk. A sprinkle of house and office lights testified that it was inhabited. As Matthew Mahan looked meditatively at it, the pain in his stomach flickered menacingly. He suddenly remembered that it had begun yesterday evening on his flight back from Washington D.C., where he had pleaded in vain for the apostolic delegate's help in controlling his insane nuns. Looking down on the city as the plane landed, he found himself murmuring: *Would that you knew the things that made for your peace.*

Now was not the time for those kinds of lamentations. There was still work to be done. "Have you checked with the chancery office switchboard to see if we have any calls?"

"No," said Dennis, visibly twitching. A tendency to forget or fail to record telephone messages was his new secretary's worst failing. A typical intellectual was Matthew Mahan's not always patient excuse for him. Off on cloud nine—or ninety-nine.

Dennis plucked a white telephone from a cradle in the armrest beside him and called the chancery switchboard. He asked the required question and jotted down a list of names on his steno pad. They were in the city now, rolling down Kennedy Parkway toward a warm bath and a soothing scotch and soda. Dennis read the list of callers to him. Mike Furia, chairman of the Archbishop's Fund Committee; Herb Winstock, the vice-chairman; Mrs. O'Connor, the mayor's wife, another potent fundraiser. "A man named Fogarty."

"Bill Fogarty?"

Dennis peered at his hurried scrawl. "Yes. I think it's Bill. He's at the Garden Square Hotel."

"Eddie," said Matthew Mahan, "get us to the Garden Square fast."

At the next traffic light, Eddie Johnson swung the big car around the stone island in the center of the Parkway and hurtled them to the Garden Square in ten minutes. Matthew Mahan explained the abrupt about-face to Dennis McLaughlin, en route. "Bill and I were in the same class at the seminary. We lost him about fifteen years ago. Woman trouble. Lately I'd heard they'd split up and he was drinking the bars dry. I wrote him a letter asking him if I could help."

As they got out of the car, Matthew Mahan told Eddie Johnson to buy himself some dinner if he got hungry. "This might take awhile," he said. In the green-carpeted lobby, filled with third-rate modern furniture, the Archbishop walked swiftly to the desk. "Is there a William Fogarty registered here?" he asked.

The long-haired young desk clerk picked at a pimple on his cheek, ran his finger down a list of names, and said there was a Fogarty in Room 1515.

"Give me a key to that room," Matthew Mahan said.

The clerk stared in astonishment.

"I am Archbishop Mahan, and that man is a priest. A sick priest. Give me a key."

The Archbishop and his secretary were soon striding down the upstairs hall, which also had a green carpet, plus wallpaper full of equally green shamrocks. Matthew Mahan knocked at the door of 1515. There was no answer. He inserted the key in the lock and stepped into the room. The drapes were drawn. The hot-air heat from the register in the wall had turned the room into a sauna. Worse, there was an overpowering odor of vomit in the thick air.

After a moment of fumbling, Matthew Mahan found the wall switch, and the overhead light revealed Bill Fogarty sprawled on the bed. There was a two-day stubble of gray beard on his chin and cheeks. A half-dozen whiskey bottles stood on the dresser, all of them empty. He had thrown up in several places, the last time on the bed. Matthew Mahan took a deep breath and stood there for a moment, staring mournfully at the sleeper. He was remembering seminary days. He could hear Bill Fogarty singing his outrageous parody of Mother Machree at the musical they had staged at the end of their third theology year.

> Sure we'll love the dear surplice
>   that drags on the ground,
> And we'll serve and we'll sugar your tea
> If you let us stay out until ten once a week.
>   Dear Father, Dear Father McKee.

Wait, it had been a duet, you and Bill had sung it as a duet, Matthew Mahan recalled. Which gave him all the more reason for thinking, as he pondered the ruins of Bill Fogarty: *There but for the grace of God go I.*

A handsome black Irish buck, that was what he had been, Matthew Mahan thought mournfully, looking down at the flaccid cheeks and sagging mouth and thinning gray hair and beer belly of the man on the bed. Was it time alone that wreaked such havoc, or was it spiritual failure, whatever that meant? Matthew Mahan did not pretend to be an expert on the subject, but he knew that it had something to do with pride and the way pride so slowly slides into arrogance and too often ends in despair. No one had been prouder than Bill Fogarty, prouder of being a priest, prouder of his unique ability to hold an audience, to make them laugh and to make them cry.

The pride had seemed innocent enough, even justifiable to his friends and admirers in the class of 1939 at Rosewood Seminary. It had also seemed perfectly understandable that Bill became the darling of the uptown Catholics, always invited to parties and on trips, always cajoling a week off here and a week off there to relax in Florida or enjoy the summer sun at the state's poshest beaches. And what harm was there riding back and forth on these outings with a very attractive and very divorced woman?

Alas, when Archbishop Thomas Hogan heard about it, he thought there was a good deal of harm. Bill suddenly found himself exiled to what the older clergy of that era called the Prairies and Matthew Mahan's generation called Siberia—the dreary downstate boondocks of the archdiocese where Catholics were a distinctly unaffluent timid minority. When Bill balked, he was singled out by the Archbishop at the next meeting of his deanery and publicly excoriated as a disgrace to the priesthood. He was then summoned to the episcopal throne and ordered to kneel and kiss the extended ring.

Bill crept out to his assignment, a cowed, embittered man. His very divorced lady friend was horrified by what she had inadvertently done, and deeply sympathetic. Result: a clandestine romance which finally became a real scandal. Saddened friends, Matthew Mahan among them, advised Bill to ask for laicization. Predictably, Archbishop Hogan responded with another jeremiad. After two years of not very patient waiting, Bill left the Church and married his divorced friend. When Matthew Mahan became Archbishop, he had looked up Fogarty's case in the files. Hogan had never even forwarded the papers to Rome.

Fogarty's wife had money, which seemed a good thing because Bill found it practically impossible to get a job. Old Hogan and the characters around him were vengeful men, and they got Bill fired or blocked his being hired more than once. In the end his wife's money only made it easy for Bill to drink all the booze he wanted. Like so many ex-priests' marriages, Bill's love was doomed from the start. He never resolved the conflict between the woman and his priesthood. He loved both, and now he was ending his life probably hating both.

Matthew Mahan gently shook the sleeping man's shoulder. "Bill. Bill," he said.

Fogarty awoke and lay there staring numbly at him. "You called me, Bill."

Tears trickled out of Fogarty's eyes and down the unshaven cheeks.

"O Jesus, Matt," he said. "O Jesus, Mary, and Joseph, Matt, what's going to become of me?"

"I don't know, Bill," Matthew Mahan said. "I don't know. I don't think you're in any shape to discuss it right now."

"Sally left me, Matt. She walked out on me. She gave me a thousand bucks and walked out on me."

"I know, Bill, I heard about it. I wrote you a letter."

"I got it. That's why I called you. I wouldn't—I wouldn't have had the guts to do it otherwise."

Fogarty turned his face away, as if he found the round collars on Matthew Mahan and Dennis McLaughlin an unbearable sight. "I'm just a drunk, Matt, an absolutely useless drunk. I was going to kill myself. That's why I checked in here. But I couldn't get drunk enough. When I woke up this afternoon with puke—"

"Somebody was praying for you, Bill. Maybe a lot of people were."

The bed shook. Fogarty was sobbing silently. "What's the point, Matt, I'm finished."

"No you're not, Bill. I don't think you are. Would you want to come back to work as a priest?"

"Would you—would you even consider it?"

The voice was choked, the head still turned away. "Of course, I'd consider it, Bill," Matthew Mahan said. "But you'd have to get yourself back in shape physically and spiritually. You'd have to join Alcoholics Anonymous. And spend three or four months, maybe longer, at a monastery down in Kentucky. When you're on your feet, we'll talk."

"I don't deserve it, Matt. I don't deserve it," Fogarty said. But the offer got his feet over the side of the bed and he sat up. In this position he was even more pathetic looking. The belly bulged, the chin dissolved into the blubbery neck, the raddled cheeks sagged. Whether he sensed what Matthew Mahan was thinking, or the attempt to sit up straight had revealed to him the totality of his collapse, Fogarty began to weep again.

"You're wasting your money, Matt."

"It's my money. If I feel like wasting it, I will."

No. That was too harsh, too arrogant, Dennis McLaughlin thought as he saw Fogarty flinch away from these words. But Archbishop Mahan either did not notice or did not care. As usual, Dennis thought mordantly.

"See if he's got any clothes, Dennis."

A search of the room revealed nothing but a raincoat and a few more empty whiskey bottles in the closet. In his drunken stupor Fogarty had also used the closet as a bathroom. Dennis McLaughlin snatched the raincoat off a hook and hastily closed the door. But the urine stink mingled with the vomit, and for a moment he had to struggle for breath. Anxiously he wondered if he was getting another attack of the claustrophobia that had sent him fleeing off elevators and avoiding planes and tunnels for the past two years. When it combined with his asthma, it could come close to killing him.

"Can I wait in the hall?" Dennis asked. "I feel a little—sick."

Matthew Mahan's mouth twisted with irritation. He nodded and sent him on his way with a curt umpire's wave of the thumb.

From the hall Dennis listened while Matthew Mahan phoned the hotel housekeeper and told her he was leaving twenty dollars for the maid to clean up his friend's room. "He was taken sick unexpectedly. We're very sorry about it." He also called the desk clerk and told him to send the bill to the chancery office. So crisp, so businesslike, the perfect spiritual executive, Dennis thought sourly.

Archbishop Mahan gestured to him as he came out the door, holding Fogarty erect by his right arm. Dennis seized the left arm, and they proceeded down the hall to a bank of elevators in the rear. Fogarty smelled like a troop ship in heavy weather, Matthew Mahan thought grimly. But there was a good chance that they could get him out of the hotel unnoticed on this back elevator.

On the ground floor the bellboy guarding the rear door stared curiously at them. His bored sallow face and dull greedy eyes were almost a guarantee that he would not be scandalized in the least by the sight of two priests hauling a nameless alcoholic into the night. At least this time the drunk was not dressed in clericals.

Outside in the parking lot, Eddie Johnson was waiting for them, the car motor running. Eddie had helped him pull so many drunken priests out of the hotel in the past ten years, the whole thing was routine for him. In a moment they were on their way downtown to St. Peter's Hospital without Matthew Mahan saying a word to him.

"Where are we going?" Bill Fogarty asked dully when they started down Hillcrest Avenue. Matthew Mahan told him, and there was a gasp of agitation, a panicky shaking hand on his arm. "Don't put me in the alcoholic ward, Matt, please. I remember visiting my old man there once. It's a terrible place."

"I don't even think they have an alcoholic ward anymore, Bill. You're going to get a private room, and you don't have to see anyone until you get enough vitamins in you to hold your head up."

Strange, Matthew Mahan thought, how drunks seemed to dread most the alcoholic ward or the mental hospital or the probing psychiatrist—the very things that came closer to them every time they bought a bottle. You would almost swear that they had a need for suffering, to expiate some awful unknown crime. But no matter how you scrutinized the lives of the few alcoholics you knew well, you could never find any evidence of such a crime. No, Matthew Mahan thought mournfully, you were never able to find a trace of a reason for this demonic, destructive guilt, not even in the alcoholic you knew best. For a moment he saw before him his brother's boyhood face with a grumpy look on it. "No like peaches, *mad*," his mother had written at the bottom of the photo. A sorrowful sighing wind seemed to blow through Matthew Mahan's mind. God's will be done, he thought, even when we are totally unable to understand it.

There was work to do, he abruptly told himself. Now was not the time to meditate on the mystery of suffering. He picked up the car phone and called Mother Margaret Canavan, the head nun at St. Peter's. Although she was rather stiff about the short notice, she agreed to have a private room ready and a psychiatrist on call to prescribe whatever was needed to get Bill Fogarty through the night.

"Tonight will be rough, Bill," Matthew Mahan said as he hung up. "The first night in the hospital is always the worst. Trust them. They're on your side. I'll see to it."

With a sideward nod of his head, Matthew Mahan ordered Dennis McLaughlin to join him in escorting Fogarty to his room. After ten more minutes of soothing reassurance, they left him sitting on the bed giving his vital statistics to the head nurse and found Eddie Johnson waiting for them in front of the hospital.

"Well, that was a change of pace, wasn't it?" Matthew Mahan said to Dennis McLaughlin as they headed uptown.

"You sound like you've done that before," Dennis McLaughlin said.

"In a way. Most of the time it's a priest in good standing who's on the sauce. I've got one of the worst alcoholic problems of any diocese in the country. About eighty per cent of my priests are Irish-American. I guess that explains it."

He sighed and lit a cigarette. "Poor Bill," he said. "You can't believe what a fantastic priest he was. He could—he had this power to make people do things. He seemed to radiate—a kind of modern holiness. Visible grace. I never had the gift. I always had to make my mark the hard way."

"I'm amazed to hear you say that."

"Why?"

"Because you seem—seem to handle people effortlessly."

"Ah," said Matthew Mahan, pleased by the compliment, "it's just practice. And this ring," he added, tapping the emerald ring on his fourth finger of his right hand.

"What happened to the woman Fogarty married? Do you know her?"

"I knew the family. The Donnellys. A familiar story. Rich girl marries Irish drunk. Or playboy, whatever. In that case I think it was a mental breakdown. They split up, she's got plenty of money, and we say she can't get married again. Result, we've created a tragedy that's very likely to involve a half-dozen more people before it's over. It takes fantastic effort, superhuman effort, to keep these women in the Church without destroying themselves—and other people. I know that from experience."

As Matthew Mahan said this, his mind again leaped from the moving car, across housetops and river and sea to Rome. For a moment he stood in the window of a penthouse apartment looking out at St. Peter's illuminated dome, then turned to a heartbreakingly beautiful woman and said: *Are you all right, Mary? You're sure?*

"Don't pastors do anything for these women?" Dennis McLaughlin was asking.

"What?" Matthew Mahan said, struggling to return to the reality of time and place. "Pastors? No, most of them are scared to death of a divorced woman. For obvious reasons. They're afraid they may go the Fogarty route."

"What about these good-conscience divorce programs that bishops are operating down in Baton Rouge and a few other places?"

"Portland, Oregon," Matthew Mahan said guiltily. "Yes. I've been very interested in them. But Monsignor Barker, the head of our diocesan Rota, takes a very dim view of them. It gets pretty complicated when you tell people that all they need to return to the sacraments is the subjective judgment that there was no way to avoid the breakup of the first marriage. I'm in favor of it from a spiritual point of view. But it creates a legal nightmare from a canon lawyer's point of view."

"Maybe if we all went the Fogarty route we wouldn't be so legalistic," Dennis McLaughlin said.

"*What?*" Matthew Mahan said.

"I mean—get married," Dennis said hastily.

"Sometimes I think that's all guys your age think about."

"It's pretty hard *not* to think about it."

"I know, I know. I went through it. There were nights—"

And days, days in the country walking under spring trees, the air rich with greening grass, budding branches, sunlight on glossy dark hair, incredibly white skin, turning to search the direct green eyes. The face too perfect to tolerate sadness on it. Your voice asking once more: *Are you all right, Mary?*

Beside the Archbishop, Dennis McLaughlin was brooding over the impossibility of discussing celibacy with any priest over forty. He had tried and failed and had seen his friends try and fail too often. The word meant revolution to them. He had been foolish to think that the Archbishop's reaction would be less extreme. His Excellency was practically strangling with rage. Or was it embarrassment, because he had blundered into admitting he had been frustrated in his time? The episcopal dignity had been compromised. Quick, Dennis, change the subject, or you will get either a growl or a howl, and this little experiment delaying the collapse of your priesthood may end.

"Do you always deal—with alcoholic priests yourself?"

"I try to—for several reasons," Matthew Mahan said. "My brother was an alcoholic. I tried to help him and made a mess of it. It's one of the few chances I have to do some real pastoral work. As we said at Vatican II—it's part of a bishop's job to be a father to his priests. It sounds great, but it isn't easy to put into practice. Priests are grown men. Most of them don't want a father—at least not in the obvious sense of that word."

Dennis nodded. "Like the laity—they don't want shepherds anymore. They're not sheep."

The larger implications of those words made Matthew Mahan recoil. They had stopped for a red light. He looked out the window and saw a half-dozen black teen-agers staring hungrily at the Cadillac. "I suppose that's true," he said. "But people still need care. They need help in so many ways. I'm not quite ready to give up that image."

"Most people my age have given it up."

The cold arrogance in those words disturbed Matthew Mahan enormously. It was not the first time he had caught an under-tone of contempt in Dennis McLaughlin's voice. But for the first time he was able to locate one of the central sources of the uneasiness he felt when he was talking to or thinking about Father McLaughlin's generation—their sullen attitude toward imperfec-tions of phrase or practice that his generation had tolerated—an attitude that eventually seemed to translate itself into a contempt for the tolerators and finally for toleration itself.

"I wonder if you'll feel the same way in twenty years," Matthew Mahan said.

"Who knows where I'll be in twenty years," Dennis McLaughlin said.

Again the tone was icy, and Matthew Mahan heard the con-tempt—and something else (an implied threat?)—in the words. For a moment he felt himself poised between anger and sadness. The past two days flickered behind his eyes, a succession of dis-connected images: the Jefferson Memorial serenely Greek beside the water as the plane landed in Washington, D.C.; the suave Roman courtesy of the apostolic delegate, subtly refusing his

55

agitated plea for assistance, while words of empty reassurance flowed from his mouth; the city, mysterious, coagulated, and impenetrable from the air; Monsignor Paul O'Reilly's stony hatred. The unspoiled faces of the confirmation class; the tormented face of Bill Fogarty; and now this stiff-necked rebuke from thirty-year-old Dennis McLaughlin.

To lose his temper now would be unfair, Matthew Mahan wearily realized. It would only widen the gulf between him and this haughty young man. Letting go of his anger, even regretting it, Matthew Mahan succumbed to muddy, stagnant sadness, letting it engulf him and his voice, his will, even his good intentions. Was there really any hope of escaping this insistent sense of bafflement, of frustraton, of failure? It seemed to infect, infest, every fiber of the fabric of faith, to defy every effort, thought, prayer.

"The trouble with that attitude, Dennis," he said, "is you may give up caring about people completely. There's a young priest in Pittsburgh—what's his name, Ross or something—who recently announced that the real reason for the priest shortage is the Catholic laity. They're not worth bothering about. That's what he actually said."

"Yes," said Dennis.

The response could not have been more inert. The car slowed to a stop. Eddie Johnson was opening the door, lifting out the briefcase with its daily burden of problems and propositions. Matthew Mahan stared for a moment at the cathedral, illuminated by two dozen floodlights that cost almost as much to maintain each year as a grammar school teacher. The product of his immediate predecessor, the huge white pseudo-Romanesque structure was unique—uniquely expensive and uniquely grotesque. Sandblasting its limestone exterior twice a year to prevent the city's polluted air from turning it a perverse gray cost another five grammar school teachers.

With the same enthusiasm for fake traditional architecture, his predecessor had also built the twin fieldstone buildings that comprised the Archbishop's residence and the diocesan offices. Blunted turrets and an imitation parapet decorated the roofs, and the high narrow windows on the first floor were protected by iron grillwork. The front door was a huge one-piece mixture of cast iron and glass that required substantial muscular effort to open. Wryly,

Matthew Mahan remembered that Monsignor Lawrence McGraw, the pastor in his first parish assignment, used to call the cathedral the White Elephant and the residence Castle Rackrent. What did they call it these days? He must ask Dennis McLaughlin sometime, when he was not feeling quite so discouraged.

Dennis McLaughlin seized the large cast-iron ring on the front door and tugged once, twice, then tried both hands before finally persuading it to creak open. In the warm downstairs hall the housekeeper, Mrs. Adelaide Norton, hurried toward them, wiping her hands on her long white apron. "Good afternoon, Your Excellency, or better, good evening." Mrs. Norton's way of reminding him that she had been keeping the supper hot for two hours.

"I'm sorry we're late. We got delayed by an unexpected emergency."

"Perfectly all right, perfectly all right. I've a roast and it was no trouble to keep warm." Mrs. Norton's overlong pointed nose twitched, as it often did when she was annoyed or excited.

As usual, the roast was overdone. Matthew Mahan ate a single slice hurriedly. He had more or less given up trying to get Mrs. Norton to cook things his way. His stomach felt vaguely uneasy, and he wondered if the chicken salad sandwich he had gulped at the airport restaurant yesterday in Washington was tainted. He had no time to get sick, not even for a day. In the center of the long table Dennis McLaughlin ate his dinner in silence as usual. Matthew Mahan felt vaguely annoyed by the way Dennis seldom if ever started a conversation. It was especially irritating tonight, when he was too tired to think.

He finally resorted to the most obvious conversation starter of them all and asked Dennis what sport (if any, he thought as he asked) he had preferred at college. Track was the answer. A sprinter? No, cross-country. It was logical. The wiry, almost skeletonic frame. "I was a team man myself. Baseball mostly. A little basketball. What do you think about while you run along?"

He realized the question sounded vaguely contemptuous. Dennis did not seem to mind. "Nothing. That's what I liked about it."

Another enigma. Matthew Mahan said good night and trudged wearily upstairs to his bedroom. He had barely taken off his coat and collar and slipped his tired feet into some loose-fitting slippers when the red light on the telephone beside the night table glowed. "For you, from Washington D.C., Your Excellency," said Mrs. Norton.

"Put it through."

"Excellency," said the apostolic delegate, apparently thinking he had already been introduced by Mrs. Norton. "I am calling you because of a message I received from Rome, scarcely an hour ago. I would not in the least way want you to think that I concealed such happy information from you, either through an idle lapse or from absurd pique, because of the delicate nature of the subject we were discussing yesterday."

"There is no need for you to worry about that," Matthew Mahan replied. "I understand your position."

"Yes, of course. But the information. May I tell you now what you will receive from me by telegram tomorrow morning? The Holy Father has seen fit to add your name to the distinguished fathers of the College of Cardinals. I would like to extend my most heartfelt congratulations."

"You're sure?" Matthew Mahan said dazedly.

"Beyond all doubt. It is one of five. Archbishops Cooke, Dearden, Carberry, and Bishop Wright are the others. May I say that for the first three, the honor is perhaps a perquisite of their sees, whereas for you—I do not believe your see has ever had a Cardinal. So it is a signal mark of the Holy Father's affection for you."

"I—I can hardly believe that. I mean I can hardly believe— I can't believe—that I am worthy of it."

"Of course, of course," said the sibilant Italian voice on the other end of the telephone. "As for the problem we discussed yesterday. You may be sure that I will do my utmost on my next visit to Rome to place your views before the persons who are most concerned with such matters. One of my dearest friends, Idelbrando Cardinal Antoniutti, is now head of the Sacred Congregation for the Religious. I can't understand why this did not occur to me when we were together."

Another shower of congratulations, and Matthew Mahan said good-bye to the apostolic delegate. For a moment he stared at his reflection in the round mirror above the heavy dark brown antique bureau. This glum-faced man with the square fighter's jaw darkened by five o'clock shadow, this potbellied fifty-five-year-old, who had mounted the stairs wondering if he was a walking, talking mistake—this was a Cardinal? A Prince of the Church?

Instinctively, Matthew Mahan sank to his knees beside his bed and gazed up at the suffering Christ on the crucifix between the high carved newel-posts. *You are not worthy. There is simply no comparison between your doubts and discouragements and disappointments and that suffering figure, taking upon himself the incomprehensible burden of the whole world's pain.* To his lips came the words from the mass, words that were always deeply meaningful to him although he never completely understood why. *O Lord, I am not worthy. Say but the word and my soul shall be healed.*

VII

Upstairs in his third-floor bedroom, Dennis McLaughlin was also communicating with Rome.

Dear Gog:

I am glad to see that your determination to save my soul has not lapsed along with most of your theology. But it may be too late. Instead of being picked off by a swinging nun, I've been plucked by an Archbishop. You won't believe it, so I will write it twice. I have become the Archbishop's secretary. I have become the Archbishop's secretary. Yes, *secretary*. I, the anarchistic depreciator of all authority, the rebel with or without a cause, have been catapulted by Somebody into the highest councils of the Establishment. I am in a position to acquire an intimate knowledge of the power structure. Before many more moons, I will know precisely where to place my intellectual dynamite to bring the whole system crashing down around our ears.

So much for rhetoric. Now for reality. I am so tired I can hardly keep my eyes open past 9 P.M. Working for this man is like trying to run the mile against an express train. For my own pleasure or enlightenment I have read nothing weightier than the newspaper since my elevation two weeks

ago, and I suspect that I will soon give that up for Total
Vacuity (TV, remember?).

Among my duties are the following: 1. Write His Excellency's speeches—he gives about one a week. 2. Scour the
papers and magazines for bits and pieces that will keep
him "in touch" with the latest in theology, education, modern
morals, student behavior (the two are not interchangeable
in his opinion), ecumenical dialogue, and contemporary
politics. 3. Draft replies to his correspondence with everyone
from the manager of our inglorious baseball team to the
Mayor and The Apostolic Delegate. 4. Accompany him almost everywhere to take notes on what is said and decided.
He has a horror of being misquoted. 5. Deal with the press,
radio, and TV newshawks who are always trying to get him
to say something for or against contraception, abortion, divorce, the war, student riots, clerical dropouts, President
Nixon, Pope Paul, and whether or not he is ever going to let
Catholics receive Communion with Episcopalians.

Let me give you a typical Mahan day. Last Thursday, for
instance. We started with a communion breakfast for the
Holy Name Society of the fire department at 7:15. Then
back to the office for a conference with our education bureaucrats about the ominous signs that the lay teachers are talking
union. Then a meeting with a wandering journalist who
wanted to know everything about "a day in the life of a
bishop." Next came an hour with the archdiocesan building
committee, debating the question, to build or not to build
anymore? After a half-hour lunch, at 1:15 came a man
who wants to equip all our priests with special credit cards.
Baltimore and several other dioceses have bought the idea.
At 2:45 we hustled down to dedicate a chapel being opened
in the underground part of the Civic Center mall. At 3:30
a conference with our four black priests and six black nuns
about getting more nonhonkies into the parochial schools.
At 5:15 we spent an hour with three state senators trying
to get some support for a parochial school subsidy bill. (Not
much hope.) By 7 we were at the Garden Square Hotel,
speaking to the workers for the upcoming Archbishop's Fund
Drive at a warmup banquet. Back to the residence at 9:30,

for two hours of dictating letters, memos, etc., which I have to wrestle with the next morning.

Sounds alarming, no? Even terrifying? But the most unnerving part is yet to come, old friend. *I seem to be enjoying it.* What this reveals about my character, or lack of it, you can imagine, after having spent your youth listening to me dissect myself and everyone else within range of my instinctive nay-saying. For the first time in my life I find myself unable to step back and contemplate that unreal fiction known as Dennis McLaughlin. More and more, I find myself doing, saying, even thinking, and worst of all feeling things *without being aware of them.* Only an hour or two later, when the sacred assembly line has stopped for a meal or some fitful sleep, do I find myself recalling that I felt angry or sad or disgusted earlier in the afternoon, listening to His Excellency exchange banter with the mayor or the governor, or tell the Chamber of Commerce that he will be ready to make his annual Lenten visit to them on April 6.

What do I think of His Excellency? That's another problem. I don't know. Some of the things he does and says appall me, others confuse me, and a few I find strangely moving. But there is one thing I can't forgive him: his colossal self-confidence. He never betrays the slightest hint of doubt, of angst, he moves with stunning aplomb from one social situation to another, as good-humored and as full of sententious remarks as Archbishop Babbit in the flesh.

Meanwhile, beyond the episcopal residence (in which yours truly has a maid's room on the third floor) the city is smoldering, and our once docile Romans are as combustible as the rest of the populace, perhaps more so. The blacks are beginning to hint that they make us another Watts or Detroit. The students are even more rancid over our endless war, and old Pusillanimous Paolo's ruling on birth control has three quarters of the women in the diocese seething. I doubt if there is a priest our age who can follow Il Papa's logic, much less agree with his conclusions. We may have another Washington, D.C., on our hands if His Excellency tries to get tough and order conformity in the confessional. (Living in the first century, you may not be aware that the

D.C. Cardinal, O'Boyle, suspended about forty priests down there last fall in a brawl over *Humanae Vitae*.)

Let me give you a quick description of His Excellency. He is about 6'2", slick black hair, on the beefy side, with exceptionally long arms and big hands. He has an interesting face, very Irish in its general configurations—a square jutting jaw, high prominent cheekbones, small intense eyes, a mouth that's extremely mobile, breaking easily into a Gaelic smile, with an upward curve to the right corner, a cocky, don't-kid-me expression. In the next moment the lips can become a hard, harsh line. Only in the nose have his mother's Italian ancestors made their contribution: no Irishman, not even those putative westerners who intermarried with the survivors of the Spanish armada, ever wore Mahan's nose. It comes down in its strong bridge and delicate structure from some forgotten senator who strode the Forum with a pride and no doubt with an arrogance that equaled Caesar.

As you can see, I mingle psychology with my physiognomy as usual. But I am fascinated by how everything about His Exc. *fits*. It is all so beautifully interwoven, the manner and the appearance, the effortless exercise of authority. I used to think of power as crude as well as cruel. But watching him in action for only two weeks now, I realize that the really good ones disguise the cruelty and modulate the arrogance beautifully.

Even when he gets mad, it is part calculation, I think. Whether this is correct or not, when the episcopal temperature rises, he is *très formidable*. A few days ago, he got into an argument with a recalcitrant pastor over a big bequest. It involved shares in a western copper company, worth over a million dollars. The pastor, a smooth-talking mick named O'Connell, had persuaded the dying Dives to leave the shares to him personally and then tried to argue that the take belonged to his parish and not the archd. His Exc. summoned O'C. to the episcopal office and argued calmly with him for a half hour, referring several times to Cusak and Snee's *Documents and Data for Estate Planning*, the only book he has on his desk. When O'C. still balked, the large Mahan head suddenly lowered, and began shaking back and forth like a bull about to charge. The decibel level rose about

30 per cent, and he started telling O'C. what he would do to him if he did not sign papers transferring the shares to the archdiocese, now. Within five minutes, O'C. signed.

He is prone to unleash this temper on his immediate underlings, such as yours truly. One of my more menial tasks is keeping the battery of six pens on his desk full at all times. Nothing drives him into a frenzy more than an empty pen. Remembering such details is not one of my strong points, as you well know, and I've had to rescue several empty pens from far corners of the office, where they have been unceremoniously flung. I think he fancies himself a little as the Lord Jehovah hurling thunderbolts in these moments of irritation. He is also prone to be rather snappish when I forget to give him telephone messages, or forget to call someone to cancel or change an appointment. I try to remind myself that the greatest man of them all, George Washington, treated his subordinates in the same way. But not having a revolutionary cause to console me, I wonder how long I can last, before I pull a Benedict Arnold.

Most of the time he *tries* to be polite to me. I've been recruited largely because he has sensed he is on the wrong side of the generation gap with his younger priests, and he sort of practices on me. You can imagine how co-operative I am. In spite of all his efforts to be republican, there is something inescapably *royal* about him. Maybe it's the setting in which we labor.

The episcopal residence is nothing much to behold from the outside. Just another fake medieval mélange. But inside, you, the antiquist, would spend hours silently drooling. Even I, who profess to have no interest in anything not made in America, am reluctantly impressed by the splendor. Most of it, perhaps all of it, was gathered by the previous Archbishop, who had Renaissance inclinations à la Cardinal O'Connell of Boston. In the dining room there is a lacquered William and Mary cabinet vitrine, containing a collection of Capo Di Monte porcelain, circa 1770. Not the best artistic match, you'll say, but think of the prices. Beside it is a chiffonier by Gaffiéri decorated with medallions and arabesques of satinwood. The mahogany dining room set is early French Renaissance, the chairs in the caqueteuse style. Facing each other at the end of the room on either side of the door that leads to the kitchen are two magnificent *cabinets à deux corps*. The carvings are all classical motifs, with caryatid supports at the corners of the lower units. On the floor is a sixteenth-century German Renaissance carpet, on the walls a couple of gold girandoles, with double mirrors and center cases decorated in chinoiserie.

Just across the hall, in a little wing that connects at the rear with the chancery office, is the chapel. It is a baroque jewel, imported in toto from a French chateau. The frescoes on the ceiling are a veritable orgy of baby flesh and wide-eyed ethereal angels. The altar is mahogany, carved from a single piece of wood, with incredibly intricate filigree work around and above the tabernacle. The stained-glass windows are all done in purple and blue, in imitation of Sainte-Chapelle in Paris.

Are you still with me? The parlor is mostly Louis XVI. We have a Martin Carlin cabinet in rosewood, with Sèvres porcelain inlays, cartouche back chairs and a *canapé à corbeille* (love seat to you) upholstered with Beauvais tapestry, a cabriole leg secretary of gilded walnut by Georges Jacob, and a pair of bergères (low armchairs) upholstered in yellow satin by the same *maître-d'ébéniste*, and several of those small tables called, I believe, *guéridons à crémaillère*. The walls are covered with boiserie, with the woodwork in gilt in the style of Germain Boffrand (of course, you remember he decorated the Palais Soubise for the Prince de Soubise). In the hall by the front door we have a canopy chair, early sixteenth-century French, worthy of the Archbishop of Paris himself. In the upstairs hall we have a cassapanca from fourteenth-century Florence with painted front and back panels and all sorts of *caso rilievo* carvings. Also a sixteenth-century *chaise à bras* by Jacques Du Cerceau.

On downstairs and hall walls we have a few paintings, a Correggio, a Zurbarán, a Pisanello, a small El Greco, all sacred or ecclesiastical in subject, but worth a bundle.

In His Exc.'s bedroom are two sixteenth-century French Renaissance *chaires à haut dossièr*, fantastically carved, with backs at least six feet high. Perhaps he uses them to converse with fellow bishops when they call. Beside these are matching *commodes en tombeaux,* massive, squat, tombstone-like dressers with a lot of satinwood inlays and exquisitely carved bronze handles. His Exc. sleeps in a Chippendale four-poster with a pleated valance of black silk with mother-of-pearl decorations on it. Oh yes, and he hangs his purple cassocks in an oak armoire by Robert de Cotte (restorer of the choir of Notre-Dame de Paris).

In his office, which he enters from his bedroom, His Exc. sits at a lovely Louis XVI *table de l'anglaise* made of tabanuco (that's a light-colored, beautifully grained West Indian hardwood) designed by Dugourc in the Pompeii style. On either side of the doors are two mahogany varguenos, those seventeenth-century Spanish folding desks, the fronts inlaid with velvet panels. His Exc. uses them to store and partially display his collection of seashells. He is apparently one of the top concho aficionados around, regularly corresponding with other collectors, such as the Chilean poet Pablo Neruda. In front of the desk, usually occupied by the sacred rear ends of chancery monsignors, are two eighteenth-century *fauteuil de bureau* desk chairs, upholstered in leather.

The rest of this room is unmentionable from a decorative point of view. His Exc. has plonked a big leather swivel chair behind the desk and covered the walls with personal mementos, pictures and plaques of the sort that local politicians accumulate. This, of course, brings up one of the oddest things about His Exc. He doesn't seem to *see* any of the expensive stuff. For him it is invisible. How else can you explain a swivel chair behind a Louis XVI table? Or (I forgot) a Barca-lounger beside his *commodes en tombeaux* in the bedroom? I have yet to hear him so much as comment on a piece of furniture or a painting.

In case you're wondering where I suddenly acquired all my antique-ology, the data on each piece is readily available in the files. Also the insurance figures. The whole joint is worth a million, if it goes up in smoke.

Not bad for the son of an Irish saloonkeeper, eh? That is what I gather His Exc.'s father did for a living (this picked up from a random remark). The question is, how long can he remain ensconced here in monarchical splendor while the archdiocese smolders around him?

The worst trouble at the moment emanates from the Sisters of the Divine Heart, who run Mount St. Monica's College and a couple of high schools in the diocese. These girls have really flipped out. They make the Immaculate Hearts in Los Angeles look like docile postulants. (Have the echoes of the I.H. brawl with Cardinal McIntyre penetrated the Biblical Institute's insulation from our century? Mac got a little upset when the IHM's announced all sorts of changes, from wearing trig habits to living in apartments and generally behaving like real people. When His Eminence ordered them to return to the Counter-Reformation or else, a wonderful war of words exploded. At this writing, the nuns seem to have told both the Cardinal and the Vatican to go to hell.) Imitating them, our local Weird Sisters have abandoned our precious parochial schools, bulwarks of our lily-white suburbs, and dispatched half of their nunneries into the ghettos, where they are behaving like the Vietcong in their prime. The Archbishop grew so agitated he betook himself to Washington, D. C., yesterday, to see what sort of whammy he could concoct with the apostolic delegate. These girls are not really under diocesan jurisdiction, which makes them very difficult to control. From the way he's acted since he got off the plane, I don't think the A.D. gave him very much satisfaction. So passeth away the light of this world.

Simultaneously, our spiritual leader is also trying to bank a fire glowing in the breast of one Vincent Disalvo, who yearns to imitate Father Groppi of Milwaukee fame. He has been trying to forge an alliance between university students and the blacks in his downtown parish to break the color line in the white sections of the city and in that all-white nirvana known as suburbia. His Exc.'s big worry, of course, is the possibility that Disalvo will turn off a lot of the diocese's heavy contributors. I gather there isn't much between us and financial collapse but the annual Archbishop's Fund Drive and a gimmick called the Diocesan Education Fund which raises money from the upper-crust parishes and doles it out to the parochial schools that are going broke

66

educating the hoi polloi (Slavs, Poles, Italians) and some blacks in the inner city. Only Boston has a higher percentage of kids in parochial schools than this archdiocese. Wouldn't it be terrible if the parochial school system fell apart and the R.C.s had to join the United States of America at this dubious point in history? You can't blame them for being up-tight, even if they realized they had it coming to them—which of course they don't.

The Archb. is a kind of symbolic figure in this mess (the parochial school thing, I mean). Practically single-handed during the 1950s, he raised the umpteen million bucks that built an awful lot of the schools that are now going broke. I guess he's also kind of symbolic in regard to the blacks. During the fifties he was their biggest advocate, defender, what have you, here in town. Now they're starting to give him the same kind of headaches they're giving everyone else. If I had an ounce of human kindness in my crab-apple soul, I'd feel sorry for him. But we intellectuals never permit ourselves such humanoid emotions, do we?

I stopped writing this bit of free nonsense verse to answer a summons from downstairs. I arrived to find the Archbishop being saluted by the Right Reverend Monsignor Terence Malone, our iron chancellor, and Monsignor George Petrie, our suave pseudo-liberal vicar-general, Mons. Thomas De-laney, the string-bean rector of the cathedral, Mons. Robert Quinn, ex-star fullback turned supe of Archd. Education, and sundry other chancery trolls, all with glasses in hand. Even our housekeeper, Mrs. Norton, was tippling. I soon had a Can. Club and ginger ale in my own mitt. The reason for this revelry was swiftly explained to me. Our noble lord and master has landed a red hat. He stood there, exuding his all-American vitality, his face more beatific (I saw more teeth) than ever. As my agent in place in the Imperial City, I hereby order you to find out why and how this happened.

The party was hideously clerical, with the Iron Chancellor (huge, ponderous, with wire-stiff gray hair in a crew cut) making jokes about starting a special fund to pay the cost of hanging His Eminence's galero from the dome of the cathedral, an expense which the archdiocese would have to meet for the first time. Our jolly vicar-g., who is as smooth, burnished, dapper (small, just a little pudgy in the belly and cheeks, black hair always slicked on the head) as the chancellor is large, crude, and clumsy, proposed a toast. We drank and the V.G. added, scarcely wasting a breath, "Your Eminence, why don't you use this good news as an excuse to take it a little easier. I think you're driving yourself much too hard."

"Oh, I suppose you're right, George," was the reply, accompanied by a somewhat self-congratulatory smile. "But the work is there—it has to be done by someone."

"Appoint another vicar. I'm not proud. I'll be glad to share my enormous prestige and power. Better still, when you're in Rome, ask for two auxiliaries. I have no interest in becoming either one of them, I hasten to add."

"I appreciate your concern, George, but I've discovered that most things get done the way I like them when I do them myself."

I saw poorly concealed smiles on several faces. It is common knowledge that Petrie is getting more and more annoyed by the Cardinal's disinclination to elevate him to the purple. If Big Matt made anyone else an auxiliary, Petrie would probably burn down the chancery office in sheer vexation.

All in all, it was a charming little party and I was flattered to find myself on the inside of the Big Story. See how readily I succumb to the lure of power and influence? You will have to write me one of your sermons on the Mystical Body as a divine comedy, and set my feet once more upon the strait and narrow. I don't know whether I'll be coming to Rome or will be left here to mind the telephones. But I would say we have a fair chance of a reunion on Ye Olde Aurelian Way.

As ever,
Mag

VIII

Charles Mahan's waxen face, the one he had worn in his coffin, had been transferred to a statue in a mysterious cathedral. It was not the archdiocese's white monstrosity, nor was it any other cathedral Matthew Mahan had ever visited. It had the cold penetrating smell of the catacombs. The heavy leaded glass of the windows had only crude outlines of the saints and biblical heroes that would have glowed with rainbow life in the sunlight. It was a cathedral of the dead, a gigantic crypt in which the statues bore witness to the failures rather than the triumphs of love. Matthew Mahan knelt before another statue. Its back was turned. Yet it was maddeningly familiar. A big man, solid shoulders, large head. Who was it?

In the distance, chanting. A procession emerged from the darkness. Monks or nuns, two by two, with cowled heads, a strange wailing hymn. Ahead of them, a cross twice his size and weight fastened to his back, struggled a dog. An Irish setter, the favorite dog of his boyhood, Shane. His wide uncomprehending eyes stared up at Matthew Mahan. A crown of thorns was imbedded in the dog's skull, beneath the soft silky setter's ears. One of the cowled figures bent down and patted the dog's head. He jerked back his hand and shook it angrily. The thorns had cut him. Who was he? Who had always patted Shane's head in that strong authoritative way? The father, dear God, yes, the father.

Matthew Mahan woke up. The cathedral bell was softly tolling one, two, three, four. He peered at the digital alarm clock beside his bed and saw it was 5 A.M. He had missed the first stroke. He thought for a moment about his bizarre dream. The dog, Shane, with a crown of thorns. It was vaguely blasphemous. Yet they had all loved him. Shane had especially loved the father.

Matthew Mahan sighed and told himself that dreams were full of incomprehensible mumbo jumbo. Rolling over on his right side, he shut his eyes and tried to go back to sleep. Impossible. A mixture of words and images churned in his mind. His Eminence. A Prince of the Church. No longer one of 2,500 bishops, but one of a select 120 or 130 Cardinals. Why? Him of all people, the swimmer against the Vatican tide. What did they want from him?

Then he became aware of the pain. It began slowly, and built remorselessly to an explosion that sent slivers of anguish up, down, and around the center of his body. The earlier pain that had vanished after supper was a caress compared to this agony. Again it built, exploded, and regrouped to focus itself like a fiery disk just below his waist. Cancer? Matthew Mahan remembered his father in the hospital, teeth clenched, jaw muscles bunched, refusing to cry out against the probing pincers of the crab. No, cancer did not come and go like this. An ulcer? Absurd. He was born with a cast-iron stomach. Besides, ulcer pains were mild. Or were they? Ruefully, Matthew Mahan reminded himself that medically he was an ignoramus.

He went into the bathroom and peered into the medicine chest. He saw a bottle of aspirin tablets, shook two into his hand, and gulped them down. Aspirin was supposed to be a pain killer. But the aspirin did not work very well. The pain seemed to grow more intense. Soon it was almost a separate thing with a personality of its own, a small ferocious animal. Who was that saint who concealed a lion cub under his cloak while hiding from Roman persecutors and let it gnaw him to death without a word of complaint?

By the time his alarm went off at 6 A.M., the pain was almost unbearable. But he managed to shave and dress and walk downstairs to his private chapel. He nodded to Dennis McLaughlin, who was just finishing his mass, and knelt for a moment on one of the prie-dieus before the altar. He studied the writhing Christ on the crucifix above the tabernacle. Baroque ecstasy, blending pain and beauty. He offered up his pain for Bill Fogarty and his brother Charlie, one in Purgatory, the other in this world's version of that place of suffering.

Dennis helped him vest and then served his mass for him. The sacred Host, the wine that was transmuted into Christ's body and blood, seemed to have a soothing effect on his malevolent internal visitor. Breakfast was even more helpful. By the time he finished his bacon, eggs, and home-fried potatoes and drank his coffee, the pain had vanished again.

Dennis McLaughlin had his usual thimbleful of orange juice and a cup of black coffee. "I don't know how you can get through the morning on that, Dennis," he said, realizing as he spoke that it was not the first time he had made this remark.

"My mother says the same thing."

Matthew Mahan got the implied comparison. "You'd better call Monsignor Cohane over at the paper and tell him the news," he said briskly. "Let him set up the press conference. See how

70

many copies of my standard biography we have in the files over here. We'll probably need a couple of dozen pictures, too."

Dennis McLaughlin nodded and reminded him, "We're scheduled to be at Mount St. Monica's at ten forty-five."

"I know," said Matthew Mahan. "We'll skip the mail today. I'll catch up on my committee reports."

Upstairs the Cardinal-designate spent the next half hour stretched out in his Barca-lounger reading his breviary. He found the opening lines of the morning prayer particularly suitable.

O Lord, open my lips
And my mouth shall declare your praise.

After completing half the day's reading, Matthew Mahan opened a door at the rear of his bedroom and entered his office. On his long table-desk, in small gold frames, were three pictures. On the right were his father and mother. Bart Mahan was on the beach, the ocean visible behind him. He wore white pants and an open-necked shirt. The barest hint of a smile was on his tough handsome face. Beside him was a much earlier picture of Teresa Mahan, taken in a city garden. She was a pretty, vivaciously smiling young woman in a below-the-knee print dress. A mass of dark hair fell to her shoulders à la Mary Pickford. On the left was a family portrait of Charles Mahan and his wife and their seven children, taken four years ago. They looked marvelously happy, as if they had just been named Catholic family of the year.

Around the walls of the office were many more pictures, almost all of them commemorating a sports event. A smiling Matthew Mahan was presenting a trophy to the winning baseball team, basketball team, football team, track team. Everything, he had once remarked looking at all the pictures, except a winning horse.

Above the door hung the Archbishop's coat of arms. On the right side of a green shield was a golden griffin, a mythological animal, half eagle, half lion, the heraldic symbol of the Mahans. He was on his hind legs, all but embracing a golden halberd, symbol of the martyrdom of St. Matthew. On the left side of the shield was the symbol of the archdiocese, a lamb feeding before a church spire. Beneath these images was Matthew Mahan's motto, *Dominus in corde*—"May the Lord be in my heart." It was taken from the gospel prayer of the old Latin mass. Above the shield was a gold Maltese cross, symbol of the beatitudes from the Gospel of St. Matthew. Surmounting this was a green broad-brimmed pontifical hat with five gold tassels running from it down each side of the shield.

All these things—the coat of arms, the pictures—were the every-day furniture of Matthew Mahan's life, and he seldom paid much attention to them. By now it was eight o'clock. He spent the next hour reading reports from the committees of the National Conference of Bishops. The one on diocesan financial reporting was the most important—and the most incomprehensible to him. As far as he could figure it out, every other diocese, and often every other parish, religious order, and institution within a diocese, used different accounting methods to keep track of their money—with the result a haphazard jumble that drove businessmen and bankers berserk. It made him grateful for Chancellor Malone, who was considered a financial genius.

Malone was one of the few chancery officials he had held over from the old regime. The chancellor's right-wing politics created a separate problem, however. Matthew Mahan spent another half hour brooding over the report of the Malone-dominated Building Committee, recommending the creation of three new parishes and the construction of three new churches and church schools in the city's ever growing suburbs. During the past year, the local chapter of the ultra-liberal National Association of Laymen had fiercely criticized the archdiocese for spending too much of its money in the suburbs and ignoring the needs of the decaying inner city. Chancellor Malone was inclined to discount protests from such "agitators" as left-wing propaganda.

"Your Eminence," Dennis McLaughlin said from the doorway, "the car is here. I've talked to Monsignor Cohane at the paper. The wire services have the story. The papers, the radio and TV people, have called him. He wants to know if two o'clock would be a good time for a press conference."

"Perfect," Matthew Mahan said. "Get on your hat and coat. I want you to come with me and take notes on what's said—and not said—out there. Nuns only hear what they want to hear, and they sometimes think they've said something when they've only meditated on it."

The Saturday morning traffic on Kennedy Parkway was light.

Without warning the pain began stirring again beneath Matthew Mahan's belt buckle. At first, he tried to regard it objectively, with no more interest in it than a computer has in the electrical impulses that dart down its intricate circuits. But within a few minutes it had resumed its explosive role, hurling long slivers of agony upward along his nerves to end sometimes in his throat like stifled cries.

Picking up the white molded phone on his side of the back seat, Matthew Mahan gave the operator a number and waited for it to ring, his eyes wandering along the sidewalks of Kennedy Parkway, collecting bits and pieces of familiar images. The same bored teen-agers staring woodenly at each other before the doors of La Parisienne, the city's most expensive ice cream parlor. Clumps of shouting, wrestling grammar school boys on the way to Washington Park to play baseball. A cop on a corner gassing with a friend. *Still the same, nothing has changed really*, the images whispered to the Cardinal-designate.

A feminine voice spoke brightly into his ear. "Mr. Furia's office."

"My goodness, Doris, has he got you working on Saturday, too?"

"Oh, I don't mind, I really don't, Your Excellency. I charge him for it."

"Good."

In seconds Mike Furia's ragged, rugged voice was on the line. "Padre," he said, "how goes it?"

"Fine," he said. "How's everything?"

"Okay, except for the wandering boy."

"He'll come around. Just be patient, Mike."

"The hell with patience. You've been telling me that for a year."

"It may take another year. Look, Mike, I'm calling from the car. It's not the place to discuss anything seriously. I just wanted you to know a piece of news. I'd rather you heard it from me than from a newspaper or TV reporter."

"What's happened? Has Father Disalvo decided to improve the liturgy by saying mass in the nude?"

Matthew Mahan laughed briefly, politely. "No, Mike, nothing that important. Somebody in Rome has gone crazy. They're making me a Cardinal."

"Well I'll be damned," roared Furia, almost shattering Matthew Mahan's eardrum. "When I knocked out that German tank only twenty feet from your foxhole at Falaise, I never thought I was saving a Prince of the Church."

"You didn't sound like you were saving a chaplain, either," Matthew Mahan said with a reminiscent smile. "I've tried to forget them, but I can still remember three or four of those names you called me for being out there in the first place."

"Yeah," Furia roared at the same decibel level, "but you gave me absolution on the spot."

"It was all I had to give," Matthew Mahan said. "Besides, you probably needed it."

"The hell I did. That was the one time in my life when I said more prayers than you. Listen, is this one of those deals where you go to Rome and throw yourself at Il Papa's feet?"

"More or less."

"We'll charter a plane and go with you. We'll sell the seats for a thousand bucks apiece."

"That sounds a little steep, Mike, but you're a better judge of those things—"

"Listen, if it goes the way I think it'll go, we'll probably need two planes."

"Let's think about it for twenty-four hours, Mike."

"Okay. But listen, congratulations. It's about time they recognized the best damn Archbishop in the country."

Matthew Mahan slipped the phone back into its white cradle and cast a slightly uneasy sidelong glance at Dennis McLaughlin. Why, he asked himself irritably, was he worried about what Dennis would think of that conversation? There was nothing unusual about organizing a group to go to Europe with a new Cardinal. They were undoubtedly talking about the same thing in New York and Philadelphia and Pittsburgh at this very moment. Maybe frankness was the best way to face it. These young people had to accept the fact that in the modern Church, money and the sacred, if that was not too grandiose a word for his elevation, were inextricably mixed. "Mike wants to charter a plane and organize a cheering section for our trip to Europe. He says he can get a thousand dollars a seat."

Dennis smiled. "I want the scorecard concession."

Matthew Mahan was half inclined to laugh. Instead his eyes fell on the dark red hair that vanished unwillingly beneath Dennis's round white collar, and he became serious. "Mike's a wonderful guy. But a little too enthusiastic. I have to rein him in a lot. The poor fellow's been having all sorts of trouble with his son Tony. Mike and his wife are separated, which is probably the root of the problem. Last year Tony dropped out of Georgetown. Mike put Pinkertons on his trail. They finally located him in a commune down in Hutchinson County."

"Hard Times Haven?"

"Something like that."

"They publish a newspaper—the Hard Times *Herald*. Everybody reads it out at the university. Would you like to see some copies?"

"No thanks."

Wrong, Matthew Mahan thought. You made it sound like a rebuke. He fiddled with his episcopal ring. "Well," he said, "you've been on the job almost two weeks now. How do you like it?"

"A lot more than I thought I would," Dennis said with a slightly strained smile.

"Good. I thought you'd like to know that I'm satisfied. Quite satisfied."

There was no evidence of pleasure, much less warmth, on Dennis McLaughlin's face. He ran his hand through his unruly hair and nodded. "Good—good. I'm—glad," he said.

"Let's see," Matthew Mahan said, "who else did I have on that list?"

Dennis took an index card from his coat pocket. "Your sister-in-law, Bishop Cronin at the seminary, the mayor."

"You take care of him," Matthew Mahan said.

"The president of the City Council."

"Ditto."

Matthew Mahan picked up the phone and dialed the seminary number. A querulous voice answered. "Rosewood?" It must be Mary Malone's fiftieth year at the switchboard. Matthew Mahan decided to see if she was as ornery as ever. "I'd like to speak to Bishop David Cronin, please," he said.

"He retired five years ago," replied Mary.

"Isn't he still living at the seminary?"

"How should I know," said Mary. "I ain't got time to keep track of all the old nuts they got parked around hee-uh."

Matthew Mahan sighed. Someday he would become indignant enough to fire Mary. But today was not the day. "This is Archbishop Mahan," he said. "Ring Bishop Cronin's room, will you please? If he isn't there, try the library."

A series of clicks and buzzes followed, with no commentary from Mary. With his free ear, Matthew Mahan could hear Dennis McLaughlin saying, "Yes, Your Honor. His Eminence just thought—no, nothing special, I can assure you. He just thought you might like to prepare a statement. It doesn't hurt to get one step ahead of the reporters. Yes, certainly, I'll let him know."

A dry voice rasped in his other ear. "Cronin here."

"Mahan here. I thought you'd like to hear some interesting news I just got from the apostolic delegate."

"Now what could that be?" said Auxiliary Bishop Cronin in his ripest Irish brogue. "Is he bringing over his sister and her twenty kids, and wants you to get the pack of them city jobs? Or worse, has he set them up in a Roman palazzo and wants you to send them everything you collect for the propagation of the faith?"

"No, nothing like that," said Matthew Mahan. He caught a glimpse of his own smiling face in the rearview mirror. The pain stirred menacingly, as if it were watching, too.

"Then it's got to have something to do with the heretofore unused miraculous powers of the papacy. From now on, you'll be able to ban books before poor cods like me have even written them."

"Oh, he knows all about you," Matthew Mahan said. "I told him a long time ago that if anything happened to me, he'd better consecrate the commandant of the Marine Corps to keep you in line."

"All right, all right," said Bishop Cronin, "let's get to the point. I planned to spend the day demolishing old Pio Nono, and I don't want to waste a minute of it."

"From now on there'll be another name I won't let you call me."

"Eminence? By God, don't tell me a wandering particle of actual grace has pierced the Roman miasma and inspired them to do something intelligent for once? That's the best news I've heard since Vatican II ended with a whimper."

"I'd like you to come to Rome with me for the consistory."

"Out of the question, Matthew me boy. Aside from the fact that a man of eighty has no time to waste, I don't trust myself to stand up to the triumphal pretensions of that accursed city."

76

"Nonsense. Don't make me pull rank on you. I want you to come."

"There's only one way you'll get me. You'll have to import a half-dozen of the holy blatherer's Swiss Guards and a straitjacket."

"I may do it. We'll take you along as a Sister of the Divine Heart complete with wimple."

"I dare you. I dare you," said Cronin, laughter breaking through the last words. He caught his breath. "Well, it's glorious news, lad. You know you're always in my prayers. It just shows you how much pull I've got with His Infinity upstairs."

"Stay in contact with him for my sake, will you please?" Matthew Mahan said.

"You know I will. God love you now. Thanks for the call."

Matthew Mahan dropped the phone back into its cradle. The pain had mysteriously subsided. They were on the expressway now, moving rapidly past the ugly outskirts of the city, humming across the miles of meadowland created by a meandering fork of the city's river. Matthew Mahan pointed to four sets of steel rails that crossed the meadows on a cindery embankment several dozen feet lower than the expressway. "I can remember going down to the shore on summer excursion trains during the depression. These meadows were dotted with tin shanties that men were living in."

"Sometimes when I hear stories about the depression," Dennis McLaughlin said, "I wonder why we didn't have a revolution in this country."

"People were too—too defeated, I think," Matthew Mahan said. "I remember in 1938 a half-dozen of us in the seminary came down here to the meadows to see what we could do for those poor devils. It was heartbreaking. They'd lost all hope. All they wanted was an unlimited supply of smoke, cheap fortified wine, to keep them semiconscious until oblivion. You couldn't even get them to go to confession."

"Is that what you did?" Dennis asked. "Tell them to repent?"

"Of course not. But we thought that if we could get them back to the sacraments, it might be a step on the road to rehabilitation."

A suggestion of a sarcastic smile formed on Dennis's lips. "I guess the theory was sound. How did it work in practice?"

"It didn't. They were too far gone. Too broken. It was—a terrible time."

"I wonder how they would have reacted if you took them back to the seminary, gave them your rooms for a weekend, and lived in their shanties."

"In those days the seminary was run by Monsignor Walter Kincaid. He was about six feet four and had a voice like a diesel engine whistle. He would have expelled every one of us."

"Oh well," said Father McLaughlin, "just brainstorming."

With no warning the pain exploded again, filling the center of Matthew Mahan's body with cold fire. They were in the suburbs now, still on the expressway. At the wheel, Eddie Johnson was relaxed, guiding the big car with one slim black hand, humming a song that the wind from his half-open window obliterated. Eddie loved the expressway. They were doing well over seventy, Matthew Mahan suspected. Two or three days ago a state cop had pulled Eddie over. When the lawman saw who was in the back seat, he had waved them on with profuse apologies. Dennis McLaughlin had sat there silently, commenting only with his enigmatic smile. Matthew Mahan had angrily suspected what he was thinking. These were the kinds of privileges that the Church must cease accepting.

What should he have done? Matthew Mahan asked himself, growing angry all over again. Insist on the trooper giving Eddie a ticket? If a judge suspended his license, he would be out of a job. He had six children to support. That was the kind of practical dilemma Father McLaughlin's generation blithely ignored.

"Easy, Eddie, easy," Matthew Mahan said. "We're in no hurry."

The car slowed perceptibly—from seventy-five to sixty was a highly probable guess. Matthew Mahan began to think about their destination, now only ten or fifteen minutes away, the College of Mount St. Monica. "This is the last time I'm going to make this trip," he told Dennis McLaughlin. "I'm trying to prove my good faith in this thing, but if I don't make any more progress than I did last week—"

He groped for the ultimate word or phrase.

"Sister Agnes will have to come to Canossa?" Dennis said.

Matthew Mahan looked blank.

"Pope Gregory VII made the Holy Roman Emperor Henry IV stand outside his residence for three days in a snowstorm before he talked to him."

"I'll settle for one day, to show my moderation," Matthew

Mahan said with a quick smile. "The truth is, I think I'm still afraid of Agnes. I sat next to her for a year in St. Patrick's. She was so damn smart she gave me a permanent inferiority complex."

"I wonder if the Pope could get President Nixon to Canossa?" Dennis McLaughlin murmured.

"He'd be a fool if he tried it," Matthew Mahan said. "Nobody wins in confrontations."

"But what if winning isn't the name of the game? What if losing is better?"

"Realistically," Matthew Mahan said, irritation welling in his chest again, "that makes no sense to me."

"Speculative theology," Father McLaughlin said with another fleeting smile.

"Freedom and order. The Church stands for both. The Church must have both." The new Cardinal emphasized his point by bringing his big hand down on his thigh.

Dennis nodded, but his eyes drifted away from Matthew Mahan to the suburban scenery. "Fantastic," he said. "Look, those trees, they're beginning to bud and it's not even the end of March."

"It's been a short winter," Matthew Mahan said.

They rode in silence for a few miles, until Eddie Johnson whipped the big car around one of those looping expressway exits, paid the toll, and swung onto a two-lane blacktop that ran through woods filled with bare birches. In a few more minutes Eddie eased the limousine through a set of massive iron gates. On some iron fretwork above them was a plaque that read:

COLLEGE OF MOUNT ST. MONICA
FOUNDED 1910
SISTERS OF THE DIVINE HEART

They rolled up a curving path through a half mile of open woods and emerged onto a wide lawn, dull green beneath the overcast sky. The massive main building, Sacré Coeur, was six stories high. Its gray fieldstone walls were topped by three weird white cupolas which made it look like something from a berserk fairy tale. The other buildings ranged from vaguely Colonial to a stridently Gothic chapel, complete with fake flying buttresses. "Every time I come out here," Dennis McLaughlin said, "I wonder how they managed to create such ugly buildings."

As Eddie slowed to a stop in front of the main entrance of

79

Sacré Coeur, the chapel bell began clanging mightily. Instantly, a horde of young women came racing out of the building to swarm around the car. Many of them were wearing blue denim shirts and overalls. More than a few were in miniskirts that drew a pleased "Wow" from Dennis McLaughlin. Now the doorway of Sacré Coeur was filled to capacity with a clump of older women, headed by the president of the school, plump, placid-faced Sister Agnes Marie. Only a half-dozen older nuns were wearing the traditional black robes and high white wimple. The others, including Sister Agnes Marie, were wearing tweedy, conservatively cut suits.

Inside the car, Matthew Mahan was temporarily stunned. "What the devil—" he muttered.

"Maybe they're going to burn us at the stake," Dennis McLaughlin said. "Or at the Cadillac."

The pain stirred greedily in Matthew Mahan's stomach, flickering up his chest and turning the palms of his hands cold. Summoning calm by an act of the will, he said, "They've heard about me. It was probably on the eleven o'clock news."

Matthew Mahan opened the door and climbed out of the car, forcing a smile. "What's this? What's this?" he asked Sister Agnes Marie.

Sister Agnes Marie raised her hand, and five hundred feminine voices simultaneously cried: "*Congratulations, Your Eminence.*"

"Now, now," he said to Sister Agnes Marie, "you shouldn't call me that until I get down on my knees before the Holy Father, and he makes it official."

"We like to be a few steps ahead of the Church," said Sister Agnes Marie.

A wave of laughter rippled through the crowd. Everyone obviously understood both meanings of the remark.

"You will say a few words, won't you, Your Eminence?" said Sister Agnes Marie.

There was no hope of escape. Matthew Mahan walked up the steps and turned to look down on the crescent of smiling young faces. For some reason the innocence he had grown used to seeing in his visits here over the years was no longer visible to him. Was it because he had changed? Or was it the cascades of black, brown, blond, red hair, the proletarian blue jeans that seemed to flaunt an alternative life-style? Although they wore less makeup than their

sisters of earlier decades, their faces somehow seemed more knowing—yes, even slyly knowing—the smiles subtly mocking. For a
moment Matthew Mahan doubted his ability to say anything.
What was the use of trying to communicate his real feelings, his
desire to reach into their hearts with the healing power of grace?

"This is—a delightful surprise," he began. "I don't feel I deserve
those congratulations. I don't feel the honor that the Holy Father
has said he plans to confer upon me is in any way a personal
tribute. It is a recognition of the steady growth of this archdiocese, not only in numbers, but in loyalty to the Church and the
word of God that she preaches. I mean that, I really do. It heartens
me—heartens me tremendously. Without the support of young
Catholic women like yourselves, all the titles in the world will not
do me or the Church any good. Without you, I am nothing."

There was a scattering of applause, not very enthusiastic, Matthew Mahan thought. Then, out of the crowd at the front of the
car stepped two girls with guitars. They strummed the opening
bars of a melody, and everyone began to sing.

> *We are one in the Spirit*
> *We are one in the Lord*
> *We are one in the Spirit*
> *We are one in the Lord*
> *And we pray that all unity*
> *May one day be restored*
>
> *And they'll know we are Christians*
> *By our love, by our love*
> *Yes they'll know we are Christians*
> *By our love*
>
> *We will work with each other*
> *We will work side by side*
> *We will work with each other*
> *We will work side by side*
> *We will guard each woman's dignity*
> *And save each woman's pride*
>
> *And they'll know we are Christians*
> *By our love, by our love*
> *And they'll know we are Christians*
> *By our love*

The faces swayed with the rhythm, and the voices rose and fell in a melody that seemed both mournful and joyful. Matthew Mahan began to feel better, more in command of himself, more certain of his feelings. When the song ended with a final flourish of the guitars, he said, "Thank you. Thank you from the bottom of my heart. I will always remember this day. I'd like to give you my blessing now."

Two girls in the front of the crowd knelt, but most of them did not even bow their heads as he raised his hand and lowered it swiftly, then moved it horizontally to form an invisible cross, saying, "May the blessing of Almighty God, the Father, the Son, and the Holy Spirit, descend upon you and remain with you forever."

He turned to Sister Agnes Marie and said, "That was very nice of you, Mother Agnes—I mean, Sister Agnes."

Why couldn't he just call her Agnes? he mused for a moment. When they sat side by side in St. Patrick's School, he had called her Aggie. Sometimes, when in the company of those who hated her for her astronomical marks, he had called her Baggy Aggie. He decided it made him feel better—or safer?—to use a title, even if her refusal to accept the traditional "Mother" which went with her position confused him.

She turned aside his thanks with a meek nod. "It was the girls' idea. We announced the news at breakfast, and they decided that you deserved a royal welcome."

"It was royal. Most definitely royal. I'd like you to meet Father Dennis McLaughlin. My new secretary."

Sister Agnes Marie nodded and shook hands with Father McLaughlin. They moved past the rapidly dispersing faculty into the lofty domed rotunda, with a faded mosaic of the Holy Spirit in the form of a dove on the marble floor. Casually, Sister Agnes Marie caught the arm of a young woman who wore her dark hair in an interesting sort of knot at the nape of her neck. She was also wearing a suit, but her skirt was several inches shorter than Sister Agnes Marie's. There was no doubt that she had very shapely legs, and equally little doubt that Dennis McLaughlin was noticing them.

"Sister Helen," said Sister Agnes Marie, "would you join us in my office, please? We need someone to do some note taking." As they walked, she introduced Sister Helen, whose last name was Reed.

"Reed," said Matthew Mahan. "Is this Dr. Bill Reed's daughter?"

"Yes."

"My goodness. I haven't seen you since you entered the noviatiate—"

"Five years ago."

"I thought between us we'd have your father converted by now." Matthew Mahan's tone was humorous. Sister Helen's reply was at the opposite emotional extreme. "You can't convert a stone."

Matthew Mahan recalled an angry discourse from Bill Reed when he had visited him for his annual checkup last year. Bill had been vastly exercised about the way "left-wing" Catholics were turning his daughter into a radical.

As they entered the office, the pain grew so intense that for a moment Matthew Mahan wondered if he could conceal it much longer. He forced himself to think about how totally the appearance of this office had changed. During the long reign of the foundress of Mount St. Monica, Mother Mary Catherine, heavy maroon drapes had cut off the light that was now streaming through the bay windows behind the desk. The furniture had all been fake medieval, with hand-carved devils and angels dueling on the backs of the massive chairs. Sister Agnes Marie had transformed the room from a gloomy European cavern to a light-filled model of modern American decor. The desk had a free-form top resembling a figure eight, with one end slightly smaller than the other end. The floor was rugless. The walls abounded with explosive prints of modern paintings by Henri Matisse, Stuart Davis, Ben Shahn, and several others that Matthew Mahan did not recognize. Along one wall was a beige couch, its cushions thin as communion wafers. On the other side were several chairs in the same spare design, the ribs and armrests so delicate that they seemed to be one-dimensional, drawn on some invisible screen.

It made Matthew Mahan think about getting rid of the collection of European antiques with which he lived. Up in Boston, Cushing had sold off Cardinal O'Connell's splendid treasures when he took over. But Matthew Mahan found a certain satisfaction in sitting on old Hogan's *ancien régime* couches and chairs. Besides, the stuff impressed antique fanciers such as the mayor's very rich wife, Paula Stapleton O'Connor.

Sister Agnes Marie's furniture was clearly unsuited to a six-foot-two-inch Archbishop, who weighed 195 pounds, Matthew Mahan thought. Even Dennis McLaughlin seemed to have the same feeling as he carefully sat down. Sister Helen Reed, as petite as Matthew Mahan was bulky, was perfectly at ease in her chair, crossing her legs and paying no attention to the way her almost-miniskirt rode up her thigh. Sister Agnes Marie sat down behind the inner loop of her desk.

"I wish we had some sunshine," she said. "It usually pours through these windows at this hour of the day. Would anyone like some coffee?"

The decision was unanimous in favor of coffee, and Sister Agnes Marie pushed a buzzer. It produced a tall brunette wearing a miniskirt that almost raised Matthew Mahan's eyebrows off his forehead. He could only hope she was a student.

"Now," Sister Agnes Marie said, as the coffee was served within seconds from a hot plate in the rear of the room, "what have you heard from our esteemed apostolic delegate?"

The pain prowled deep into Matthew Mahan's body. He hastily swallowed almost a third of his coffee. The question was typical of Sister Agnes Marie. It was asked in the mildest tone. She was no longer the know-it-all of their grammar school days. Diffidence was her style now. But her words, in spite of their aura of humility and submission, so often suggested the very opposite of those virtues.

"Mother—I mean, Sister Agnes," he said, "I have no desire to decide this matter purely on the basis of authority. I would hope to reach a consensus with you and the other sisters. A consensus that would preserve the peace of this archdiocese, and yet permit the discretionary freedom you want to some extent at least."

Did the semismile on Sister Agnes's face mean that she knew exactly why he had avoided answering her question about the apostolic delegate? If so, she was being unfair to him. He agreed with the A.D. The last thing he wanted was a donnybrook such as the one Cardinal McIntyre of Los Angeles had created between himself and the Sisters of the Immaculate Heart of Mary.

"Perhaps you might begin by giving us some idea of what this discretionary freedom entails," Sister Agnes Marie said.

More mockery? "I approved, without a word of criticism, your decision to alter, and finally to abandon, your habits. I have gone out of my way to find you a chaplain that *you* approve. I have never tried to stop you from participating in civil rights protests, antiwar rallies."

The expression on Sister Agnes's face seemed to imply that these were hardly gestures of liberality. His temper flickering, Matthew Mahan abandoned the positive approach and said: "But I would prefer to begin by telling you what I will *not* tolerate. What I will not tolerate for another day, in fact. I will not tolerate sisters moving into a parish, unannounced, uninvited, and with no warning starting a guerrilla war against the pastor. That is the only possible description of what is going on in St. Thomas's parish."

"We wrote a letter to the pastor telling him that we intended to open a community clinic in the parish. We never heard a word from him," Sister Agnes Marie said.

"Of course, you didn't," Matthew Mahan said. "He forwarded the letter to me and I asked the vicar-general of the diocese to investigate it."

"He wrote us a very intemperate letter," Sister Agnes Marie said. "So intemperate, in fact, that we did not feel we could receive it in the spirit of holy freedom, so we—or to be more exact, I—decided to ignore it."

"And that is why two hundred and fifty people showed up in front of St. Thomas's rectory last week, demanding free access to the parish bowling alleys, social hall, and gymnasium?"

"I suppose, to some extent, you could assign it as a reason. But only by a very strange, inverse logic. The real reason for the protest was the situation in St. Thomas's parish. How long must people wait for pastors like Monsignor Farrelley to die?"

Matthew Mahan's temper began to flame. Part of the reason was Sister Agnes Marie's bluntness. Part was the knowledge that he was about to defend the indefensible. Jack Farrelley was one of those cool Irishmen who run their parishes to suit their own convenience, which in his case included spending a month in Europe each summer and a month in Florida each winter. There were a half-dozen aging pastors like him in the downtown parishes. They were all inclined to the sumptuous life-style of the former Archbishop. "Monsignor Farrelley has been pastor of St. Thomas's for thirty-five years."

"About thirty years too long, I'd say," Sister Agnes Marie said.

"Thirty-five years," Matthew Mahan continued, "and there has never been a single criticism leveled against him, in spite of the fact that the parish became heavily Italian during those years."

"It is now heavily Puerto Rican," Sister Agnes Marie said.

"We know that, we know that. We have demographic maps for the whole archdiocese down at the chancery."

"A pity you don't send some of them to your pastors, Your Eminence," Sister Agnes Marie said, pouring herself a glass of water and taking a tiny sip of it. "Please don't regard what I am saying as impertinence, or worse, disobedience. We are only responding to the summons of the Gospel, seeking out, in our Lord's image, the lost sheep of the House of Israel."

"Truly, truly, I say to you," said Dennis McLaughlin, "he who does not enter the sheepfold by the door but climbs in by another way, that man is a thief and a robber."

There was a moment of astonished silence. Sister Helen Reed, her pencil poised above her pad, was glaring at Father McLaughlin in a most un-Christian way. Sister Agnes Marie smiled and said, "I didn't know we had a scripture scholar among us."

"I learned that line in fourth grade," Dennis said.

"That was well put, Father McLaughlin," Matthew Mahan said. "Let me go on to another point—in fact, two points that disturb me. At least one of these community clinics is soliciting funds from people in the parish and from well-to-do people outside it. Monsignor Mulcahey, at St. Rose's, says that this has resulted in a thirty per cent drop in his weekly collections. Now, you may think that this sounds unsavory. You may see me as a walking cliché, the cold-blooded bishop as banker—I don't care what I am called when I am fighting for the good order and spiritual health of this diocese. Money is a very important part of good order, and, for your information, of spiritual health as well. The average man soon becomes disenchanted with a church that bombards him three hundred and sixty-five days a year with pleas for help. When I became coadjutor bishop nine years ago, there were dozens of Catholic organizations, some local and some national, competing for funds. I brought order out of this chaos by insisting that every fund-raising appeal had to be authorized by the chancery office. We soon found that we could include most of the local appeals in our annual Archbishop's Fund Drive."

"We asked for a grant from Catholic Charities," Sister Agnes Marie said. "Monsignor O'Callahan turned us down with a three-line letter."

"I saw that letter. I also saw your grant application. It was poorly done. Your program was vague and your goals were undefined. It didn't meet the tests of professionalism, in Monsignor O'Callahan's opinion."

"Professional what?" Sister Agnes Marie asked.

"Professional social work."

"But we have no intention of doing social work," Sister Agnes Marie said. "We see ourselves as translators—translating the words of the Gospel into acts, making it flesh once more."

"Isn't that what the Church is doing and has been doing since the Resurrection?" Matthew Mahan snapped.

Sister Agnes Marie shook her head wearily and leaned back in her chair for a moment. The gray March daylight made her face look old—although she was only fifty-five, the same age as Matthew Mahan. According to rumor, well propagated by her followers, Sister Agnes Marie was a saint. She lived in a bare unheated room with planks for a bed. She frequently fasted for days. If it was true, Matthew Mahan could only wonder why the Holy Spirit declined to send her a little common sense.

"Could we take up another point?" Sister Agnes asked. "I fear we are poles apart on this matter of money."

Cardinal Mahan lowered his head and shook it back and forth. Dennis McLaughlin braced himself for the explosion. "Sister Agnes," the Cardinal said, "I have not come out here to be told we are poles apart. On this matter I am giving you an *order*. You will not raise another cent in another parish in this archdiocese without my permission. Do you understand me?"

Sister Agnes Marie's mild expression did not betray an iota of emotion. "Yes, Your Eminence. I understand you. But I reserve the right to appeal that decision to Rome."

"You have a perfect right to do that. I intend to have a long talk about this situation with Cardinal Confalonieri of the Sacred

Congregation for Bishops and Cardinal Antoniutti of the Congregation for the Religious."

Matthew Mahan found he enjoyed rolling these Italian names off his tongue. Maybe this red hat will serve a purpose after all, he thought grimly.

Sister Agnes Marie nodded. "I'm afraid we have no hope of winning an argument with you, Your Eminence, but we feel conscience-bound to try."

Matthew Mahan saw all too clearly that Sister Agnes Marie was spiritually one-upping him. But there wasn't time to play psychological warfare. They had to get to the next item on the agenda. "Let us take up the matter of St. Clare's Hospital."

A moldering pile in the depths of the First Ward, St. Clare's was over a hundred years old. Its clientele was almost totally black and non-Catholic. After much soul-searching, Matthew Mahan had decided to close it. Minimum repairs were costing $300,000 a year. The over-all deficit this year would exceed a million.

"You know how much money we are losing in that place. Yet you let your nuns join that demonstration last week, demanding in the name of the community—whatever that means—that the hospital stay open."

"Your Eminence—I led that demonstration," said Sister Helen without a trace of apology in her voice. "Those people have no place else to go. As you may recall, I'm a nurse by profession— before I went into inner-city work. I've seen what comes into that outpatient clinic."

"I know, I know, I've read the studies," Matthew Mahan said testily. "But where are we going to get the money, Sister? The age of miracles is over. Can you raise the money? Show me you can do it, and the hospital can stay open."

"If *you* can't raise the money, how can *we* hope to do it, Your Eminence?" said Sister Agnes Marie.

Another spiritual left jab? Wasn't she saying that was all Mahan stood for—Cardinal Moneybags?

"I sent a plan to Catholic Charities—a stopgap plan to convert the whole operation into a clinic. I never heard a word from them," Sister Helen said.

"I'm sure it was impractical," Matthew Mahan said crisply. "Or else I'd have heard of it."

88

"Are you sure that you didn't hear of it because Monsignor O'Callahan down at Catholic Charities disapproved of our counseling women to use the pill?"

"I—haven't heard a word about that," Matthew Mahan snapped. There was nothing in this world he disliked more than being caught off guard. "But let me say this. If you are doing that—and I heard about it—I would have supported Monsignor O'Callahan a thousand per cent. What else could I do? Really, Sister, don't you see that I have no alternative?"

"As women, I'm afraid *we* have no alternative, Your Eminence," said Sister Helen. "We find the Pope's position intolerable."

For a moment Matthew Mahan wanted to say: *So do I.* But he could never say that to anyone. Especially to anyone as antagonistic—that was the only word for it—as this young woman.

"I'm afraid I must issue another order. You will cease this sort of counseling forthwith. The most you are permitted to do is tell a woman—if *she* raises the question—that there are two points of view on the subject. That she must follow her own conscience—"

"Your Excellency," Sister Agnes said. For the first time she betrayed a trace of emotion. "These are poor people. They don't have the background, the intelligence, the time, to read *Humanae Vitae.*"

Inwardly, Matthew Mahan struggled to control the loathing aroused by the mention of that ruinous encyclical. Why, why, why? he wondered for the three or four hundredth time.

"I agree, I agree," he said. "I am not suggesting any such thing. I am only pointing out the complexity, the delicacy, that marital counseling on this subject entails. The possibility of a scandal that could engulf the diocese in controversy—that's what I want to avoid."

Sister Agnes Marie said nothing. There was no trace of sympathy on her face. Sister Helen Reed's face was patently hostile. He glanced at his watch. Time was running out as usual.

"Sister Agnes," he said, "with this news from Rome, my time will be devoured for the next month or two. Perhaps it would be best if you developed guidelines for marital counseling—and discussed your future plans with my secretary, Father McLaughlin here. He's worked in those downtown parishes, so he's familiar with the milieu. Just remember this. I don't want to see anything happening down there that I haven't heard of—and approved—in advance."

Sister Agnes Marie nodded. Did that mean she was saying yes, or merely signifying that she had heard him?

"I'm afraid my time is going to be terribly limited, too," she said. "I'm supposed to give a paper at a conference of Catholic college presidents next month, and I haven't even started to think about it. I'm sure Sister Helen here would be glad to serve as my deputy. She's serving as my vicar for our inner-city missionaries."

The word "missionaries" came close to making Matthew Mahan explode again. Only another exercise of willpower got him out of the office and down the corridor to his car without a farewell exchange of insults.

"Did you hear what she said?" he asked Dennis McLaughlin as they pulled away. "Did you hear it? Missionaries. She's sending missionaries to my diocese."

Dennis McLaughlin nodded, desperately trying to think of a response that would not state his opinion of the idea. He glanced at his fingernails, which were gnawed to the point where raw flesh was visible, and tried to make light of it.

"Who knows? They might work."

The Cardinal missed the humor—totally.

"Maybe you ought to put on a skirt and go back in there and join the revolution right now," he snapped. "I hope you realize that I just gave you a very serious responsibility. If anything else goes wrong with those screwball women, it will be your fault. Do you understand that?"

"Yes."

That was the last word spoken by either the Cardinal or his secretary on the ride back to the city.

IX

This isn't real, this is a happening, Father Dennis McLaughlin told himself. Standing in the center of Matthew Mahan's office facing the white glare of the television lights, his eyelids felt as if they might peel off like grape skins at any moment.

Out in the hall, he could hear the Cardinal-designate answering questions for the newspaper and radio reporters. He was saying much the same thing that he had said to the girls at Mount St. Monica's, earlier in the day. The honor belonged not to him, but to the people.

A busty blonde in a pants suit ducked past a television camera, almost tripped over a cable, and rushed up to Dennis. "Have you got another bio?" she asked in a voice that struck him as exceptionally sultry. But on second glance he decided it was only his perpetually lusting imagination. Besides, her legs did not come close to the sensuous perfection of Sister Helen Reed's limbs (as the nuns probably called them, he assured himself in a burst of desperate complacency). He handed the blonde a two-page mimeographed biography of Matthew Mahan that had been produced by some previous secretary. Great writing it wasn't, but it told the essential facts.

Older son of devout Catholic parents, father a professional baseball player and then a minor league umpire who put his modest reputation and his savings into a local restaurant, which failed to survive the sudden evaporation of prosperity in 1929, thereafter a Parks Department official. Young Matt ordained a priest at Rosewood Seminary in 1939, one of the first to volunteer for the chaplain service in 1940 when war loomed, chaplain of an infantry regiment in the state's National Guard Division, a local hero by the time the war ended, thanks to numerous letters from the front, praising "Father Matt's" courage and compassion. The ultimate accolade, a column by Ernie Pyle.

Home, something of a celebrity, Father Matt quickly proved that he had what it took to succeed as a civilian. Given charge of the diocese's Catholic Youth Organization, he transformed it into a social dynamo, spewing out athletes and awards. Gymnasiums magically sprouted from one end of the diocese to the other, leaving the YMCA (and presumably the YMHA) flat-footed. Promoted to monsignor in charge of diocesan education, he proceeded to repeat the performance, building enough high schools and parish grammar schools to win a word of praise from that master apostle of bricks and mortar, Francis Cardinal Spellman. Simultaneously known as a forthright spokesman for the rights of labor and of disregarded minorities, particularly blacks. Injudicious remarks in this area sometimes placed him under a cloud with the then Archbishop. But his money-raising talents neatly balanced those black points, and his aging mentor made no protest when *mirabile dictu* Pius XII finally died and that Deus ex Italiana, Pope John XXIII, appointed his friend, Monsignor Matt (they had met in France during World War II), to be coadjutor bishop, thus making him heir to the throne which he officially ascended in 1960.

Now the man himself was standing in the doorway, calm, composed, like a veteran diver ready to do some familiar acrobatics into an equally familiar pool. To Dennis McLaughlin, on the wrong side of the lights, he was only a dark, elongated blur, booming cheerfully: "Is this television or a trip through Purgatory?" For a moment, half smiling, poised between discomfort and distrust, Dennis McLaughlin found the blur a satisfying image. That was all he really wanted to see when he looked at Matthew Mahan. He suddenly found himself wanting to see less and think more about what was happening to himself. What gave this bulky, affable (publicly) man the power to disturb him? As usual, there was no time to do more than record the intuition on the scar tissue of his cerebellum and stand there smiling (he was sure) vapidly while the Cardinal-designate disposed of a questioner or two in the doorway, and with swift sure strides stepped through the wall of light into the center of the hothouse.

It was all part of it, the way he walked and the way he talked, part of that enormous self-assurance that he projected, part of the vitality, the charisma (ugh), that wove a circle of charm around everyone near him. Was it simply envy, Dennis wondered, envy from a man who had neither bulk nor charisma?

"Are we ready to go, Dennis?" Matthew Mahan said in a low voice intended only for him. "I can't take much more of this."

The words jolted Dennis McLaughlin out of his introspection. The Cardinal-designate was looking unusually pale. Or was it only the glare of the television lights, which would have given a pallor to a full-blooded Indian?

"They're ready," Dennis said, "but I'm afraid I couldn't persuade them to shoot a single interview. Each of them insists on doing it his way."

Matthew Mahan's lips tightened, and his big squarish jaw jutted. "Didn't you tell them I *want* it my way?"

"I did," Dennis McLaughlin said, hating the plea in his voice. He could see the headlines now:

McLAUGHLIN BLOWS ANOTHER ONE
Proves Himself Unworthy of the Great Man's Trust

Matthew Mahan glared past him for a moment at the white wall surrounding them, then sighed and said, "Oh well. I guess another five minutes won't kill me."

"Hello, Your Eminence," said a short, balding man, who appeared almost magically through the glare and made a lunge for the episcopal ring on Matthew Mahan's right hand, while simultaneously bending his right knee about two thirds of the way toward the floor. His foot caught on a television cable, and he had to cling to the Cardinal's hand to keep from falling on his face. There was raucous laughter from the technicians beyond the white wall. The proles are easily amused, Dennis thought.

"Now, Jack," said Matthew Mahan, "that isn't necessary anymore."

"I still like to do it," said Jack Murphy, the anchor man of KTGM's news team. He nervously fingered his pale brown moustache, which looked like something pasted together from random bits of an Airedale's coat. "It gives me the feeling that everything's kind of in place, you know?"

The moment they had returned from Mount St. Monica's, Matthew Mahan had ordered Dennis McLaughlin to locate a folder in his personal file cabinet marked "Newsmen." He found it with no difficulty, and while the new Cardinal rested for fifteen minutes in his Barca-lounger, Dennis capsulized the already condensed biographies of the men he would be meeting at two o'clock. The more salient details were underlined in red: the man's religion, if any; marital status; number of children; place of birth (a local boy or a cold-eyed outsider?); schooling and political inclination. Thus the Cardinal could joshingly smooth Jack Murphy's dented self-esteem. "How's Jack Junior these days? Is he having a good season? I haven't had much time to follow the sports news lately."

"He's averaging twenty points a game." You would almost swear Murphy was growing perceptibly taller, Dennis McLaughlin thought, as he watched his pinched chest expand, his bony

93

shoulders brace, and his head ride high at the mere mention of his son.

"Going to your twenty-fifth reunion down at the Prep this spring?" asked Matthew Mahan.

"Wouldn't miss it, Your Eminence. No, sir, I wouldn't," said Murphy.

You had to admire the finesse, Dennis McLaughlin thought ruefully. Within Jack Murphy there now glowed a gratitude that guaranteed that there was not the faintest possibility of Jack asking His Eminence a difficult question. Instead, he would do what he was doing right now, clear his questions in advance.

"I thought I'd ask you a couple of quick ones about Pope Paul. Nothing that will put you on the spot, don't worry. Is there anything you'd like to talk about?"

"Well, now that you mention it, Jack," said Matthew Mahan, "it wouldn't hurt to mention the annual fund drive. It'll be starting in about two weeks. You might ask me something about what we hope to do with the extra million we're trying to raise. We want to expand the psychiatric social services, to set up mental health clinics in local neighborhoods. The federal government will match us dollar for dollar. And then there's the old-age center that I'm hoping to build. Without a single step in the whole building. Inclines, elevators, everywhere. A specially equipped movie theater to help the hard of hearing enjoy films again. Marital counseling services. Old people have marital problems, too. In the basement, a modern machine shop and hobby craft center."

"Fantastic, Your Eminence, fantastic," Jack Murphy said, scribbling notes on an index card in his hand.

"It'd be nice if you gave me a chance to talk a little about what we've been doing in the spirit of Pope John's *aggiornamento*—you know, updating the church here in the archdiocese. About seventy-five per cent of our parishes now have parish councils. We've got a functioning priests' senate, and we're doing wonderful things liturgically. Particularly at the cathedral, where we've got some of the finest young liturgists in the country. It isn't just a case of saying the mass in English, Jack, as you well know. It's getting the people to participate in the act of worship. In fact, that sums up what we're trying to do with all levels, get

94

the people involved with the government of the church. They're helping to run their local parishes. We've got five laymen and five laywomen on our diocesan board of education. Participation, Jack, that's what the life of the spirit is all about, a sense of being part of a genuinely loving community. We're working at it. We're making progress on all levels. We might even mention the catechism. We've changed that competely. No more rote memorizing of answers kids can't understand. No, now we try to encourage reverence, awe, a sense of the mystery of God, a questioning, searching spirit."

Listening, Dennis had to admit with his usual bitter reluctance that His Eminence was a magnificent salesman. He was even forced to admit that some of these things were actually happening. They were producing creative liturgical experiments at the cathedral, the new catechism was an enormous advance over the old catechism. On the other hand too many of the parish councils were handpicked by the pastors, the priests' senate was totally controlled by Mahan loyalists. But Jack Murphy had no interest in discovering the dark shadows in the sunny story of local reform that the Cardinal was telling him. Nor would Jack ask any difficult questions about the war in Vietnam or why the city's construction unions, which were about 90 per cent Catholic, did not have a single black member.

"Another thing, Your Eminence. Would you like to say a few words about General Eisenhower? What you thought of him, that sort of thing?"

"I'd like to do that very much, Jack. I was hoping you'd give me a chance."

A technician thrust a microphone into Jack Murphy's hand. "Quiet, everybody," somebody yelled through the door, where the newspaper reporters were still milling around. The red light on the TV camera announced that its omnipotent eye was now open.

"First of all, Your Eminence, let me say that this is the best news this city has heard for a long time. . . ."

A hand seized Dennis McLaughlin's arm. He turned and stared into a face that distinctly resembled his own. It had the same freckled skin and bony contours and was topped by an even more unruly mass of reddish-brown hair. The one difference was the angle of vision. There was another eight or nine inches of torso between the chin and the floor. "Hello, Big Brother," the newcomer said, the grin on his lips making it clear that he enjoyed the phrase.

"Where've you been?" snapped Dennis. "The press conference is over. TV now—"

"Goddammit, I could have sworn—"

Leo McLaughlin looked at his wristwatch and groaned. "Oh hell, it's stopped again."

Three years younger than Dennis, Leo was the managing editor of the diocesan newspaper, the *Beacon*. How much longer he would retain that title was questionable. To hear him tell it, he was locked in ideological combat with the editor in chief, Monsignor Joseph Cohane, day and night. In the early sixties the *Beacon* had won numerous awards from the Catholic Press Association for its crisp writing, professional layouts, and its often daring objectivity in covering issues that too many Catholic papers carefully avoided—integration, North and South, the need for more public housing, for a public defender system in the courts. But according to Leo, those halcyon days of high courage were over. All his attempts to report on liturgical experiments by young priests, the ferment of revolutionary thoughts and feelings in the archdiocese's Catholic colleges, or resistance to the draft or criticism of the Vietnam War had gone into ex-liberal Cohane's wastebasket.

Monsignor C. had also politely refused to raise Leo McLaughlin's salary from a hundred and twenty-five a week, in spite of the fact that his wife had given birth to their second child in two years. It had been painful watching Leo and his wife, Grace, struggling to live decently within their financial straitjacket. More than once, Dennis had heard Grace suggest rather strongly that it was time for Leo to abandon his crusade to move the Catholic press out of the nineteenth century. But his effervescent idealism, plus Chianti and a joint or two, usually persuaded her to postpone an ultimatum.

"Christ," said Leo, "how am I going to explain this one to Jerky Joe? It's like missing God's birthday."

"Calm down, I'll give you the standard press release. Maybe you can pick up a few things from the vidiots."

A wave of hot air greasily enveloped them as they stepped to the door of the television room. The Cardinal was now talking

96

to Carl Magnum, the stocky gravel-voiced roving reporter of station KPOM. Magnum was not a Catholic, and he made no secret of his far-out (on local terms) attitudes on war, race, and other potentially explosive topics. But Matthew Mahan seemed to be handling him as easily as he had dealt with Jack Murphy.

"I'm always ready to admit I'm *not* infallible, Carl."

"Does that mean you'll never be Pope?"

Perhaps Magnum thought this was a difficult question. If so, it only proved his imbecility, Dennis McLaughlin thought gloomily. Incredible, how little so many supposed sophisticates knew about the Church.

Gravely smiling, Matthew Mahan corrected Magnum like a benevolent pastor talking to an altar boy. "The Holy Father's infallibility is a theological gift, and it only applies to matters of faith or morals. As a human being, the Pope can make mistakes just like I can. But I'm sure I make a lot more than the Holy Father."

What could Magnum say now? Confronted by this confession, he could only change the subject. "Do you approve the idea of a married priesthood, Your Eminence?"

"For an old man like me, the question is rather irrelevant. Let me say this. I don't approve of it, but I don't oppose it, either. If married priests can make the Church more effective, I'm for it. But I'd like to see some real evidence before I make that judgment. The tradition of a celibate clergy is a thousand years old. You don't throw that sort of thing away like a wrapper on a candy bar."

"Yes, I see what you mean," said Magnum, outdistanced once more.

Why, Dennis McLaughlin wondered moodily, why did they all put him on a pedestal? Why couldn't someone talk to him as one human being to another human being? When would he (and his brother bishops) face a jury of their peers?

"The whole thing bores me," Leo said, collapsing into a leather chair beside Dennis's desk. He waved a copy of the Hard Times *Herald* at his brother. "Here's what I really should be writing for. They want some more stuff from me."

Under the transparent pseudonym Leo the Great, Leo had done a number of articles for the *Herald*, diatribes on the Church's failure to condemn war and join the revolution, the sort of journalistic trash that was ruining the underground press, in Dennis's opinion.

"I hope you put some facts into your next effort," he said.

"I thought you were going to stop playing Big Brother–Ph.D.–Jesuit–Junior Jesus," Leo said.

Last year they had had a bitter argument about Dennis's fondness for giving Leo large amounts of unwanted advice. Dennis had been shocked by the bitterness of Leo's resentment and had tried to abandon the role. But Leo's headstrong tendencies did not make it easier. Nor did his recent inclination to attack his older brother and put him on the defensive in almost every conversation.

"Sorry," Dennis said.

Leo tried to restore their earlier cheer. "I thought old Pope Placebo was going to let the title of Cardinal wither away. What the hell are they but glorified flunkies?"

"Andy Goggin calls it the godfather complex. You don't see Luciano or Luchese dismissing his capos. Why should you expect more from a Montini?"

"How's old Gog? Enjoying Rome?"

"Moderately."

"You could be there with him. Any regrets?"

"An occasional twinge."

Leo laughed mockingly. "Poor old brother Dennis. He quits the Jesuits, turns his back on intellectual prestige to become a priest of the people. Two months later he finds himself handing out episcopal press releases. The tragedy of a would-be saint. It happens every day all over this lousy country. Guys start out like you, determined to make the organization go straight. You generate some attention and they decide you're brilliant. The next thing you know you're running the goddamn show. Or helping to run it. So bye-bye idealism."

"Maybe I'm more interested in finding out where idealism ends and realism begins," Dennis said a little testily. "Maybe you ought to get interested in the same thing."

"Now, now, Big Brother, no lectures," Leo said with a mocking grin. His eyes grew wild and he pulled a pad and pen out of the pocket of his khaki jacket, threw one denimed leg over another, revealing that he was wearing no socks with his army hiking boots, and said, "I've got a better idea. I'll interview you. An off-the-record with one of the Cardinal's intimate deputies. Confidentially, what was His almost-Eminence doing when he heard the news?"

"He was about to have a scotch and soda nightcap and go to bed," said Matthew Mahan. He was standing in the doorway, a not quite believable smile on his face. "The phone rang. It was the apostolic delegate calling from Washington, D.C. He sounded as surprised as I was."

"Your Eminence. This is my brother Leo," Dennis McLaughlin said, feeling painfully foolish.

"I know him. I know him," said Matthew Mahan. "I like what he writes, too, most of the time."

"I skipped your press conference, Your Eminence," said Leo. "I thought I'd rely on a little nepotism to get a story with some new journalism feel. You know, personal details."

"Let's see," said Matthew Mahan with pseudo-solemnity. "I drank my scotch and soda and decided it might be better to keep the news a secret until the next morning. Then about ten o'clock I realized I was being silly. I wasn't important enough to play the secrecy game. I decided to have a little celebration with the people who are working their heads off for me, day in day out. So I called in Chancellor Malone and Vicar-General Petrie and the rest of the chancery crowd, and we hoisted a few."

"Usquebaugh—the water of life. Do you think that's what Jesus meant when he said, 'I am the good shepherd. I come that you may have life and have it more abundantly'?"

"Somehow I doubt it," Matthew Mahan said. "But I'm sure we could find a theologian at Catholic University who'd agree with you."

"Give me his name, rank, and serial number," Leo said.

Matthew Mahan's laugh was a little forced. He patted Leo on the back and said, "I'm glad you don't write the way you talk. We'd have to change the name of the paper to the *Asylum*. Dennis, would you be a good fellow and call Dr. Bill Reed for me? Tell him I'd like to stop by his office tonight. I'm going to lie down for a while. I'm not feeling very well."

"I'm sorry, terribly sorry. Can we—I do anything?"

"No. If Bill asks what's wrong, tell him I've got an awful pain in my belly."

With another forced smile he wagged a finger under Leo's nose and said, "That's off the record, you understand?"

"*Credo ut intelligam,*" said Leo.

"I beg your pardon?" said the Cardinal.

"St. Anselm," said Leo. "I believe in order to understand." His brother's cockeyed grin was close to derisive, Dennis thought nervously, but His Eminence did not seem to be offended.

"Oh yes. Oh yes," he said. "I haven't heard that for a long time. Sometimes I wish you intellectuals would remember that most bishops are just parish priests who got lucky. We're working stiffs, like the rest of the troops."

There was an awkward moment of silence. Leo obviously did not know what to say. Matthew Mahan took his silence as agreement and turned with a weary smile to Dennis McLaughlin. "Tell Mrs. Norton I won't be down to dinner tonight."

Dennis nodded and watched the Cardinal walk out of the room with the plodding step of a very tired man. Why was he continually noticing these details, he asked himself angrily, details that seemed to lure sympathy out of the recesses of his mind, no matter how harshly he ordered it to keep its distance? He told himself to remember the angry rebuke in the car at Mount St. Monica's and was forced to recall that Matthew Mahan had apologized to him at lunch. "I'm off my feed today," he had said, and as if to prove it had eaten only a few bites of his ham and potato salad.

Leo McLaughlin watched the Cardinal-designate's departure with a very different emotion. "So much for the hierarchy's opinion of the intellectuals. Who needs to think when you're a working stiff?"

Dennis McLaughlin eyed the doorway. "Lower your voice a little, will you?"

This only made more mockery dance in Leo's blue eyes. "Have you heard the latest from the Vatican? Or have you been too busy grinding out your own propaganda here? The Pope has announced an enormous step forward, a massive reform."

"What now? Antibiotics in the holy water?"

"Nothing quite *that* drastic. They've replaced 'I do' with full marriage vows, just like the Protestants use. They even adopted some of the Protestants' service, word for word, as—I quote—'an expression of Christian brotherhood.' However, non-Catholics are still required to swear by all the angels in heaven that they will raise the offspring as devout R.C.s."

"That's what I call statesmanship," Dennis said.

"Which is another word for crap." Leo peered at his non-working watch and untangled his elongated legs. "Listen," he said, "it's almost five o'clock. Five o'clock, *Saturday*. You must be off duty. Let's have a few beers."

"I'll have to get out of uniform."

"So?"

"All right. Give me ten minutes."

Dennis McLaughlin trotted up another flight of stairs to his room on the third floor. Quickly he snatched a navy blue turtle-neck shirt out of a drawer, threw off his tight white collar, black coat, and rabat, stepped out of his sweaty pants, and pulled on a pair of dark blue gabardine slacks. On went a bluish-green tweed sports coat, and he stood before the bureau mirror transformed from cleric to civilian. *If only it were as easy to change the inside as it was the outside of your persona, Father McLaughlin.*

X

"Does that hurt?"

Bill Reed's stubby fingers pressed down on Matthew Mahan's abdomen. The pain lolling drowsily beneath his flesh leaped into angry life again. "Yes," he said.

It seemed to hurt almost everywhere Dr. Reed's fingers probed. Matthew Mahan was lying on the leather-covered examination table in Bill Reed's office. He looked past him at the gleaming instruments on the white cupboard in the corner, the shiny aluminum sterilizer beside it. The white walls beneath the glaring overhead light, Bill Reed in his white coat, all this whiteness in contrast to the somber black of his coat and pants, hanging from a hook on the back of the door. His mind roved in unexpected directions, as in a dream.

Why this humiliation, this reduction by pain to the status of a child on this day of all days? Perhaps God was trying to tell him something, perhaps the pain was a coded message, warning him against the most obvious sin that might tempt him now—pride, complacent self-satisfaction. But did he really need the warning? The way things were going in this archdiocese, every day seemed to send him a similar message. Still, there was a distinction between pride of office and a purely personal pride, and perhaps the pain was intended to demolish the latter. Matthew Mahan was not conscious of this offense, either. Perhaps that was not an acquittal but an indictment. He would listen, he would watch himself more closely for evidence of this all too common flaw. *Thy will be done*, he prayed as Bill Reed finished his probing and told him to sit up. Bill took the stethoscope around his neck, put the spokes in his ears, and listened for a moment to Matthew Mahan's heart. Then he told him to breathe in and out, in and out, while the cold metal disk moved up and down his back.

"Okáy," Bill said. He scribbled his conclusions on the chart that was spread out on a white metal table beside the examining table. "Okay," he said again, his shrewd eyes glinting behind his silver-rimmed glasses, "what's eating you?"

His dour sallow face, with the faint tracing of a scar on his right cheek where a shell fragment had ripped it just before they crossed the Rhine, almost made the question an accusation. But Archbishop Matthew Mahan and Dr. William Reed had too much in common to let a tone of voice trouble them. For eleven harrowing months, June 6, 1944, to May 8, 1945, they had shared a special agony. Young Dr. Reed had been in charge of the forward aid station where the 409th Regiment's wounded were brought. When Matthew Mahan was not in the lines with the men, this was where he spent most of his time. How many awful nights and days had he watched while Dr. Reed, his face saturnine, separated the wounded according to the heartbreaking but lifesaving triage system, working first on the seriously wounded, next on the slightly wounded, and last, when he had time, on the men who were almost certainly going to die.

With his fondness for the sardonic, Bill had called the mortally wounded Matthew Mahan's patients. "Three more for you out there, Padre," he would say as the medics carried a writhing figure to the operating tent. Chaplain Mahan would stumble into the darkness or the daylight and kneel beside the dying men and give them his blessing and, if they were Catholics, absolution from their sins.

On slow days, Dr. Reed and Chaplain Mahan discussed God.

Dr. Reed did not believe in him. He called himself "a scathing atheist from birth." Chaplain Mahan and the Protestant chaplain, Steve Murchison, dismissed Dr. Reed's verbal hostility. *"When I see you talking to the wounded, Bill, I know you're not an atheist,"* Matthew Mahan used to say. This inevitably made Dr. Reed furious and would inspire even more vehement denunciations of the "God stuff" that the chaplains were "selling."

After the war, at Matthew Mahan's urging, Dr. Reed had migrated from his downstate hometown to the city. Father Matt had not a little to do with making him a very successful internist. Reed had married a local girl, a shy, dark Irish beauty who remained a devout Catholic and raised their only daughter, Helen, almost too strictly, Matthew Mahan thought, as if she were constantly afraid that her unbelieving husband would steal the girl's soul. Otherwise, the marriage had been extraordinarily happy. When he was with his wife, Bill Reed became almost sociable.

Four years ago, Shelagh Reed had died of cancer. The effect on her husband had been catastrophic. Each time Matthew Mahan saw him, Bill seemed more dry, empty, laconic, a man going through the motions of living. Studying the drawn face now in the harsh light of the examining room, Matthew Mahan saw that things were no better.

"Don't you know what's eating you?" Bill asked, his eyes glinting upward beneath the glasses. "Or are you afraid to tell me?"

"How about giving me your diagnosis first."

"You've got an ulcer. I'm ninety-five per cent certain of it. I want you to go into the hospital Monday. We'll do a gastrointestinal series and take some X rays to make sure I'm right."

"Monday? I can't possibly do it, Bill. It's the beginning of Holy Week. We've got the Archbishop's Fund Drive coming up in two weeks. I've got speaking appointments scheduled right straight through, three and four a day."

"When was the last time you took a vacation?" Bill asked, tapping his ball-point pen on the metal table beside the chart.

"I went to Brazil last year—"

"And spent all your time in the bush visiting missions."

"What else could I do?" Matthew Mahan asked. "We've got twenty-five priests down there. I had to go see all of them, or none of them."

"When was the vacation before that one?"

"I made my *ad liminem* visit to Rome in sixty-seven."

"What the hell is that?"

"Every five years or so, a bishop has to go to Rome and report on how things are going in his diocese."

"That's no vacation, either."

"Oh, I took it easy. I hit all the best restaurants."

"And between meals worried your ass off about what the Pope was going to say about your report."

No, Matthew Mahan thought, *not about that, Bill, I worried about a woman. A woman with haunted eyes who responded bravely, always bravely, to my perpetually fatuous question: Are you all right, Mary?*

Bill Reed sighed and looked at the ceiling, as if he were invoking an unknown god for assistance. "I can see that we're not going to settle anything here. A lame-brain atheist like me can't win this kind of an argument. But generally speaking, there are only a couple of reasons why people get ulcers. They're either drinking too much or worrying too much or working too hard. Usually it's a combination of all three."

"I like a scotch and soda in the evening," Matthew Mahan said, "but that's about the only drink I take regularly. Unless I'm eating in a restaurant or speaking at a dinner."

Bill Reed gave him a fleeting smile. "Okay, Padre. I know you're not on the sauce. It's obvious to me and everyone else who knows you that you're working too hard. Frankly, if I had a choice of diseases for you, I'd pick this one. It's a lot safer than a coronary. Put on your duds and let's go into the office and talk this over."

In his wry way Bill told Matthew Mahan how an ulcer worked. The new Cardinal only half listened. His eyes were on the furrows in Bill Reed's haggard face. The man looked like he was dying of some mysterious disease that dried out the flesh and annihilated the spirit.

"Now, this Titrilac comes in liquid form and in pills," Bill was saying. "Use the liquid whenever you can. Carry the pills in your pocket. Take the pills any time you feel like it. Take the liquid a half hour before eating.

"This second prescription is for some pills called Donnatal,"

Bill said, scribbling as he talked. "They cut off the nerve that pumps acid into your gut. They have a side effect you don't have to worry about. Periodic impotence."

"I wish you'd prescribe it for a few curates I know."

"Are you having trouble sleeping?"

"I wake up around four A.M. an awful lot of nights and never get back to sleep. I lie there solving problems."

"And you feel lousy for the rest of the day. I do the same thing. Here's a prescription for my favorite sleeping pill, Seconal. Don't use them every night. Wait until you feel really sleep-starved, then take one and arrange things so you can sleep about ten hours. It'll put you back on your feet."

Matthew Mahan nodded glumly. Next Bill handed him two mimeographed pages listing foods he was forbidden to eat and sample meals of what he was permitted to enjoy—if that word still meant anything. Matthew Mahan doubted it as he glanced down the pages and saw veal, spaghetti, lobster, and a half-dozen other favorite foods on the forbidden list. "Booze is out, and so is smoking," Bill said.

"*Smoking*," Matthew Mahan said. "Come on, Bill, give me a break. You remember what happened when I tried to give it up two years ago. I didn't sleep for a month."

"How much are you smoking now?"

"Oh, about a pack a day."

"Cut in half this week, and cut that in half next week."

"Okay. But if the condemned man can make an observation, I think you're taking entirely too much pleasure in giving these orders."

Bill almost smiled. "How often does anybody get a chance to order a Cardinal around?"

"How are things with you, Bill? You look awfully tired yourself."

"What the hell is this? Are you trying to play witch doctor on me in my own office?"

"You know damn well what I'm talking about," Matthew Mahan said. "When is the last time *you* took a vacation?"

"Oh, I go up to my shack in the woods and putter around on weekends during the summer."

"Alone?"

Bill's eyes were on the blue and silver ball-point pen that he kept turning around and around in his hands. "Yeah. It guarantees you a real rest."

"I never see you at dinner parties, lunches. Nobody does anymore since Shelagh died."

A nerve twitched in Bill Reed's drawn cheek. He gave a little sigh. "I know, Matt. I just don't have the heart for it anymore."

"Bill, you're a young man. You can't be more than fifty. Why don't you get married again?"

A dry sound, something between embarrassment and distaste. "Mrs. Right just hasn't come along, Matt. Maybe I'm a hard man to please."

It was hopeless. He was like a turtle retracting into his shell. Matthew Mahan groped for a new approach. "I saw your daughter today. Sister Helen."

A mistake. Bill's already saturnine face became a mask of fury. For the next ten minutes Matthew Mahan sat there while Dr. Reed told him that the Catholic Church had destroyed his daughter's mind. Intensely conservative like so many doctors, Bill's temperament fed upon the nostrums of the far Right. He was too intelligent to join the John Birch Society, but he was ready to believe that the American system was threatened by wild-eyed critics who seemed to be sprouting like weeds everywhere. He had seen too many men die for the country to tolerate wholesale castigation of "Amerika."

Six years as a nursing nun at St. Clare's had turned his daughter, Helen, into one of the castigators. She was now living with four other sisters in a rat-infested slum in the heart of the First Ward. She totally rejected everything her father stood for, everything she had enjoyed so casually in her girlhood—the baronial house on the Parkway, the beach-front mansion at the shore, the yacht clubs and country clubs, the sports cars and stylish dresses that Daddy's money had munificently supplied. Worse, she called him a hypocrite, a parody of a doctor, because he spent most of his time peering down the throats and tapping on the stomachs of the Establishment. Understandably, Bill was hurt, confused, outraged.

"Bill, if it makes you feel any better, I can't figure out what's going on in their heads, either. People her age. I've got a secretary, Dennis McLaughlin. A very bright young kid. At least three or four times a day he says things that are totally incomprehensible to me. Something's—snapped, Bill. The links, cords, whatever you want to call them that we assumed were there, connecting us to the next generation. Kennedy's assassination, this war, Nixon in the White House."

"Not everybody thinks that's so bad, you unreconstructed Democrat."

Matthew Mahan forced a smile. Now Bill was trying to cheer him up. He was also trying to tell him that no matter how bad he felt about his daughter, they would always be friends. It was a consolation, a deep consolation, Matthew Mahan thought ruefully as he involuntarily rubbed his aching stomach, to know how many men like Bill, Catholics, Protestants, Jews, and men of no particular faith, were his friends in this city, friends on a deep, unshakable level reached a quarter of a century ago in that fiery trial they had all endured in Europe.

Gruffly Bill Reed demanded a firm date for the gastrointestinal series. Matthew Mahan told him he would have to consult his appointment book, shook hands, and departed. Walking back up the Parkway to his residence, six blocks away, he felt vaguely humiliated by his illness. A sense of personal defeat dogged him— something he had rarely felt before. It was multiplied by an even more unpleasant feeling, helplessness. There was nothing he could *do* to solve this problem except take his pills and stay on his diet. A servile, mindless kind of obedience. Beyond that, the solutions seemed to lie in not doing, in not working so hard, in not caring so much, ideas that only seemed to compound the feelings of failure and futility that were dogging him these days. *Lord, Lord, thy will be done,* he prayed, but why this, why now? When he needed all his strength, all his physical and emotional resources to hold back the waters of chaos?

At the residence, Mrs. Norton peered from the other end of the hall seconds after the big iron front door clanged shut. He gave her the two sheets of diet data and asked for some cream of wheat for his supper. "I'm afraid this is going to be an awful nuisance for you," he said.

"Oh dear, dear," she said. "Oh dear, dear. I was saying only the other day to Mrs. Finch that you didn't look well to me, for all the flesh on you, you were eating like a bird. This won't be any trouble. Not a bit of trouble at all. I'll have the cream of wheat up to your room in only a minute or two."

Calling Dennis McLaughlin on the telephone intercom, he asked him to come down and take the prescriptions to the drugstore. The new Cardinal trudged wearily up the stairs to his second-floor apartment, wondering why he was the last person to discover that he was visibly overtired. He did feel exhausted now, but it had been a lulu of a day. He thought for a moment about Sister Agnes Marie, and the pain made a rapid reconnaissance from one side of his abdomen to the other.

On the second-floor landing he met his secretary, wearing a blue turtleneck sweater and green tweed sports jacket. He gave Dennis the prescriptions and said: "I seem to have an ulcer. At least that's what the doctor says, based on an educated guess."

"Oh. Oh. I'm—sorry."

"So am I. I'm afraid you and the rest of the crew will have to do more, so I can do less."

Dennis nodded and started down the stairs. Suddenly Matthew Mahan felt compelled to say something about his outfit. "Dennis," he said, "would you, as a personal favor to me, only wear those kind of clothes when you are off duty?"

It was almost unfair. Taking advantage of your illness. Was it also unwise? Speaking from weakness instead of strength? "It's more or less what I've asked all our priests to do. I sent a letter to them last year, laying down some guidelines."

Father McLaughlin looked more wistful than angry, gazing up at him from the darkened staircase. "I'm sorry. I went downtown with my brother for a few drinks. Do you want me to change now?"

"No, no."

"Oh, I almost forgot. Again." He smiled guiltily. "Father Reagan, the president of St. Francis, called. He'd like to speak to you about the demonstration that Father Disalvo is planning to hold on the campus tomorrow. He sounded very up-tight."

"All right. I'll call him. As soon as I've finished my mush. That's what I'm condemned to eating for supper."

Matthew Mahan turned away abruptly, again displeased with himself. *Wrong, wrong.* You must learn to handle this illness without any pleas for pity.

In his bedroom he switched on the television to get KTGM's

ten o'clock news. B-52s flew high over South Vietnam in response to the latest enemy offensive. The bombs drifted down, as he had seen them fall in countless other film clips while a voice-over named their unseen target. "As of last Sunday 33,063 Americans have died in Vietnam fighting. A figure fast approaching the Korean War Total of 33,629," the invisible announcer said. Matthew Mahan turned off the sound and called "Yes?" to a sharp rap on the door. Mrs. Norton came out of the dark hall like an apparition, his steaming cream of wheat on a tray. "Here it is, Your Eminence," she said. "It takes only a jiffy. Any time you want some more, let me know. I've a nice pitcher of cream here. It gives it a scrumptious taste, in my opinion."

Midway through the cream of wheat, the international news ended, and the local news began. He turned on the sound and listened to himself answering nice harmless questions from Jack Murphy. Downstairs, the telephone rang. A moment later the red light on his phone came aglow, and he picked up the receiver. "It's the president of St. Francis University," Mrs. Norton said. "He called before and I connected him to Father McLaughlin. No doubt he's forgotten to tell you."

"No, he told me," said Matthew Mahan mildly. "I'll take the call now." He sat down in his Barca-lounger beside his bed and switched off the sound on the television.

"Good evening," said Father Philip Reagan. He was one of those almost too handsome boy geniuses in which the Jesuits had seemed to specialize during Matthew Mahan's two student years at St. Francis. In fact, Reagan had taught him freshman Latin. He had been considered a brilliant classical scholar in those days. But as far as Matthew Mahan knew, Reagan had never fulfilled his early promise. Typical of too many Jesuits of that era, he thought. Posted from one job to another, fund-raising for the missions one year and giving retreats the next year and running a university the next, they became jacks of all trades, masters of none. "Can I jump the gun a little and call you Your Eminence?" Father Reagan asked. "At least, I want to extend my personal congratulations, and the best wishes of every member of our faculty."

"Thanks," said Matthew Mahan. "What's the problem? Not another financial crisis, I hope."

Last year, Chancellor Malone had caught the Jesuits negotiating a private two-million-dollar loan from an out-of-state bank. In a fierce test of influence and willpower, Archbishop Mahan had won an unconditional victory both in the countinghouse and in Rome. The Jesuits had been forced to withdraw their loan application and borrow the money through the archdiocese, thereby admitting to Matthew Mahan that the university was in parlous financial health.

"Oh no, oh no," said Father Reagan. A little more humility crept into his voice, however, which was why Matthew Mahan exhumed the topic in the first place. "It's this rally they're going to have out here. Solidarity Day, they're calling it. Father Disalvo says that he's planning to lead ten thousand blacks out here. He estimates there'll be five thousand students to greet them. Our campus security people tell me they can't possibly handle a crowd that size."

"Are you sure your information is correct? Father Disalvo promised me the last time we conferred that he would clear all his plans for future demonstrations with me. I haven't heard a word about this."

"I only know what my security people tell me."

"Don't you know by now that cops and lawyers love to anticipate the worst? Lately, I'm inclined to add mayors and university presidents to that list."

As he spoke, Mayor Graham ("Jake") O'Connor's rugged Irish good looks filled the television screen. His lips moved soundlessly, but Matthew Mahan was sure that His Honor was heaping hypocritical praise on Cardinal Mahan's head, proclaiming how pleased he was that the Pope had seen fit to reward their Archbishop for his long years of service to the Church, etc., etc.

"What am I supposed to do about this big demonstration, presuming it exists?" Matthew Mahan asked.

"I was hoping—that you'd forbid it. Forbid Father Disalvo to participate in it, at any rate. That would pretty much defuse it."

"Meanwhile, you can go on pretending to be in favor of free speech and free association, while poor slobs like me get pilloried in every underground newspaper from here to California."

"We are prepared to issue a statement supporting your stand to the limit. After the violence of Columbia—and Fordham."

"Oh yeah. They trashed the administration building at Fordham, didn't they? No wonder you're nervous."

"Your Eminence," said Father Reagan forlornly, "I wish you'd try to understand our position. We've got several thousand very restless young people out here. We're doing the best we can."

"Oh, I suppose so," Matthew Mahan said. "It's just an irresistible temptation to stick some pins into you guys after all those years of you acting as if the diocesan clergy didn't exist, pretending that you were the whole Catholic Church."

"I don't think we ever—"

"How's my nephew doing? When I heard him describe the grab bag that you're offering in place of a comprehensive philosophic education, I couldn't help but wonder if he'd be better off at the state university, where they don't discuss religion at all."

"He's doing quite well, I believe, Your Eminence."

On the television the mayor had been replaced by owlish Dominic Montefiore, the head of the City Council, and then by none other than Father Reagan. Having pummeled him into humiliation, Matthew Mahan felt a little conscience-stricken. "Calm down, Phil," he said. "I'll get hold of Disalvo tonight and straighten this thing out."

Grateful murmurs from Father President. Matthew Mahan hung up and turned on the sound in time to hear his old friend, Steve Murchison, the city's Methodist bishop, filling the screen with his slow, Gary Cooper grin and telling the people how pleased Protestants were by Pope Paul's latest choice for the cardinalate. "His Eminence and I were chaplains together, you know. The 409th Regiment. I've seen him do things under fire that only a man inspired by tremendous love for his fellowmen would even think about doing. He saved my life one night outside Düsseldorf. I came walking down a road that the Germans had zeroed in with a half-dozen machine guns. Father Matt, as we called him then, jumped out of a shell hole, hit me with a flying tackle, and the two of us went sailing into another shell hole on the other side of the road—full of water. I was going to drown him, I was so mad. Then I saw those machine gun bullets kicking up the dust where I'd been standing ten seconds before."

Matthew Mahan turned off the sound and dialed Steve Murchison's number. He answered the phone himself. "What are you trying to do to me," he said, "making me sound like Superman and Batman rolled into one? The next time I get on television,

111

I'm going to tell them a few things you did—one in particular—for me."

"How are you, Matt?"

"I could be better, but you know why."

Murchison chuckled. "Remember what I used to tell you, about you Romans being too *visible* with all your schools and colleges and what have you? That's why you're a target these days for every radical nut that can find himself a TV camera to talk at. You've got to learn to travel light, Matt."

"You may have something there, Steve. Anyway, I wanted to let you know how much I appreciate all those things you said just now on the tube, even if most of them weren't true."

"I don't need absolution, you Irish faker, and you know it."

"Good night, Steve. God bless you."

Matthew Mahan dialed the mayor's private wire. His Honor answered the phone. "Jake," he said, "I just wanted to thank you for the nice things you said on television. I only wish you meant them."

"You know how it is, Matt. We politicians have to stick together."

"I wish you'd stick a little closer to me when it comes to getting that parochial school aid bill through the state legislature."

"I told you before, Matt, and I'll tell you again. All your goddamn crummy schools ought to go out of business tomorrow. Having gone to them, I speak with authority. You won't get me to say a word for them."

"You know I'm a born Democrat, Jake. But if the other fellows are inclined to help us on this thing, you may find me awfully cool when you run for governor or senator or whatever it is you're going for next."

"If that's the price I have to pay for winning, I prefer to lose. Believe it or not, Matt, I actually care about this city, this state, this country. Your goddamn parochial schools have wrecked the public school system in this city. Would the blacks be able to scream de facto segregation, if we had your catechumens in the public schools? Would we be getting all this shit about black culture and African studies, instead of learning how to read and write? Why don't you make yourself a real hero, Matt? Why don't you announce that you don't want the legislature to pass that bill? Why don't you get out of the education business before you tear this city and state apart?"

Matthew Mahan felt his temperature rising in five-degree leaps to the boiling point. In public His Honor pretended to be a model Catholic. This was his private personality. He talked to his Archbishop as if he were an uncooperative ward leader.

"Why don't you stop trying to be an expert about a field in which you know nothing? Why don't you try just once to see the situation from my point of view? I'm responsible for the souls of those children you're telling me to send into the public schools."

"Oh what the hell," the mayor said, "we've already had this argument four times and you keep coming up with that same garbage. You make it sound like you're throwing a lot of little lambs to an army of wolves. The public schools aren't that bad. Have you ever been in one?"

"No, I just read the papers about them. Have you been in one lately?"

"Yes. They're trying to do a good job in an impossible situation —a situation you helped to create by segregating seventy per cent of the white kids in this city."

"We're integrating our parochial schools."

"Yeah. What are you up to now, five, ten per cent?"

"Thirty, thirty-five percent downtown."

"Wow. We're up to ninety per cent in most of the public schools down there."

"Well," Matthew Mahan said, as pain prowled in his stomach and he realized once more that arguing with Mayor O'Connor on this topic was futile, "I didn't call you to get into this tonight. I wanted to find out if you have any information about a parade being planned by Father Disalvo tomorrow. From downtown out to the university."

"No," said the mayor, instantly alarmed. "Have you? I'll call the police commissioner and check back with you. It sounds like a lovely way to burn down half the city."

"Now, don't get excited, Jake. I have no intention of letting Disalvo do anything of the sort. I've kept him on a very tight leash. Not that you ever give me any credit for it."

"I'll give you a few white points. I'd give you a lot more if you'd shut him up. If you don't, I may arrange to do it with a couple of nightsticks."

"Now, now, Jake, don't revert to the style of your predecessors."

"When it comes to Disalvo, I wish you'd revert. On parochial schools, I wish you'd stop reverting."

Cardinal Mahan hung up, seething. In his anger he remembered being present in the office when Archbishop Hogan had phoned City Hall about getting a dropout priest fired from a job as a playground instructor in the Parks Department. (Was it Fogarty? The man's name was never mentioned.) *Catholic children play in that park. I won't have them exposed to that kind of immorality, Your Honor.* From the other end of the phone come nothing but *Yes, Your Excellency. No, Your Excellency. Right away, Your Excellency.*

Of course, His Excellency had been ready to sound off whenever they needed him. Such as the year he helped the boys at the Hall defeat a new state constitution which would have required public officials to reveal their personal wealth. Six months later His Excellency had politely accepted a check for one million dollars for his Seminary Fund. Maybe, Matthew Mahan decided, his anger subsiding, it was better to have a mayor who told him off to his face than one who mixed money and phony subservience to buy him up like any other power broker.

Still it rankled, the way the mayor put a sneer into that word "politician" when he threw it at him. Before they were through, Matthew Mahan vowed he would teach Mayor O'Connor at least one political lesson.

Dennis McLaughlin in his green sports jacket hesitated at the door, the prescriptions in a gray paper bag. Matthew Mahan ripped it open and gazed distastefully at the neon-red Seconals, the tiny white Donnatals, the big brown bottle of liquid Titrilac, and a brown plastic container full of aspirin-size Titrilac tablets. The humiliation he had felt leaving Bill Reed's office reawakened. It must be a dread of becoming a child again, of losing control of your life, he thought. For a moment he was tempted to send it all back to the drugstore and rely on prayer and cream of wheat.

"Do you know Father Vincent Disalvo?" he asked Dennis McLaughlin.

"I've heard of him. Who hasn't? But I've never met him."

"You will soon. I want you to put on your clericals and go down to St. Sebastian's parish right now. Bring him back up here with you. I don't care where he is or what he's doing. If you're wondering why I don't telephone him, the explanation is simple. He's never in the rectory, and he never returns calls."

As the door closed, the telephone rang again downstairs. With uneasy prescience, Matthew Mahan knew who was calling. A moment later, the red light glowed and he picked up the receiver. "It's your sister-in-law," Mrs. Norton said. "Shall I—"

"No. I'll talk to her."

"Father Matt?" said the tired familiar voice. "Matt? I didn't want the whole day to go by without at least callin' you to tell you—"

"I should have called you, Eileen," Matthew Mahan said, guiltily remembering that her name had been on the list Dennis McLaughlin had read to him on the way to Mount St. Monica's, "but I've been up to my ears in reporters."

"I know. I'm lookin' at you on television right now. I can't help thinkin' how proud Charlie would be."

Would he really? Matthew Mahan asked himself, trying to imagine what his brother would have said on this triumphant day. He could only remember the hate-filled diatribes that had been flung at him over the telephone at three in the morning. The ruined political career. *They didn't see me, they saw my big brother the bishop. I never had a real friend. They were all your friends.* "I wish he was here. I wish it with all my heart and soul, Eileen. But we have to accept God's will, even when it makes no sense to us. How are you feeling?"

"Oh. Pretty well. The job's boring, ya know. Ya get tired sayin' hello t'people all day, and never really gettin' a chance t'talk t'them. They only stay in the reception room a minute or two, mosta the time."

"How's Timmy?"

"Matt, I don't want to spoil your big day. I didn't call to talk about him. But—"

"Don't be silly. Tell me."

"Oh, Matt. I'm terribly worried. He won't—he won't talk to me. He seems to be in another world most of the time. I found some pills on his dresser. Bright red little tubes. I was so scared. I threw them down the toilet."

"How's he doing in school?"

"I don't know. They've adopted pass-fail at the university, so he doesn't get any marks. I never see him study. He's never home. And he won't tell me where he goes. Sometimes I get so worried I—I just sit and cry."

Matthew Mahan was staring at bright red Seconal pills on his dresser, and simultaneously picturing his nephew, Timmy Mahan, as he last saw him, six months ago. The urchin face, the half-wise, half-mocking smile—the same smile that he had seen on so many faces at Mount St. Monica's earlier today.

"I'll call you in a day or two, when things quiet down. We'll have a good long talk. Incidently, tell your boss that you want a leave of absence, so you can take a trip to Rome."

"Rome? You mean for your—"

"Of course. I want you and Timmy to come. We'll get a nurse to take care of the younger kids."

"Oh gee, I can't wait to tell him. He'll be so excited—"

"Good night, Eileen. I'll remember Timmy in my mass tomorrow morning. I always remember his father."

"Oh yes, Matt, I know. Thank you—"

It would be better, Matthew Mahan thought as he hung up, much better, if she hated you and told you so. Hate could be conquered by love. But what can love do with a cringing defeated blob? No, that was too harsh. Eileen Mahan could not be blamed for her defeat. She was doing her best to bear a heartbreaking burden of sorrow, a burden she was too weak to carry and, alas, too stupid to understand. But Matthew Mahan knew, even as he tried to right his spiritual balance, that Eileen Mahan had been defeated before she married his brother. In some strange, unfathomable way, she had perfectly suited the methodical self-destruction that Charles Mahan pursued all his life. Why, why, why? *O Lord, we grope here in the darkness. Have mercy on us.*

He picked up his breviary and saw he was on the last page of the day's reading.

> *Come let us return to the Lord,*
> *For it is He who has rent, but He will heal us.*
> *He has struck us, but He will bind our wounds.*

For a moment Matthew Mahan's eyes blurred with emotion. He wiped away the tears and read the final prayer of the day.

> *We want to be strong enough, Father*
> *to love You above all*
> *and our brothers and sisters because of You.*

XI

Upstairs, Dennis McLaughlin put on his black suit and round collar. He called Eddie Johnson and asked him to bring the car around to the residence. Eddie groaned and remarked in a resigned voice that he was on his way to bed. "That man we work for don't know the dark from the light, he really don't. I'll be there in fifteen minutes."

"I could take a cab."

"Oh no. When he say he want the car, he want the car."

A half hour later, Dennis McLaughlin sat in the back of the Cadillac as the limousine bounced from pothole to pothole along the downtown streets. At last he was going to meet Vincent Disalvo, the city's radical priest. He had marched to City Hall in one or two protests led by Father Disalvo, protests against the war, against inadequate public housing for blacks. But he had never tried to become a member of the inner circle, a name on the letterhead of his Council for Peace and Freedom. In fact, Dennis admitted gloomily to himself, his career as a revolutionary thinker-activist was pretty much over when he returned to the city from Yale last year. His marching and protests had been reflex reactions, largely at the behest of his brother Leo.

This thought led to some depressing recollections of his outing with Leo earlier in the evening. They had gone downtown to a converted warehouse called The Place, where lesser faculty, students, journalists, and others committed to saving the world gathered for liquor and mutual support. He had stood there, beer glass warming in his hand, while Leo conferred with ad hoc committee heads and assorted spokesmen and spokeswomen. A feeling of futility had seeped into his veins as Leo smiled conspiratorially and swept each one close in the casually physical style of his generation. Arm around the shoulders of the men, around the supple waists of the long-haired girls. A hug-and-kiss hello or goodbye.

It reminded Dennis all too painfully of a visit Leo had paid him at Yale two years ago. Then Leo had been the pale smiling observer, while big brother–father Dennis demonstrated how he spent his days and nights concocting manifestos and denunciations, manufacturing protests, marches, marathon discussions. In vain Dennis told himself that his reasons for giving up this heady way of life were good and sufficient. He was thirty years old, and the appalling egotism, the superficial thinking, the neurotic hatred of so many radicals, their substitution of hysteria for politics, had rightly chilled his fervor.

It did not work, this dutiful reminder. He did not like playing pale observer. But now if—as was (theoretically) his privilege —he decided to change his mind, he could not play the other game, the save-the-world-or-at-least-the-country game. He was a man under obedience. At Yale he had been the clerical civilian, reveling in the opportunity to demonstrate to the WASPs and Jews that a Catholic priest could not only think, he could feel. But thinking, feeling, were verboten now, except as directed by Cardinal-designate Matthew Mahan. He and Father Vincent Disalvo and Fathers Novak and Cannon and all the rest of them, some 2,600 lesser shepherds, were vowed to obey Supershepherd, the man who guarded the sheepfold and who (theoretically) controlled the water of life for both sheep and shepherds.

Stop, Dennis told himself, stop. It was not *that* bad. You are out of humor, as the poet would say. Leo had gotten to you, he was making up for those years when Dennis had been mother's darling, the model to be perpetually emulated and praised. Leo's condescension was almost blatant. Now he was the man of action, the mover and the shaker, while poor old big brother—father Dennis was the pathetic captive of the Establishment.

But Leo's cruelest gambit, the one for which Dennis found it hard to forgive him, was the celibacy probe. Last year, in a moment of careless candor, Dennis had confessed to his anguish— yes, you had revealed your need, your wound—and Leo never let him forget it. As the liquor flowed, Leo made a point of giving certain girls more than a casual fondle, and then suggesting that they were ready to solve Dennis's problem, at his, brother Leo's, earnest request. And all big brother–father Dennis could do was play the dry stick, smiling wanly, no thank you, I prefer—what?

What do you prefer, Dennis? That is the unanswered question.

"This here's St. Sebastian's," Eddie Johnson said.

It had started to rain. Dennis peered through the blurred windows at the lights of St. Sebastian's rectory. He rang the bell once, twice, three times. Finally, a short, bald-headed priest with a large paunch opened the door. Dennis introduced himself and asked for Father Disalvo.

"He's over in the school conferring with his black beauties" was the answer. "But probably not in the first-grade classroom, where they belong."

St. Sebastian's school was separated from the church and the rectory by a large blacktop playground, illuminated by glaring white lights. The pastor was obviously trying to keep away prowlers. The school was dark except for five glowing windows on the top floor. He trudged up six flights of stairs. On the final landing he heard voices passionately arguing. "I say we gotta let the brothers do their thing, man. Screw this discipline."

Father Disalvo and his lieutenants were scattered around the eighth-grade classroom. Disalvo was sitting on top of a desk in the first row. Others were sitting sideways in their seats, their feet up on the seat across the aisle. Two lounged against the rear wall. About half of them were black. Along the wall nearest the door were two shaggy-headed young whites and a slim scowling blonde wearing granny glasses. Student leaders, no doubt. One of them looked vaguely familiar. On the other side of the room, surrounded by blacks, sat Sister Helen Reed. She had the same expression of intense dislike on her face that she had been wearing when they parted at Mount St. Monica's earlier in the day. Trying to avoid her glare, Dennis found his eyes on the furniture. For a moment the scarred brown desk tops, the curlicues of black iron on the front and back legs, numbed his mind. He was a boy again, reliving those lost years when he sat at one of these desks, devoutly believing everything Sister said about God and man.

"What can we do for you, friend?" Disalvo asked.

His rather high pitched voice was disconcerting. Father Disalvo was wearing a dark blue work shirt and dirty chinos. The outfit was made doubly incongruous by his looks. He had wavy dark hair and a cherubic olive-skinned face. "The Pretty Ginny" was what his fellow priests called him behind his back. No matter how tough he tried to look or act, Disalvo still somehow suggested a Christmas card choir boy on his night off.

Inwardly Dennis was nonplussed by Helen Reed's hostile eyes. But he had always amazed himself by a strange ability to conceal inner turmoil behind a cool, even an icy, facade. "I'm Dennis

McLaughlin, the Cardinal's secretary," he said. "His Eminence sent me down here. He wants to see you immediately. The car is waiting outside."

"What does he want to see me about?" Disalvo asked tensely.

"I have no idea."

Disalvo glowered down at his feet for a moment. Dennis noticed he was wearing dirty white sneakers. "I would like to finish this meeting."

"His Eminence is not feeling very well. I think he'd like to get to bed early."

"Oh my, now would he?" mocked a tall, thin black in the rear of the classroom.

"Okay," Disalvo said. "If you cats don't mind waiting. This shouldn't take more than a half hour, maybe an hour at the outside."

There was evident dismay on every face, but they murmured vaguely that they would wait for their leader's return. On the way down the darkened school stairway, Disalvo said, "I guess I'd better change into clericals."

"It wouldn't be a bad idea," Dennis said, recalling the brisk admonition about his green sports jacket that he had gotten earlier in the evening.

Father Disalvo trotted down to his rectory in the rain and came hurrying back five minutes later in black, his white collar shining in the streetlight's glow. "What's on the great man's mind?" he said as Eddie Johnson headed uptown.

"Something about a march or a demonstration he's heard that you're planning tomorrow."

"It's not a march. I promised him there wouldn't be any marches. I guess you'd call it a patrol."

They sat in chilly silence for a minute or two. Eddie Johnson stopped for a red light at Delaney Street on the northern edge of the ghetto. A half-dozen black teen-agers stood huddled in the doorway of a candy store. One of them dashed out and ran his hand down the rain-slick front fender. Eddie Johnson blew his horn angrily and shouted, "Get your hand off this car, boy."

"Those kids could be in trouble before the night's over," Disalvo said. "St. Peter and Paul parish, just two blocks away, has a gymnasium that could be turned into a social hall. Instead, it's open two nights a week, once for the Catholic Boy Scouts, and once for a parish dance—whites only."

"I know," Dennis said. "I was a curate there for a couple of months. The pastor, Monsignor McGuire, is a beaut. During baseball season, he's out at the stadium four or five days a week."

"Did you tell that to your lord and master?"

"No. I gather he's one of his best friends. They were classmates at the seminary."

"It's worse than the Mafia," Disalvo said bitterly. "You don't say a word against anybody around here if he's got the Godfather's okay. How do you stand working for him?"

"So far it's been bearable. Interesting. You know, seeing the power structure from the inside."

"Doesn't the arrogance get to you?"

"Not really," Dennis said.

Is that because you more than match it with an arrogance (intellectual brand) of your own? he wondered.

"I don't know how much longer I'm going to take it," Disalvo said. "Getting dragged up to the palace in this goddamn car like a tribune summoned by the Emperor."

"Time to become a tribune of the people?"

"You're goddamn right it is. Time and past time."

They were at the residence. The Cardinal awaited them in his office, his feet up on his Louis XVI desk, his high-backed leather chair tipped precariously. "Hello, Vinny," he said in a hearty voice that struck Dennis's ear as totally phony. "*Buono sera, caro.*"

Defiance, ferocity, vanished from Disalvo's demeanor. "Hello, Your Eminence," he said, holding out his hand. "Congratulations."

Matthew Mahan shook hands without bothering to take his feet off his desk. "Sit down, Vinny, sit down," he said. "Would you like a drink?"

"No, nothing," Disalvo said, his eyes roving nervously around the shadowed office.

"I hope I didn't get you out of bed, Vinny."

"No, no. As a matter of fact, I was having a meeting. Of the Peace and Freedom Council."

"Oh. I'm sorry to interrupt it. Maybe you could tell me what it's about now, and save yourself the trouble of reporting to me."

"Well—we were discussing this trip—that we're going to take

out to the university tomorrow. Talking about how we could break through the apathy out there."

"Trip?" Matthew Mahan said. "Are you going by bus?"

"No. We thought we'd go on foot."

"A march?" Matthew Mahan said. His voice was still cordial, but there was a definite threat in the tone. "Remember what I told you about marches, Vinny? You're not going to turn this archdiocese into another Milwaukee."

"This isn't a march, Your Eminence. We thought of it as—well, a kind of patrol. No more than a few dozen people. According to the city's statute, you have to get a parade permit only if you have more than fifty people."

"Vinny, don't try Jesuit logic on me. I've been through that mill. Are you going to carry placards?"

"Well—we thought we might carry one or two."

"No," said Cardinal Mahan in a voice that eliminated an argumentative reply.

The Cardinal lit a cigarette. "How many people do you expect to have on the campus?"

"I have no idea," Disalvo said. "A hundred. Maybe two hundred."

Matthew Mahan roared with unfeigned laughter. For a moment Dennis felt enraged. He had no great love for Father Disalvo. He was one of those rhetorical terrorists with which the nation abounded these days. A clerical Mark Rudd who sometimes veered close to the absurdities of Abbie Hoffman. But the man was probably sincere. It was bad enough to cow him. Laughing at him was detestable.

"I'm sorry, Vinny. I'm not laughing at you," Matthew Mahan said. "I'm just thinking of old Flappy Reagan, as we call him around here. Always in a flap about something. He told me they expected you to arrive with ten thousand screaming blacks to join at least five thousand inflamed students. Do you see what I have to put up with?"

The Cardinal took a deep drag on his cigarette and looked at it ruefully. "I'm not supposed to be smoking these things anymore." He stubbed it out in the ashtray. "Okay. Let's settle this right now. What do you want to do, Vinny?"

"I want to lead a delegation from the Peace and Freedom Council. An integrated delegation. Maybe twenty blacks and about sixteen whites. From St. Sebastian's Parish Hall to the university campus, where I'm scheduled to make a speech at three P.M."

"Take a bus. The thirteen bus will drop you off right at the campus gate."

"Your Eminence," Father Disalvo said desperately, "I can't go back down there and withdraw this proposal. I'll look like a total fool. I'll lose every bit of influence I have with these people. Especially the blacks. They're getting more militant every day. They're tired of marching on City Hall to demand that fair housing law. They see what's being done in Milwaukee."

"And you see what Groppi's doing out there, don't you, *amico mio*. You 'd love that kind of publicity, wouldn't you, Vinny?"

"I'm not in this for publicity," Disalvo said doggedly, obviously repeating something he had said several times before.

"Oh sure, oh sure. I bet you've got a dresser drawer full of press clippings down there in your room right now."

It was fascinating, Dennis McLaughlin thought, his mind cool once more. Watching His Eminence handle Father Disalvo was a little like seeing an old pro, the total professional, up against a brash, nervy newcomer to the power game. Father Disalvo never really had a chance. His confidence had undoubtedly been shattered by four or five previous sessions like this one. Now he was being jabbed, uppercutted, and one-two-punched without ever seeing where the next blow, or the one before it, came from.

Earnestly, His Eminence was now assuring the victim that his heart was in his corner. "You know how much I care about those people, Vinny. I stood up for them in this diocese—in this country —when there weren't a half-dozen other Catholics saying anything for them. God knows I'm one of the founders of the Catholic Interracial Council."

"I know, Your Eminence. But the situation has *changed*—"

"I know it's changed. And I know you're meeting it realistically. That's why I've given you all the freedom of speech I think you can handle. It's a lot more than some of my pastors think you should have. You don't seem to realize how much time I spend defending you up here. From Father Reagan, from the mayor. From half the people in the chancery office, for that matter. I'm on your *side*, Vinny. But never forget what I told you about that collar you're wearing. If I ever took it off you, you'd be a has-been in two weeks. You're getting attention because you're a priest, Vinny. And because you're a priest, you've got to demonstrate responsibility, prudence, if you expect me to stay on your side. Now look me in the eye and tell me that you really believe your effectiveness would be hurt if you backed down on this patrol."

Matthew Mahan's tone reduced the idea to utter idiocy. He was now the benevolent father, talking to a headstrong child.

"It would, Your Eminence, I swear it."

"All right. Then you can do it. But limit the number to *twenty*. Get me?"

"All right, Your Eminence."

"Dennis, get that apostle of law and order, Father Reagan, on the phone for me."

Dennis retreated to his cubbyhole between the Cardinal's study and the hall, dialed the university, and got an anxious Father Reagan on the phone. "Phil," Matthew Mahan boomed into the phone on his desk, "I've got Father Disalvo sitting here in front of me. He's coming out to visit your so-called educational institution tomorrow. Do you know how many people he's bringing with him? Twenty! That's right. He originally intended to bring thirty-six, but when he heard how nervous you were, as a gesture of Christian charity, and at my request, he's reduced it to twenty. He also says that if more than two hundred students show up, he's going to apply to the Sacred Congregation for the Causes of Saints for certification as a miracle. Just to be a good fellow, he'll attribute it to some phony Jesuit candidate. Who are you pushing these days, anyhow? No one? I'm overwhelmed by this outburst of humility. All right, Phil. Sleep tight. No one's going to trash your office tomorrow."

Matthew Mahan gave the mayor pretty much the same treatment, only sticking the needle in from a slightly different angle. "I don't know what you'd do without me to hold this city together, Jake."

Matthew Mahan hung up and sighed. Again Dennis sensed a touch of the theatrical. "What a disappointment that fellow has been to me on a personal level. So antagonistic. And he won't take advice. On anything."

With an effort the Cardinal brightened. "Well, Vinny, are you satisfied?"

"Yes, Your Eminence."

"Do we still understand each other?"

"Yes, Your Eminence."

"Good. What are you going to talk about tomorrow?"

"Mostly I'm going to attack Nixon. The war. Try to get more students involved in seeing the connection between the war and black poverty."

Matthew Mahan sighed again. "I don't agree with it but—okay. Just remember, no talk about violence. I don't want to hear even a hint that this city might burn."

Father Disalvo nodded glumly. "I got that message the last time, Your Eminence."

"I just want to make sure you've still got it. Okay, Vinny, good night. The car's still waiting outside, isn't it, Dennis?"

Dennis nodded.

The Cardinal held out his hand. "Thanks for coming up, *amico mio.*"

Father Disalvo trudged into the night. Dennis McLaughlin looked at his watch. It was eleven-thirty. His followers, including Sister Helen Reed, would wait an hour and a half for his return—if they waited. Not exactly the sort of experience that kindles the illusion of charisma. Did His Eminence understand this, too? Dennis wondered. Was his application of the negative nuances of power that sophisticated?

"Tell me frankly, Dennis, how do you think he feels about the deal we just worked out?"

Dennis was too surprised by the question to find a diplomatic answer. Perhaps he did not really want to find one. "I think he's mad as hell."

"Really?"

To Dennis's amazement, there was dismay, genuine dismay, on Cardinal Mahan's face.

XII

"And the money—you just can't believe the way he handles money. He's the corporation sole, you know. He literally *owns* everything in the archdiocese. Every building, every cent in every bank account. I was looking at this year's financial report the other day. He takes in about eight hundred thousand a year in his cathedraticum—"

"His *what?*"

"Cathedraticum. It's a tax of five per cent the archdiocese levies on each parish. That means that the total take must be around forty million dollars. Exclusive of the annual fund drive."

"Wow. This is fascinating stuff," said Leo McLaughlin as he thrust another Bourbon and ginger ale into his brother's hand.

You are talking too much, a drowsy voice whispered in Dennis's skull. But he did not care. He was not talking to Leo and his wife, Grace, although they sat openmouthed on the couch. No, his audience was the young woman in the pale pink suit with a skirt that stopped at least a foot above her knees. He was talking to the dark hair that fell in a glossy fountain down her back, to the curve of those nylon-stockinged legs so insouciantly crossed, to the breasts that filled the white blouse and created a lovely hollow within which a gold cross rested. If Sister Helen Reed was impressed by the revelations of the Cardinal's secretary, she did not show it. A Mona Lisa smile was all she deigned to bestow on Father Dennis McLaughlin. So he talked on.

"When it comes to money, he's got the instincts and style of a Renaissance prince. I think it's a reaction to the bad time he had in the depression, when his father lost his life's savings in a restaurant and had to take a crummy city job. He's paying me six hundred dollars a month. I couldn't believe it. That's three times what a curate gets. He just laughed and said I was working three times as hard."

"Well, you are," Grace McLaughlin said.

"Oh, I suppose so. But I'm getting used to it."

"You like it," said Leo. "You don't have to think anymore."

"Is he going to publish a financial report this year?" asked Sister Helen.

"Not if he can help it. The chancellor, Terry Malone, who's to the right of Bismarck, is against it one hundred per cent. It's easy for Matt to go along with him. There are figures in the draft report I saw that he wouldn't like to make public. The cost of running the episcopal residence, for instance: $32,567.80. And something called travel expenses that came to $26,896.50."

"And he won't give us $25,000 for our inner-city project," Sister Helen said.

"Careful," Dennis said. "No revolutionary statements, please. Didn't I tell you that my head is on the block if you girls try anything drastic? Let Father Disalvo play local radical."

"He's a jerk," Sister Helen said.

That had a very satisfying sound in Dennis McLaughlin's ears. He had somehow assumed that Sister Helen was enamored of the city's leading militant. The thought that there might be a vacuum in Sister Helen's heart inspired still more revelations from the inner corridors of the chancery.

First a word-for-word description of the way the Cardinal cowed Father Disalvo. Then the contretemps at Holy Angels, where Monsignor Paul O'Reilly was still doing his utmost to create a confrontation over birth control. Next the worries over the fund drive which did not seem to be going well. The failure of the Republican-controlled state senate to even report out of committee the bill to subsidize the parochial schools, in spite of the Cardinal's covert offers of political support in the next election.

On and on Dennis talked while laughing Leo stuck more dark Bourbon and ginger ales into his hand. Negative aphorisms, snide cracks, tumbled from his lips. Sister Helen was smiling now, yes even laughing at Father McLaughlin's description of the wreckage of the Jesuit order, the Bona Moris (Happy Death) Society, as they called the over-fifties, who sat in their rooms wondering where all the certainties had gone. She murmured her amusement at his recipe for soothing Pope Paul. "Let him take lessons in humility from the Archbishop of Canterbury." She even chuckled at his solution to the celibacy problem. "Voluntary castration. Peace will descend upon the Church, and the Pope will once more have a choir second to none."

They were at the table by now, dining on veal parmigiana as only Grace née Conti cooked it. The wine was flowing, and for some reason he still had a full Bourbon and ginger ale beside his plate. "Leo," he said raising his glass, "allow me to toast you as a diplomat second to none."

It had been Leo's idea, this "Easter truce session," as he called it, between Father Dennis and Sister Helen. He had summoned her to his office for a conference earlier in the month, and she had icily told him she was too busy. Mentioning it to Leo on the phone, he discovered that he and Helen and Grace were old friends. Grace had been in Helen's class at Mount St. Monica's. It was easy for Leo to discover that Sister Helen had no place to dine on Easter Day, thanks to her feud with her reactionary father. So the peace banquet had been arranged.

But Father Dennis had been totally unprepared for the chic, astonishingly beautiful girl who greeted him in his brother's living room. He had murmured awed idiotic things about her hair being different, her clothes. Only after the first drink did he regain some shreds of his savoir faire. Now, smiling at Leo through the alcoholic haze, he felt wonderful. The compulsion to play the frowning big brother had strangely diminished, and apparently so had Leo's fondness for sneering at Mother's favorite, the Jesuit genius.

"What are we going to do about it?" Leo said as he raised his glass in response to Dennis's toast.

"Do about what?" he said, puzzled by his brother's harsh tone.

"The Church."

"Little Brother, you are speaking to an intellectual. We don't do anything. We just talk about it."

"Maybe it's time you started doing something," Sister Helen said.

Her voice was amazingly seductive. Dennis realized that she had yet to say a word about the role he had played at the conference with Sister Agnes Marie and Matthew Mahan. It was generous of her to keep such lethal ammunition out of Leo's hands (or mouth).

"Don't you realize, Big Brother," Leo said, "that you are in a position to get information that could blow up the whole crummy show? You are on the inside—on the inside of one of the most important archdioceses in the United States. Not the *most* important, like New York—which is precisely what makes it so valuable. An exposé of New York wouldn't excite the rest of the country one bit. Everyone assumes that everything is rotten in New York, and it wouldn't surprise anyone to hear that the Church had the same disease. But this guy, your guy, is *typical*. What he's doing is what most of the other shepherds are doing— the phony image, the controlled press, the secret finances. Do you get a look at his checkbook?"

128

"I draw the checks."

"Fantastic. Then you see him in action. Absolute master of a ten- or twelve-million-dollar-a-year operation, with no accountability to anyone but himself and his guardian angel. Has he spent any money recently that might be questionable?"

A shrug from ossified Father McLaughlin. "He gave his sister-in-law a hundred dollars for Easter. All the bills she runs up at the department stores come to us. She's a widow."

"Black widows are living on welfare," Sister Helen said. "Did he say one word when the governor cut the welfare budget ten per cent last week?"

"I assume that's a rhetorical question," Father McLaughlin said, and for his reward got another smile. "It was also part of a deal. No protest, and they'd support the parochial school subsidy bill. But the WASPs double-crossed him."

Leo began asking questions like a parody of CIA section chief. Was there a copying machine in the office? Yes, a Xerox. Did he have access to it at any time? Any time. Did he have access to all Mahan's correspondence? All. How far back? Years. What about tapping his telephone? Now wait a minute. It's simple, you and he are on the same lines, right? You can tap his phone at your desk. All you need is a cassette tape recorder and a jack with a suction cup. If he catches you, he can't put you in jail—that would ruin the episcopal image.

"You'd be back in the ghetto, working with people you really care about," Sister Helen said.

Somehow, through the alcoholic blur, a cry almost sprang to Dennis's lips. *My priesthood, my priesthood, don't any of you understand?* whispered the lamenting voice. But obviously no one understood, and the words remained unspoken.

Instead, over a glass of port they listened to Leo expound the "theology of action." The Church, he declared, with its stupid clinging to Aristotelian ideas, made a childish distinction between essence and existence. She saw herself as the champion of essentials, which were constantly being stained and muddied by the accidental travails of existence. She moved when she moved at all like a cautious dinosaur. Only when you realized what Jesus was really saying when he declared, "I am the way, the truth, and the life," did you understand what Christianity really was, a continuous series of implosions that released dynamic revolutionary energy. Truth, way, life, were all one thing—action that defined itself by existing. Without action there was nothing, the void, nausea.

It was terrifying, Dennis thought, gripping his refilled port glass as if it were a stanchion that was holding him upright. You are listening to yourself two years ago. All these ideas that Leo is spouting, to the obviously hypnotic delight of Sister Helen, were the nihilistic nostrums of Father Dennis, the man-who-saw-the-revolution-coming-and-when-it-came-did-not-like-it. Yes, you must say that very rapidly, because if you stop to think about it, you may throw up.

On Leo talked. The world with its multiple agonies was forcing America to stop staring into the magic mirror of childhood with its always flattering answers. The same thing was happening to American Catholics. For the first time they were discovering that their faith did not automatically make them loyal to God and country. So far more warmed-over Dennis talk.

But suddenly Leo was on his own, beyond big brother Dennis, moving through new exciting territory. The Catholic Church in this country was one of the few institutions where "a revolutionary situation" existed.

What was a revolutionary situation? One in which the Establishment has lost its charisma, its prestige, and the expectations of the people were rising faster than the rate at which the Establishment was prepared to meet them. That was the moment when the revolutionaries must renew their efforts with the utmost savagery. The sentimentalists will cry out, wait, give them more time, they are doing their best. Nonsense, of course. No establishment ever voluntarily surrendered its power. Ultimately, power must be ripped from their hands.

Sister Helen turned to smile admiringly at Dennis. "It makes sense, it makes so much sense." She was paying him a compliment. Why? His numb cerebellum gradually deduced that she regarded *him* as the source of this wisdom. Suddenly the possibility—no, the several possibilities—of the situation coalesced in Father McLaughlin's double vision. In the glow of Sister Helen's revolutionary smile, he coolly agreed to supply his brother Leo with all the confidential material he might need from Matthew Mahan's files to create a book-length exposé that would rock the archdiocese—and hopefully the entire American Catholic Church. Not that Leo would ever write the book, or that Father McLaughlin believed it was worth writing. Leo was much too disorganized, and the realities of Matthew Mahan's day-to-day activities were much too ambiguous to be worthy of righteous condemnation. No, Father McLaughlin had another motive. As he made his blithe promises, he was remembering his brusque conversation with the Cardinal about celibacy. Suddenly, he saw how to resolve the question for himself in a way that was doubly satisfying.

The evening ended with a long, cold cab ride downtown. Dashing Father Dennis insisting on taking Helen to her dingy door in the ghetto. More jokes about conferences in the coming weeks to negotiate a truce between Cardinal Mahan and Sister Agnes Marie. "We'll be very good, we'll come up with the most harmless imaginable programs," Sister Helen said. She was silent for a moment, and then in the semidarkness of the tenement hall, he felt her eyes upon him. "May I ask you about something that puzzles me? Why did you make that devastating comment out at the college the other day? About the sheepfold?"

"I don't know. This last year, I don't know why I've done or said a lot of things. I have this sensation of floating in space in one part of myself while the other part of me goes through the motions of living and talking down below, reacting to a situation without any attempt at—coherence."

"The void. Not even you—have been able to escape it. When Leo first told me about it—and about you—it explained so much."

The hero must now speak with just a touch of tragedy in his voice. "We're all so locked into the system, body, mind, and soul. Only—"

"—exceptional ones can break out."

Incredible. She had memorized his Great Thoughts. He insisted on escorting her up the three flights of dark stairs. The stench of sweat and several other human effluvia was unbelievable. On the second-floor landing a man sat hunched against the wall, singing softly to himself. On the third floor, illuminated like the other landings only by the random rays of a streetlight coming through a dirt-smeared window, Sister Helen paused, took out her key, and slid it into the lock. She turned to him and he said, "Would you be shocked if I kissed you?"

"A kiss of peace?"

"You might call it that."

He kissed her firmly on the lips. Incredible sensations occurred in his body. When was the last time you had kissed a woman? Seventeen, the night of your senior prom, with your arranged-by-Mother date. The kiss, come to think of it, had come from her, inexplicably, suddenly, as they had said good night. The answer to your question really is: Never. Discounting Mother, you have never kissed a woman before. The realization brought Father McLaughlin very close to weeping.

XIII

On this same Easter Sunday evening, Matthew Mahan sat alone in his office, writing a letter to Rome.

Dear Mary,

Thanks for your cable with those extravagant words of praise and for the letter that followed it. The whole thing is still more or less dreamlike for me. It's hard to believe that in three weeks, give or take a few days, I'll be in Rome kneeling before the Pope.

The past week has been the worst one in the year for me as usual. I try to preside at all the ceremonies in the cathedral and keep up a normal work schedule. This invariably leaves me and my secretary frazzled by Easter Sunday. The last time I saw him as he trudged out of here a few hours ago, the poor fellow looked like a fugitive from a concentration camp.

He's new. Have I told you his name—Dennis McLaughlin? I can't remember the last time I wrote to you. He's an escapee from the Jesuits who got tired of playing intellectual Ping-Pong in the rear areas and decided to see what it was like in the trenches with the troops. I snatched him out of one of our downtown parishes, and I'm not sure yet whether he will forgive me for it. But he's exactly the sort of help I need. He's in touch with the youth movement and at the same time is a hard worker and a talented writer. He's already taken a lot of the pressure off me. My only fear now is that I may not be able to hang on to him. Like so many young people these days, he's practically tongue-tied when it comes to talking to someone my age. I think he's also gotten an awful lot of notions into his head about the conservative American Catholic Church and its arrogant authoritarian bishops. Maybe I'm confirming them!

As our schedule now stands we'll be leaving here on April 23. We're staying overnight in Ireland to give the professional micks in my entourage a chance to do their stuff, and then we're dropping by Paris for two days so the old soldiers can drive out to visit a few World War II battlefields. We'll arrive in Rome on the 27th and we'll probably stay until May 6. That should give us more than enough time to pay a few visits to the Tre Scalini.

I could write you a sermon on patience in response to a lot of the things you've said recently about the way things are going in the Church. But you can get sermons by the yard in Rome. Why import them? Besides, we'll have lots more fun arguing about it face to face.

With much affection as always,
Matt

The Cardinal addressed the envelope, sealed it, and went rummaging in Dennis McLaughlin's desk for a stamp. On his way back to his own desk, he paused to gaze wistfully at the visible portion of his shell collection in the cases on each side of the door. He had several thousand more shells down in the cellar, all carefully stored and catalogued. In the past he had managed to spend at least one relaxing evening a month changing the upstairs display, cataloging new purchases, deciding what he was now prepared to trade. But for almost a year now, he had not had a single night to spare.

He picked up an imperial volute from the Philippines—a large brown and white beauty with markings that resembled ancient Greek and Roman pottery—and let his fingers run along the smooth expanding spirals. For a moment he was back on a Florida beach, excitedly picking up a local version of the same shell, while a stern-faced man gave him a rare smile. Outside the residence a taxi horn beeped three times. He sighed and put the volute back in its case.

Riding downtown through the empty streets, he found himself thinking uneasily about the gastrointestinal series that Bill Reed planned to inflict on him the day after tomorrow. Bill had dourly warned him that it included barium enemas and all sorts of other unpleasant, undignified procedures. Bill was unimpressed by his feeble attestation that his ulcer was thoroughly quiescent, thanks to a steady diet of Titrilac and Donnatal. They had to know exactly where it was and how much damage it was doing.

Matthew Mahan popped a Titrilac tablet into his mouth and chewed it moodily. He began brooding over the words he had just written about Dennis McLaughlin. For all the hard work, he sensed an emptiness, a lack of enthusiasm for the job he was doing. Why couldn't he reach him—or any of these young people? What was he doing wrong? No answers came, and he glumly began reading his breviary.

The words of the last verse of Psalm 95 made him smile.

> Forty years I loathed that generation
> And I said: they are a people of erring heart
> And they know not my ways
> Therefore I swore in my anger

Even God had his generation gap, it would seem. But where was the blame to be laid today? Who were the people of erring heart? It was too easy to point the finger at the young. He refused to do that because he knew from his own cruel experience with Archbishop Hogan how bitter it could make a young priest—or any young person—feel. Perhaps those early wounds inflicted by old Hogan would at last serve a purpose. Emotionally he was in an ideal position to be a mediator. Why this dismaying sense of failure every time he tried to play the part?

Eileen Mahan and her seven children were waiting in the lobby of the Downtown Athletic Club. All except the oldest boy, Timmy, were dressed in new clothes, bought at Conway's Department Store and charged to his account. Matthew Mahan made no attempt to keep track of how much money he gave his widowed sister-in-law in an average year. He only knew it never seemed to be enough. Eileen Mahan was not a very good money-manager. But this was not the moment for negative thoughts. He threw himself into an enthusiastic greeting to each of the children.

"Timmy, how are you?" he said, squeezing his nephew's limp hand.

Timmy's hair completely covered his ears. He was wearing an army fatigue jacket with a dozen or so buttons and emblems on it, all in favor of peace, power to the people, and other causes.

"I couldn't get him to wear anything but that," Eileen Mahan said. "Not even a sports jacket. I'm so embarrassed."

"Now, calm down, Eileen," Matthew Mahan said. "We'll probably see a half-dozen kids upstairs wearing the same costume—and with even longer hair."

The expression on Timmy's face told Matthew Mahan that his easygoing condescension was being scorned. He turned to the rest of the family, five girls and six-year-old Matty. He greeted each of the girls by name and told her how pretty she looked. Alas, if it were only true. All of them had inherited their mother's buck teeth and narrow jaw. Timmy and his little brother resembled their father. Little Matt was an especially beautiful child, with jet-black hair and a face that exuded Irish pugnacity. He was Matthew Mahan's favorite. His mother called him a heller and his older brother said he was a spoiled brat, but Matthew Mahan never paid much attention to these complaints. "How are you, young fellow?" he said, taking the small outstretched hand.

"I'm fine, Your Eminent."

"Your what?"

The girls started giggling, and even Timmy allowed a smile to flit across his sour face.

"Your Eminence," his mother said.

Matt was totally unbothered by the correction. "Your Eminent," he said again.

"Now listen," Matthew Mahan said, speaking to all of them. "No one in this family has to call me by that silly name. I've always been Father Matt to you and I always will be." Speaking to Matt II, he added, "You don't call a baseball player by a different name when he gets traded to another team, do you? Well, I've been traded to the Cardinals, but I'm still the same guy."

Matt grinned. "It's okay with me. What position are you going to play on the Cardinals?"

They were in the elevator now with a half-dozen strangers. Everyone started to laugh.

"I don't know," Matthew Mahan said. "What position do you think I ought to play?"

"Center field. That's where sluggers play."

"I'm too old and too fat for center field. I think I'd better be a coach."

In spite of this amusing start, Matthew Mahan found the dinner depressing. He made a half-dozen attempts to start a conversation with Timmy and got nowhere. The girls gossiped and giggled and quarreled among themselves while their mother wearily corrected them. They were all picky eaters and left two thirds of the food untouched. Only Matt seemed to have a good time, voraciously downing his child's portion and confiding to his uncle all the gossip from the first grade at St. Damian's parochial school.

He did his best to converse with Eileen Mahan, but it was hard going. A receptionist at the Furia Brothers Construction Company, she did not see or hear much that was even faintly interesting. Their only link was her pastor, Monsignor Frank Falconer, who was a seminary classmate of Matthew Mahan's. Frank had been a tremendous help to Eileen in the first year of her widowhood, visiting the house frequently, persuading her to become active in several parish societies, something she had been ashamed to do when her husband was coming home staggering drunk two and three nights a week. Frank, not Matthew Mahan, was responsible for the spiritual resignation that Eileen Mahan had achieved. But after a quick rundown of the thriving state of things in St. Damian's parish, a comment on a new curate who was fond of liturgical experiments—on Palm Sunday the children had led a procession around the church with forty or fifty banners that they had collected or improvised—a ritual exchange of praise for Monsignor Falconer, the conversation limped.

Outside her job, Eileen never saw anyone except the neighbors in her flat, and they were as boring as she was. Occasionally, she asked him to do one of them a favor—get a son or daughter into one of the diocesan high schools or an eighty-year-old parent into St. Joseph's Home for the Aged. He usually obliged her, but the people behind the names remained a blur, unrelieved even when they took the trouble to write thank-you letters—which was seldom. Eileen insisted on talking about them as if they were all his intimate friends. He tried to listen, but invariably his mind wandered and the conversation would end with: "Gee, you're just like Charlie. You never listen to anything I say. It must run in the family. Timmy doesn't, either."

Timmy's face was a mass of pimples. He, too, ate practically no food until he got to the dessert. He wolfed down a huge chocolate sundae and raided the strawberry shortcake and the peach melba and the chocolate cake that his sisters were eating. His conversation consisted of monosyllables. Was he enjoying his freshman year at St. Francis? No. He'd rather go someplace else? Yes. The state university? Yes. The answers, not to mention their style, did nothing to improve Matthew Mahan's mood. He had had to twist a few Jesuit arms rather hard to get Timmy a scholarship at St. Francis, leaving him in the uneasy position of owing a favor. It was never a position he liked, and he especially did not like to owe anything to the Jesuits.

Although the Society of Jesus had educated him through high school and two years of college, Matthew Mahan never forgot or entirely forgave the snobbery with which the order had rejected his attempt to join their elite ranks. He would be happier, they told him, as a diocesan priest—coolly implying that he did not have the brainpower to be a Jesuit. One of the first things he did when he took charge of the diocese was organize a Vocation Day at St. Francis Prep. He made sure it was the very opposite of a Jesuit retreat: no emotional appeals—just an informative presentation of how a diocesan priest lived and worked, the variety of roles he played. Each year he had taken one or two, sometimes three or four of the Jesuits' best prospects away from them.

A few years ago, before Timmy Mahan had lapsed into adolescent sullenness, his uncle had hoped that he might be one of his Vocation Day converts. Timmy had gotten extraordinarily good marks in his first two years at St. Francis Prep. He had been a daily communicant. But with no warning, as he crossed from sixteen to seventeen, he had undergone an almost malevolent transformation from true believer to defiant cynic.

"Timmy," Matthew Mahan said as the waiter served their coffee, "would you like to come to Rome with your mother for my official crowning?"

"Crowning? Yuh mean they're gonna make yuh the Pope?"

"No, I'm only kidding. There'll be a ceremony in St. Peter's where the Pope will put a red hat on my head. I'll be dressed in a long red cloak with a train, called a cappa magna."

"Sounds like something out of the Middle Ages."

"Timmy!" said his mother.

"In a way it is. But it's kind of interesting; it reminds us of how old the Church is."

"Too old sometimes, it seems to me."

"Timmy! I'm gonna wallop you when we get home. I don't care how big you are, I'm gonna wallop you."

"I know what you mean. At least I try to understand what people your age mean when they say that, Timmy. But stop and realize that the Church has seemed too old many times in its history. When the Roman Empire fell. When the Protestant Reformation swept Europe. Each time, the Church was reborn, it evolved new ways of doing things. That's happening today, too. That's why I'd like you to come to Rome. To give you a chance to see the heart of the Church in action there."

"That's all we're gonna do? Go to Rome?"

"No, no. We'll spend a little time seeing the rest of Europe. Not all of it. But some of France, maybe Ireland. It depends on what we can work out."

Timmy shrugged, still unimpressed. "Sure, I'll come. Why not?"

"I wish I could bring all of you," Matthew Mahan said, speaking to the girls, whose faces had grown more and more forlorn throughout the conversation. "But we're going by plane and there's a limit to the number of seats."

"I wish I could come," said Matt.

"I wish you could, too. What would you call the Pope if you met him?"

"His Heightness," said Matt.

"Holiness," said Alice, his eight-year-old sister. "What a dope you are."

"I'm not a dope," said Matt, his cheeks flushing and his eyes swimming with tears. "You're a dope."

"Stop it both of you!" said their mother.

Matthew Mahan welcomed the appearance of the waiter with the check. He scribbled his name and audit number on it and in another five minutes was shoveling his nieces and nephews into a taxi. As Eileen Mahan was about to climb in after them, he slipped two fifty-dollar bills into her hand. "If you want to buy a couple of dresses for the trip," he said.

"Oh, *thank* you, *thank* you, Matt," said his sister-in-law. "I dunno what we'd do without ya."

No matter how small his gift, Eileen was always effusively grateful. "I wish I could do more. A whole lot more," he said.

Riding back to his residence in another taxi, Matthew Mahan tried to shake off the depression that seemed to be wrapping itself around him like a huge serpent. The sense of helplessness that had tormented him so often lately only sharpened every time he saw his brother's wife and children. What could he *do* beyond seeing them three or four times a year for a dinner like the one he had just endured, and send birthday and Easter and Christmas presents, and listen patiently on the telephone to Eileen's sighs and lamentations. Although he urged them to call him Father, he was nothing of the sort, and he knew it. To them he was a vaguely benevolent figure, an authority whom their mother invoked in moments of desperation, when all other appeals to discipline had failed. Why, why, why, had his brother married such a *stupid* woman? If Charlie were only alive. . . .

But that line of thought only made him more depressed. If Charlie were alive, the situation would probably be worse. Drunks do not make good fathers, and even if you had prayed, exhorted, pleaded, threatened, twenty-four hours a day, Charlie Mahan would still be a drunk if he were alive. You know, too, that those seven children were what destroyed him. Especially the five girls. What did Charlie used to call them? The Weird Sisters. Like many drunks, Charlie had a wicked tongue, especially when it was loosened by liquor. Every cent his wife spent on those five girls was savagely resented and denounced. It was almost pathological toward the end. Not only were they the reason for his self-destruction, they were his excuse. Both had blended into the nightmare in which Charlie had spent the last two years of his life. It was a nightmare into which he malevolently tried to lure Matthew Mahan. Again and again, he had poured out his defeat and self-hatred to him on the telephone.

What's your opinion on birth control, Bishop? You go right down the line with His Woppiness? You tell your story, and then listen to mine.

After number seven, why my wife said no more. My good

Roman Catholic wife, Eileen née Corcoran Mahan. And what did Eileen née Corcoran Mahan do to make sure there was no more? She kicked me out of bed. You and I, dear brother, excuse me, dear Bishop, are now fellow celibates. How does that grab you?

Rhythm? Eileen née Corcoran Mahan is too stupid to keep a chart. Even if she could keep one, she's too irregular to make one worthwhile. This is the considered advice of her fine Irish-Catholic obstetrician, Brendan O'Reilly Kendrick, M.D. So it's whack off or screw whores for poor old Charlie Mahan. How do you like that, old Uncle Shepherd? I came that you might have life, and have it more abundantly. Haw, haw, haw. Haven't you got anything to say, you fucking miter-headed fraud?

An exception? An exception? There are six guys in this bar, all drunker than me, in the same state of unsolicited celibacy. Tell you what, why don't you invite us all up to the residence? We'll get together for a little pray-in. How does that grab you? It doesn't? Don't want to rescue your strayed spavined sheep from their distress, Shepherd? We need advice, Shepherd. We need to find out the secret of how you survive without doing it. On the level, don't you diddle one of those rich Catholic divorcees like Mary Shea now and then? Come on, you can admit it to the kid brother. If a bag of skin and bones like me gets the urge two or three times a week, you must get it every night. Give us the inside story, big husky Shepherd. Don't some of those little ewes look inviting when they poke their tits at you at confirmation? That's the real hope of my heart, Shepherd. Someday they'll catch you fooling around with nine- and ten-year-olds. When that happens, I swear to Christ I'll stop drinking.

A vague nausea mixed with pain stirred in Matthew Mahan's stomach. Please, Charlie, please be quiet, he prayed. Every three or four months this rancid ghost's voice awoke inside him to recite the same searing words. It was enough to make a man wonder about evil spirits and diabolical possession. Or at least to half believe that some souls are too misshapen to enter Heaven, too tormented on earth to deserve Purgatory, and too innocent to be condemned forever. So they wandered the world recalling the lies and delusions and rages that had destroyed them while living.

When it came to tormenting his elder brother, Charlie Mahan

might as well have been sitting beside him in this taxicab, instead of lying silent beneath a stone in Holy Name Cemetery. But it was understandable, Matthew Mahan told himself, struggling to regain control of his mind, perfectly understandable. There was the Kit Kat Lounge on the corner of Van Nostrand Boulevard and the Parkway. Four years ago Charlie had stumbled through those doors at 3 A.M., into the path of a Parkway bus. Although Matthew Mahan had been in South America when the accident happened, the sight of the semifashionable saloon with its neon cats blinking alternately on a flickering seesaw was instantly transmuted into sound. He could hear the shriek of brakes, his brother's drunken dying cry. *Lord, Lord, have mercy on us. Lord, forgive us, for we know not what we do.*

"At'll be three twenny, Ya Eminence," said the cabdriver.

Matthew Mahan gave him four dollars and trudged up the walk to the residence. As he pulled open the heavy outer door, a wave of total gloom engulfed him. What had happened to the confidence with which he had taken command of the archdiocese ten years ago? He had been so sure he could do a better job than old Hogan. Perhaps there had been too much arrogance in that confidence. God was on record as being distinctly unfond of arrogance. Did He insist on failure as the only alternative? *Maybe losing is better,* Dennis McLaughlin had remarked in the car the other day. If that was true, Cardinal Mahan could only confess his total inability to understand it.

A strange sound reached his ears as he hung his coat in the hall. Laughter, filtering through the closed doors of the sitting room. Was someone giving a party? Had Dennis invited a few friends without bothering to ask permission? Had the revolution finally reached his residence? But those voices were vaguely familiar. As he stood outside the door, he heard an unmistakable Irish brogue declare: "He may send us into the night with a volley of anathemas."

Matthew Mahan opened the door and found himself a witness to a crime. An aged cleric with a long nose which stopped just short of looping into a beak was cheerfully demolishing the archdiocese's supply of Irish whiskey. In one of the period armchairs sat a large dark-haired man in a very expensive monogrammed shirt with his tie askew. "Don't worry, I'll write him a check and calm him down," he said in a cheerful rasp.

"The hell with anathemas," Matthew Mahan said, stepping into the room, "I may just call the cops."

"Matthew me boy," said Auxiliary Bishop David Cronin, raising his glass high.

"Padre," said Mike Furia, rising from the chair to extend a ham-sized hand.

Bishop Cronin remained close to the Irish whiskey bottle, eyeing his former pupil warily. "'Tis all his fault, Your Eminence," he said. "I told him a man who will soon be hobnobbing with the Pope had no time for the likes of us."

"I decided I'd take him out for Easter dinner and give him one more chance to turn wop," Mike Furia said. "It's his only hope of getting past St. Peter. But he still thinks the devil is better company."

Matthew Mahan absorbed all the nuances of these remarks with a smile. In earlier years the three of them had spent more than a few cheerful Sunday evenings in this room with their feet up on old Hogan's antiques, simultaneously insulting each other and solving the problems of the archdiocese. But in the last three years the parties had become more and more infrequent and in the last year had dwindled to a full stop. Old Davey Cronin's radical rage at the way things were going in the Church had become an embarrassment for Matthew Mahan, even in private. Since last July, when Pope Paul had issued *Humanae Vitae*, his birth control encyclical, his former mentor had become totally berserk. Mike Furia, who had no interest in the theology but knew that Cronin was hurt by Matthew Mahan's avoidance tactics, was simultaneously rebuking him and trying to restore their old camaraderie. Fortunately, Matthew Mahan was able to greet them wholeheartedly. They had come to him at a moment when he was desperately in need of remembering better, happier days.

"You know what he's just telling me?" Mike Furia said. "Christ visited Ireland."

"'Tis a strong belief among the peasants in the West," said Bishop Cronin. "And there's historical evidence for it. The wine in Palestine was the strongest of its day. According to the story, some time between his twentieth and thirtieth year the young rabbi perambulated to the Emerald sod and brought the formula for it back with him. Which explains why no one could tell the difference between the water and the wine at the marriage feast of Cana."

"You're a terrible old man. You're lucky it's not the thirteenth century. I'd have you out there on a pile of faggots, cooked to a turn."

"Ah yes, holy freedom. Wasn't it nice of good Pope John to discover it just in time?"

"Just in time for what?" Matthew Mahan said.

"In time to keep the whole bloody works from going up by spontaneous combustion."

"I used to think so, but I must confess I'm starting to wonder if holy freedom wasn't a phrase that would have better been forgotten."

"By God, he's got the glooms for sure. What's happened, have the Giovannicides in Rome withdrawn your red hat? Saying it was all a clerical error? You could get much worse news than that, believe me. The more I think of it, the more I dread the thought of you associating yourself so closely with the present occupier of the Chair of Peter."

"Now, there you know we disagree. He's doing the best he can."

"The best he can what? The best he can to turn a mess into a disaster, and a disaster into a catastrophe. The man's a fool, Matt, and it's better to face it. He knows no more about leadership than I do about atomic physics. Take old Pacelli by comparison. Much as I disliked the cold Roman bastard and everything he stood for such as business as usual while the Jews were getting cooked and his castrated connubial bliss while Africa and Asia and South America were already drowning in babies— with all of that against him, the man was still a leader. He knew you couldn't prance six paces forward and tiptoe five back, then pirouette three to the left followed by a pas de deux to the right. He went straight at the objective and carried the whole church militant, whatever the hell that means, banners high behind him."

"He could do it because he had the people with him from the start."

"Oh, the hell he did. No one ever has the people with him. The people have all been home drinkin' beer and listenin' to the radio or the tom-toms or watchin' television or a rain dance since the bloody planet cooled down enough to begin having babies. The people are only with you when you grab them by the throat and convince them that their worthless souls or their even more worthless skins are in deadly danger unless they listen to you."

"But how do you get them to listen to you these days?"

"You whisper," said Bishop Cronin, getting up and pouring himself some more Irish whiskey. "Did you know that was how Dan O'Connell rallied the Irish in the last century? He'd come to a great assemblage of country clods, all scratching and gabbing about the weather and the latest English outrage. Now, O'Connell had a voice that could be heard from Dublin to Killarney had he raised it. But where would he be then? Just one more yowling fool among the mob of them. No, he began to speak in a quiet, steady voice. Couldn't be heard beyond the length of his arm at first, and those in the first row would pummel those behind them and tell them to shut up, and those followed suit upon the fools behind them, and soon the lot of them, a hundred thousand, perhaps, were as silent as so many tombstones. That's what you must do, Matt. Not rush out among the mob and add to the clamor with advice on this and advice on that. Take your stand on whatever the matter in the quietest, simplest way. But let it be your stand until that cursed cathedral next door turns funereal black."

Matthew Mahan smiled. "That would happen in about six months if I didn't keep paying those sandblasters. Do you know what they get? Forty dollars a day."

The evasion was deliberate. Old Davey was tireless in his determination to turn him into the nation's leading liberal Catholic spokesman. It saddened Matthew Mahan to realize that his refusal to cooperate had become a threat to their friendship. But it did not alter the determination of his refusal. In the nineteen forties and fifties it had been exhilarating to be the public spokesman for largely Cronin-selected causes. How many hours they had spent together, working out speeches aimed at jarring the smug complacency of the city's Catholics—and incidentally infuriating Archbishop Hogan. When Hogan was replaced by Archbishop Mahan, Davey seemed to assume that the next step was to take on Cardinal Spellman and the rest of the hierarchy. It was then that Matthew Mahan saw, not without pain, the gap between the intellectuals and the pastors.

The front door clanged, rescuing them from an awkward pause. Matthew Mahan peered into the hall. Dennis McLaughlin was hanging up his coat. "Back so soon?" he said. "I thought it would be an all-night party."

Dennis shook his head. "Leo ran out of booze."

"Obviously God is watching over him. Why don't you come in and have a drink with us?"

Dennis walked slowly to the door. "I really—don't think— I should—Your Eminence," he said. "I've already—had enough."

"Well, you can have some strong coffee and a sandwich then. I need someone to give me some answers to this eighty-year-old heretic and his accomplice."

"I could use some coffee," Dennis said and walked cautiously into the room with the step of a man who felt like he had pillows tied to his feet. Matthew Mahan introduced him to Bishop Cronin and Mike Furia. "He's a refugee from the Jesuits," the Cardinal said.

"Oh?" said Davey, sipping his drink. "Catalog the rest of his virtues. A man with sense enough to depart the company of those intellectual egotists may be just the sort of fellow you need around here."

"Sit down," said Matthew Mahan. "I'll go see if I can get some coffee started in the kitchen, and do a little icebox raiding on the side."

He had told Mrs. Norton that his dinner at the Athletic Club would satisfy him, but she had made up two or three cold plates anyway. Sometimes he swore that the woman was a witch and could foretell the future or at least read his mind. The coffee was in the percolator ready to be plugged in. He put everything on a tray and carried it all back to the sitting room and parked it on the gilded walnut secretary.

Old Davey was practically crowing with delight. "Matthew," he said, "you didn't tell me this cod was a historian."

"A real historian, unlike a few others I could name."

"Listen to him," said Cronin. "He's perpetually trying to cast aspersions on the grand project of my old age."

"What would that be?" said Dennis, smiling in a relaxed way that Matthew Mahan had never seen before. A little liquor obviously did him some good.

"To bring down and pin into the mud where it belongs once and forever the whole cursed doctrine of infallibility."

"You see what I have to put up with in my own parlor?" Matthew Mahan said. "He comes and drinks my whiskey, insults me for not running the diocese his way, and then he tries to blow up the cornerstone and bring the whole Church down around our ears."

"The cornerstone, my foot," said Cronin. "It's the millstone around your neck, Your Eminence. Around your neck and the neck of every other bishop in this godforsaken world. Since the day that prince of fools, His Holiness Pius IX, proclaimed that insufferable doctrine on July eighteenth 1870, the Church has been reeling toward destruction like a man drunk on absinthe. Infallibility with the help of the Jesuits has infected every part of the mystical body of Christ. 'Tis like a cancer that destroys freedom everywhere it crawls."

"How do you explain Pope John?" asked Dennis.

"There are moments when even the most terrible drunkards have episodes of shining sanity. Their friends rejoice, the members of the family cheer and praise God. But unless you smash every liquor bottle within reach, or, better, blow up the still where the noxious stuff is being cooked, the mania soon reappears, just as it already has in Rome. Do you think the next one will be any better than the fool they have in there now? Don't be silly. If anything, he'll be worse, or at least more obvious. They aren't going to allow this power to pass from their hands without the most desperate kind of struggle. Someone must strike it from their grip."

"But how?" asked Dennis McLaughlin. He was clearly interested, but puzzled.

"By writing the true history of Vatican Council I. By proving that there was no more holy liberty in St. Peter's during that council than there is in the Kremlin when the Supreme Soviet whatever-you-call-it meets to ratify the decisions of the Presidium. That Pio Nono—I spell that *p*- double *e-o*—used everything from bribery to threats to physical force to whip a majority out of those poor sods, trapped there in the heat of summer with half of Rome dying of the plague all around them. And a council without holy liberty—a council engineered by the one

146

man who stood to gain by its decision—that was no more of a council than was the Battle of the Boyne."

"And do you think you can prove this?"

"I *know* I can prove it. At the very least, I'll make enough of a noise to scare the spaghetti out of them over there and maybe interest some real historian like yourself to tackle the job and do it with every footnote footnoted."

"Unfortunately, I majored in American history," Dennis said.

"I don't give a damn what you majored in. That Yale Ph.D. would mean more than my poor old S.T.D. from the Gregorian University, God save the mark. When I think of what a charade that place was in my day, I have to laugh."

"Really? I thought that was the *crème de la crème*. A lot of Jesuits went there."

"It's run by the Jesuits, lad. You know what we had to do to get our degree in sacred theology?"

"Write a thesis, I hope," Dennis said.

"That's right, that's right. A thesis of nine hundred words' length."

"You're joking."

"I wish I was. I would have taught a little more theology and a lot less blather in my day if they gave me an education instead of a degree."

"You think there's something to what he's saying about Vatican I?" Mike Furia asked as Matthew Mahan poured the coffee.

"The theory makes sense," Dennis said, reaching almost too eagerly for his cup. "There are a number of councils that have been declared invalid for one reason or another—mainly because the things they passed would blow the whole theory of infallibility into outer space."

Bishop Cronin crowed with delight. Matthew Mahan plunked the plates of cold roast beef and potato salad on the antique end tables. Dennis wondered uneasily if the sound conveyed disapproval of what he had just said or was simply one more example of the Cardinal's disinterest in the valuable furniture that surrounded him.

"Do you read German?" Bishop Cronin asked, thrusting a piece of roast beef into his mouth without benefit of fork.

"A little. I passed a test in it to get my degree."

"Germany's where the gold is. The best Germans went home

after Vatican I and broke away, you know. They formed the Old Catholic Church. They were true to that church, they said, not to the New Church that Pio Nono had created. That was a monstrosity."

"Did they take any bishops with them?"

"Does anybody ever take a bishop with them? Did Luther?"

"All I can say," said Dennis, finishing his sandwich and taking a long swallow of his coffee, "is wow. If you can do half or even one third of what you're saying, it would be fantastic."

"Give him a day off, Matt, and let him come out to the seminary and look over what I've written. I've got three hundred pages done."

"Do you expect to get my imprimatur for this book?"

"I should say not. The days of imprimaturs are dead and gone. But if you'd like to give it to me for friendship's sake, I won't refuse it."

"How can you be so brazen, when you've got one foot in the grave?"

"That's what makes me brazen, Matthew me boy. I wish I'd had the courage to be brazen twenty years ago when I had something to lose. That's the real test, and I flunked it."

"I'll admit this much," Matthew Mahan said. "It explains what happened at Vatican II."

"What do you mean?" Dennis asked.

"The Germans ran Vatican II. They organized all of continental Europe except Spain, and they knocked the Curia's control of the council into the Adriatic. If John hadn't died, I'm almost afraid to think of what that council might have decided. They were fully capable of kicking infallibility even farther than they kicked the Curia. They made a run on it a couple of times in the second and third sessions, but by that time Montini was Pope and he intervened at just the right moment in just the right way and the Germans settled for what they could get. Which was a lot."

"But not enough, not enough," said Bishop Cronin. "They should have nailed an annually elected assembly of bishops to the Chair of Peter like James Madison glued the Congress to the presidency."

"Now you're being ridiculous," said Matthew Mahan.

148

"Why is it ridiculous? Would you rather be ruled by your peers or by Van Lierde and the rest of that curial crew?"

"Van Lierde?" Dennis asked.

"He's a Belgian, Peter Canasius Van Lierde, papal sacristan, vicar-general to His Holiness for Vatican City. He didn't mean to do it, but the fool—"

"He's not a fool. He's a good man," said Matthew Mahan.

"The good man summed up the whole reason for the spirit of somber prophecy which sits upon my head. In fact, I have committed a passage from his book on the Vatican, pages 160 to 161, to memory. Would you like to hear it?"

"Of course," Dennis said.

Cronin stood up and recited in a mock basso voice;

" 'Two simple words, Holy See, serve to designate the Supreme Pontiff and the Ensemble of the Curia. The Pope and the Curia cannot be separated, as two parts of the whole of which the Pope is the head.' Have you ever heard such rot? It's a travesty on the Scriptures, a travesty on truth, and a damn menace!"

Bishop Cronin brought his fist down on his antique table hard enough to cost the Cardinal five or ten thousand dollars. His fork jumped onto the rug.

"All right, you old soothsayer," Matthew Mahan said, "if all the terrible things you say about the Curia are true, why are we going to Rome in two or three weeks to watch me stagger around in my cappa magna?"

The wizened old Irish face with its shiny beak of a nose bored into him for a moment. "Romanita," he said.

"I hate to keep sounding like a dummy," Dennis McLaughlin said, "but what's *that?*"

"Romanita, my lad, is the Roman way of doing things. Now, this fellow here, who's midway between being His Excellency and His Eminence, so that there's no need to call him anything but his Christian name, he's marked by the boys in the Curia and their yes-man, Montini, as undependable."

"Why?"

"First of all, I don't believe a word of it," said Matthew Mahan. "This ancient revolutionary is trying to picture me as a church burner, because I took a very strong stand on the birth control issue. I collected a lot of cases right here in this diocese."

"One of them your own brother," Mike Furia said.

"Yes, one of them my own brother—cases where attempts to follow the Church's teaching and have unlimited numbers of children with the only alternative rhythm or abstinence led to family tragedies. Drunkenness, mental illness, complete family breakdowns. I sent them to the Papal Commission on Birth Control with the strongest letter I could write, telling them that in my opinion the Church had to change its position. I even did local surveys to back up the national surveys. I thought that this city was particularly significant because we have such a high percentage of Catholics. You can't say that we're succumbing to the dominant secular culture when two out of every three people in town are Catholics. Believe it or not, our surveys showed a higher birth control position here than in the country at large."

"Perfectly understandable," said Cronin with a chuckle. "The poor Catholic cods in Iowa are so busy standing tall among the WASPs, they haven't time to ask themselves whether what they're saying makes any sense."

"I might as well have thrown all my surveys and case histories and letters into the wind, for all the good it did. His Holiness gave us his decision last summer, as you well know," Matthew Mahan said.

"And you published it in your paper and noted with an absolute minimum of enthusiasm that the Pope had spoken," said Cronin with a look that struck Dennis McLaughlin as remarkably affectionate. It was the first time he had ever thought of anyone feeling affection for Cardinal Mahan. He began wishing he was not quite so drunk.

"Right," said Matthew Mahan. "Where does Romanita come into it?"

"Seventy-eight American theologians published a paper calling Pope Montini a damn fool. Every one of those cods would have stopped shaving for a month if they could have included a bishop in that statement, an Archbishop, in fact. But you held your peace."

"Now you're being silly. Do you seriously—"

"I'm seriously saying that you *could* have made one devil of a rumpus over here. You shut your trap—and now you have your reward. That's Romanita."

Matthew Mahan sipped his milk and shrugged. "You might be right. It's the best explanation I've heard yet."

150

"Romanita," said Father Cronin, turning back to Dennis McLaughlin, "really has only one principle." He ran his hand along the gilt edge of his antique table. "Smooth, keep everything smooth. No bumps, no shouts, no yells, scarcely a word said above a whisper. But the business gets done their way."

"That happens to be an attitude I share," said Matthew Mahan.

"So stop wondering why you're getting a red hat. They're saying more or less the same thing old Pio Nono said to all those bishops and Cardinals he bribed with honors and favors at Vatican I—'Welcome to the club.'"

Matthew Mahan was finding the conversation less and less amusing. "Are you suggesting I should have taken a trip to Rome à la Cardinal Gibbons?"

"Of course not. It wouldn't have worked," said Cronin. "Those spaghetti benders only understand money and power. If you sat in New York, Matt, or Los Angeles or Chicago, I would have said go the minute you mentioned it. In fact, I would have mentioned it a few hundred times meself until you were even sicker of the sight or sound of me than you are now."

That one hurt. Matthew Mahan struggled to keep the conversation casual. "But Baltimore wasn't that big in Gibbons's day."

"No, but Gibbons was. If you'd only take my advice and follow his example, you could come close to the same kind of leadership, Matt. Now, here's a lad with a good head, and if he's as Irish as he looks and sounds, a good pen, no doubt. Let him write a book for you, put your name on it, and if it goes well, do more of the same. There's an intellectual vacuum in the American Church right now. Fill it, fill it with bold brave words about the Church and the modern world."

"No," Matthew Mahan said, shaking his head. "I've told you a half-dozen times, that's not my style. I couldn't put my name on a book I didn't write."

"Why not? Do you think St. John F. Kennedy wrote those books that he published?"

Matthew Mahan shook his head. "I'm sure Dennis has no desire to become my ghost."

Amen to that, thought Dennis.

"And will you get it through your head, once and for all," Matthew Mahan went on, "that I don't see it as part of my job?

I'm a pastor, not an intellectual. I can't see any point in embroiling this diocese in any more turmoil than it's in already."

Cronin was serious now, too serious. "Matt, when will you get it through *your* head that you can't be the pastor you dream of being unless you stand up to those monarchical bureaucrats in Rome? Do they let you say what you really believe about married love? What the people are desperate to hear? Can you speak to your younger priests honestly about celibacy? Can you lift your hand to help the thousands of divorced and separated? Even the good friend sitting beside you?"

Matthew Mahan shook his head in a way that Dennis had come to consider ominous. He braced himself for another explosion. But the words came from Bishop Cronin.

"Ah! When it comes to taking good advice, there's nothing worse than an Archbishop. They're all the same. Hearts of stone and heads of oak."

Mike Furia roared with laughter. Dennis McLaughlin gulped his coffee and stared at Matthew Mahan in frank astonishment. The Cardinal was smiling. It was a somewhat tense smile. But it was still a smile. At the same moment, Matthew Mahan found himself looking at Dennis, thinking, *Maybe this will convince you that I'm human.*

"Well," said Father Cronin in a gloomy voice, "perhaps we'll find new answers to our dilemmas—or new dilemmas for our answers—in Rome."

XIV

At the window seat in the first row of the plane's first-class compartment, Matthew Mahan looked out at the airport lights glowing and flickering mystically through the rainy darkness. Around him in the compartment, and in the tourist compartment behind him, were 130 of his well-wishers and supporters, participants in this "Pilgrimage to Rome." That was Mike Furia's name for it. When Joe Cohane headlined it in the archdiocesan paper, the grandiosity made Matthew Mahan slightly uncomfortable. Behind their jet on the runway, he could see a second 707, also loaded with pilgrims. In the glow of the runway lights, the golden griffin of the Mahans reared ferociously, just behind the cockpit window. Both planes had the Cardinal-to-be's coat of arms painted on them. They remained essentially the same as his Archbishop's shield. Only the color of the papal hat and tassels had changed from green to red, and the number of tassels running down from the hat had increased from ten to fifteen.

He was on his way to the Eternal City, as the newspapers kept calling Rome, with well over two hundred well-wishers to cheer him at this self-described "greatest moment" of his life. Why wasn't he happier? Why this sagging, soggy sadness even now, when he could look forward to a full week of relaxation and celebration?

The Cardinal sighed. He knew part of the answer. So did Mike Furia, who was sitting beside him. As chairman of the Cardinal's Fund, Mike had had to tell Matthew Mahan the bad news last week. The big givers simply weren't coming through this year. The Nixon recession had made the stock market a disaster area. The extra five or ten thousand dollars that people could skim off the top of their Wall Street profits had vanished. Now the money had to come out of savings accounts or the sale of stock on which they had already taken a bath. Normally the committee depended on the big givers for two or three million—a third of the fund target. Based on early returns, the computer whiz kids in the marketing department of Furia Brothers Construction Company were predicting a 50 per cent drop in this crucial category.

Another reason for the poor public response was the outburst of rioting in Chicago on the eve of the first anniversary of the assassination of Dr. Martin Luther King, Jr. A new outbreak of campus disorders, highlighted by the seizure of Harvard's main administration building by three hundred militants, also contributed to a general feeling that the nation was on the brink of anarchy, and this, in the words of a morose Mike Furia, inclined everybody to "take care of Number One." Mike also maintained that Pope Paul VI had not made a positive contribution when he said on Maundy Thursday that the Church was in "a practically schismatic ferment." This made more than a few Catholics wonder if the Church, too, was about to come apart. And people, as an ever more harassed Mike Furia had growled, "don't like to put their money on a loser."

The bad news had cast a pall over the trip. Every day that

Matthew Mahan was away meant a half-dozen major contributors escaped his personal attention. For the first time he found himself feeling like Cardinal Cushing, who had remarked to him during Vatican II that every day he was away from Boston cost him twenty or thirty thousand dollars.

After a sleepless night he decided to shorten the trip to give himself four extra days. The visit to Ireland and the stopover in France to take a nostalgic look at some of their old battlefields were abandoned. He had spent the extra days in a near frenzy of telephoning and conferring and cajoling, but the results had been meager. Earnest promises were all he got most of the time. *If the market goes up, Your Eminence, even twenty points, I swear—* So here he sat, exhausted, depressed.

Stop it, now, he told himself. He forced himself to think of Rome, only six or seven hours away. Think of it as a city of refreshment, he told himself, a city where you will regain your spiritual balance by visiting churches that still echo with Pope John's husky voice. You would stand before the altar of the cattedra in St. Peter's and feel once more those heavy peasant hands consecrating you a bishop, see the serenity in those dark brown eyes, hear the words *To help you remember this moment, to help you hold fast to the hope and faith I see on your face, Matthew, let me make you a promise. I will be in Paradise long before you. Think of me as your friend there. When you join us at last, I will be the first to greet you.*

As a young priest, John had explained later, he had been the secretary of a bishop who had received a similar promise from an earlier pope. It had been a source of constant reassurance to the bishop and "wonderfully consoling" on the day of his death, a difficult death, from cancer.

Four years after he had told that story, John himself had died the same difficult death. Was it that memory and the memory of his father's death from cancer that made Matthew Mahan wish during the unpleasant poking and X-raying of his gastrointestinal series that Bill Reed's diagnosis was wrong? You are so persistently arrogant, Matthew Mahan told himself. You even insist on the right to choose your fatal illness. Reproachfully, for the hundreth time, he made a vow to accept his ulcer as God's will.

How little he had thought about Pope John in recent years. When he was packing for the trip, he had found crumpled against the back of a bureau drawer a list of quotations that John had given him to meditate on, during the retreat he made before his consecration. He had told himself ten years ago that he would use this wisdom to sustain himself and enrich his episcopacy. But the nonscholar, the old smoothie, the whirlwind organizer, the Irish charm boy, had managed to forget all about this noble resolution before the year was out.

And Mary. Mary Shea would be waiting in Rome, greeting you with her enigmatic smile.

Matthew Mahan began feeling better. He started kidding Mike Furia who was cheerfully pouring airline Bourbon into one of several silver flasks in his five-hundred-dollar attaché case. Mike always filled his flasks when he traveled first-class to Europe. Good Bourbon was practically unbuyable on the Continent. And the absurd price the airline charged for first class made him determined to gouge them in every possible way. "Once a Mafioso always a Mafioso," the Cardinal said.

"Don't knock it, it's in your blood, too," Mike replied. "The assistant chaplain thinks it's a good idea."

Red-haired Jim McAvoy, almost as slim and definitely as freckle-faced as he was during his dangerous year as Chaplain Mahan's assistant during the war, was doing the same thing with the airline's scotch. The equipment in his attaché case was not as expensive as Mike Furia's furnishings. But Jim was doing very well, with some subtle help from Matthew Mahan. The Cardinal had used his friendship with several local bankers to help Jim buy control of the state's biggest Cadillac agency. Beside Jim sat his chic blond wife, Madeline. Her Dresden doll prettiness belied her remarkable personality. In spite of six children, she had a co-ed's figure. She ran her family—and to some extent her husband—and was simultaneously head of the woman's division of the Cardinal's Fund and president of the Marian Guild, the city's poshest Catholic women's organization. An honors graduate of Mount St. Monica, she could discuss church history and politics as intelligently as any layman—and many priests—that Matthew Mahan had ever met. With so many Catholic couples taking the divorce court route these days, it always reassured the Cardinal to see Jim and Madeline McAvoy together. They never made a public display of their affection for each other, but it was obviously there, still solid and dependable after twenty years of marriage.

"I was hoping you'd say something, Your Eminence," Madeline said. "I think they're acting like a couple of six-year-olds. Maybe it's going back to Europe with you. They think they're in the Army again and are planning to spend all their time raising hell."

"That was my department," Mike Furia said. "Jim had to behave. He was exhibit A for the Padre's sermons."

"That wasn't it and you know it, Sarge," said Jim. "I never had *time*. When I wasn't ducking shells and bullets, I was lugging some guy to the rear on a stretcher."

"I'm warning him," Madeline said, "if he goes off with the boys, I'm going to spend my time shopping."

"I've got a better idea," Matthew Mahan said. "For every hour he leaves you alone, Madeline, we'll penalize him a hundred dollars, payable to the Cardinal's Fund."

Madeline laughed delightedly. "The women's division of the Cardinal's Fund. You watch. This year we're going to beat the socks off these big-businessmen."

"That won't be hard," Mike Furia said.

In the first row of the tourist compartment Dennis McLaughlin savored the high cushioned back of his seat and looked forward to seven hours of rest. He was totally exhausted. For the past week he had worked every night until 3 A.M. "getting ahead," as His Eminence-to-be put it, on reports, memorandums, speeches, and random thoughts that the Great Man confided to his dictating machine.

Beside Dennis sat the Cardinal's sister-in-law, Eileen Mahan, and her son Timmy. He was still wearing his hair shoulder length but had succumbed to his mother's pleas and was wearing a new suit. Timmy's reading material consisted of Zap comics, which his mother feebly remarked were "awful." Dennis hoped to vacate his seat the moment they were airborne. The thought of listening to Eileen Mahan's drone for seven hours horrified him. She was plaintively disappointed because Monsignor Frank Falconer, her pastor, was not on this plane. He was with his fellow members of the Cardinal's seminary class in the jet behind them. But Dennis was not particularly troubled by being on the losing side of the implied comparison between him and Monsignor Falconer. He had more alarming emotions churning through his body.

For several days and nights, Dennis had been trying to prepare himself for his first flight across the Atlantic. It made his previous plane trips—to New Haven, to Florida to see his mother—seem trivial by comparison. The thought of hurtling out across those thousands of miles of empty ocean awed and chilled him. Would the claustrophobia be proportionately worse this time? What was it, after all, but the strangulating fear of sudden death, extinction, when life, love, had been barely touched? Now, Dennis thought uneasily, now you have a double reason for terror. Death may mean more than extinction; it may include—in spite of all your denials and rationalizations—damnation.

Looking around him, Dennis wondered if any of these well-fed and soon-to-be well-drunk Americans with their complacent wives and rebellious children felt even a touch of the fear that crept through him, as he contemplated both the metaphor and the reality. How hopeless it was to think of yourself as a priest to these people. You were outside them, hopelessly outside them all. And what has happened during the last three weeks has only widened the distance.

In a momentary lull from the first-class compartment, he heard Bishop Cronin's rich Irish brogue proclaiming the need for Vatican Council III. What was the source of that old man's fire? Did he draw something from that primary ancestral soil, something that you with your city feet and your city lungs can never touch or breathe? But now, now, you have touched—yes, and even breathed—a different kind of fire, and what has it done for you?

Mordantly, he let his mind re-create the recent scene in Matthew Mahan's office when His Eminence asked him for a report on what was happening between his secretary and Sister Helen Reed. Would you be on this plane now, Dennis, if you had blurted out the truth? You know the answer. No. Neither would you be wearing this tight white round collar that so effectively neutralizes all your words and thoughts.

What was it you had said to her that first night, when you picked up your collar and flipped it off the bed? *You know what I always think when I see a priest in one of those collars? I think it's a kind of spiritual chastity belt that divorces his head from the rest of his body. That's why only pale, neutral abstractions come out of his mouth. No gut thoughts or heart thoughts or testicle thoughts. No man thoughts.*

I want to love you. Do you love me?

Of course. Just let me look at you, look at you. And touch this, and this, and this.

Who are you, Dennis, now that she has given you her body to explore like a geologist, hunting buried pleasure? It had never been innocent, from that night when she had kissed you. No, admit it, you hurried to your conference, notebook in hand and hot hungry desire in mind, telling yourself that there was nothing particularly new or startling about this except the discovery of an object for your familiar gnawing lust.

The apartment had been empty. Only you and Sister Helen, knee to knee, you in the easy chair, she on the couch in the lamplight. Green eyes glowing with expectation. She knew. She awaited you, ripe with rebellious love.

And what happened next? Fear, Dennis, the fear of the celibate, the unmanning fear, Mother's hand still clutching, slapping you there, preventing what your lurid imagination had proclaimed a thousand times, what your dreams had evoked into how many soiled sheets. For a moment the shame had been unbearable. Suicide, madness, had loomed in the shadows.

Then came the miracle, her gentle compassion, her patience, her understanding. Perhaps it was better for them, this almost-love, perhaps it was all God permitted them. And you agreed, you almost believed, for three weeks now it had been enough to taste, to touch. But how much longer could the hero conceal his humiliation?

The jet engines roared and the tremendous acceleration pressed him back against his seat. His pulses pounded, his guilt-charged brain seemed to vanish in a flash of fire. Death, death waited for them all at the end of this rain-shrouded runway, death and damnation, and nothing, neither prayers of supplication nor flagellations of contrition, could save him.

They were airborne. Like a huge animal, the jet groaned and vibrated as it devoured altitude. Below them the city and its suburbs became fantasies, a glimpse of the improbable earth as seen by an indifferent God.

Slowly the terror ebbed from his body. In a few moments the aisle was full of people with drinks in their hands. He cheerfully joined them, accepting a Canadian Club and ginger ale from a

158

purring stewardess. "Hey, that Cardinal's a doll," she said, rolling her eyes. "How did the girls let him get away?"

Did he get away, or did he get away with it? Dennis mused, thinking of the several scented blue letters that had arrived from Rome and the one or two replies from His Eminence, addressed to Mrs. Mary Shea, 41 Via Margutta. Revealing that the Cardinal had a love nest in Rome—that would win eternal admiration from Leo and eternal opportunities from Sister Helen.

It was shocking, even disheartening, to see how callously aware he was of his real motive for playing his brother's silly espionage game. In fact, he took masochistic pleasure in following the twists and turns of his conscience. After that Easter-night session with His Eminence and Mike Furia and Davey Cronin he had adopted a selective approach to betraying the inner secrets of Matthew Mahan's episcopacy. Only decisions, habits, policies, that in your intellectual majesty you saw fit to disapprove were communicated to Leo. You had not told him the most damaging story, the one you had heard from His Eminence's lips the day after he returned from the semiannual conference of the American bishops in Houston.

"Call Terry Malone and tell him to put three hundred thousand dollars in my personal account. Tell him I'm giving another hundred thousand dollars to Peter's Pence, and when he screams, tell him I know that's fifty thousand more than we collected. Draw another check for fifty thousand to the Propagation of the Faith, and another for fifty thousand to the shrines in the Holy Land, ditto to the Bishops' Relief Fund."

The expression on his secretary's face made His Eminence laugh. *"I can see what's going through your suspicious mind. So this is the price you pay for a red hat. Well, it's a little more complicated than that. Down in Houston I got a reading on what the other guys were giving. Wright over in Pittsburgh has handed out a half million to one thing and another. We've got to at least match him. If our fund drive was going better, I'd top him by a hundred thousand. We've got more people than he has."*

This revelation you concealed in your devious heart, Dennis. Why? It had something to do with the way it was said to you. It somehow connected with the feeling you had on Easter Sunday night when you were invited to join the conclave with Furia and

Cronin. *A man among men.* To betray that feeling seemed not only sacrilegious but downright dangerous.

Instead you gave Leo a Xeroxed copy of the proposed diocesan financial report, which His Eminence had again decided not to issue this year. He was going to wait and see what the ten or twenty other dioceses who were taking this dangerous plunge said first. The thirty-five-page document was laborious reading and almost totally unrewarding from Leo's point of view. The value of the diocesan stock portfolio was a trifling two million dollars, and its blue chips had declined 6 per cent in the past eight months. Although last year's finances were affluently in the black, the one-and-a-half-million-dollar surplus had been applied to reducing the eight million dollars still owed on the last regional high school. Parishes owed another twenty million on recently built churches and grade schools. It was really almost malicious to torment Leo with this sort of thing, but his extremism deserved it.

There were, of course, those two rather large items identified as the Cardinal's living expenses and travel expenses. But he had diabolically demolished these in an attached memorandum, which explained that the living expenses concealed numerous gifts to priests who needed money for one reason or another, salaries for the housekeeper and assistant housekeeper, and gifts of cash to his sister-in-law and her family. The travel expenses included trips to semiannual bishops' meetings, conferences in Washington, D.C., and a tour of the archdiocese's South American missions, where the Cardinal was even more inclined to be munificent with his cash while face to face with his young volunteers.

Anyway, the whole purpose of the plot, if it still deserved that heroic name, was to give him access to Sister Helen. This had been thoroughly, if not gloriously, achieved. Again Dennis found himself thinking with savage self-satisfaction that it was somehow fitting to have Matthew Mahan's unwitting cooperation in solving the problem of priestly celibacy—which he so blithely dismissed. True, he had been one of about twenty of the three hundred bishops at Houston who had met with a group of married and shacked-up priests to discuss the celibacy problem. But he seemed unimpressed by what he had heard. *They just aren't in touch with reality* was his comment. That had produced a secret smile behind the sober mask His Eminence's secretary habitually wore.

It was amazing how his intoxication with Sister Helen made the thrown pens, the snappish orders, the outrageous hours he worked, so much more bearable. When His Eminence berated him for forgetting yet another telephone call—from Mike Furia, of all people—he was able to smirk behind his pained apology. He had a consolation that made him indifferent to His Eminence, impervious to His Eminence, superior to His Eminence.

How brave you are, Father McLaughlin, he mockingly congratulated himself. How marvelously metallically analytic, now that we are stabilized at 35,000 feet and the booze is flowing. You can even enjoy yourself, accept the friendly greetings from the titans of the city's power structure, so many of whom pass through your office to worship at the episcopal throne. There was Jim McAvoy's sexy blond wife waving to him. Moderately sophisticated, they could chuckle at some of the idiocies of the Church, yet somehow retain an active faith in it. Madeline McAvoy began telling him about a letter that Jim had just received from one of his Notre Dame classmates. The alumnus wanted Jim to give His Eminence a secret solution for ending the Vietnam War victoriously. Massive, carefully tabulated, archdiocesan-wide daily communions. It was based on a tried and true formula developed at the mecca of Catholic education in the late 1940s. They had found an undeniable correlation between the number of daily communions each week and the scores by which the Fighting Irish rampaged to victory on the gridiron.

"Isn't that fantastic?" Madeline McAvoy said.

"I bet he thinks *Humanae Vitae* is a great encyclical," Dennis said.

"Oh, he does, he does," Madeline said with a conspiratorial smile. She had sat next to Dennis at a recent dinner for the women's division of the Cardinal's Fund and had, first cautiously, then candidly, confided to him her dismay over Pope Paul's refusal to change the Church's teaching on birth control. It was not that she, personally, had any regrets about having her six children. She was fortunate enough to have the money and the energy to cope with them. But she knew too many other women who lacked one or both of these vital ingredients.

And Mike Furia, coming toward him now to clap him on the

161

back. Mike was already a little drunk. His glistening black hair was rumpled, his twenty-five-dollar flowered red silk tie askew on his fifty-dollar dark blue handmade shirt. Without his exquisitely tailored coat, the fat on his massive chest and shoulders visibly pressed against the broadcloth. "Hey, Dennis," he said, "how's it going?"

The man exuded a kind of animal warmth that made him hard to resist. The big arm was around his shoulder now. It was somehow flattering to find him treating you as an equal. A *man among men.* Although Furia could talk like a tough guy when he was in the mood, he was a shrewd, sophisticated man. Dennis had taken some fund-raising reports up to his apartment ten days ago and was amazed to discover the good taste with which the place was decorated. The style was moderate modern. On the walls were Modiglianis, Chiricos (his favorite), and several other names that were new to Dennis—Osvaldo Licini, Giuseppe Capogrossi, Atanasio Soldati. Casually Furia admitted that all the paintings were originals and quietly intimated that he probably had the best collection of contemporary Italian art in America.

This discovery grew less surprising once Dennis learned that Furia Brothers was one of the ten or fifteen biggest construction companies in the world. They had gotten their start building schools for the archdiocese in the early fifties with the help of some ardent arm twisting by Monsignor Matthew Mahan. From there they had expanded up and down the eastern seaboard, and then across the nation, building dams, apartment houses, office skyscrapers. Next had come a quantum leap to airfields, harbors, base camps in Vietnam, then railroad tunnels, superhighways, and shopping centers across Europe. Today there were Furia brothers, cousins, or nephews running subsidiary companies in Hawaii, Australia, Rio de Janeiro, Rome, and London. Furia spent most of his time on planes during the decade—1955 to 1965 —he spent building his empire. His wife had a pathological fear of flying and never traveled with him. His marriage had broken up three or four years ago. But he had settled—largely at Matthew Mahan's urging—for a separation rather than a divorce.

"Looking forward to kissing Il Papa's ring?" Furia asked.

"Not really."

"Just between you and me, I think the whole papacy rigamarole ought to go. It's ruined Italy. I'm not kidding, it really has."

Furia had a remarkable ability to sense a person's mood. He had been saying things like this to Dennis every time they met. "I don't have the nerve to tell that to your boss."

"Why don't you try it sometime," Dennis said. "Bishop Cronin gets away with it."

Furia laughed. "That old screwball could get away with thumbing his nose at God. On the level, is there anything to that book he's writing?"

"It's hard to say. I only spent a couple of hours looking through the material last week."

"He's had my people in Rome shipping him stuff by the trunkload. We've run up an air freight bill of a thousand bucks. I told him I'd pay a hundred grand to knock a few holes in that crummy setup."

"What do you hear from Tony?"

"The usual bullshit. Excuse my French."

From his refuge in the Hard Times Haven commune Furia's son Tony made a habit of writing his father outrageous letters, calling him a tool of American imperialism and an agent of the military-industrial complex. Furia had shown a recent letter to Dennis at the residence and asked him for some advice. With that cool objectivity that both intrigued and repelled him, Dennis had put aside his personal opinions and given Furia an unorthodox suggestion. Start returning Tony's letters unopened, cut off his allowance, and in general start acting more like an outraged father—which he was—and less like a patsy, which was what Tony was intent on making him.

"When I get back, I think maybe I'll take that advice. About getting tough with him. I'm just afraid—you know my wife works on the kid all the time, turning him against me. I hate to give him more ammunition."

Dennis nodded sympathetically. "It's a tough decision. I just thought it was time to try something different."

"Anyway, I appreciate your interest." Furia's beautifully manicured fingers slipped something in the pocket of Dennis's coat. "Buy yourself something in Rome. Something you don't need." The big hand banged him on the back, and Furia was moving past him down the aisle, calling cheerful insults to Herb Winstock whose gnomish face evoked Jewishness as totally as Furia's satiny olive skin and gleaming black hair said Italian.

Sitting in an aisle seat talking to Winstock was Kenneth Banks, member of the City Council and a power in the NAACP, the city's leading Oreo. Sitting behind Banks was Mrs. Dwight Slocum, wife of the city's richest Protestant. Her gaunt, horsey, rather oddly handsome face could easily have joined any collection of Early American portraits in the city's art museum. All of these people, devout Jew, black Baptist, idealistic WASP, served on the executive committee of the Cardinal's Fund. It was fascinating, how thoroughly Matthew Mahan had studied the money-raising style of Francis Cardinal Spellman and adapted it to his native city. Ecumenical? You bet. There is nothing more ecumenical than cash. That was His Eminence's (unspoken) motto.

In his pursuit of the dollar, Matthew Mahan had had an advantage that even the prince of New York would have envied. Furia, McAvoy, Winstock, and almost every other man on this plane, reserved for the mostly rich, had served with Matthew Mahan in the 409th Regiment or at least in the 113th Division. It had provided him with a fantastic city-wide ecumenical head start which no one in the archdiocese including the resident Archbishop had been able to match. No wonder he waxed sentimental about G. I. Joe at the annual division reunion dinner and steadfastly refused to say a word against the war in Vietnam.

"Hey, Dennis. Dennis."

Mike Furia was waving to him. "We wanna check something. Your boss ever talk to you about the war?"

Dennis shook his head.

"That's what I mean," said Mike Furia, bringing a formidable fist on the back of Winstock's seat. "He's so afraid of bragging, he won't tell anybody anything. You ought to write a book about him, Dennis. You really should. Somebody should. I mean—the things we saw him do."

You are going to spend the night listening to these stories, yards and yards of them, Dennis told himself. He ordered himself to look interested.

"We're in the Hürtgen Forest, see. Goddamn Germans dug in ten feet deep everywhere. We're coming down this ravine when all of a sudden they open up on us with machine guns. We dive for the bank of the ravine, and they can't depress the guns enough to get us. Out in the middle of the ravine we got a half-dozen dead and maybe four badly wounded. We lost another

164

dozen guys trying to get to those wounded. This thing started at dawn, and for a while it looked like a replay of the Lost Battalion, you know, the World War I job, on a small scale. The Krauts were counterattacking all around us, and we lost contact with everybody as they rolled back with the punches. Meanwhile those wounded guys were out there all day in the sun dying little by little. It was absolute agony, listening to them.

"Well, we hang on there for twenty-four hours. Every two or three minutes all night Adolf's friends send up flares to make sure nobody gets to those wounded guys. By noon the next day we're out of water, and some guys were talking surrender. I told 'em I'd shoot the next guy that used the word, but I was thinking about it myself. Suddenly into the ravine comes this—this figure. We were all half crazy with thirst and I thought it was an hallucination. But it was the Padre wearing his mass vestments. He was walking in a very slow, stately way, like he was in a procession in the cathedral. He kept shouting, '*Ich bin ein katholisch Priester.*' He was betting there were some Catholics behind those German machine guns. It was the bravest thing I've ever seen a man do. Those Nazis didn't give a damn for priests, most of them. By any kind of odds, he should have gotten himself blown apart.

"He got to the wounded guys. Two of them were dead. He touched some oil on their foreheads and said a prayer over them. Then he picked up the other two guys, one under each arm, and dragged them over to our foxholes.

"Under his robes he's got about ten canteens full of water and a couple with whiskey in them. And a couple of pounds of C rations hanging off his belt. Next, he ties us into the operations for the day. There was a big counterattack coming in about an hour. We went up the bank just as Adolf's boys got hit from the flank by a couple of other companies and they didn't stop runnin' until they got to Düsseldorf. I was for giving the Padre a Medal of Honor, but the chief of chaplains cut it down to a DSC because there was some sort of hanky-panky about wearing his vestments that way. It violated the Geneva Convention or some damn thing."

"Hell," said Herb Winstock, "he won a DSC damn near every day that we were in action."

More stories from Winstock, from Jim McAvoy, from a half-dozen other well-fed middle-aged faces, all conspiring to make Matthew Mahan a cross between a saint and a superman.

"The guy just wasn't afraid. He wasn't afraid of anything," said Jim. "I remember when he made me chaplain's assistant. I thought I had it made. Then I found out the three guys who had the job before me were in the hospital. The next thing I find myself taking more chances than the whole rest of the division put together. There was no place he wouldn't go. And half the time he didn't crawl—he walked straight up—right through barrages."

Jim gulped his drink, obviously reliving some of the fearful emotions of 1944–45, then he said quietly, "I'll tell you something —following him made a man out of me. I mean, I was the original callow kid, and maybe a little bit of a mama's boy in those days. I was sure I was going to fink out under fire. I forgot all about it, after watching him in action for ten minutes."

"You should write a book about him, Dennis, I really mean it," said Mike Furia. "He should have been the Father Duffy of World War II. Even Ernie Pyle said so. But when he got home, he wouldn't talk to a writer. Not even to the reporters from the *Journal*."

A harried stewardess came by, begging them for the third or fourth time to sit down for dinner. Dennis reluctantly rejoined Eileen Mahan and her son. They discussed Catholic education, and Dennis was surprised to discover that Mrs. Mahan was not in favor of reinstating the Baltimore catechism. "They got to give these kids more freedom. Why shouldn't they? They treated us like we were in reform school or something."

"Maybe you would have been better off if you had been," said Timmy, wolfing down his filet mignon.

He looked mockingly across his mother's tray at Dennis as he said this. Mournfully Dennis saw the pathetic dimensions of Timmy's illusions. The Archbishop's secretary had to be a square faggot. The Catholic Church in particular and everything else in the world that represented tradition, order, were garbage. This reduced the number of books worth reading, the music worth listening to, the thoughts worth thinking, to a pitiful minimum.

After dinner they turned out the lights, and Dennis tried to sleep. Eileen Mahan was soon snoring gently beside him. Timmy continued to peruse Zap comics. By this time Dennis estimated that he must have read each copy at least seven times. After an hour of squirming, Dennis found his mind yearning for sleep and his body refusing to obey it. First his back ached, then his eyes ached, then his neck ached. His mind drifted like a Ping-Pong ball accidentally loose in a spaceship with zero gravity.

First Helen Reed's breasts were touching his moist palms, then his mother smiled primly at him and snapped his picture in the white suit he wore for his First Communion. Then Leo was there, a disembodied face peering in the cosmic window, shouting above the humming engines: "When are we going to start telling the truth, Jesuit?"

Next came memories of the day he visited Bishop Cronin at the seminary. He was sitting on the sagging daybed once more, politely drinking cold coffee and staring around him at a room piled high with books and stacks of miscellaneous papers. Names whizzed past him; Mansi, Cecconi, Mosley, Veuillot, Icard. The immense effort that the old man was making staggered him. More saddening than dismaying was the evidence that the task was too huge. The text, what he read of it, was too emotional to be history and too burdened with abstruse arguments to be a successful tract. He did not have the heart to tell him, but Cronin, with an almost awesome intuition, seemed to read his mind. "I know I'll never finish it," he said. "All I can hope really is to get enough on paper to catch the nose of a bright young dog like yourself who likes to feed on red meat."

Then his sudden outburst. *I'm afraid you've got the wrong dog. For me the whole thing is an argument about nothing. I don't believe this fanatic first-century Jewish revisionist named Jesus is the son of God. The more I think about it, the more I realize I'd better sit down and tell that to Cardinal Mahan, and be on my way.*

In the background the ironic angel had clapped his wings. They sounded exactly like the erasers he used to clean for Sister by pounding them together in the school yard once a week—a job that left him coated with chalk dust.

Do you really believe that, lad, asked the old man with a very serious face, *or is that the result of last night's or last month's book?*

What do you believe?

First of all I believe that history has some sense, that it isn't a totally mad collection of anecdotes as it sometimes appears to be. I believe, with that Frenchman who like me never had the guts to publish what he really thought when living—once past seventy you might as well consider a man legally dead, because people no longer take him seriously—I believe with that Frenchman in the Holy Event. Exactly what the devil that means I don't pretend to know. But it changed the course of human history, and you can't walk out on history, you can't act as if the whole damn slate can be wiped clean, not if you're Irish. Out of it came the Church—and for all its terrible blunders, there's something grand about it at the same time—soaring as it has above history, and at the same time so much a part of it—it's the one thing around that puts poetry in the mouths of common people, lad, and gives them someplace else to look for consolation and hope. The nation can't do these things, try as it might. It's too bound up in the lust for power and the pursuit of its own best interests. Only the Church can change men's hearts—and how well she might do it, we both know, if only we could free her from her self-forged shackles. The truth is—and it must be told by someone—that the Church has been seduced by the nation. In fact, seduced is hardly a proper word. The hussy never so much as resisted old Constantine's first buss, but she leaped into bed with that bad imitation of a Roman emperor and like a shrewish wife immediately began coopting his power. It's this fatal imitation of Caesar that's destroying us, and since there's no hope of convincing the Italians of this, we must tell the rest of the world.

But listen, now. What disturbs me more than anything else in that bit of foolishness you just bespoke is the idea of talking to Mahan about it. Don't do that. If you must go, think up something more suitable, like being seduced by an oversexed nun. The likes of Matt were not made to deal with problems that torment garçons like you and me. He was born to lead the common people, to fill their hearts with hope and faith of the sort that they must have to live at all. Shackled though he is, it's toward freedom that he leads them, the kind of freedom that no bureaucrat in the Internal Revenue Service of the Curia will ever understand. If God is willing, the likes of you and me may yet strike off some of the shackles that keep him from being the true shepherd that he is at heart, that cursed subservience to Rome and the canon law that sits like an imp of Satan on every bishop's crook. Such as Matt can't free himself from those shackles. He loves too much, too readily. He has a heart that's too full, too good. Those are the most obedient, you know. It's the cold cods like us who have little or no love to spare; we're the ones who must stand back and decide with good reason on what we shall bestow our mite.

Still no sleep. Only these baffling words revolving through his tormented body. Gradually, Dennis concluded that the night flight to Europe was one of the most exquisite forms of torture devised by modern man. The Inquisition was mercy in comparison to it. Another two hours, and he would confess to any sin.

In the first-class compartment Matthew Mahan was reminiscing with Mike Furia about their first trip to Europe. "Did you ever think that we'd be going back this way, Matt?" Mike asked. "I sure as hell never did. But I bet you did. I can remember watching you in action on the troop ship and saying to myself, 'That guy will be a bishop someday.'"

"Oh come on. I was so green and so seasick I didn't know what I was doing half the time."

"You took charge. That's what a bishop does, right?"

"To be honest, Mike, I never dreamt of being a bishop. I didn't think I had enough brains. I was pretty much convinced that the Lord intended me to get shot somewhere in Europe. That's all big lugs like me—and you, for that matter—seemed to be good for then. And after our first day under fire, I was absolutely convinced I was going to get killed."

"You and me both."

Mike Furia brooded into a silver cup half full of Bourbon. "So here we are," he said. "We didn't get our heads blown off like we thought we would. Here we are, twenty-five years later, and when I ask myself why, what difference it made, I don't have an answer."

"Now, Mike," Matthew Mahan said. "It's four A.M. Remember what I told you about four A.M. thinking?"

"I know, I know. You told me. But you didn't necessarily convince me."

"You put together a big business, Mike. You gave jobs to

thousands of people. Good jobs, and you treat them fair and square."

"Three cheers," said Mike, pouring himself another hefty belt of Bourbon. "I just happened to find out that's the best way to do business. But that doesn't give you the kind of satisfaction I'm talking about. Nobody in the company really gives a damn about Mike Furia. He's a good meal ticket, that's all. That goes for my brothers, my nephews, my cousins. I'm talking about the people who mean something to a paisan like me. You're half Italian. You know what I mean. A man without a wife, a father without a son. What the hell is he? In ten, twenty years, I'll be dead. The rest of the clowns in the family will either sell out or run the company into the ground."

"Mike, isn't there any hope that Betty will calm down and help you and Tony get back together some one of these days?"

The contempt on Furia's face suddenly made Matthew Mahan wonder if he knew the real story of why the Furias' marriage had collapsed. Was it simply Betty Furia's resentment over her husband's constant traveling—and her fear of flying? Did marriages break up over such things?

"She's never going to let that happen, Matt. That's her revenge—making sure my son hates his old man's guts."

Another belt of Bourbon, and the expression on Mike Furia's face was almost menacing. "What's the answer? You got one, Padre?"

"Prayer, Mike. Nothing else but prayer."

Mike slumped back in his seat and shook his head. "Padre, you've got more faith—a hell of a lot more—than I have if you can say that and mean it."

"Don't be silly, Mike. You've got faith all right. I'll do the praying for both of us."

"Okay, okay."

Down another note, from grudging assent to unconvinced agreement. How often you have heard that in recent months, Matthew Mahan thought.

"Mike. You'll feel a lot better tomorrow afternoon when you get a couple of hours' sleep. Look, there's the sun coming up."

Ahead of them the horizon was a rim of fire. Racing toward the dawn at six hundred miles an hour, they never really saw the sun rise in traditional, multicolored majesty. Within an hour

170

they were winging through mid-morning brightness, and the stewardesses were passing out hot washclothes to give the sleepless travelers an illusion of refreshment. A light breakfast came next and then the pilot was saying, "In a few minutes we'll be landing at Rome's Fiumicino Airport. The temperature on the ground is a cool fifty-eight degrees. Light rain and some fog have lowered visibility to about a half mile. I regret to inform you that there has been a wildcat strike of porters and baggage handlers. I'm afraid it will mean some pretty annoying delays. . . ."

How right he was. They sat in a leaden stupor in the three-story glass terminal building, inhaling acrid fumes caused by the radiant heat pipes just below the rubber floor. Mike Furia sat between Dennis McLaughlin and Davey Cronin, giving them a lecture on the history of the terminal building and the airport, which Matthew Mahan found very unpleasant listening. "They paid twenty-one million dollars for this hunk of marshland that they knew was fogged in half the time. Why? It didn't have anything to do with the fact that the land was owned by the Torlonia family, very big in the Vatican. Oh no. The runways were built by Manfredi Construction, and Castelli Construction put up the hangars. Guess who owns both of them? The Vatican. Provera e Carassi, another Vatican outfit, bid five point twelve million to build this abortion of a terminal. We bid against them, and we knew they had to be lying. A year later they went back and got another four point three eight million from the government to finish the job. And what have they got? An airport where big cracks appear in the runways every year or two. The whole damn place is built on shifting sand. A terminal that stinks, literally, because of this stupid rubber floor."

A small slim priest of about forty approached them and introduced himself. He was Monsignor Roberto Gambino from the Vatican. He mopped his neck with a handkerchief, polished his silver-rimmed Pius XII glasses, and lamented the baggage situation in mournful, surprisingly good English. "Sometimes I think it is the capitalist system," he said. "Italy is losing faith in it. There is no way to win rewards within it except by violence. It is turning us into a nation of sadists."

"Watch your step, Monsignor," Mike Furia snapped. "You're surrounded by American capitalists here."

"Oh yes?" said the Monsignor, blinking nervously.

"You know what I've got here in my pocket?" Furia said. "Ten million bucks. To expand the Italian branch of my company. This sort of thing inclines me to drop the whole idea of doing business with you people. And I'm Italian. How do you think it affects other American businessmen?"

"Perhaps it would be better to give the money to the missions," said Monsignor Gambino with a nervous smile.

Was he joking? Matthew Mahan wondered. It was impossible to tell. Before Mike Furia could start shouting, the Cardinal decided to take charge of the situation. "Let's go get our own baggage," he said, standing up.

"I'm with you," Mike said.

"Round up a squad, Sergeant."

With a nod and a grin, Mike strode among their slumped pilgrims and soon had a dozen of them, including Dennis McLaughlin and Timmy Mahan, waiting for orders.

"I assure you, Your Eminence, it is utterly impossible," murmured Monsignor Gambino.

"The hell it is," said Matthew Mahan. "Where's the Bank of the Holy Spirit?"

In a few moments he was cashing a traveler's check at the airport branch of the Banco Santo Spirito. He strode resolutely to the baggage section of the terminal, with Monsignor Gambino panting sweatily beside him, assuring him again and again that it was impossible. They marched through a door leading to the runways and were challenged by a security guard wearing a gun. Monsignor Gambino began explaining to him in Italian what these crazy Americans wanted. Not knowing that Matthew Mahan and Mike Furia spoke the language, Monsignor threw in several uncomplimentary comments. The remark about capitalism was obviously not an accident.

Even though the priest in black beside him was a *neo porporato* (new Cardinal), Monsignor Gambino said, he had no right to interfere with the struggle of Italian workers for a just wage. These *americani presuntuosi* (arrogant Americans) must learn that they do not own the world simply because they have money. He hoped that the guard would not succumb to their dishonorable way of doing things.

172

"Excuse me, Monsignor," said Matthew Mahan in Italian. "I think you had better let me talk to this gentleman."

Monsignor Gambino's mouth sagged. He began to stammer an explanation. He was afraid that the press would hear about His Eminence's refusal to honor the rights of strikers and pillory him.

"Monsignor," said Matthew Mahan, "I think the best thing for you to do is take a taxi back to the Vatican, explain that you have become ill, and send a replacement to meet us at our hotel."

Matthew Mahan turned to the guard. With a broad smile on his face he said in Italian: "My mother was born in Rome, so that makes me part Roman. Where are you from?"

With a nervous smile the guard admitted that he, too, was a Roman.

"Isn't there an old saying that when two Romans argue there is always a solution—unless they happen to be enemies? Now surely, we are not enemies. That would be impossible, because every Roman is my friend today. I have come here from the United States to salute the people of Rome and embrace their father, Pope Paul. You are about to give me the greatest honor of my life, a Cardinal's red hat. If I offer you money, it is not a bribe, it is a gift from a full heart."

He put a ten-thousand-lira note—sixteen dollars—into the guard's hand. "I'm at your service, Eminence," he said. "What do you wish me to do?"

Within sixty seconds Mike Furia was at the wheel of one baggage truck after giving Matthew Mahan a rapid lesson in how to start one parked beside it. Timmy, Dennis, and the other volunteer baggage unloaders scrambled aboard and they headed for their planes, which were fortunately parked close to the terminal, their crews still aboard waiting for orders. There was no problem persuading the pilots to open the baggage hatches. Working furiously, the volunteers soon had both trucks piled high with suitcases. Two more quick trips, and the big metal bellies were empty. By this time, all 250 of their pilgrims were down in the baggage area, eagerly grabbing their luggage and piling it on rolling carts. As the last pieces departed for the buses, Matthew Mahan casually slipped another ten-thousand-lira note into the security guard's hand and murmured, "God bless you," in Italian.

By the time they reached the Hotel Hassler in Rome, it was 1 P.M. Matthew Mahan felt exhausted, and he was not surprised to discover alarming pains in his stomach. But he insisted on waiting in the lobby until everyone was checked into their rooms. This took another hour. Dennis McLaughlin, who looked equally weary, stayed beside him and did his best to expedite occasional tangles over missing luggage or Italian confusion over the spelling of Irish-American names. Mike Furia also stayed on the job, performing similar services. Finally they felt free to stagger to the elevator and down the hall to their fifth-floor rooms. "I hope you don't mind bunking with Bishop Cronin, Dennis," Matthew Mahan said.

"I hope he sleeps a little more than he did on the plane."

In the early hours of the morning the bishop had entertained the pilgrims with some thirty-six verses of "The Same Old Shilelagh My Father Brought from Ireland."

"Oh, he will. He will," Matthew Mahan assured him with a chuckle.

Mike Furia stopped opposite his room, about halfway down the hall. "What's the program?" he said. "Three hours' sleep and then tie on the feedbag?"

"That sounds sensible," Matthew Mahan said, "but I'm afraid I can't join you tonight. I've got a date with a lady friend."

"Wow! A real Roman operator."

"Mary Shea. Do you remember her?"

"Sure. I thought she lived in Venice."

"She's lived here for years. I promised her we'd have dinner together my first night—"

Matthew Mahan had thought that by being frank he would escape possible embarrassment. But he still felt strange. Or was it Dennis McLaughlin and Mike Furia who were feeling (or thinking) strangely and letting him know it with the expressions on their faces?

"I'm afraid she still thinks of me as her spiritual adviser. Though I don't think I ever gave her a word of good advice."

Mike Furia nodded. "We'll have a nightcap, maybe. I'll tag along with Dennis here and old Davey, like a good little celibate."

When Mike's door was safely shut, Matthew Mahan said quietly to Dennis, "He's upset about his son, the poor fellow. I can't say I blame him."

"He ought to get divorced," Dennis said as they walked down the hall. "As long as he goes on letting his wife ruin his son's opinion of him, he's going to be miserable."

"Is she really doing that?"

"Haven't you ever talked to him about it?"

"I'm afraid not, really. I tried to help—when they were separated. Lately all I've heard about is Tony."

"Tony didn't get to be what he is by accident. My brother Leo knows him pretty well. His mother is the nearest thing you can get to a monster."

His weariness made it difficult for Matthew Mahan to control his feelings. For a moment, all he knew was a great confused shame. *And you call yourself a priest?* mocked a voice in his mind.

He paused at the door of his room. "Let's see, you're right across the hall, Dennis."

"I'm afraid the porter has my bags on your truck," Dennis said.

"Oh. Come in then, come in."

He walked into the suite followed by Dennis. On the dresser was a huge spray of red roses with a large white envelope tucked among them. He ripped open the envelope and read: *To the best Cardinal they've found yet. With much love, Mary.*

Dennis McLaughlin, bags in hand, was looking curiously at the roses. "From Mary Shea," Matthew Mahan said. "This really looks suspicious, doesn't it?"

As usual, his attempts at humor made no impression on Dennis. "Someday I'll tell you more about her. It's a rather amazing story." He gave the porter a thousand-lira note and waved him out the door. "Let's get some sleep," he said. "If you go out tonight, do your best to slow old Davey down. He's got a heart condition—which he consistently ignores."

Dennis McLaughlin nodded and lugged his bags into the hall, closing the door behind him. Matthew Mahan gulped down a handful of Titrilac tablets to quiet his complaining stomach, turned on the water in the bathtub, and stripped off his clothes. He plunged himself into the hottest bath water he could endure, and lay there for ten minutes, with a washcloth draped over his face. By the time he finished shaving, he felt almost human. Stepping into clean pajamas, he threw himself down on the bed and lay there, thinking about himself, his mother, Rome.

He remembered the first time he had come to this supposedly Eternal City, leading a group of pilgrims for the Holy Year in 1950. He had been filled with awe, vibrant with deep emotion. He was finally visiting his mother's city, the place where his priesthood had been born. It was his mother who had created —but never forced—his vocation, who told him on her deathbed, gasping for the breath that her failing heart had long denied her, "Someday you will go to Rome a bishop. That will be my first task in Heaven. When you do, think of me, pray for me at the Church of St. Peter in Chains. It was our family church. There—I received—my First Communion—only a week before we sailed to America." He had visited the church on that first trip to Rome, and on the second trip, the second visit to St. Peter in Chains, a visit that still seemed half dream, half miracle.

But now, after ten years as a bishop, something had happened to these old feelings. Throughout these ten years, he realized now, he had been moving slowly away from his mother, from her excitable voluble ways, even from her fanatic devotion to all things Italian. She had become like the statue of a saint on the side altar of a cathedral, revered, but with a distant, almost automatic piety. More and more, he sensed his spirit turning to that stolid, silent man, who never said a word of approval— or of disapproval—about his priesthood. Only the cryptic sentence *If you know what you're doing, I'm for it; everybody's got to live his own life.*

The memory blended uneasily with the memory of his father dying stoically of cancer of the stomach, with never a sign of fear—or of faith. No, Bart Mahan had perfunctorily accepted the Host that his son had placed on his tongue each time he had visited the hospital. There was never even a hint that he prayed. Only silence, broken by small talk about baseball, city politics. More than once at that time and in the intervening years Matthew Mahan had puzzled over the mystery of that mortal silence. But he had always thrust it from his mind. A wordless threat lived inside it, somehow. But today, for some reason he did not completely grasp, he said a prayer. O *Lord, help me to understand.*

What was there about his father that attracted his mind, his spirit, now? The calm, almost emotionless way that he accepted disappointment? He had lost the savings of his lifetime when the restaurant failed. But he never showed a tremor of regret of bitterness. He had accepted his job in the Parks Department and gone to work for the local Democrats, indifferent to their colossal corruption.

You could certainly use some of that calm. Too much of your mother's violent emotionalism has always been surging around inside you, controlled only with enormous effort and, to quote Bill Reed, at the expense of your stomach.

But his father had paid a price, they had all paid a price, for his calm. Another memory now, a tense game, between the front runners for the International League Pennant. A play at the plate, his father's thumb above the dust: out. "*Son of a bitch!*" A huge man with a knife in his hand charged past the box seats where he and his mother were sitting. He was across the distance to the plate before a cop could move. Bart Mahan had thrown aside his chest protector and dropped into a fighter's crouch. A left to the belly, a right to the jaw, and the would-be knifer was on his back in the dirt. The crowd screamed with joyous excitement. He was screaming, too—until he looked at his mother. There were tears streaming down her face.

That was the moment when he realized the spiritual chasm between this woman and this man. She had seized his arm (he had only been seven or eight when it happened) and dragged him out of the ball park, denouncing baseball as a sport for fools, morons, lovers of violence. If he became a baseball player, she had screamed at him in her hysteria, she would disown him. What did it mean? It was the sport of atheists, Protestants. How could a man give his life to it?

Later that day she had calmed down and tried to apologize. She did not mean to criticize his father. She was only criticizing baseball, which she considered a peculiarly American insanity. She hoped and prayed her son would have higher, more serious goals. But it was too late. The knowing had been born, knowing that deepened and grew more saddening with the years. Somewhere, somehow, there had been a breakdown of love between this silent man and voluble woman. Had he grown weary of her chatter? Had she become bitter over his months away from home each baseball season? It was never explained, it was simply there, the chasm, filling the house with silent tension.

Matthew Mahan moved restlessly in the strange bed, trying to find a familiar feeling of comfort. Too late, too late to heal the wounds of the dead. But not too late, perhaps, to find his balance between them. It was more than calm, more than steadiness, that turned his mind and spirit toward his father. It was—it had to be—his independence. Not something flaunted, argumentatively proclaimed, but a quiet, incontestable fact. Bart Mahan was his own man on the baseball field and off it. And a bishop: Didn't a bishop have to be his own man, too, most of the time, except . . . when he was the Pope's man?

A low, gentle snore filled the room. Cardinal-designate Matthew Mahan was asleep.

XV

Matthew Mahan was dreaming again. It was another procession in a ghostly church to the foot of a huge cross. Looking up, the tortured body of the Savior with his father's face. *Forgive me, Father, I know not what I have done. Forgive me,* he prayed.

Bells were ringing, the kind of bells that rang in prison movies. A breakout. They were free, free at last. . . .

He awoke to find the room full of shadows. The Roman sunlight had vanished and gray dusk dulled the windows. The telephone was ringing. He picked it up and a woman's voice said, "It's supper time, Your Eminence."

"Mary," he said, struggling up on one elbow. "How are you?"

"Mildly ravenous, but I thought first you'd like to make a visit. I go there myself quite often in the early evening. I've gotten to know the sacristan. For a thousand lire he keeps the church open an extra half hour. When I told him I was bringing a *neo porporato* . . ."

"I'm all shaved and showered. All I've got to do is put on my uniform," Matthew Mahan said. "When can I pick you up?"

"I'll pick *you* up in a half hour. You're right on the way."

"No, I'll pick you up."

There was a tiny pause, which told him she understood exactly why he said it. "All right," she said in a voice that strained too much to be offhand. "We'll have a drink at the apartment first."

An hour later she welcomed him at the door of the penthouse, which was only a five-minute walk from the Hassler. She was wearing a dark red linen suit with a single gold brooch on the lapel. She had warned him a year or two ago that her hair was turning gray. It stunned him to find that it made her more beautiful than ever. There was scarcely a line in her face. Her figure was still as slim as it had been when he first saw her in 1949. She had been twenty-six that year. That meant she was forty-six today.

He took both her hands, and for a moment they simply faced each other. "This was the right place to meet," she said. "I should have known I was going to kiss you and cause a scandal."

She touched his cheek with her lips and stepped back again, their hands still joined. "You look—as wonderful as ever, Mary."

"Stop it, you clerical flatterer," she said, freeing her hands and strolling ahead of him into the living room.

"I don't flatter people I care about," he said. "I tell them the truth."

"You look tired," she said. "And you've gained weight."

"Good God, you sound like my doctor," he said with a grin. He patted his waistline. "Only ten pounds in three years. That's not a mortal sin."

Mary studied him for another moment and tossed her head in that feminine way that made her hair swing around her neck. Twenty years ago the sight of her glossy flowing black hair had turned his brain to jelly. Now in the lamplight he saw the gray hair swirl, and the feeling was a sad yet somehow sweet memory.

For a moment he wanted terribly to share his feelings with her as he had shared them in the past. He wanted to confess his ulcer, his troubles with liberals and conservatives, his weariness, as he had lamented his persecution by Archbishop Hogan in that lost decade that seemed almost prehistoric now. But the letters Mary had been writing him for the past two years, lamentations over the failure of renewal, the betrayal of the spirit of Pope John and the council, forced him to assume another role. He must be the sympathizer, the consoler now. Perhaps he had even passed beyond these roles, to the spokesman, the defender of the Way Things Are Done. For a moment he thought guiltily of Dennis McLaughlin. Too often, that was unquestionably the part you played for him.

"The way you talked about your hair—you made it sound like you were turning into a grandmother."

She smiled and gave it a pleased pat. "My hairdresser deserves the real credit. It was his idea to silver it."

"What have you been doing besides writing me those—those gossipy letters."

The pause gave him away, and once more it was clear that she caught the meaning he had tried to avoid. "Oh, I keep on painting, telling myself a small talent is better than none at all. I've done another translation—a marvelous young poet named Aspirante."

"I want ten copies. I only wish that you'd try to publish some of your own poetry, Mary."

"Oh, stop flattering me, you big Irish lug. I've told you there are too many minor poets around already."

Matthew Mahan sighed. "I give up. What's the latest gossip?"

"Let's see. They're giving Wright the Congregation of the Clergy."

"Good. He's a good man."

"Oh. How you people stick together. You're worse than politicians. He's a standpatter with a few bits of liberalism for window dressing."

"They say the same thing about me, Mary."

"I know. But I'm trying to change you. And I'm going to succeed, because I know your heart is in the right place."

Matthew Mahan strolled over to the window and studied the illuminated dome of St. Peter's. "It's wonderful that you of all people can say that, Mary. But don't expect too much. The situation is—so delicate. So very delicate."

"You sound like Pope Paul. Fix me a drink."

"The usual?"

"Of course."

He found the full bottle of Cinzano Bianco beside a silver ice bucket on the bar. Cinzano was certainly on Bill Reed's forbidden list. Aside from his desire to conceal the ulcer, Matthew Mahan flinched from refusing to join Mary in a drink which had become almost a ritual. She had ordered it for them before their first dinner in Rome. The situation was very delicate here, too.

In a moment they were clinking glasses. They drank in reflective silence for a minute or so. Then Mary made a visible effort to brighten their mood. "Let's see. What else have I heard from my revolutionary monsignori? Oh. You're going to be required to take a CIA-style oath."

He sipped his drink. The cool sweet liquid felt pleasant, even soothing in his stomach. But it was not soothing to realize that Mary was forcing him to ask about this new oath. "I can't imagine anything CIA-ish about the oath we take."

"This is not the regular oath. It's an oath of secrecy. Under pain of excommunication, you'll have to promise right there on the altar before Il Papa that you will never disclose a word of anything he says or writes to you."

"That—that's incredible."

"I know," Mary said. "It gives you a good idea of the prevailing psychology. They act like they're a fortress under siege."

"God help us all."

St. Peter's dome, sailing serenely above the darkened city, was suddenly a reproach. Too frank, too frank, Matthew Mahan warned himself. You are here to sustain this woman, to give her the hope and faith and love she needed to survive. "I've brought your old friend Bishop Cronin along with me. In the mood you're in, I'm not sure you should see him. The two of you may try to depose poor old Paul with a coup d'état."

"I know. We correspond. I've gotten him a lot of material for his book."

"You have?"

Matthew Mahan did not like to be taken by surprise. For a moment he almost asked what in the devil's name Mary thought she was doing, playing games with Cronin behind his back. The realization shocked him. He concealed it by hastily draining his drink. "What time are we due at the Tre Scalini?" he asked.

"Eight-thirty."

"If we want to make our visit, we ought to leave now."

"Yes," Mary said, glancing at her watch. "I don't like to keep the sacristan waiting."

They hurried into the cool Roman night past the shops and strollers on the Via Margutta and Via del Babuino to the Spanish Steps. Matthew Mahan squeezed his long legs into a tiny Fiat cab that happened to be at the head of the line. Perhaps the size of his cab or the presence of a priest made the driver more cautious. They drove almost sedately to the Via Cavour and trudged together up the tunnel beneath the slope of the Borgias to the Piazza of St. Peter in Chains.

They paused for a moment at the edge of the piazza. Through the darkness the sacristan was little more than a patch of white shirt, at the door of the church. Matthew Mahan looked across the piazza at the flats where his mother had been born. The windows were open to the warm April night, and sounds of voices, bits of music being played on radios or television, drifted across the empty square to them. A man in his undershirt with a glass of wine in his hand stopped at one of the windows, threw back his head, and laughed. A little girl ran to him and threw her arms around his waist. Matthew Mahan's throat tightened. Life, love, is truly indestructible; it endlessly empties and fills and empties, year by year, decade by decade.

"The more things change," Mary said softly beside him.

"Yes," he said. "The old cliché. Except it's true. It's true."

"Remember the first time we came here, Matt?"

"Could I ever forget it?"

You must go, said the old man with the huge nose and the sagging cheeks, you must go to this church at twilight, my favorite time to visit it, whenever I have been in Rome. I wish I could go with you, but trust me, I will be there in spirit. You must do two things. You must stop before the statue of Moses and try to see it above an immense tomb with forty other statues of similar magnificence. See it for what it was intended to be, the very essence of the old law, all that Christianity must never become, all the terror, the agony of the law and the majesty of it. Let's hope you also sense what I have always found in Moses' gaze, which is fixed on no one, which stares into a distance that is almost infinite. There is a sadness, a longing, even an emptiness in that gaze.

I think this longing is only visible because the work is on our level. If it had been raised to where it was originally intended to go—atop a mountain of marble—it might have become im-

perial. It was intended to be the summit of the tomb of Julius II, the man who built St. Peter's. Look about you at St. Peter in Chains, a humble church at best, and think for a moment about the way God has of teaching even popes a lesson. This Julius was more an antipope than a pope, a brigand, a tyrant who rode out of Rome at the head of his own army to pillage anyone who refused to pay him homage. And I mean pay. He died the most hated man in Italy, and his successor immediately canceled Michelangelo's work on his magnificent tomb. In the end, they shoveled his bones into the grave of his uncle, Sixtus IV.

Now go down to the reliquary under the high altar and look at the chains which supposedly bound Peter. Whenever I went there in the past, I used to think: Alas, St. Peter is still in chains. I used to reproach myself for that thought, which always seized me in spite of all my resolution to avoid it. I used to wonder if I was a secret heretic. Now I know I was only telling the truth.

Go now, and when we meet again, let us talk of some thoughts I have to free St. Peter from his chains.

All this spoken with a magic combination of sadness and vivacity. Overcome with emotion, they had fallen to their knees, ignoring the old man's protests, and kissed his ring. Then they had left Pope John XXIII smiling sadly after them, an ugly yet beautiful old man, bulky in his white robes as the peasant son he was, and driven directly to this church. Then, as now, the sacristan was waiting for them and they had entered the gloomy interior of the thirteen-hundred-year-old building and approached the magnificent statue of Moses.

At first, Matthew Mahan recalled, he had been seized by a kind of panicky humility. He knew nothing about art. What was this amazing old man in the Vatican trying to tell him? Why couldn't he say it, instead of sending him on this strange errand? Then he had looked around the church and remembered that his mother had knelt here as a girl. He remembered, too, the incomprehensible coincidence that had brought him to the attention of this old man, not once but twice, and had now made him Archbishop of one of the ten largest dioceses in America. A remarkable calm had descended upon him, and he found himself totally involved with the statue, giving himself to every twist and fold of the marble, to the incredibly realistic arms and hands, the curve of the muscles, the ridges of the veins, the massive reality of the shoulders and chest. Finally, the face, abstracted, yes, even somber, gazing into some unknown distance. There was not a hint of triumphant power in it. In fact, not a sign that the prophet was even aware that beneath his right arm he held the tablets of the Law.

Matthew Mahan had suddenly remembered a print in his grammar school Bible history book showing a bearded Moses holding high the commandments while the people fell on their knees before him. This was not the same man. There was an immense sadness on his face, Matthew Mahan suddenly saw. Yes, even a weariness, born of living and knowing the children of men. *Is this all, is this all I have to give them?* he seemed to be saying. *Is there no choice but to lay this burden upon their backs?* he mused, listening, perhaps silently praying, for a voice that would say: *My yoke is sweet, my burden light.*

Was it all in the statue? Matthew Mahan had dazedly asked himself. Was the marble and the mysterious power of the artist saying these things, or was it infused by that radiant stooped old man in the Vatican?

Beside him he had heard Mary saying in a low, soft voice, "Come to me, all you that labor and are heavy laden, and I will refresh you. Take up my yoke upon you, and learn of me because I am meek and humble of heart, and you shall find rest to your souls. For my yoke is sweet and my burden light."

Matthew Mahan had glanced down at her in astonishment. She had draped a white lace kerchief over her black hair. A fold of it shadowed her face. She had drawn it back and smiled at him. "That's Don Angelo's favorite passage from the Gospels. He told me that he first realized what it meant, standing here."

Ten years ago, only ten years ago. At times, looking back at this staggering decade, born in such hope and then bloodied by such tragedy, it was impossible to believe it was a mere ten years. It had to be twenty, thirty years ago that he had first heard (and largely failed to understand) Pope John's cryptic words of hope and radical faith. But now the years coalesced and it was only yesterday, only a few hours ago, that they had turned from the statue after that exchange of Gospel words and walked down to the high altar, where the strip of sacred chain was framed by two magnificent bronze doors. *St. Peter is still in chains.* Then you had wondered what the old man meant by those words. The Pope was still more or less a prisoner of the Vatican, unable to leave without elaborate preparations to protect him from the enormous crowds the sight of him inevitably attracted. But in that sense the President of the United States was also a prisoner of the White House. It was too trivial an observation to make Angelo Roncalli fear he was a secret heretic. Moreover, why was it juxtaposed to this statue of Moses?

"Remember how baffled we were—or at least I was—by what he said about St. Peter being in chains?"

Mary nodded, smiling. "You found out in the next two or three years—the whole world found out about it." She sighed. "If only he hadn't died so soon."

"I don't feel that way, Mary," Matthew Mahan said. "Remember what he told that fellow who said he should abolish the College of Cardinals and fire the whole Curia?"

" 'It's not for me to do everything.' "

"What he wanted done," Matthew Mahan said slowly because the thought was coming to him as he spoke, "involved all of us. It was part of the thing itself—us doing it."

"Yes," Mary said, "but with him alive there wouldn't be—a perpetual spirit of obstruction."

For a moment Matthew Mahan felt as if she had thrown something at him. It was almost a physical sensation that caused him to move his head abruptly to one side, in what seemed like a shake of disagreement. "Let's go inside," he said.

Mary exchanged a *buona sera* with the sacristan, and they entered the darkened church. It was illuminated only by the glow of candles and perhaps a single invisible light before the statue of Moses, and another light at the reliquary of St. Peter's chains beneath the altar. With Mary beside him, Matthew Mahan walked slowly over to the Moses and stood before it. At first he thought of it as a test. Would he again be able to feel with his eyes what the old man, six years in the grave now, had created for him here? At first he felt nothing. A wave of unidentifiable emotion—regret, perhaps fear—flooded him.

Then an extraordinary thing began to happen. He found himself *within* the statue. He could almost feel the folds of Moses' robes around his legs, the weight of the stone tablets beneath his right arm, the almost unbearable tension in the left arm, making that cordlike vein or sinew leap out just above the wrist. He was not watching a prophet gazing into history's distance with sad longing; he himself was there, his own eyes aching for a glimpse of the face, his own ears yearning for an echo of the voice he had heard in this church ten years ago. This was what his straining body needed—to relax, to find peace, peace that the lawgiver can never know, in his perpetual struggle with rebellious men. The realization that he had become this lawgiver, this wielder of authority, in spite of all his inward wish to escape the role, struck him like a blow from one of those huge marble hands. His throat filled with tears. It was so natural. A leader—a bishop—has to give orders and then he has to see that those orders are enforced, and to guarantee enforcement on a regular basis, he has to enforce laws not of his own making.

Father, forgive us, he whispered, *for we know not what we do.*

"Every time I come here," Mary Shea said, her eyes on the statue, "I always feel that either he or you—sometimes both of you—are here with me."

"Yes," Matthew Mahan murmured, "yes." How could he explain this desolating sense of loss to her now? For Mary this was a church of fulfillment, of happiness, peace. For him it had suddenly become a house of dread, of accusation. He almost expected Moses' massive right hand, with the index finger resting now on the prophet's stomach (another ulcer patient?), to raise and point accusingly at him. Matthew Mahan felt his pulse racing, his heart pounding in his chest. Again he looked around the darkened church, but there was no glimpse, no sense whatever, of his mother now. She was a vanished ghost, only an echo in those noisy tenements across the square. He was utterly alone, unable to share his grief with anyone. He could only reach out in the darkness to the lost image of the old man in the Vatican; he could only say with extravagant hope that he was somehow listening: *I understand, now I really understand.*

Mary, seeing him turn away, thought that he wanted to look at the relic of St. Peter's chains. He didn't. He wanted more than anything else to escape from this church with its shadows that seemed to press claustrophobically around him. How could this be happening? he thought in utter bewilderment. How could this sentimental gesture be turning into agony?

Mary walked ahead of him into the darkness, saying, "The old chain is still there, and over at the Vatican they're reforging the few links he managed to break. Why can't they see that they're destroying themselves, Matt?"

"I don't know," he said. "I don't know."

The banks of devotional candles before the altar flickered eerily on the bronze doors on each side of St. Peter's chains. Matthew Mahan stared numbly at them, thinking, *Not just Peter's chains but yours, too.* He had no idea how long he stood there while these words reverberated within him. Mary finally touched him on the arm. "Matt," she said, "I hate to keep the sacristan waiting too long. It is suppertime."

"Oh yes, yes," he said, "of course."

Outside it was totally dark. Matthew Mahan slipped a thousand-lira note into the sacristan's hand and apologized to him in Italian for keeping him waiting.

There was a flash of white teeth in the darkness, and the man replied that he was enjoying the cool night air, it was no trouble at all.

They said good night to him and strolled down an alley past a technical school to a small *ristorante* with an outdoor café. At the end of the street the Colosseum loomed eerily in its floodlights, looking like a great ship wrecked and abandoned by history's unpredictable winds. Matthew Mahan felt incredibly exhausted. Maybe the whole experience had been nothing more than exhaustion, he told himself, an unparalleled seizure of nerves. But he knew even as he toyed with the thought that this was an evasion. What had just happened to him in that church was a truth that he could never deny without risking his soul.

"How about an aperitif?" he said. "It's a long way to the Piazza Navona."

Agreeable as always, Mary sat down with him at one of the green and yellow tables. She fingered the swans on the tablecloth and let him order two Cinzano Biancos from the gravely formal middle-aged waiter. While they waited for the drinks, they watched a half-dozen boys in a field across the street trying to play soccer. An eerie glow fell across the field from searchlights playing on a massive hunk of rock, lined with a thousand and one ridges. It looked older than Rome.

"What's that?" he asked, knowing that Mary's knowledge of the city was practically encyclopedic by now.

"Probably part of Trajan's baths. They were the first ones to admit women."

"And right after that," Matthew Mahan said, "Rome started collapsing?"

"Don't be such an *obvious* male chauvinist," she said.

She began asking him about people they both knew. He gave her the little information he had, mostly a list of divorces. A dismaying number of well-to-do Catholic marriages had broken up over the last five years. Most of them had not even bothered to seek the advice or permission of the Church. Mary was frankly amazed. "I can't believe it," she said. "I thought I'd still be a pariah if I came home. Now I realize I wouldn't even be noticed."

"That's certainly true," Matthew Mahan said.

"What's the explanation for it, Matt? Is there one?"

"I don't know. I've always been wary of putting people into moulds and attributing personal decisions like divorce to some sort of national trend. An awful lot of people in their late forties and early fifties are getting divorced, and they're not all Catholics by a long shot. The Episcopal bishop and the Methodist bishop, who have lunch with me once a month, tell me the same thing is happening in their churches."

"But take the Currans, Joe and Wilda, four kids, twenty-five years of marriage. Why would they suddenly walk away from it?"

"I wish I knew," he said, thinking ruefully that when Joe Curran got divorced he stopped giving $25,000 a year to the Archbishop's Fund. He was the most successful patent lawyer in the state. "In his case, from what I could find out from friends, it was the old sexy-secretary cliché. Obviously, more and more Americans don't see any reason for saying no when they want something badly. Personally, I think they're seduced by this myth of experience, the great enricher. And the fantastic propaganda coming out in books and magazines and on television about marriage being passé. There's nothing we can do about it. But I'm willing to bet that the priests of the next generation will spend a lot of time with these people's children—they're the ones it breaks your heart to think about. Speaking of children, how's Jimmy?"

"Oh, just great, from a distance," Mary said, fingering the stem of her glass. "I've tried hard to take your advice, Matt, and not smother-love him. He enjoys his job. All those languages he learned spending every summer over here with me are paying off beautifully. No other editor his age can match his publishing contacts in Europe. I see him four or five times a year when he comes over on business. But I suspect that his moral life leaves something to be desired from a Catholic point of view."

Matthew Mahan sighed. "I'm afraid there's nothing much you can do about that, and there's even less for me to do. His letters got pretty perfunctory after he graduated from college. I could see that he'd had just about all the clerical advice he could swallow—though I did my best to sound as unclerical as possible."

"I'm sure you did, Matt," she said, touching the back of his hand lightly with the tips of her fingers, damp from her glass. "What you've given him—what we've both tried to give him will come through eventually, I'm sure of that. I really am sure."

"I am, too," Matthew Mahan said, hoping that he sounded convinced. Trying to find a more cheerful subject, he began asking for some of their Roman friends. "How is Monsignor den Doolard?"

"Gone home to Holland. There's nothing for him to do in Rome these days."

Den Doolard was a brilliant Dutch theologian who had been on the staff of the late Cardinal Augstin Bea, the leader of the Vatican outreach to Protestant and other churches. He had been one of the hardest working *periti*—experts—at the Vatican Council, a constantly cheerful undiscouraged man, an earthy version of the saintly Bea.

"Did he request a transfer?"

Mary nodded. "It's just as well. He might have ended up like Father Guilio."

"What's wrong with him?"

Guilio Mirante was an Italian Jesuit, a quintessential Roman with a gentle, melancholy air, a touch of Roman cynicism in his usually self-deprecating irony. He had long operated on sort of detached duty, in the Jesuit order but not of it, serving as chaplain of an orphanage to which Matthew Mahan had contributed handsomely, and as a friend of prominent Romans of every class and political persuasion. He, too, had been a council *perito*, appointed by John himself.

Mary glanced at her watch. "It's a long story, and I think it would be better if he told you himself. If I get into it, I may spoil our evening—and we'll be late for dinner."

"Tell him to call me."

"I will."

In a somewhat uneasy silence he paid the waiter and they strolled down the street and through part of Trajan's Park to steps that led them down to the street level and the Colosseum. They peered into one of the outer arches and found themselves being appraised by a half-dozen prostitutes in silver and gold miniskirts and satin blouses. Several small boys, none older than twelve, approached them and cheerfully inquired whether they were interested in a guide to the Colosseum or to the young ladies, all of whom were ready to satisfy a customer's preference, no matter how bizarre. For a single girl, a thousand lire; for two or three the price went up, depending upon whether they wanted to participate or just watch. Matthew Mahan stood there, transfixed by the utter lack of caring in their boyish voices.

"Don't be ashamed, Father," said the tallest of them, with black hair falling over his ears. "Last night we had a Cardinal."

Laughter echoed from stone arches, the same savage, empty tones that must have filled them when an unpopular gladiator died ingloriously.

Mary was pulling at his arm. He decided it was better to say nothing, and they walked along the curving path until they found an archway occupied only by postcard salesmen. These could be brushed aside, and they stood for a moment gazing across the battered interior of the stadium. There was nothing realistic about it, neither in the daylight nor now in the moonlight, helped here and there by floodlights. Death was all Matthew Mahan saw, ancient, grinning death, man's oldest enemy. The whole thing was a gigantic skeleton, leering here with an empty mouth, staring there with an empty eye, a gigantic monument to death. "It always depresses me," Matthew Mahan said, "but every time I come to Rome I feel compelled to stare it in the face for a minute or two."

"What do you see?" Mary asked.

He told her. She nodded. "Yes," she said, "Pope Paul came down here a few months ago and said the Stations of the Cross. It was a mistake. The place dwarfed him. He looked lost, futile."

They crossed the street and found a cabstand on the Via dei

Fori Imperiali. The taxi whisked them past the Church of St. Maria in Aracoeli, once the site of a temple to the goddess Juno and of a palace of Caesar Augustus. There, according to myth, the Virgin and the Child descended and informed the trembling Emperor that henceforth "this is the altar of the son of God." Now the magnificent Byzantine Virgin over the main altar shared with the Virgin of St. Maria Maggiore the responsibility of watching over the people of Rome. A few minutes of hairbreadth driving down the Corso Vittorio Emanuele, and they were at the entrance of the Piazza Navona. No traffic was allowed inside, the driver explained, and they hastily assured him in good Italian that they understood. With Mary's hand resting lightly on his arm, Matthew Mahan entered their favorite Roman enclave.

Shaped like a huge outdoor salon, the piazza occupied the former circus of the Emperor Domitian. The palazzos, the church, and the other buildings along each side and at the loops on both ends composed an almost perfect harmony of form and space. Three fountains added their own circular contrasts to the composition. At this hour of the evening there were strollers everywhere, the very old hobbling on canes, the very young pushed in carriages. Between the darkened facades of the palazzos and the church, the restaurants glowed busily. In the shadows wrinkled old beggar women chewed on grapes and other fruit and vegetables snatched from the shops of the nearby Campo dei Fiori market.

Before the first fountain, a huge bare-chested fire-eater performed. They gave him only a passing glance and headed for the central Fountain of the Rivers, one of Rome's masterpieces. Four huge rocks supported a pedestal on top of which stood an obelisk from the Appian Way. On the rocks stood four statues symbolizing the Ganges, the Danube, the Nile, and the Rio de la Plata.

"They're still waiting for it to fall," Matthew Mahan said, pointing at two of the statues, who seemed to be reacting with fright and horror to the facade of the church opposite them. According to the story, this was the way the creator of the fountain, the great architect-sculptor Bernini, had spoofed the architect of the church, his rival Borromini.

Mary sighed. "I'm afraid that story has been disproved by the architectural historians. The church was built after Bernini finished the fountain."

"It's still a good story," Matthew Mahan said. "I'm telling it to my tourists tomorrow."

Mary was barely listening. She was gazing mournfully at the numerous hippies in their standard blue jeans, beads, and long hair sitting around the fountain rim. "I try to understand them, I even try to love them," she said, "but they're so vacuous, Matt. What's wrong with them? What do they want?"

"I wish I knew."

They turned back to the Tre Scalini and were soon sipping another set of Cinzano Biancos. They had a choice table, inside, so that the noise of the human traffic in the square was muted, while a window gave them a view of the Four Rivers Fountain. The food was superb, as usual, and Mary entertained him for a while with funny stories about her outrageous landlady, a countess who collected the rent for her apartments personally and always managed to be condescending even at her most mercenary. "She's decided to take charge of my life," Mary said, "as I'm sure she's taken charge of everyone who made the mistake of letting her get close to her. She keeps telling me I should marry. 'It is never too late,' she says."

A temporarily forgotten sense of guilt assailed Matthew Mahan. He suddenly remembered something he had wanted to say to Mary Shea for years. The last time he had come to Rome he had almost said it, but prudence, that virtue to which bishops come naturally, and a fear of the eternally unpredictable feminine had held his tongue. But tonight he suddenly knew that he would say it. He would shuck off once and for all this role of protector, all-wise adviser that had been half hypocrisy for too long. It was only a matter of waiting for the right moment. He did not want to play the standard cleric and abruptly interrupt Mary's gaiety with a solemn outburst. Instead, he entertained her with some of the nut mail he got every day. She particularly enjoyed the plan to end the Vietnam War Notre Dame style with a massive bombardment of daily communions.

They finished a bottle of Valpolicella with their main course, and Matthew Mahan surreptitiously swallowed two or three Titrilacs to soothe his ulcer. By now it was ten o'clock. The crowd in the piazza was beginning to thin. "Why don't we have our coffee and *gelato* on the terrace?" he said. He signaled the waiter and issued the order. In a moment they were seated at an outside table in the deliciously cool night air. The Romans, the tourists, even the hippies, slowly vanished from the piazza. In a few more minutes it was almost empty. They sat there, lulled by the splash of the fountains, the magical mingling of light and water and marble that enriched their eyes as the sound charmed their ears.

"What a wonderful reunion, Mary. I can't tell you how much it means to me to see you so well, so lovely, so serene, after all these years."

She lifted her face just slightly to him, and her eyes seemed to anticipate his words. Or was he only hoping that this was the case? "I hope the—the emotion in those words doesn't upset you, Mary, or surprise you. But for years now there's been something I wanted to tell you, something on my part that has been less than honest and has—well, troubled me. In those days in the early fifties when I was the hustling young monsignor ready to tackle anything the bishop assigned to me, I—I wasn't ready for someone like you, Mary, a woman with such depth, such sweetness, a woman who was my spiritual superior in so many ways. I thought it was just a matter of giving you the standard soft soap, spiritual consolation, daily mass, Communion, frequent prayer. All the time I was saying those things, Mary, a voice inside me was saying, 'But not for her, she deserves something better. She wasn't born to live this mutilated life, just because she had the bad luck to marry a drunken Irish bum.' The more I saw you, Mary, the more panicky I became. I diguised it pretty well. Remember, you used to tell me I should have been a comedian?"

"That imitation you used to give of Archbishop Hogan, Matt. That's still the funniest act I've ever seen or heard."

"Act is the right word. I did everything I could think of, not only to make you happy—for a little while—but to avoid telling you the truth. I knew there was no hope of you ever getting an annulment, but I told you to come here—come to Rome—because if you stayed in the city, I didn't know what was going to happen to me, Mary."

The *gelato tartufo*, the special ice cream of the Tre Scalini, the best in Rome, was untouched on the plates before them. As he talked, Mary had slowly leaned back in her chair, not a gesture that suggested she wanted to get away from him, no, it seemed more a desire to see him in perspective.

"I never thought you'd stay over here for the rest of your life, Mary. I just thought—even a year, maybe two, would give me a chance to get a grip on myself."

A small sad smile played across Mary's lips. Now, in the same deliberate way, she leaned forward again and took his right hand, which was closed in a fist on the table, in both her smaller, softer hands. She did not lift it from the table. She simply wrapped her fingers around it and slowly unbent the contorted fingers.

"Oh, Matt," she said, "Matt. To think that all these years I've let this trouble you."

"You let—?"

"Do you think I didn't know, Matt? Do you think I came over here just because you suggested it? Women may not be terribly bright about things like moral theology and church politics. But when it comes to knowing when a man is in love with them—it's the rare woman who's too dumb to miss that." She leaned almost imperceptibly closer to him. "And they also know when they're in love with the man."

Her smile was more solemn now, more earnest. "Matt, I was the one who decided to come over here. I came of my own free will knowing that nothing could be done about my marriage. I came because I saw that you were a great priest. I saw that—no matter what you thought or felt about me—your priesthood was the real center of your life. I didn't want to be guilty of destroying that part of you, Matt. It was too important to you—and to the world. When I came over here, I knew I was going to stay a long time."

He felt unbelievable. A chaotic mixture of joy and sadness surged in his body. "My God," he said, "what an egotistic ignoramus I am."

Mary threw back her head and laughed heartily, reminding him of the way she used to laugh when he did his imitations of the Archbishop and other chancery office factotums fifteen years ago. "No," she said, "no, you're not an ignoramus. You're just a man. And like all men, you naturally assume you're running things."

Now came a question he had also been afraid to ask for too long. Almost in spite of his will, it rose to his lips. "How has it really been, Mary? All those years I asked you—are you all right? I always took the answer you gave me—too easily. It was what I wanted to hear."

"I know Matt. That's why I gave it to you."

She ran her finger around the rim of her wineglass. "It was terrible for the first few years. I—I drank and—there were men. I was so bitter and empty, Matt. Giving up you—seemed to take all I had left. This isn't a good country for a woman in that frame of mind. It's so easy to be exploited—and Italian men are artists at it.

"That's why I moved to Venice. I lived with a businessman whom I met in Rome. I also wanted to be someplace where you wouldn't visit me. There was always too much of a chance of you showing up in Rome. Well—the thing went sour in Venice. Too close to the wife, that sort of banal problem. Then he came to Venice. I met him. And everything began to change."

"Roncalli?"

Mary nodded. "He told me that we all had to spend some time in the desert. Forty days, forty months, or in his case thirty years. Thanks to him, Matt, I was able to come back to Rome, back to you, without—the old fear."

They began to eat their *gelato*. They savored the chocolate taste in silence for a moment. It seemed to Matthew Mahan the perfect physical expression of what they were feeling—sadness, regret, but a dark sweetness, too. Outside in the shadows of the piazza the fountains splashed, the light-filled water of the four rivers ran out to the Eternal City. Matthew Mahan sat with the woman he had loved and still loved, and slowly realized that there was one more question to ask.

"And now, Mary. How are you now?"

For the first time she avoided his eyes. "Not—not good, Matt. Oh, I know what you're going to say to me. The same thing my psychiatrist says. Don't be so involved with the Church. Let the clerical politicians play their games."

"Don't put words in my mouth, Mary. What's this about a psychiatrist?"

"I've been depressed, Matt. On and off, for the past year or so. It's no fun. You can't sleep. You find yourself thinking all sorts of sick thoughts. It even bothered my digestion for a while. I was living like an ulcer patient."

"Really?" He was not sure which symptom upset him most. "And your psychiatrist blames the Church?"

"No. My morbid interest in the Church. In where it seems to be going. Or not going. It's really a sense of loss, Matt. Loss of him, Don Angelo. Every day they seem to do something else that—that's obscene—that makes him seem more remote, more—dead. Don't you feel it, Matt? Don't you sense that his spirit is being driven out of the Church?"

For a moment something close to panic seized him. Was he part of this betrayal? Wasn't that the only conclusion to be drawn from what he had just experienced in the Church of St. Peter in Chains? But to confess it would be devastating to this anguished woman confronting him.

"Mary, try to be—a little more charitable. Toward Paul. The men around him. Maybe it would help if I suggested including me. We're all victims of the same thing, Mary. An incredible explosion of problems. And we're just ordinary men, Mary. Not saints or geniuses like John. You do the best you can. But it's so hard to get a perspective on whether that best is good or bad. The situation sort of engulfs you."

"But charity, Matt. Charity and love. I'm sure you make them your first principles. And reasonable freedom."

"I—I tell myself I do. I try. But maybe even you would say I don't always succeed."

It was almost a confession. Did she hear it? No, she was too embroiled in her own tormented emotions. "And birth control. That unspeakable encyclical? You fought that. You told me. You're not browbeating your priests like that old ogre O'Boyle in Washington, D.C."

"No. I'm trying to handle it—another way."

"But how could it have happened? How could he turn his back on the commission, the best thinking of the best men? With the world drowning in people? How could he be so utterly heartless? How could he condemn women to my mother's fate?"

"Your mother? Oh yes—"

Kathleen Murtagh had died giving birth to her fifth child in six years. Her husband's second wife had made Mary's childhood and adolescence a misery. She had married the first available man to escape from what she called a concentration camp. Inevitably, he turned out to be the worst available man.

Another wave of weariness washed over Matthew Mahan. "Mary," he said. "Popes make mistakes, just like Archbishops and priests and everyone else. We have to live with them. We have to live with everybody. But we shouldn't let anything shake our faith or our confidence in the Church. Christ himself told us that the gates of hell wouldn't prevail against it."

"What about the gates of heaven? Why don't we look in that direction? Matt, it's hope that's being destroyed, not faith. That's for the next world. But hope—that's what the people want and need. I can't tell you how much your becoming Cardinal meant to me, this way. Now you're in a position to speak out—and be heard. You've got to do it, Matt. Somebody has to raise his voice against that crew in the Vatican."

For another moment he sat there paralyzed, his spoon in midair. Mary, too? Where did all of them—Cronin, Mike Furia, Dennis McLaughlin—get these incredible expectations? But this was the most unbearable summons. She was placing her soul in the balance and demanding the impossible from him to stop the scale from plunging her into darkness.

"Mary—I'm not going to be that important—to start lecturing the whole Church."

"One of eleven American Cardinals. Of one hundred thirty-five in the whole world? If you speak, Matt, speak forcefully, they've got to listen."

"But I'm not sure—it's not really my style, Mary. I try to avoid brawls—not start them."

"You fought old Hogan. You spoke out for important things— when you knew it would enrage him. Negro rights. The liturgy. Psychiatric help for Catholics. Honest labor unions."

The causes of the fifties. How simple, how nostalgic, they sounded. How could he tell her the difference now? How could he explain how threatened the Church seemed to him, how much time he spent defending, preserving, rather than changing it? He saw from the anguish on Mary's face that it was impossible to explain. And then he saw what he could never endure: tears. For a dazed moment he saw his mother weeping, heard his father's voice snarling: *Okay, okay, we'll do it your way.* What were they arguing about? What hadn't they argued about?

But he would not snarl. He could not, would not, be that man of iron, or rock—yes, that marble man to whom he felt so strangely close these days. He would consciously refuse to be him, snarling his laconic decrees. No, somehow, no matter what it cost him, no matter how soft, how vulnerable, it made him, he would be a man of love. He took Mary's hand and held it between his bigger hands. "Don't, Mary, don't," he whispered. "We'll do it. We'll find a way."

XVI

Dear Leo:

It's the beginning of my first full day in Rome, and I am so tired I am seeing double. The flight over was sheer barbarism, no possibility of sleep for the entire night. We all staggered into bed late in the afternoon, napped a few hours, and then had dinner. The Cardinal went off alone with this mysterious Mary Shea whom I have mentioned to you. By now I've met her, and if there is something going on there, I have to congratulate His Eminence for his good taste, at least. She's a real beauty, one of those svelte, gray-haired women who simultaneously manage to look sexy and mature without trying, all very subdued and controlled. That same night, I went to dinner with our millionaire godfather, Mike Furia, and Bishop Cronin. What a combination, I thought, at first. But it turned out to be an interesting evening. Cronin left his intellectual hat in his room, and we spent most of our time talking about Matthew Mahan. Mike F. told me that he'd probably be a hit man in the Mafia today if he hadn't met Padre Matt in W.W. II. His father was a soldier in one of our city's best families. Incidentally, if you think you're cynical about the Church, you should talk to Furia. He knows an incredible amount about the Vatican's business dealings.

Furia and Cronin got talking about the odd way that Mahan became a bishop in the first place. It's a series of coincidences, built around Pope John XXIII, of all people. It seems that Roncalli, who was an Italian army chaplain during World War II, decided to give a dinner for American army chaplains just after the war ended, in 1945. (He was the papal nuncio in France by this time.) Since his English wasn't very good, he wanted someone who spoke French or Italian to help him out. The local chief of chaplains tapped

Captain Matt, with his decorations and his mother's good Italian, and the two of them got along like father and son. The dinner was a big success. Father Matt suggested inviting Protestant and Jewish chaplains as well as Catholics, and Roncalli loved the idea. Thereafter Roncalli invented all sorts of excuses to keep Matt on his staff practically full time until the division sailed for home.

Back in the States, Big Matt corresponded with him sporadically. Then Mary Shea came into the picture. She is the very rich niece-in-law of our fair city's old boss, and Matt was assigned to soothe her spiritually when her marriage collapsed. Since she was loaded with money, he told her that her best chance for an annulment was a direct appeal in Rome. Sensible advice, even if it didn't work. But Mary decided that she liked living in Europe, and she settled down—guess where? In Venice. And guess who was appointed patriarch of Venice on January 15, 1953, within a month or so of her arrival in Gondolaville? Naturally, Patriarch Roncalli got to know the very rich American lady. In that respect, good Pope J. was, I gather, no different from any other prelate. She was soon being invited to lunches and dinners at the patriarchal palazzo, no doubt responding magnificently via her checkbook.

Guess who she talked about when she got the ear of His Eminence? Who else but that wonderful monsignor who was charging about our archdiocese, building schools and CYO gymnasiums by the dozen, and raising money by the ton. That's right, good old Matt. Imagine her surprise when Roncalli, who apparently never forgot a name, brightened instantly and began agreeing with her paeans.

When the miracle occurred in 1958, and the old man became Pope, he was better informed on our archdiocese than he was on any other see in the United States, including New York. He knew that old Hogan was senile and was never any good in the first place. So he promptly made Matt an auxiliary bishop, and within a year had made him coadjutor with a guarantee of succession. Talk about casting your bread upon the waters—or in this case, upon grass widows. There are some curious questions unanswered, of course. Wouldn't it have been logical, if Mary Shea went to Europe at the suggestion of Big Matt and failed to obtain her annulment, for her to look upon him without much warmth? What has been the source of her continuing attraction, not to say fascination? Renaissance possibilities are the most obvious. If this is the case, he is an even bigger fraud than he seems to be, and thoroughly deserves all the opprobrium you plan to heap on him. But keep that diabolical pen of yours in your pocket for the time being. Let's try to find out the truth. I know you liberals are not much interested in that sort of thing these days, but I'm old-fashioned enough to believe it may be important.

Best,
Dennis

He had just finished licking the envelope when there was a knock on the door, and in marched Andy Goggin, escorted by Bishop Cronin in a tam-o'-shanter. "I found this innocent wandering about the lobby," he said, poking Goggin with his blackthorn walking stick, "and thought at first he was one of those clerical panhandlers. But then he gave me the password, McLaughlin, and I agreed to deposit him at your door."

Goggin was, if possible, taller and skinnier than ever. Both aspects drew appropriate comments from Bishop C. "I asked him if they were putting Christians on starvation diets in the Mamertine Prison again. He said no, so I asked him if they were using the rack, for I couldn't imagine how else he'd been stretched to such a length."

"He says you're writing a history of Vatican I with him."

"He's liable to say anything," Dennis said.

"We're on our own today, lads," said Bishop Cronin. "His Eminence-to-be is taking his millionaires about the city in a chartered bus with himself as guide. I offered to supplement his comments with a few of me own, and he insulted me by saying he couldn't afford to have any of his biggest givers scandalized. However, I managed to shake him down for fifty thousand lire, which will save us the trouble of eating at the Irish College, a fate I wouldn't wish on anyone but my worst enemy."

"I am putting myself totally in the hands of you two experts," Dennis said. "Before the day is over, I expect to know the essential Rome."

At this point there was another knock on the door, and Jim McAvoy came wandering into the room looking sheepish. "We missed the bus. I set the alarm clock wrong. Madeline's down-stairs in the lobby, ready to kill me. Do you think we could join you fellows for the morning, at least? We can pick up the Cardinal and the rest of the crowd at the Cavalieri Hilton. That's where they're having lunch."

Bishop Cronin looked annoyed. But Dennis could see no reason why the McAvoys would not fit easily into their entourage. He introduced Goggin and they descended to the lobby, where Madeline McAvoy looked both relieved and pleased. "We may learn more from a strictly clerical tour," she said archly to Dennis. "I'm sure the Cardinal is going to give the rest of the group a pretty standard lecture."

"Which we've heard," said Jim McAvoy. "We came with him in sixty-seven."

"Well now," said Bishop Cronin briskly, "there's only one place to go first. Only one place that means Rome to the likes of us. Saint Peter's."

They found a large taxi and headed for Vatican City. Crossing the Tiber on the Ponte Cavour, they drove along the river to the Via della Conciliazione which, Cronin told them, had been built by Mussolini to celebrate the treaty he signed with Pope Pius XI. The street had destroyed The Borgo, one of the most charming sections of old Rome. As they rounded the curve along the river, Cronin pointed out the ancient Castel Sant'Angelo, the tomb of the Emperor Hadrian, and more recently a place "where the Pope put people he didn't like, so he could kill them at his leisure."

"See that bridge there?" said Cronin, pointing to the Ponte Sant'Angelo. "I never cross on it. I don't trust the damn thing. In 1450 it collapsed and drowned a hundred and seventy-two Christmas pilgrims."

Soon St. Peter's was visible straight ahead of them on the Via della Conciliazione. It looked particularly immense from this dis-tance, Cronin said. In fact, this was the best possible perspective. Closer, the long nave, installed at the order of a pope who wanted the biggest possible audience, destroyed the original architectural plan, which called for a church with four equal wings, surmounted by the stupendous dome.

Against the clear blue sky, Dennis thought the dome looked weary and a little forlorn for all its size. Cronin, seeming to read his mind, remarked, "Belloc in his *Road to Rome* said it was a delicate blue in 1901, but by the time I got here in 1911 it had faded to its present gloomy gray. Either that, or the old boy was looking at Rome through tinted glasses—which I suspect he was."

"What do they think of Belloc these days?" Jim McAvoy asked. "They told us he was a great Catholic historian."

"He was a better poet," said Bishop Cronin and proceeded to rip off the dithyrambic epithalamium or threnody with which Belloc had closed his *Road to Rome*. The bishop was still reciting it as they got out of the taxi and let Jim McAvoy pay the driver.

> Drinking when I had a mind to,
> Singing when I felt inclined to;
> Nor ever turn my face to home
> Till I had slaked my heart at Rome.

They walked into St. Peter's Square and stood there for a moment, feeling miniscule within the immense embrace of the circling columns.

"When I was here the last time," Mrs. McAvoy said, "a guide told us that those columns represented the Holy Father's arms reaching out to the whole world."

"There's something to that, there's something to that," said Cronin with a wicked twinkle in his glance toward Dennis and Goggin. "They were designed by Giovanni Lorenzo Bernini, educated by the Jesuits, creators of the doctrine that the way to salvation was blind obedience to the Pope."

"Yea, verily," said Goggin. "As our sacred founder, St. Ignatius, wrote in Rule Thirteen of the Spiritual Exercises, 'If we wish to be sure that we are right in all things, we should always be ready to accept this principle: I will believe that the white that I see is black, if the hierarchical church so defines it.'"

They strolled toward the basilica until they reached the obelisk in the middle of the square. "Now stand a moment, if you will," Cronin said, "and imagine what was here before the Christian Church collapsed into the arms of the Emperor. St. Peter was crucified somewhere along the route we have just come, in or near the Roman Circus of Caligula. No one knows where the devil he was buried, though the popes would like mightily to believe it was beneath that great mass of stone facing us. But the best evidence tells us it was not the grave but a little shrine to St. Peter that stood here on Vatican Hill.

"It was in the corner of a cemetery—the poorest corner, at that. To get to it, you had to walk past all sorts of impressive tombs of wealthy Romans. The shrine was not much more than two niches in the side of the hill. There was a bit of an altar table on two legs in front of it, and the upper niche was like a tabernacle. Under the altar ledge was a movable slab of stone, behind which the old fisherman's bones may have lain for a time. The whole thing was no bigger than an ordinary house door and not much higher than one.

"This is what that noble pseudo-Roman, the Emperor Constantine, that wonderful example of Christianity in practice, who killed his wife by putting her into a steam bath and raising the temperature until she was boiled alive, found after he'd slaughtered all his enemies and became the boss of bosses. He decided to build around the humble shrine a church big enough to hold an army. For it was armies and not religion that good old Constantine was thinking about, you may be sure. He was the first but by no means the last imperialist to discover that Christians made good soldiers. Even when I was a green seminarian here just before the Great War, I often found myself wishing that damned old pagan had left well enough alone."

Madeline McAvoy was obviously enjoying Bishop Cronin's highly unorthodox approach to church history. Jim McAvoy's reactions seemed a little more wary. "But if it wasn't for Constantine," he said, "the Romans would have kept on persecuting the Christians. They would have remained a minority."

"The best damn thing that could have happened," Bishop Cronin said. He led them across the piazza until they were about a hundred yards from the portico. Then, raising his hand like a traffic cop, he pointed with his blackthorn toward the facade and rapidly read the inscriptions, which consisted of the titles of the Pope in Latin. "Pontifex Maximus, that's the key phrase to notice up there, children. That term is borrowed lock, stock, and Latin from the Empire. It was one of the many titles of the Emperor. You see," he said, speaking directly to Dennis, "this marriage of the Church and the state is no joke, lad."

"Where did you find *him?*" Goggin whispered as they mounted the steps of the portico beside the McAvoys.

"Ex-professor of theology at Rosewood."

"Can such things be?" murmured Goggin.

"Now here," said Cronin as they entered the church and stood at the head of the tremendous nave, "we see the beginning of the great conspiracy. The Renaissance church designed by Michelangelo to replace old Constantine's Romanesque barn was in the form of a Greek cross with equal arms. A nice touch, suggesting among other things that our friends in the East might someday join us to worship here. But this was all changed by the popes of the seventeenth century, for whom absolute monarchy was a way of life. They had a second-rate architect named Maderno triple the size of this arm so you come from sunlight into this darkness and are led slowly into a world of illusion, of infinite distance, where nothing is clear or certain." He gestured with his blackthorn stick to the aisles and side chapels beyond the massive pillars.

"But we proceed—like trusting pilgrims—toward the light." Cronin led them down the nave at something very close to a run. They arrived breathless before the magnificent marble and bronze *baldacchino,* or canopy, over the high altar. Cronin ignored it and pointed up into the immense dome. *"Tu es Petrus et super hanc petram aedificabo ecclesiam meam et tibi dabo claves regni caelorum.* Thou art Peter and upon this rock I will build my church and I will give thee the keys of the kingdom of heaven," translated Bishop Cronin. "That is what we see, when we first look up into the light. I always enjoy reading it, because it isn't even an accurate quotation. As usual, the Curia left out the most important thing. Upon this rock I will build my church and the gates of hell will not prevail against it—that's the one thing all Christians believe."

Turning, he poked a finger at Goggin and said, "We have here the noted young scriptural scholar, the Reverend Andrew S. Goggin, S.J. When, Father Goggin, did that quotation begin to play a major role in the Church?"

"Not until the fourth century, and even then the popes had rough going. Everyone east of Athens gave them the horse laugh when they claimed it proved that they were Number One. It took them about another five hundred years to build up a following, and even then they probably never would have done it, if it weren't for the forged decretals of pseudo-Isidore."

"The forged what of what?" Dennis asked.

"The forged decretals of pseudo-Isidore, you Americanist heretic," Goggin replied in his severest scholarly tone. "In the ninth century some bright fellows here in Rome turned up a treasure trove of documents that *obviously* proved that the Bishop of Rome had been universally acknowledged as the teaching authority of the Church, from the first century. Popes immediately began using them to beat down opposition everywhere. Only trouble was, we now know a hundred fifteen of them are total forgeries and another hundred twenty-five are semiforgeries."

By now Dennis had his brain in gear and began remembering some of the church history he had studied as a Jesuit. "This isn't exactly news," he said. "Weren't they discovered by the German Protestants around 1588?"

"Yea, verily," said Goggin, "but in the 1918 revision of the code of canon law, of three hundred and twenty-four passages quoted from the popes of the first four centuries, three hundred and thirteen of them are from the forgeries. However, this is minor compared to the way these fakes made history when they got incorporated into the *Summa Theologica* of old Tom Aquinas. That's where they created the philosophic background that in turn created Vatican I's declaration of papal infallibility."

Now even Cronin was listening closely. "By the eternal fires," he said, "this beanpole has some useful things in its topmost knob. We must have a conference or two before we leave. But now—on with our tour! This is only the first stop."

He gestured to the baldacchino with the incredible web of children's faces woven into the bronze pillars. "Magnificent as this altar and canopy is above St. Peter's tomb, the eye, if you will go back down the nave a few dozen feet, is not drawn to it but to that." He pointed between the baldacchino's twisted columns into the western apse. "There is where Bernini, the Jesuit's favorite architect, wanted your eye to go, to the Cattedra Pietri, or, as ordinary folk call it, Peter's Chair. This was a nice piece of solid oak in which the apostle sat while taking his ease in the house of Pudens, a good Christian who gave him free room and board when he first visited Rome. At least, that's the story they tell. There's not a word in writing about this holy chair until the year 1217. At any rate, it was a simple enough thing. It had four good legs of yellow oak, and the back and crest were of acacia wood. 'Twas a perfectly ordinary chair, which even Constantine did not see fit to meddle with. It sat in the baptistry of the old cathedral. See what the Jesuits' boy did with it."

They strolled around the baldacchino and over to the cattedra to gaze up at its baroque splendor. High above the altar the Chair of Peter was encased in black and gilt bronze. At its feet were four huge statues. These, Cronin explained, were the great doctors of the Church. On the right, wearing a bishop's miter, was St. Augustine, and on the left, similarly attired, St. Ambrose. Behind them, without miters, overshadowed by them and by the chair itself, stood two fathers of the Eastern Church, Saints Athanasius and John Chrysostom. "You will notice," said Cronin, "that the Greeks are not given miters. The implication is, whatever they say has no authority. But here, my children, here you see what the popes aimed at all along by heaping up so much marble and brass and glass. Not to glorify St. Peter, a poor sod with scarcely brains enough to catch a fish. But this, a throne. A simple chair, sat upon by a fisherman, has become, thanks to the genius of the greatest artist of his day, a veritable explosion of spiritual arrogance."

By now Jim McAvoy was frowning severely. "We never heard a word about any of this when we toured Saint Peter's with the Cardinal."

"Of course not," said Bishop Cronin, "he's much too kind-hearted to tell the whole truth about this place."

"Are you trying to tell us that the whole idea of a pope, the successor to St. Peter, is a mistake? A lie?"

"Let's call it an exaggeration," said Bishop Cronin. "An exaggeration that became first a distortion and then a disaster."

"I think it's very exciting," said Madeline McAvoy. "I don't completely understand it. But it's exciting. Where did you learn all this, Bishop? Is there a book you could recommend?"

"He's going to write it," said Bishop Cronin, pointing to Dennis. "Now let's take a quick look at the only piece of sculpture worth discussing in this godforsaken place."

He led them back around the baldacchino to confront a black marble statue of St. Peter. The simply robed saint sat in a humble chair staring straight ahead, the keys in his left hand and his right hand raised in a blessing.

"This is one of the few things left over from old Constantine's basilica. It's really a statue of an ancient philosopher. The Pope's boys put another head on it and stuck those keys in his hand. No matter, this at least is a man. If you want to get a good laugh, you should come in here when they put a papal cloak of silk and gold around the poor cod and slap a triple tiara on his head. You've never seen anything more ridiculous in your life."

"Do you think it's worth kissing his toe?" Madeline McAvoy asked. "You're supposed to get an indulgence for it, aren't you?"

"I could use one," Jim McAvoy said defiantly. He had obviously made up his mind that Bishop Cronin was not going to convert him. He marched forward and kissed the worn right foot.

"You'll never catch me performing that unsanitary act," said Cronin. "It was all started by him in the 1860s." He pointed to a mosaic of a pope on the pillar above St. Peter's head. "That's old Pio Nono. He had his picture put up there, to announce that he was the first Pope who reigned longer than St. Peter's twenty-five years. We'd all be better off if he'd only lasted twenty-five days."

"Why do you say that, Bishop?" asked Madeline McAvoy.

"Because, my dear lady, I thought it was time they elected an Irishman."

Madeline McAvoy smiled. "Do you think they'll ever do that?"

"If they do, my dear girl, say your prayers because the next thing you hear will be Gabriel's trumpet."

Bishop Cronin about-faced and led them down the nave toward the doors. Without warning he stopped at the Chapel of the Presentation where, he told them, there was the only monument he had come to see. At first Dennis thought he meant the body of Pope Pius X, which was exhibited beneath the altar, the death-withered hands and face covered by silver shields. "Pay no attention to old Pio Cento there, he was a time server without an idea in his head but daily Communion. I mean up here, man."

Dennis followed Cronin's finger and discovered a large bronze relief of Pope John XXIII on the chapel wall. While a squadron of angels descended from above, the Pope in his tiara and robes blessed a humanity that struggled to reach him from behind bars. To Dennis's amazement, Bishop Cronin knelt down in front of it and bowed his head in prayer.

Glancing over his shoulder at them, he said, "Come now, all of you. Say a prayer with me here." They knelt down beside him, the McAvoys on the right, Dennis and Goggin on the left. Dennis made no effort to pray. He was a spectator here, nothing but a spectator.

"It's good, very good and very fitting," Cronin said. "He visited the jail here in Rome, you know, his first year as Pope. Right into the maximum security section he went, surrounded by killers and rapists. A murderer fell on his knees before him and asked him if there was any hope of forgiveness for him. The old boy simply lifted him up and held him in his arms."

Cronin was silent for a moment, then looking from left to right, he said, "Well, here I am, surrounded by the Church militant and the Church reluctant. Holy Giovanni," he said, looking up at the memorial, "help us to know the difference and care about it."

Suddenly, Dennis felt frighteningly tired. Last night's sleep had not been much more restful than the night on the plane. He suddenly remembered Mike Furia complaining that the jet lag always ruined his sleep for a week. With the wave of exhaustion came an almost unbearable tightness in his chest. He tried to take a deep breath, and it came out in a long ratchety gasp. Was there a chill in these shadowy chapels? What else would bring on an asthma attack now? The doctor who had treated his last attack carefully explained to him the psychological connections, noting how often his attacks coincided with a visit to or from his mother. But why should he sense smother love in the terrible things old Davey was saying about this gigantic parade of marble and bronze and gold?

The doctor had also warned him not to get overtired, Dennis numbly recalled as Cronin led them out of the church at the same brisk trot and paused before two great bronze doors to the right of the ones through which they had entered. "These," said Father Cronin, "are the doors of death. The artist who did them, a fellow named Manzu, came near to cutting his throat over them. Between the time they were commissioned and when he got to work on them, he totally lost his faith. A mutual friend brought him to John, and something flowed out of the old man that stirred the atheist's soul. He rushed home and locked himself in his studio for days and nights on end, and this was the result, a protest against death in all its shapes and forms. See here, we have the death of Abel, then the death of St. Joseph. Then this poor fellow, hanging upside down like a slab of meat. Death by violence. Every Italian knows what this suggests in the bargain. It's how they finished off old Mussolini.

"Next we have the death of St. Stephen. Can't you all but feel that mighty rock smashing his skull? Next the death of Pope Gregory VII, who finished his days as a starving beggar on the side of the road. Here we have death on earth, a mother dying while her child weeps. Finally, death in space. That's the worst of them, in my opinion. Have you ever seen anything more terrifying than that fellow's silent scream as he chokes for breath?"

Dennis stared at the falling man, the outstretched hands, the terrified sucking mouth, and heard Goggin say, "Every one of them is universal at the same time. Pope Gregory could be Thomas Becket, about to be murdered by Henry II's knights, or Dietrich Bonhoeffer dying in that Nazi concentration camp."

"The Curia Cardinal who was supposed to approve the whole thing wanted Manzu to put a rosary in the hand of the woman dying on earth. And an airplane behind the fellow dying in space," Cronin said.

"Notice how Cain is dressed in modern pants and shirt, and Abel is naked," Goggin said. "The rape of the third world. Or an industrialist beating up a worker."

Dennis heard all this, but his eyes remained riveted on the man dying in space. The void. He found it more and more difficult to breathe. He turned and walked away from them toward the steps leading to the square. He found himself staring down at the shield of John XXIII in the portico pavement. It was rectangular, crowned at the top by a papal tiara. Running from it, to appear again at the bottom of the rectangle, was a priest's stole. Peeping out at the four corners of the rectangle were parts of two enormous keys. But the most charming thing about it was the lion at the top, the friendliest lion he had ever seen.

Suddenly, the lion seemed to grow enormously large. Dennis realized he was falling and threw out his hands to protect his face. The last thing he saw was the lion's childish green eyes.

Several hours later he awoke in his hotel room. The light was fading from the window. Bishop Cronin, minus his tam-o'-shanter and his blackthorn stick, was sitting beside the bed, looking worried. Matthew Mahan was standing behind him, looking even more concerned. "How are you feeling, lad?" Cronin asked.

"Not very good," Dennis croaked. "I'm afraid I've ruined your first day in Rome."

"The devil with the day."

"I'm having an asthma attack."

"We know that. We've had Bill Reed in to look at you. Every ten minutes we've been clapping this oxygen mask here on your face."

Cronin held up a plastic mask connected by a hose that ran down beside the bed to an oxygen tank.

"I haven't had one in two years," Dennis gasped. "An awful time to pick—"

"Stop talking," Matthew Mahan said. "It's my fault, not yours. I've just been examining my conscience with the help of this heretic, and realized I've been working you like a galley slave."

Dennis smiled forlornly. "I was doing all right until last week. Three A.M. every night."

"Why didn't you tell me?"

"Now, Matt. Who can tell you anything?" asked Bishop Cronin.

"Why don't *you* go down and get something to eat," the Cardinal said. "I'll take over here."

With a wink at Dennis, Cronin departed. Matthew Mahan took his seat beside the bed. "How did things go on your tour?" Dennis asked.

"Good enough. The laborer was worthy of his hire. Now they can say they've seen Rome with the world's most expensive guide."

"They'll find that out next year when—" Dennis began, but he ran out of air before he could finish the sentence.

"Clap that on your mug," said Matthew Mahan, handing him the mask. "I've got some pills over here you're supposed to take. Bill Reed thought there might be an allergic factor. They're antihistamines."

Dennis nodded. "The same one's I used to take back home. If they work, I may be all right by tomorrow morning."

He gulped down the pills with a glass of water and lay back on the pillows again. "I'm really sorry—" he started to say.

"Do I have to start acting like the Pope and order you to shut up?"

Dennis smiled feebly. He was in no shape to disagree.

"I was supposed to go over to the Vatican this afternoon to see Cardinal Antoniutti or one of his boys about our nuns," Matthew Mahan said. "In fact, before I left this morning, his office called to see if I could have lunch with him. It shows what the prospect of some red silk on your head can do for you in this town. But while I was saying mass this morning, I decided not to go."

Dennis managed to look surprised without saying anything.

"If we can't solve that problem on our own, I don't deserve a red hat—or a bishop's crosier, for that matter. The whole thing boils down to me doing a better job of explaining myself to those ladies. I haven't tried to do it, really. Instead I played the authority game to the hilt, I'm afraid. I've got to show them that I want the same things that they want for those poor people downtown. If I can't do it, if I haven't done it, it's my fault."

Dennis was glad that he was forbidden to say anything. What could he do but agree—and that might start an episcopal explosion.

Dennis noted the Cardinal's hand moving back and forth across his stomach. "I'd better take some of my own medicine," he said. "They're giving a reception for us over at the embassy tonight. The four other American Cardinals arrived today. They all headed for the North American College. They're all graduates, except Cooke, and he would have gone, except for the war." He shook his head and smiled wryly. "One of the many clubs I don't belong to, I'm afraid. During the council I got awfully tired of inside remarks about the house on Humility Street. They're a little like West Pointers when they get together. They've even got their own language. You'll probably hear some of it in the coming week. They kid each other by saying, 'Now you're a real bag.' That's what they called themselves when they got decked out in their regulation cassocks, with the sky-blue piping on them. Don't let them put you down with any of that junk. Personally I think more college in America and less in Rome would make better bishops in the long run."

Dennis suddenly found difficulty breathing again. Was it what Matthew Mahan had just said, or some unlistening physiological mechanism that was determined to strangle him for reasons of its own?

"Well," Matthew Mahan said, "I'd better stop scandalizing you. But it's the truth. It's one thing to be loyal to the Pope on a spiritual basis. Letting the Curia run the American Church is another matter. On that point I agree with old Davey. But I don't feel we have to wreck the papacy to get our freedom." He patted Dennis's arm. "Go to sleep now and I'll read my office."

Dennis fell asleep a few minutes later. His dreams were bizarre. They always were whenever he took antihistamines. Helen Reed was in almost all of them, sometimes naked, sometimes clothed. Most of the time she was laughing about him, or at him. But once she appeared with a tragic expression on her face. *O withered is the garland of the war*, she sighed over and over again. Every time she said it, he grew angry. Suddenly his anger became panic. She would always be there beyond the reach of his fingers, the touch of his lips. He was a dry stick, a man fashioned in the shape of a cross, doomed forever to stumble through the world while the faithful chipped relics from his meaningless timber. *Please*.

He awoke to find the oxygen mask over his nose and mouth and Matthew Mahan's face so close to his face that it was a visual collision. The Cardinal's steady blue eyes seemed to penetrate his own to the very depths of his soul. Did he know? More panic.

"It's all right, Dennis, it's all right," he said gently. "You must be getting better. You haven't had any trouble for a couple of hours. Were you dreaming?"

He nodded, the oxygen still hissing coolly down his throat.

"It must have been a bad one, you looked scared."

He glanced at his watch. "There, that's two minutes." He took the mask off and hung it over the bedpost again.

"Haven't you gone to dinner yet?" Dennis asked. He was pleasantly surprised to hear his voice so clear. The pills were working.

"Oh, I've been to dinner and came back a good while ago. I put the world's oldest heretic to bed. I don't want him dropping dead on me in the middle of Rome. How could we ever explain the odor of sanctity arising from the likes of him?"

Bewildered and appalled, Dennis looked over at the other twin bed. It was empty.

"I put him in my room."

"Really—you shouldn't be losing this much sleep, either," Dennis said.

"I can afford to lose sleep a lot more than I can afford to lose a good secretary."

If emotion was the real cause of his asthma attack, Dennis thought gloomily, he should be strangling to death now. God, or whoever was in charge of his peculiar pilgrimage (the ironic angel?), certainly had a sense of humor. How does the sour young snot who is already actively involved in betraying his benefactor respond?

"Really, I feel fine," Dennis said desperately. "Why don't you try to get some sleep?"

"It's five-thirty in the morning," Matthew Mahan said. "I'm going out to say mass at six. Don't worry about it. I'll get a nap after lunch."

"What will you be doing today?"

"Oh, I'm still playing tour guide. We're going to St. Peter's this morning."

"Don't take Bishop Cronin along, unless you want to shock the true believers."

"Oh, don't worry, I've had his tour of St. Peter's. He'll be on duty with you all day. I hope he didn't shock you too much."

"It was interesting. I'm not sure what Mr. and Mrs. McAvoy thought about it all."

"Good God, I didn't realize they were with you."

"Mr. McAvoy just got a little more conservative. But Mrs. McAvoy seemed inclined toward getting radicalized. She was that way before she went on the tour. *Humanae Vitae* has really got her upset about the Church."

Matthew Mahan nodded glumly. "She and most of the intelligent women in the diocese." He sighed. "Anyway, I'm looking forward to our visit today. I was consecrated there by Pope John, at Bernini's altar, the cattedra."

"Was that before or after you heard Cronin's lecture on it?" Dennis asked.

"Before. He didn't emerge as a full-fledged radical until the council. He says that Pope John liberated the Church's unconscious—including his own."

"Why were you consecrated in St. Peter's?"

"Because I couldn't get consecrated at home. Old Archbishop Hogan was a terrible man. He made a habit of cutting to pieces anyone who started to get too much publicity or power."

"How did old Hogan take the news?"

"How do you think? On the way home I was supposed to stop over in New York with Mike Furia and a couple of other people. Mike's company has a suite in the Waldorf Towers, and we were going to see a few baseball games and a play or two. A telegram was waiting for me at the Waldorf desk. His Excellency the Archbishop ordered me to return to the diocese immediately and assume my episcopal duties."

"What were they?"

"He gave me every confirmation in the diocese for the next three years. And all the fund-raising, of course. And the seminary. Matthew Mahan looked at his watch again. "It's almost six. I'd better get over there to say mass."

"Where are you going?"

"To the Church of St. Peter in Chains. Have you ever been there? Don't miss that statue of Moses by Michelangelo in the nave. Take some time to study it. When you get a chance, tell me what you saw."

He picked up the face mask. "Need a whiff before I go?"

Dennis shook his head. "Your Eminence," he said as the big man in black strode to the door. Dennis's throat was tight, but his chest was remarkably free. "Thank you—for—for staying up with me."

Matthew Mahan turned in the doorway, his lips curving into that cocky Irish grin. "It's the least I could do. After almost killing you."

Five minutes later, Bishop Cronin was in the room, telephoning for two continental breakfasts. "By God," he said, "you're cured. It's a miracle, nothing less than a miracle."

"I hope you're kidding," Dennis said.

"What do you mean, you irreligious young cod? Here we are in Rome, where there's not a foot of ground that can't be claimed by some damn fool martyr who didn't have brains enough to keep his head down when the centurions were out hunting Christians or some Italian hysteric who floated four feet in the air at the thought—the mere thought—of perpetual chastity."

"Okay, who shall we give the credit to?"

"I'm torn between St. Patrick and Pope John, to be honest. I think we'd better give it to the latter. You fell on your kisser square across his coat of arms, a gesture of devotion which is typically Italian, to say the least. If we credit St. Patrick, we'd be in danger of summary vengeance by the maddened populace. After all, what was he? A mere leader of men, who preached into oblivion the oldest religion in Europe—I mean the Druids, lad—

214

put together the best—I mean the holiest—national church in Christendom. What's that compared to flying through the air or having the Virgin Mother appear to you, speaking pure Aramaic? No, we'll give the credit to old Pope John. For one thing he's an Italian, and they don't know what to do with him. They blame it on all the years he spent out of Italy, you know, as papal legate in Bulgaria and Turkey and France. He didn't get back to Italy until he was seventy-three or so, too late to rebrainwash him."

Breakfast arrived and Dennis decided he was hungry. He smeared a piece of fresh Italian bread with butter and marmalade and took a large swallow of coffee. "I can't get over the nursing care I've gotten," he said. "The Cardinal sitting up all night with me—"

"I knew he would. I've had two heart attacks now, each of which carried me to within a handshake of St. Peter. Then for reasons best known to the Almighty, I was sent spinning back to my hospital bed, and who do I find sitting beside it at three or four A.M., looking like an undertaker about to bury his last client but himself. How can you help but love a man like that?"

Yes, Dennis thought gloomily to himself, how, how?

XVII

After leaving Bishop Cronin with Dennis, Matthew Mahan took a quick shower and shaved. Freshened, though a little light-headed, he stepped into the hall and headed for the elevator. He was looking forward to saying mass at the Church of St. Peter in Chains. He wanted to combine what he had experienced there two nights ago with the words of the consecration. Out of this might come stronger, clearer insight.

He had not taken more than ten steps when a woman appeared in the hall about a hundred feet ahead of him. She had high delicate cheekbones, a sensual, rather arrogant mouth, and dark hair elaborately done in Empire style. A white evening dress fell from beneath her maroon cloak to the tops of her high-heeled silver sandals. She stared coolly down the hall at him for a moment, and her hand went instinctively to her hair, which was in some disarray. A mocking smile played across her lips. She turned and walked ahead of him to the elevators.

Well before he reached the door, Matthew Mahan knew that she had come from Mike Furia's room. He was shaken by a strange combination of emotions. First anger, then a kind of fear. Was there anyone he could trust, anyone who did not betray him in one way or another? A new brutal loneliness assailed him. But now there was nothing, not even the faintest touch of the sweetness he had felt with Mary Shea. It was the bitter isolation that Jesus must have felt alone in the High Priest's dungeon exposed to the whips and rods and insults of the temple police. All through his mass, Matthew Mahan struggled to accept the pain as Jesus had accepted it.

After mass, he met the somber gaze of Moses with a new, more anguished understanding of his sadness. He said a silent prayer to Pope John, asking him for guidance. Slowly he became convinced that he must do something. He could not look the other way, as he had done more than once during the war in France and Germany. Then he had told himself that men who faced death every day had to be forgiven a great deal. When he saw lines of G.I.s outside a local whorehouse, he had always turned down a side street before he got close enough to recognize anyone. Maybe Mike Furia had been in one of those lines. Maybe Father Mahan should have descended on the customers in the style of a few chaplains he had known and lectured them angrily, ordered them to disperse. But for every convert that technique made, there were a dozen enemies. Besides, all that was long ago in a different world.

Mike Furia was more than a face in the congregation, a soul he was ordained to shepherd. He was a personal friend, a man with whom he had shared his life, who had often sought his advice, his help. To be silent now would be more than cowardice; it would be betrayal of Mike's soul.

Pressing another thousand-lira note into the sacristan's hand, Matthew Mahan left the Church of St. Peter in Chains and walked down through the tunnel to the Via Cavour. The streets were beginning to fill with people. The explosion of motor scooters and motorcycles, the roar of accelerating autos, filled the air around him. He walked on past pawnshops and palazzos. At one point he found himself staring dully at the Fountain of Trevi,

216

practically deserted except for a quartet of determined young Americans who looked ready to pass out from lack of sleep or too much marijuana, yet did their best to raise their voices above the splash of the water. They were singing a kind of lament. The only words Matthew Mahan could catch were "goin' home, goin' home." It suited his mood, but he declined their invitation to join them.

By the time he reached the Hotel Hassler it was almost eight o'clock. Mournfully, with nothing to reassure him but a kind of grim determination, he knew what he was going to do. He would have to risk his friendship, his episcopal dignity—yes, even his self-esteem—without the slightest confidence of success. His stomach twinged. It was well past time for his breakfast mush, but that would have to wait. Up to the fifth floor in the elevator he went and down the hall to knock on Mike Furia's door.

"Hey," Mike said as he opened the door, "I just had breakfast delivered. Do you want to join me? I'll call for another order."

"Thanks, Mike," he answered, "I'll just drink your leftover milk."

"Okay," said Mike, returning to the dresser where his bread was already broken and his coffee steaming in his cup. Matthew Mahan took a glass from the bathroom and poured a few ounces of warm milk into it. He sipped it, while Mike munched on the roll and washed it down with coffee. The intense concentration he gave to swallowing the hot liquid made it seem a kind of primitive rite. He gasped with pain and pleasure. The massive body, the big dark face with the somewhat hooded eyes, was strangely threatening.

"What's up?" Mike said. "How's Dennis?"

"Fine, thank God. Listen, Mike, you're not going to like what I'm about to say, but I've got to say it. I couldn't face myself in the mirror or consider myself a priest if I didn't say it."

Mike Furia put down his coffee cup and stared at him, completely baffled. Two furrows appeared on his wide, tan forehead. He hunched his huge shoulders and leaned forward in his chair, so that he looked even bigger than he already was. "I'm listening," he said.

"On my way out to say mass, I almost bumped into a woman coming out of this room. She—she obviously spent the night here."

"Well, I'll be a son of a bitch." Mike jumped to his feet and strode across the room, turned and walked back half the distance. "Matt," he said, "it's none of your goddamn business."

Matthew Mahan shook his head. "Mike, it is my business. What kind of a friend would I be, what kind of a priest would I be, if I let you lose your soul in front of my eyes without saying a word?"

Mike's eyes could not have been more icy, more contemptuous.

"What possible—value—what good can a woman like that do you? Do you even know her name?"

"Of course I know her name. She's a dress designer. One of the best in Rome. She's separated like I am and she can't get married again because Holy Mother Church will put her in jail here in Italy."

"I'm sorry," Matthew Mahan said humbly. "I thought—I thought she looked a little like a call girl."

"I have them, too, when she's not available. I haven't taken a vow of celibacy like you, Matt. I thought you understood that."

"Mike, you've got a wife, a son. This sort of thing—only takes you farther away from them. Spiritually, psychologically. There is the possibility of one of these women—what would Betty, Tony, say?"

Mike Furia threw back his head and laughed. Never before had Matthew Mahan heard such a cold, bitter sound. "They'd say, 'Look, the Animal is at it again. Isn't he disgusting?'"

The Animal. Matthew Mahan remembered the conversation with Dennis McLaughlin about Betty Furia being a monster. He had sat at a dozen dinners with this simpering woman who oohed and aahed over his every word. In her home she had shown him her "grottoes"—the one to the Little Flower on the landing of the stairs, to the Blessed Virgin in her dressing room. He had beamed his approval of them all, and at her relic of the True Cross, her devotion to St. Blaise, who cured her of her sore throats, and St. Anne, who had saved her from death when she gave birth to her son, and St. Teresa of Avila, who always cured her headaches.

"You want to know the last time I had sex with my wife, Matt? That's all I ever did with her, have sex. I've never made love to her. At least, not after the kid was born. The last time was May 5, 1959, ten years ago next week. Before that, we used to go two, three months without touching each other. We were separated a long time before we made it legal."

"Mike," said Matthew Mahan, "how could we be friends for so many years, close friends, and you never told me this?"

"I hinted around it often enough, Matt. But what did we usually talk about when we were together? Business. How to get another gymnasium built, another million raised. You didn't want to hear my sad story. What the hell, you're no parish priest."

Nothing compared to the pain of those words, not the pain of the ulcer, nor the humiliations inflicted on him by old Hogan. "I was a priest first, Mike. I still am."

"Well, if you expect me to get down on my knees and beg your pardon—or God's—forget it."

"I didn't—I don't. I only came here to say I'm your friend—what can I do to help?"

For a moment Mike Furia seemed to sway in the middle of the room. At first Matthew Mahan thought the sway was inside his own head, a product of his weariness and humiliation. The big hands opened and closed and he wondered what he would do if his friend drove one of those massive fists into his face. Then Mike spun away and sat down in a chair on the other side of the room. It was a gesture that seemed to say—I want to get as far away from you as possible. "I guess it's about time we've had it out, Matt. I don't believe any of it, the whole schmeer."

"You mean the Church—being a Catholic?"

"You got it."

"And this has been going on—for a long time?"

"A hell of a long time."

"You had women even when we traveled together?"

"Sure. Every time. I need a woman every second or third night, Matt, and I usually get one."

"But how do you explain—our friendship? The help you've given me? You've raised millions of dollars for the Church."

"I raised millions of dollars for *you*. For our friendship. I believe in that—even if it's in the past tense now."

"Why?"

"Because you saved my goddamn life. What the hell, do you think that just because you talked me out of being a hit man, a boom-boom guy, I'd drop the whole code? No, Matt, you have a hand on me, as we used to say in the Family. You've got it for the rest of your life whether I like it or not."

Instinctively, Matthew Mahan felt himself withdrawing his hand, as if it really was outstretched to clutch the prize he had won that day in Germany. And all the time you thought it had been sanctifying grace, a triumph of your priesthood. Instead it was the pagan code of the Mafiosi. Swallow the humiliation, he told himself, swallow it, and remember there was still a soul here, a soul in torment.

"In a way, you blame me, don't you, Mike? You blame me for almost everything that's happened to you—the marriage, the boy."

For a moment the hard mask on Mike's face wavered. The question hit very close to the truth.

"You picked out St. Francis Xavier University for me. That made it practically inevitable for me to meet that frozen Irish bitch from our sister school, Mount St. Monica's."

"Mike," said Matthew Mahan, "there's a lot of truth in what you're saying. I took a tremendous amount of satisfaction from your career. You were one of my saved souls. The fact that you were also a personal friend and an enormous help to me as a fund-raiser—well, I just assumed that was God's way of patting me on the back, giving me a little reward for my rescue work. But now I see how much I let my self-satisfaction deceive me. It's my worst fault. A form of pride—arrogance. I'm sorry, Mike."

"Sorry for *what?*"

"For failing you—as a priest."

"You didn't fail me. I never gave you a chance to fail me."

"I never looked for the opportunity, either."

He got up and walked leadenly to the door. Mike Furia let him go without another word.

At the end of the hall, a check on Dennis McLaughlin found him, Bishop Cronin, and a young Jesuit named Goggin discussing a trip to Isolotto, a town outside Florence. Dennis looked remarkably healthy.

In his own room Matthew Mahan threw himself down on the bed and instantly fell asleep. Hours later, so it seemed, a phone rang in his ear. Jim McAvoy said hesitantly, "Your Eminence— the bus has been waiting." He leaped to his feet and saw with chagrin that it was nine-thirty. He had slept about forty-five minutes. Splashing cold water on his face, he descended and resumed his role as tour guide. They spent most of the day at St. Peter's, the Vatican Museum, and, thanks to some advance preparation he had made by mail, an exclusive visit to the Vatican gardens, where the Pope strolled when he wanted some outdoor exercise. They then made a dash to the catacombs of St. Priscilla near the Church of St. Agnes. After descending into the darkness and listening to lectures by a very amusing Irish brother at various points in the winding tunnels, they surfaced and visited the mausoleum of Costanza, the daughter of Constantine, one of the most beautiful Roman-Christian survivals in the city. The mosaics were not particularly religious. The dominant theme was the joy of wine and food. Later painters added some religious inserts. Matthew Mahan's favorite was Christ portrayed as a beardless young man standing with St. Peter and St. Paul and their lambs at the four rivers of Paradise. The calm, serene confidence on their faces aroused a wistful sensation in him. Would there ever again be a time when the faith was as simple and as heartfelt?

That night after the reception at the American embassy, Matthew Mahan gave a small dinner party for the closest members of his official family and his intimate friends in a private room at the hotel. Monsignors George Petrie, Terry Malone, Father Dennis McLaughlin, and Bishop David Cronin represented the clergy, and Mary Shea, Mike Furia, the McAvoys, and Bill Reed represented the laity. There was a great deal of kidding about Bill Reed's stubborn unaffiliation with any church. Bishop Cronin, to Terry Malone's humorless outrage, maintained that this proved Bill had more sense than anyone else at the table. To confuse matters, Bishop Cronin defended himself by quoting Pope John. "I do not fear the habits, the politics, or the religion of any man anywhere in the world as long as he lives with an awe of God." Bill Reed declared himself ready to subscribe to that article of faith. Without it, anyone who practiced medicine would soon lose his mind, he said.

Monsignors Malone and Petrie left early, as if they sensed that they were outsiders, compared to the rest of the party. This troubled Matthew Mahan a little—but not as much as Mike Furia's obviously hostile mood. Throughout dinner they had scarcely exchanged a word. Mike had persisted in talking to Dennis McLaughlin and Mary Shea, and from what Matthew Mahan could hear, it was largely a cynical diatribe against the Church in

Italy. He had been pained at one point to hear Mary nod and say: "*Il Vaticano riceve—ma non da a nessuno.*" (The Vatican gets but never gives.) It was one of the oldest clichés in Europe, and it was very upsetting to hear Mary repeating it and Dennis McLaughlin smiling in approval. Jim McAvoy with his stubborn, if not always intelligent, loyalty had been the only one within earshot to disagree with Mike, and poor Jim had promptly been buried by a barrage of negative statistics.

At a signal from Matthew Mahan, the waiter poured another round of Asti Spumante, the best Italian champagne. Bill Reed eyed him ominously as he took a swallow of it. Avoiding his glare, Matthew Mahan smiled at Mike Furia and asked: "What did I hear you saying about the Church in Italy?"

"Oho," crowed Davey Cronin. "I told him he was talking too loud."

"Listen," said Mike, trying to sound offhand, even jocular, in response to his challenge. "If this kid is any good with a pen, I'm the one he ought to talk to. Nobody gives a damn about old Pio Nono and the Vatican Council of 1870. They're interested in today's scandals—and I'm the guy that's sitting right in the middle of them."

"Much as it pains me to admit an Eyetalian can be right on anything," said Bishop Cronin, "this builder of Towers of Babel may have a point."

"Have you ever heard of the Societa Generale Immobiliare?"

Mike was not even looking at Matthew Mahan. He was talking to Mary, clearly challenging His Eminence, deliberately preaching a contrary gospel.

"I've heard it mentioned by one or two friends at the Vatican—"

"It's the biggest construction company in Italy. In fact, one of the biggest real estate and building companies in the world. It's capitalized at sixty-seven billion lire. In 1967 they spent thirty billion lire on projects in Italy alone. I've made joint bids with them on a couple of dozen jobs. The Vatican owns twenty-five per cent of the shares and about ninety-eight per cent of the control. When you go into a deal with those guys, you need the best lawyers in the world behind you."

"You mean they're crooked?"

"Oh no. They just press the contract to the outer limits.

They're working for the Pope. It's their duty to get everything they can in every deal—and a little extra."

"What sort of things do they build?"

"Well, let's see. We're just finishing up the final stages of the Watergate Apartments down in Washington, D.C. It's running about sixty-seven million. Seventy per cent of the common stock and fifty per cent of the preferred is owned by Immobiliare. Then there's Immobiliare Canada. They own the Stock Exchange Tower in Montreal. That came in for about fifty mill. Have you ever seen it? It's the tallest reinforced concrete building in the world. Immobiliare owns about eighty-five per cent of a Montreal outfit called Red-Brooke Estates. They just finished a huge thirty-three story apartment building up there. It has a big piece of Lomas Verdes, which is building a satellite town outside Mexico City and a connecting superhighway, the Superavenida."

"But Italy, that's the real story, from what you told us at dinner the other night," said Davey Cronin.

Mike Furia grinned. "We'd be here until dawn if I started listing what SGI has built since the war. In 1966 in Rome alone, they put up three apartment houses, two or three office buildings, a dozen or so luxury homes, and a couple of suburban developments. In Milan they did even better—eighteen offices, a shopping center, a seven-building apartment complex. In sixty-seven they showed a profit of six point two million. Not bad when you consider that they only paid one point five million to get operating control in 1949. Around the same time they also bought Italcimenti, which happens to be the biggest cement and construction material maker in Italy. And then there's Pantanella, just about the biggest pasta manufacturer—assets of more than fifteen million. And about twenty other companies, not all of them winners."

"What's the one that's a real loser?" Cronin asked. "The toilet bowl outfit?"

"Manifattura Ceramica Pozzi. They've lost about fourteen million in the last six years, but they'll come around. Last year the Vatican put Count Galeazzi, one of their toughest boys, on the board."

"And the banks. What about the banks?" said Cronin.

"Well, they own one bank outright, the Banco Santo Spirito. They're tied into three other big banks—Banca Commerciale

Italiana, Credito Italiana, and Banco di Roma. Those four account for about twenty per cent of all the bank deposits in Italy and they handle about fifty per cent of all the foreign trade transactions. Only last year Italcimenti bought eight new banks through a financial holding company, Italmobiliare. Then there's at least a couple of thousand small banks all over Italy that either the Vatican or the local parish or church owns outright."

"And they all charge interest, do they not?" asked Bishop Cronin.

"Sure."

"Which ignores the clear teaching of St. Ambrose, St. Jerome, St. Augustine, a half-dozen Greek fathers, the Second Council of the Lateran, and numerous other councils, all of which specifically condemned charging interest on money—usury, they called it— as a serious sin. A half-dozen popes speaking ex cathedra made the same pronouncement, citing scripture from both the Old and New Testaments. But when it became clear that all Europe was ignoring them, their successors forgot about it to the point of getting into the business themselves. These are the same heroes— I mean Pius XI and XII—who refused to allow the Catholic couple with eleven children to touch a contraceptive, even though there's not a single line of scripture to support them, and only two vague pronouncements by previous popes before 1930."

All eyes in the room had turned to Matthew Mahan. For a moment he felt only outrage. Why did they expect him to answer every charge that anyone—even an obviously crazy old Irishman— made against the Church? But then he saw something else on Mary Shea's face. Not the desire for an answer but the assumption that no real answer was possible.

He sighed and sipped his champagne. "Before we all form up and march out of here to burn down St. Peter's," he said, "remember that the Church is more than an investment company—and a lot more than an enemy of contraception. No matter how wrong or right she is on any of these things, each day she brings into the world enormous amounts of God's grace."

"But if the vessel in which the grace comes is polluted, the grace itself may be of no avail," Bishop Cronin said.

"I don't believe that," Matthew Mahan said. "I don't think you do, either."

"What else explains the gigantic failure of this grace in the world around us?"

The anguish on Cronin's contorted face, in his trembling voice, was unavoidable. The conversation was off the rails.

"Let's not judge by appearances. Let's not be stampeded by panic," Matthew Mahan said. "That's—that's almost a loss of faith you're describing, Davey."

"Call it what you will," said the old man, slumping back in his chair. "Call it what you will."

"Is it you or Asti Spumante talking? No matter how much we disagree—I can't believe we'd ever part company on this point."

"No, no, of course not, Matt."

His automatic answer was more painful than defiance. Wasn't he saying, *You're not worth the time it takes to argue with you, Your Eminence?*

"Dennis, why don't you go upstairs with Bishop Cronin? We'll take his word for the Asti Spumante, but I do think he's overtired."

"I am not in the least overtired. But I do think it's time for me to shut up and go to bed."

He got up and strode out of the room. Bill Reed glanced at his watch and announced that he was joining him.

"Well, I'm a bottle finisher myself," said Mike Furia, holding up his glass for the waiter to fill.

"Likewise," said Mary with defiant gaiety. Dennis McLaughlin said nothing, but he also raised his glass. Matthew Mahan waved the waiter aside and wondered if he should try to explain what had just happened between him and Davey Cronin. He tried, but from the expressions on the faces of his listeners, he was not very successful. "It's a little like a father who can't realize his son has grown up. I just can't take his opinions and spout them anymore. I've got to think for myself. It's part of my responsibility—"

"From what I've heard," Jim McAvoy said angrily, "he's practically a Protestant."

"Not really, Jim. Underneath that scathing language there's a tremendous faith, a tremendous love for the Church."

"I sense it," Madeline McAvoy said softly. "I sense it very much."

Matthew Mahan felt a surge of concern and affection for the McAvoys. These were the kind of people he was trying to save from the rising waters of chaos. The reasonably intelligent, the reasonably loyal. He turned to Mike Furia with new determination. "That stuff about the Church in business, Mike. There are two ways of looking at it. It costs about twenty million dollars a year to run the Vatican. That means you've got to generate a lot of income from somewhere. You can't just depend on contributions."

"Maybe it wouldn't cost twenty million, Matt," Mary said, "if they didn't have apostolic delegates all over the world and the Curia with its perpetually growing bureaucracy."

"Or the Vatican radio," Mike Furia said. "What the hell do they need a radio station for?"

"John told me the Vatican Council was costing thirty million dollars. *Osservatore Romano*, the Vatican paper, loses two million a year."

"Why do they need a newspaper? The Italian Government doesn't publish a newspaper. No free world government does," Mary said.

It was incredible, the defiance in her voice, in her eyes. Mary, of all people. Was he losing her as he had already lost Mike? Through no fault of his own, but because of what they had seen and heard and felt about the Church here in the land of her leaders. What did it mean for him, for them all?

For another twenty minutes he tried to explain the origin of the Vatican's involvement with the business world. It had begun only in 1929, when Mussolini and Pius XI had signed the Lateran Treaty, ending the Church's sixty-year argument with the Italian Government over the loss of the papal states. Mussolini had paid an indemnity of some ninety million dollars, and with this money the Pope had set up a special department, administered by a shrewd financier, Bernardo Nogara. It was Nogara and his successors who had multiplied this capital into a worldwide network of investments and business enterprises. Under Pius XII the involvement of the Pacellis had led to scandalous nepotism. But now Paul was doing his best to retreat from this way of doing things. The Pacellis had largely been eased out. So had most of the other laymen.

His audience was clearly unimpressed. Not even the McAvoys responded to this historical approach. Matthew Mahan had to admit to himself that it was pretty uninspiring. The party broke up with lackluster good nights. It was an off-key ending to what should have been a very happy evening. Mary Shea sensed his emotion and with her good night said softly: "Don't let it upset you so much, Matt. You can't change the facts."

Alone in his room, Matthew Mahan gulped a half-dozen Ti-trilac tablets to defend his stomach against the Asti Spumanti and decided Mary had given him good advice. He tried to turn his mind to tomorrow, Sunday. He had reserved it, thank God, as a day to relax, think, pray. He needed time to ponder the spiritual significance of this major event in his life as a priest. He thought of tomorrow as a mini-retreat that would, he hoped, recall memories of the five-day retreat he made before his consecration as bishop. Pope John had sent his own personal confessor, Bishop Alfred Cavagna, to see him each day to give him subjects for meditation.

The fragile old man had led him through the labyrinthine passageways of the human soul, with his eyes fixed on the Beatitudes and the Sermon on the Mount. Matthew Mahan had asked for and received profound advice in dealing with his chief failing, the sin of pride. With beautiful simplicity the old priest had spoken to him of the necessity of letting go of every wish, every personal desire, of the importance of handing them over to God, so that whenever one was fulfilled, the victory belonged to God, and if it was unfulfilled, it was God's will, as well as an opportunity to be embraced, a chance to learn through suffering God's true intentions.

How hard it was to keep this wisdom in mind while sitting on an archdiocesan powder keg. Matthew Mahan took out the wrinkled list of maxims Pope John had given him. He had compiled them when he was a seminarist. It was ominously symbolic, the way they had drifted to the back of his dresser drawer, he thought, fingering the faded paper ruefully.

The emphasis, the recurring word throughout the list, was love.

I will love thee as I am loved by thee.
Love is the fulfilling of the law.
The aim of our charge is love.
A sweet word multiplyith friends and appeaseth enemies.

Some of them made discouraging reading for Matthew Mahan. Number 34, for instance. *"The best remedy I know against sudden fits of impatience is a silence that is gentle and without malice. However little one says, pride always comes into it, and one says things that plunge the heart into grief for a whole day after."*

Or 47. *"The things that thou hast not gathered in thy youth, how shalt thou find them in thy old age?"*

Fortunately, to console him Matthew Mahan also now had Pope John's book, *The Journal of a Soul.* This, too, had come to Rome with the Cardinal-designate. In it there were more than a few sentences underlined. He turned now to one that lifted his spirits a little, the entry for January 24, 1904. *"My pride in particular has given me a great deal of trouble because of my unsatisfactory examination results. This, I must admit, was a real humiliation; I have yet to learn my ABC in the practice of true humility and scorn of self. I feel a restless longing for I know not what— it is as if I were trying to fill a bottomless bag."* The extraordinary resemblance to his own feelings as a seminarist and young priest had inspired Matthew Mahan to jot an exclamation point in the margin of the book.

He had paid even closer attention to notes Pope John had made at the Villa Carpegna, March 13–17, 1925, when he was preparing for his consecration as a bishop. The first words of John's meditation troubled Matthew Mahan when he read them. "I have not sought or desired this new ministry." He had desired his elevation, desired it intensely because he saw the appalling things that Archbishop Hogan was doing to the Church in the diocese, the almost desperate need for a new approach. But he had given up all hope of achieving it by the time it came to him in such extraordinary fashion. So he could join heartily in the next words: *"The Lord has chosen me, making it so clear that it is His will . . . so it will be for Him to cover up my failings and supply my insufficiencies. This comforts me and gives me tranquillity and confidence.*

From the window of his hotel, Matthew Mahan could see the illuminated dome of St. Peter's. Suddenly, with the words of the book on his lap before him, he remembered sitting in the papal library, the day before his consecration, and listening as the bulky old man recited with amazing power of memory his favorite passage from the *Pontificale Romanum,* the ritual for the consecra-

228

tion of bishops. "*Let him be tireless in well doing, fervent in spirit; let him hate pride; let him love humility and truth and never forsake them under the influence of flattery or fear. Let him not consider light to be darkness or darkness light: let him not call evil good or good evil. Let him learn from wise men and from fools, so that he may profit from all.*" With a flash of humor in his brown eyes, John had added, "That last sentence is perhaps the most important, when it comes to running a diocese."

Now, Matthew Mahan's eyes moved down the passages from the *Pontificale* that John had noted in his retreat at the Villa Carpegna in 1925. Two immediately caused him pain.

"*Always to be engaged in the work of God and free from worldly affairs and the love of filthy lucre.*"

"*To cherish humility and patience in myself and teach those virtues to others.*"

How often he had failed to live up to the highest levels of these ideals. Where, how, had he lost touch with them? Perhaps the truth was in another sentence he had underlined, from Pope John's meditations during his first retreat as Patriarch of Venice. "*I could never have imagined or desired such greatness. I am happy also because this meekness and humility do not go against the grain with me but come easily to my nature.*" Yes, Matthew Mahan thought moodily, there was a fundamental point; meekness and humility did not come easily to his nature. Not by accident was his nickname in high school "the Mouth." On the playing field, in debates, in classroom discussions, he was always yakking away, monopolizing the limelight, and loving it. Was it a reaction against his father's unnatural silence? Or an imitation of his mother's constant loquacity?

The rapidity and intensity with which his mother could talk was a standing joke among her family and friends. Nobody could get the floor from Teresa Scaparelli Mahan once she started talking. Again he felt the curious experience of separation from his mother here in the city of her birth. The movement toward a new self. The progress had been slow and painful over the past ten years, but it was time, and past time, to complete the passage.

It was also time to let go once and for all those dreams of glory that had raced so tumultuously through his brain for the first year or two after his consecration as bishop. He had seen himself succeeding Cardinal Spellman as the kingmaker of the American Catholic Church. But reality had soon shriveled this wild expectation. John was too absorbed in his council to give much thought to episcopal appointments, so he let the Curia make the suggestions, and in America the Spellmanites, Romans all, continued to run the show. At the council, mingling with his fellow American bishops, listening to their North American College reminiscences, he had realized how isolated he was and had gravitated into the company of Europeans, particularly the Germans and Dutch with their call for an international Church less controlled by the Curia, reaching out to men of all faiths.

John's death a year later had turned his pipe dreams into the petty ashes that they had always been destined—and deserved—to become. Reality had been the order of the day for the past six years. Not so much as a deliberately conceived policy but as a way of life with no visible alternative. Five months after cancer killed John XXIII, John Kennedy had died and America had reeled off course like a rudderless ship in a midnight storm. Looking back, it was hard to say whether the Church had merely succumbed to the madness or had contributed to it. Perhaps that unanswered question was another reason why he had lost touch with the memory of John XXIII. Had he, like many other bishops he met at the national conferences, begun to make a deprecation out of the phrase "Good Pope John"? In his case, he did not say it aloud but perhaps he had been saying it in his inner mind, which could be more destructive spiritually.

Yes, Matthew Mahan thought with a sigh, it would do him a great deal of good if he spent most of the following day reading *The Journal of a Soul* and meditating on those maxims.

The telephone rang. "Your Eminence, a cablegram. . . ." said the desk clerk. Five minutes later it was handed to him by a bellboy. He opened it and read the brief message, then slowly folded it again and slipped it into his wallet. He sat down at the desk and wistfully fingered the pages of *The Journal of a Soul*. He would not be reading it tomorrow after all. The cable gave him one of those rare opportunities a bishop has to reach out as a priest to a fellow priest. He could not pass it up for his own spiritual gratification. John would understand. *Santo Padre*, he prayed, *forgive me for my neglect. Stand beside me now and in the years to come.*

XVIII

At ten-fifteen the following morning, Dennis McLaughlin and Matthew Mahan rolled out of Rome in a rented Mercedes with a handsome talkative young Italian named Tullio as their chauffeur. Dennis looked puzzled but vaguely pleased. He seemed to think Matthew Mahan was still worried about his health and was taking him for a little trip into the country for a quick rest cure. They headed south along the Via Appia Nuova, past numerous ancient ruins, and glimpses of new white high-rise apartments, and in their shadows tin shacks built by the poor from discarded construction materials. Tullio assured them that he would have no difficulty finding the town of Nettuno. He often drove down there during the summer. It was one of his (and Rome's) favorite bathing beaches. But too crowded in recent years. He preferred the sand at Anzio, softer, no rocks. But that, too, was crowded. The smart swimmers were now going to Sperlonga or San Felice Circeo. While Tullio talked, he drove at a pace that (Dennis remarked) made Eddie Johnson look like a National Safety Award winner.

In a half hour the white buildings of the town of Nettuno were visible ahead of them on the lush flat coastal plain. Matthew Mahan peered out the window until he spotted a sign that read: *Sicily Rome American Cemetery*. "That's what we want," he told Tullio. In another five minutes they were there.

The cemetery rose in a gentle slope from a broad pool. In the center of the pool was an island with a somber cenotaph on it, flanked by rows of Italian cypress trees. From the parking lot they walked down a wide grassy mall toward a white-pillared memorial at the end. The thousands of white crosses were in precise rows on each side of the mall beneath rows of Roman pines. It was a brilliantly sunny day, and the whiteness of the crosses was redoubled beneath the dark, brooding trees. On one side of the memorial was a chapel. On its walls were the names of 3,094 missing in action whose bodies were never found. On the other side was a museum room with wall maps describing the operations of the American forces in Italy.

A pudgy gray-haired man smoking a cigarette emerged from

an office off the museum and introduced himself as George Carmody, the superintendent of the cemetery. He wore the doleful expression of an undertaker. "Would you like to look at the grave now, Your Eminence? I'll be glad to lead the way."

"No," Matthew Mahan said, "we'll find our way by ourselves, if you don't mind. Just give us the directions."

Carmody gave them a map on which he had drawn an arrowed path in red. Halfway down the mall, they turned right and strolled down a shadowed lane between two rows of Roman pines. Dennis McLaughlin looked bored. He now obviously thought that this was just another episcopal aberration born of World War II combat neurosis. They stopped and Matthew Mahan counted the rows of crosses they had passed thus far: ten. Eleven, twelve, thirteen. At the head of the thirteenth row stood a cross with the name carefully lettered on the horizontal arm:

Richard McLaughlin
Lieutenant, USAAF

Dennis McLaughlin stared at the knee-high marble cross, his face frozen in astonishment. "He's here," he whispered. "Here?" He turned to look at Matthew Mahan as he said the last word.

Matthew Mahan nodded. "I wrote to the American Battle Monuments Commission in Washington, D.C. I still hadn't heard from them when we left home, and I sent them a very stiff telegram. Their cable arrived last night."

Dennis returned his eyes to the marble cross, his head nodding automatically. He heard what Matthew Mahan was saying, but the words meant nothing. He was in the void now, falling like that figure on the Manzu doors of St. Peter's, dying in space. "I never knew him," he heard himself saying. "I never knew him. I was three years old when he—went in the Army."

"Yes, you told me," Matthew Mahan said. "But I thought—you should know this much about him. At least know where he died. He was copilot on a B-26. The plane was hit by German antiaircraft fire only a couple of miles from here. He was badly wounded and the pilot was killed. He held the plane on course long enough for the rest of the crew to get out. He got the Distinguished Flying Cross for it."

"I never knew anything—about him. My mother hated him for dying."

232

Tears were strangling his throat. The airlessness of St. Peter's was nothing compared to this agony. Suddenly there was a big hand on his arm wrenching him up like a drowning victim toward sunlight, air. "It's all right, it's all right, Dennis," said Cardinal Mahan in a voice he had never heard before. "Don't be afraid to cry. Everyone should cry for their dead. I cried almost every day during the war. So did a lot of other men, even tough mugs like Mike Furia."

He opened his arms, yes, Dennis McLaughlin, the sardonic smiler, who perpetually confronted the world with arms crossed on his chest like a shield, opened them and flung them around the solid bulky blackness that confronted him. He was weeping, yet he was breathing, miraculously breathing. "I never knew him," he said for the fifth or sixth time. "I never knew him. She didn't want me to know him."

"She couldn't help herself, Dennis. Some people can only give their love once, and when it's refused or lost by the person they give it to, they can't forgive them."

"Sometimes—I try to be him. But you can't be—something you don't know. Every time you reach out, all you get is emptiness."

"Now you know where he is, Dennis. Here with his friends." Softly, gently, the big hand patted him on the back. He was being held, yes, caressed, like a child, yet miraculously he felt no resentment. "The older I get, the less I grieve for those who died in battle. I think there's a poet who said they remain forever young. It's true, especially if you've known them, loved them before they died. You loved him, Dennis, even if you didn't know him. Someday in Heaven you'll know him—and love him even more."

But how do we know he's in Heaven? How do we know he didn't die in mortal sin? What if you go to Heaven and find out he's in Hell, what would you say to God? Out of my way I'm going to Hell with my father. The favorite fantasy of fifteen-year-old Dennis McLaughlin, president of the Sodality, winner of general excellence medals galore. Through his tears he tried to tell something of this to Matthew Mahan, interlacing it with sardonic laughter. Was he collapsing into hysteria?

"I'm sure he's in Heaven, Dennis. This is a dangerous thing for a bishop to say, but I believe that every man who dies in battle fighting for a good cause goes there, just like the Mohammedans say he does. Courage is a better absolution than any priest can give."

Ten minutes ago, Dennis McLaughlin would have laughed this idea into oblivion. Now he accepted it in silence broken only by his sobs.

"I'd like to say a prayer for him, Dennis."

The Cardinal knelt before the cross. Dennis knelt beside him. He could find no words in his numbed brain. He stared down the long rows of crosses, trying to comprehend the immensity of death's grasp. *I had not thought death had undone so many.* "I can't pray, I can't pray at all," Dennis whispered.

"Would you let me pray for both of us, Dennis?"

He nodded.

Matthew Mahan was swept back to a dozen, no, a hundred days in France and Germany when he knelt before the bodies of men he had joked with or blessed only hours before. Here the sunlight, the soft green grass and the white crosses were different, creating a serenity that was never there in the blasted landscape of war. He was grateful for it, because it helped him to struggle against the memory of the anguish, the helplessness that he had felt in those days, yes, even the terrible doubts about the worth of his priesthood, of all priesthoods. Slowly, he let his mind empty, as he had done in those awful days. Anguish made all formal prayers —except the prayers of mass—meaningless. The words would come, as they had always come, even on the worst days.

"O God," he said, after almost a full minute of silent waiting, "we kneel here in search of comradeship. Two lonely men, dedicated to your service, in search of comradeship with this brave man, Richard McLaughlin, and his friends. Help us to see them as they were before they died, Lord, young and full of laughter. Help us to remember their courage. We know it wasn't a constant thing, Lord. They weren't heroes twenty-four hours a day. Sometimes they were afraid, and cried out to you. You came to them, especially to those who died trying to help their friends. Greater love than this, no man has, Lord. No one knows this better than you."

For another minute there were no words. But Matthew Mahan knew the prayer was not over. So, apparently, did Dennis McLaughlin. He did not raise his head. "O Lord, we believe that no sacrifice is in vain, that its graces are stored in Heaven to be used for the works of love. Pour into our hearts, O Lord, especially into the heart of Richard's son, Dennis, the grace he needs, as we all need it, to love himself, his fellowmen, his priesthood. Thank you, O Lord, for giving us this day. Your ways are a mystery to us but we shall always believe in your justice and your love."

Silence again for another full minute. The prayer was over. Dennis raised his head and smiled wanly. "Thank you," he said. "Thank you."

Together they walked back to the memorial building where Superintendent George Carmody was waiting for them. He gave them a package containing a colored aerial photograph of the cemetery and a black and white photograph of the cross with Richard McLaughlin's name on it. "We don't get many of these kind of requests anymore," he said. "Most of the people who wanted them wrote to the commission and got them a long time ago."

"I'm sure Father McLaughlin's mother has one," Matthew Mahan said, "but I thought it would be nice if he had a set, too."

Mr. Carmody nodded and they chatted for a few moments. He told them there were very few air force men buried here. "Most of those poor fellows got it down at Anzio, the beachhead. What a foul-up that operation was. The generals who thought that one up should have been shot."

Mr. Carmody got quite emotional. He pointed to a map on the wall and described how the Germans ringed the Anzio beachhead with artillery and pulverized everything that came ashore. "Eighty-eights they had, the best gun of them all," he said. "We never had anything to match it. They could double as antiaircraft." He lectured them for five minutes on the virtues of the 88-millimeter gun. Dennis McLaughlin listened, slowly letting this dumpy, earnest man return him to the real world with its stupidity, its idiotic fascination with violence.

Still, something had happened to him out there kneeling before that cross. He did not understand it. He did not understand why that intense emotion did not crush his chest and send his breath whistling up his throat. What a strange paradox, emotions of equal intensity seemed either to kill him or—what? What do you feel, Dennis? He tried to let the words come into his mind, unhindered by preconceived ideas . . . more free, more real.

Back in the car Matthew Mahan told Tullio to drive them to a good beach. "We'll eat our lunch down there and take a walk."

235

Dennis nodded agreeably. As they rolled toward the shore, he looked out at typical resort scenery. Villas and hotels and restaurants (most of them closed until late May, Tullio told them) filled the landscape. It was hard to believe that thousands of men had died along these roads and in the miles of farmland through which they had just traveled. Dennis began asking Matthew Mahan about his experience as a chaplain. "I never realized you were such a hero," he said half jokingly.

"Don't listen to those stories. They get better every time someone tells them. The fact is, Dennis, if you really don't care about dying, almost anybody can be a hero."

For the first time, Matthew Mahan talked frankly about his chaplain's experiences, especially what they meant to him as a priest. For over twenty-five years, he had never talked about them to anyone. He did not think it was very edifying for a layman to know that a priest could have strong doubts about his faith. He never shared them with a fellow priest because he did not trust anyone in the diocese to hold his tongue about them. How childish these fears seemed now. Childish, even humiliating. As he talked about them, Dennis McLaughlin's face in the shadowy back of the car seemed to brood over them, like the fixed expression of a statue.

"The terrible part of it was the way it kept happening, day after day. The dailiness of it. Again and again you'd think: This time God will listen to me, this time my prayers will do something. But at the end of every day, there was a new batch of bodies to be blessed by me and tagged by the grave detail. After a while I went a little crazy. It wasn't enough, not to care about whether you lived or died. I started trying to get myself killed. I was saying to God, take me, take my sacrifice, and let the others go. I'm absolutely positive I'd be dead by now if it wasn't for Steve Murchison."

"The Methodist bishop?"

"That's right. He was the Protestant chaplain of our regiment. He's ten years older than me. One day, just before we crossed the Rhine, he took me aside. We'd been under heavy artillery fire all day and taken terrible casualties. For a couple of hours, I'd walked around in it and never got a scratch. 'Matt,' he said, 'you're not Jesus.'"

Matthew Mahan leaned back and stared up at the car's gray

roof. Dennis McLaughlin, the sunny resort landscape, were gone now. He was back in that shattered French town, staring into Steve Murchison's rawboned Yankee face while the grave teams methodically recorded and tagged the shrouded bodies.

"I saw you out there today waltzing through the shrapnel. And I thought to myself, that guy *wants* to get killed."

Matthew Mahan heard his own voice, half angry at being corrected by this heretic, half hysterical at confronting the truth. "What of it, what's wrong with that?"

"Is that the kind of example a pastor should give his people?"

"I was helping wounded men—"

"Sure you were, but a *man*, a man who wanted to give the right kind of example, could have done that crawling on his belly. Think for a minute, Matt. What are you saying to the men when you stroll around out there like an umpire on a baseball diamond? You're saying: If you were as holy and as brave as me, you'd be doing this, too. So you make them feel like shit, Matt, like shit, because they've got their heads down in their holes and they're saying prayers to God to give them the guts just to stay there. And if they do come out of a hole to help a buddy, they squirm along in the slop like so many snakes, with the shrapnel whizzing about a half an inch above their heads, and they look up and see Father God Almighty Mahan walking toward them looking about ten feet tall, his Irish grin saying, O ye of little faith."

It was dusk. They were loading the bodies on the trucks. Up ahead, the Germans started shelling again. In the distance, the shells made a crunching sound like bones breaking, flesh tearing. More than anything else he had ever wanted, Matthew Mahan had suddenly wanted to be angry at this man; he had wanted to grab him by the open flaps of his battle jacket and scream insults into his face. But he could say nothing. All he could feel inside himself was an enormous emptiness in which his heart pounded crazily.

"You think it doesn't break my heart, Matt? You think it doesn't break everybody's heart? To see them come back that way, day after day?"

Murchison pointed to the bodies, and Matthew Mahan noticed that his finger was shaking. "Getting yourself killed won't solve a damn thing, Matt. It doesn't have anything to do with faith. If anything, it may mean a loss of faith for you and the men who see you get it. Faith means going on, Matt, no matter how bad it gets. Faith means still trying to serve, when service doesn't mean anything anymore. Dead men, dead priests, don't serve, Matt— only living ones do that."

He stepped back a few feet, as if he no longer wanted to be close to such a priest. "You're going to hate my guts for saying all this to you, Matt, but so help me God it's spoken out of love."

Gone, the big gangling figure vanished into the dusk, stalking up the road toward the shellfire.

"That was the worst night of my life," Matthew Mahan told Dennis McLaughlin. "The worst. I had to face the fact that everything Steve had said to me was true. *True*. Where did he get the grace, the wisdom, to know that much about faith? Why did I know so little? That was the night I joined the ecumenical movement."

"It is a marvelous example of the difference between Protestant faith and Catholic faith," Dennis said. "One ventures, the other tries to apply a set of formulae, and when they don't work, hysteria sets in."

"It's not quite so neat, Dennis. It's the difference between real faith and false faith, between grandstanding and caring. There are plenty of formula boys in both churches."

Silence. Matthew Mahan hadn't intended his answer as a rebuke. But it was disconcerting, the way Dennis and his generation could draw such different conclusions from the same experience. "Anyway," he said, trying to restore their mood, "I never got up off my belly under shellfire for the rest of the war. For some reason, from that night I was able to bear the dying. Steve and I kid about it sometimes. He says that at one point in our argument he grabbed me by the shoulders and this was a laying on of hands that gave me the consolation of the Holy Spirit.

"I told that story to Pope John. Would you believe it, he took it seriously?"

"Why not?" Dennis McLaughlin said.

Ahead of them the Mediterranean glistened like dark blue metal in the sunlight. Tullio drove slowly along a road that ran parallel to the sea, until Matthew Mahan saw a wide swatch of deserted white sand. "This looks perfect," he said.

Tullio took a blanket from the trunk and spread it out on the sand a few dozen feet from the road. Dennis lugged the hamper that had been delivered from the hotel's kitchen a few minutes before they departed. There was a bottle of Soave Bolla packed in dry ice, a dozen small chicken sandwiches and as many drumsticks, wings, and breasts wrapped in tinfoil, cardboard boxes containing olives, celery, miniature tomatoes. They drank the cool dry wine, which went beautifully with the chicken. The air was hot and still. Not a flicker of a breeze ruffled the motionless water. It reminded Dennis of the beaches of their home state in July or August. He remarked this to Matthew Mahan as they finished the wine and insisted on giving Tullio the last chicken breast.

"Too hot for a couple of guys in clericals," Matthew Mahan said. "Let's strip down."

Quickly they took off their coats, collars, and rabats. To Dennis's surprise, the Cardinal also took off his shoes and socks and rolled up his trousers to the knees. "I can never go near a beach without doing some shell hunting," he said. "Want to join me?"

They left Tullio to clean up the fragments of lunch. Matthew Mahan smiled when Dennis mischievously wondered if there would be enough food to feed five thousand people when they got back. "In Italy anything is possible," the Cardinal said.

"How did you get interested in shells?" Dennis asked as they reached the sea's edge and Matthew Mahan walked in until the water covered his ankles. It was icy cold but clear.

"I guess I started when I was ten or eleven," Matthew Mahan said. "We used to spend our summers at the shore. When my father got a few days off and joined us, he and I would get up around seven and walk the whole beach, from Paradise all the way down to the tip of the peninsula. I loved those walks."

How much, how much. Matthew Mahan was astonished to find his eyes blurring, deep emotion throbbing in his body. "My father wasn't much of a talker. We'd just tramp along. Every so often we'd pick up a shell. If we found one that was especially interesting, he'd say keep it as a souvenir. I did. Pretty soon I had several dozen. When he went to Florida at the start of the baseball season, we'd join him down there for a week or so. That's where I really got interested in conchology, as they call it. The Florida beaches are a treasure trove. My mother bought me a book on the subject, and presto, I was a collector."

"What's this one?" Dennis said, picking up a brown and white cone-shaped shell with a small stem at the bottom.

"That's a ranella. There's a beautiful variety from the Philippines with bigger knobs and reddish-brown markings. But I like the little fellows. He bent over and scooped out of the sand a *Fusinus syracusanus*, a tiny brown and white and gold shell which rose from a narrow stem to a bulging middle and then narrowed again with the same white rectangular markings around each bulge, growing smaller and smaller to a point at the very top. "Like a piece of architecture, isn't it?" he said. "I always think of it as pilgrims ascending a holy mountain. I saw something like it one night in Ireland, thousands of people going up the mountain to the shrine at Knock, carrying torches."

"Dante's vision of Paradise," Dennis said.

"Now here," the Cardinal said, picking up a brown and white speckled shell which was almost round in shape with an opening at one end and a tiny knob at the bottom from which spiral lines ran out. "Here's a Mediterranean version of the New England moon shell. I believe this one is called *Natica millepunctata*. On this one you can see clearly what I find so fascinating about shells. They illustrate a principle of growth that not many people understand—the dynamic spiral. To produce a spiral, you need three things. Growth has to follow a continuous course—it can't backtrack. It also must proceed freely, with a minimum of outside interference. Finally, it must never lose touch with the beginning of the spiral. You know, that part hardens and stops living; for all purposes it's dead. But the lip of the spiral stays alive, keeps growing. One of the best examples of this is the American chambered nautilus."

"A principle of growth," Dennis said, staring at the shell. The idea stirred a vague excitement in his mind.

"You have to picture it starting from that tiny knob at the bottom of the spiral. That's called the protoconch."

"Can I keep this?"

"Of course. I've got one from Mauritius, *Natica fluctuata*. It's especially interesting because almost the entire shell consists of the last whorl. Spiral growth doesn't always follow a lockstep rhythm. There are great leaps forward."

"Do they all curve in the same direction?"

"Practically all of them. There's only one I can think of, the left-handed whelk from Florida, that goes the other way."

They were strolling along on the water's edge, letting the small waves lap over their feet. The sun was fierce, but Dennis felt strangely exhilarated. The Cardinal began talking about the importance of shells in various parts of the world. In the Roman era they were ground up for dyes. Then and now artisans made them into jewelry. In other parts of the world, particularly the South Pacific and Africa, they were used as money. Shinto priests in Japan sound the call to worship on Triton's trumpets. In India left-handed spirals are considered sacred. In the Fiji Islands the golden cowry, a smooth very rare shell that looks from the top like a piece of expensive china, is worn by chiefs as proof of sovereignty.

"Do you have one?" Dennis asked.

"Sure," said the Cardinal with a grin. "It cost me a fortune. Do you think I ought to wear it when I do battle with Sister Agnes Marie?"

The Cardinal was enjoying himself tremendously. It was the first time Dennis had seen him relaxed, carefree, since he had watched him performing for the confirmation class at Holy Angels. Again, he felt a kind of awe at the natural radiance of the man. But now there was no envy riding like a vengeful imp on top of that awe. Because the radiance, the good humor, the bonhomie, was being given to him alone? Or did it subsist independently of an audience, as God supposedly did? No, no, no, Dennis told himself. Tell that Ironic Angel to shut up, once and perhaps for all. Accept the human reality, the *happiness*, that this man is sharing with you, and something else, something deeper that seemed to lie just outside his mind's reach. He fingered the Mediterranean moon shell in his pocket.

For another hour they walked and talked, picking up an occasional shell which invariably turned out to be too common for the collector's eye and was tossed into the water, but mostly rambling reminiscently around their own lives. Matthew Mahan told him the story of his relationship with Mary Shea—the whole story, including what they had told each other three nights ago at the Tre Scalini. Dennis thought of the sneering suggestion in his letter to his brother Leo and writhed with silent regret. That, of course, was only a small part of his betrayal of this man. But he told himself feverishly that he would atone for it, he would swear Leo to silence, force him to return every leaked document, convert him from an enemy to an admirer of Matthew Mahan.

The Cardinal also talked freely about his early life. He told him about his Italian-born mother—her hatred of baseball, how she had refused to see him play in a single game, even the day he won the county championship for St. Francis Xavier Prep. How the Jesuits had turned him down. And that day at the end of his freshman year, standing on that small hill in the center of the university looking down on the depression-wracked city at twilight, how he had been filled with a wish to reach out, to comfort, to counsel, to lead, the poor bewildered people, trapped between economic disaster and the know-nothing Irish thugs who masqueraded as the city's politicians. The day, the hour, he knew with finality that he would be a priest.

"I should have waited for a couple of years and gone to college that way," Dennis said. "Maybe by then I'd have had a chance to meet a few intelligent women."

The Cardinal looked unhappy. He obviously thought Dennis was about to embark on a diatribe against priestly celibacy.

"I don't mean I would have married them," Dennis added hastily. He spent the next few minutes explaining to Matthew Mahan his belief that physical celibacy was not the heart of the problem. It was the feeling on the part of most priests that they never had a chance to really know or understand women as mature equally human beings. "I mean really appreciate them. We just see them as the Temptation."

"I know, I know," Matthew Mahan said. "I know exactly what you mean. It wasn't much different for me, Dennis. I scraped up a few dates—girls from the neighborhood, for proms, that sort of thing. But most of the time I hung around with a bunch of guys my own age. It was the depression, you know. Everybody was leery of getting involved with a girl. There wasn't much hope of finding a decent job to support a family. I was pretty unprepared to deal with women—in a mature way."

Totally unprepared, totally unprepared, whispered a corrective voice in Matthew Mahan's mind. "I guess I was—influenced by my mother. She was a good woman—but a little—silly. High-strung, violently emotional. All the things that feed the male stereotype of women. When I met Mary Shea—I couldn't believe she was real at first."

The Cardinal picked up another moon shell and reminded himself that he was here to help Dennis, not lament his now ancient travails. "You went into the Jesuits right after high school, then? You probably made the decision on your senior retreat."

Dennis nodded.

"I was afraid of that," Matthew Mahan said. "I'm so glad now that the Jesuits turned me down—and I made up my mind on my own. Those senior retreat vocations are always troublesome. You start thinking you're the victim of a con job, right?"

Dennis tried to explain that his decision was a bit more complicated. It was an instinctive flight from Mother—but a flight that simultaneously had her approval. From there it became an ego epic, an intellectual-spiritual experiment. The Cardinal listened, but Dennis could see that he was finding it difficult to follow. They were so painfully different. But the difference did not diminish the intensity of his concern. Again Dennis was engulfed by a wave of lacerating guilt.

The Cardinal wanted to know what Dennis planned to do with the rest of his life. He did not expect him to stay more than a year or two as his secretary. Did he want to be a full-time writer? Would he be interested in teaching at the seminary? Would he rather be a parish priest? Dennis had to confess that he didn't know the answer.

"It'll come, it'll come," Matthew Mahan said.

He told him more about his impromptu friendship with Pope John, the deep impression the man made on him, when he met him in France. "He knew every bishop in the country. In Belgium, too. He had them all sized up. Suenens, for instance. He would have spent the rest of his life as an auxiliary if it wasn't for Papa Giovanni."

They could see the car now, a glistening black toy on the white sand. In ten more minutes they were putting on their clericals again and were racing back to Rome. Dennis said little. Matthew Mahan talked to Tullio about the social unrest that was tormenting Italy. Scarcely a day went by without a strike, or a week without a riot or a demonstration. Tullio pretended not to know the answer, but eventually admitted that he was a Communist and firmly believed that the time had come to get rid of capitalism.

And the Church, too? Oh no, not the Church. He was a good Catholic. He saw no conflict between being a good Catholic and a good Communist. But the Vatican—they would have to change their ways. They would have to stop being capitalists. "*Il Vaticano riceve—ma non da a nessuno!*" Hearing the familiar canard on Tullio's lips was almost as painful as it had been to hear Mary Shea repeating it. Perhaps because there was even less he could do about it.

Matthew Mahan gave up trying to understand the Italians and tried to begin a conversation with Dennis. But he was abstracted, brooding, staring out the window. For a moment the Cardinal wondered if he had helped or hurt his secretary today. Perhaps he had told him too much about himself, had disillusioned him even more than he was already disillusioned, if that was possible.

Who could judge? He could only hope and pray he had done the right thing. Musing on the day, he was stirred by another insight. He was saying good-bye forever to that confused, hysterical young chaplain who saw a sacrificial death as the only answer to his inner agony. They had lived together a long time with their backs turned, grotesque spiritual Siamese twins. Suddenly he remembered the dream in the Cathedral of the Dead—praying to the reversed statue. There was an element of unforgiveness in that stance—as if the statue were alive, and disdained to face its guilty worshiper. And shame—shame was there, too. Somehow he had failed that arrogant young priest. Now it was time to face each other, the haggard, sleepless thirty-year-old and the man who had lived the twenty-five years that priest had tried to surrender. Was there just a faint ghost of a wish that the priest had had his way and he, too, would be forever young, forever unspoiled by the world of peace and profit, building and collecting, scheming and competing, judging and begrudging? No, no. But he would allow himself this one sentimental gesture. *Good-bye, old friend*, he whispered, *good-bye*.

"There it is," Dennis McLaughlin said. He peered out Dennis's window. They were well into Rome now. In the distance St. Peter's dome was visible, looming above the rest of the city, challenged only by a few high-rise luxury hotels.

"Old Davey says that Rome will never be able to stand up until we get that thing off its back."

Matthew Mahan sighed. They were in the real world again.

While Dennis narrated a compendium of old Davey's outrageous remarks on their tour of St. Peter's, they sped through the empty Sunday streets. In ten minutes they were ascending in the hotel elevator to the fifth floor, Dennis still doing his utmost to shock him with the sayings of their eighty-year-old heretic. Matthew Mahan declined to take them seriously.

At the end of the hall Dennis suddenly grew solemn. "That was quite a trip," he said. "I can't tell you which I appreciate more—what happened at the grave or what you told me on the way to the beach."

Matthew Mahan nodded. "It was good for me, too, Dennis."

In his own room Matthew Mahan knelt beside his bed and thanked God for his guidance, for giving him the words that had —hopefully—healed. How strange the life of the spirit was. By letting go, by giving up the old idols, the old guardians, by venturing forth fearful and alone, you discovered after traveling in the anxious void that new different communions awaited you. *My yoke is sweet, my burden light.*

XIX

The next morning Dennis McLaughlin arose at seven and joined Bishop Cronin, Monsignors Petrie and Malone, and two busloads of pilgrims to journey to the Church of St. Peter in Chains, where the priests concelebrated mass with their Cardinal-to-be. They then returned to the hotel, had a light breakfast, and Dennis helped Matthew Mahan put on his Cardinal's robes. It was a simpler outfit, thanks to a directive that Pope Paul had issued on April 5. The Pontiff had banned the mantelletta (the knee-length cape), the cappa magna (the huge red cloak), and the galero (the flat hat with thirty tassels). Also banished were the red shoes with silver buckles. Matthew Mahan had been delighted to forgo most of these archaic ornaments, especially the shoes. But the loss of the galero caused a momentary pang. He remembered his first visit to St. Patrick's Cathedral in New York, gazing up at the ceiling above the high altar, where the galeros of dead Cardinals dangled. It had pleased him to think that his hat would be the first to hang in his cathedral. But *Roma locuta est causa finita est.*

Earnestly and efficiently Dennis helped him into his red rabat, the sleeveless, backless garment worn beneath the red wool cassock, then the red cassock itself with trimmings, lining, buttons, and thread of red silk, then the mozzetta, the small cape worn over his shoulders. Around his waist went the red watered silk ribbon sash with silk fringes at both ends. On his head he put the red watered silk skullcap. "Well, that does it. How do I look?"

"Fine," said Dennis, circling him and adjusting the sash, which was a bit low. "Have you got your red socks on?"

"Oh no," said Matthew Mahan. The red socks were not in the dresser drawer where he could have sworn he had put them. A hasty search of his luggage discovered them in a corner of his flight bag. "Now I remember. I almost forgot them and stuffed them in there at the last minute," he said.

He quickly changed socks and regarded himself in the full-length mirror on the closet door.

"You're sure we don't wear the rochet now?"

"I checked three times with our Vatican monsignor. He says no. But I think I'll take it along in my briefcase."

Another Vatican monsignor had replaced the anticapitalist who had greeted them at the airport. His name was Giovanni Tonti. He was a stocky, boyish man from Naples, with a hearty southern Italian sense of humor. Dennis took the long-sleeved white linen rochet from the top of the Cardinal's dresser and went into his room to get his briefcase.

When he came back, he found Matthew Mahan kneeling beside his bed. "Would you let me have five minutes alone, Dennis? I'd like to collect my thoughts. I'll see you in the lobby."

The lobby was jammed with their pilgrims, all eager to get a first look at Cardinal Mahan in his red robes. They cheered and clapped like rock fans when he emerged from the elevator. He had no time to do more than wave to them like a candidate on his way to the next meeting. Outside the hotel, Monsignor Tonti was waiting for them, smiling tensely. "We have only five minutes," he said. "We must hurry."

"Baloney," said Matthew Mahan as he got into the hired limousine. "The Vatican's just like the Army, hurry up and wait. I bet we stand around for at least a half hour before anything happens."

"No doubt, no doubt," agreed Monsignor Tonti. "Where is Bishop Cronin? He is also supposed to be in this car." They peered out the window. No sign of him.

"Go look for him, Dennis," said Matthew Mahan.

He found Davey in the coffee shop, lecturing Mike Furia over a cup of tea. "He's trying to talk me into giving a million dollars to the IRA," Mike said.

"My argument is simple," said Cronin. "If the cods ever got their hands on that much money, they'd turn respectable and that would be the end of them."

"The Cardinal is waiting in the car."

"Oh, it's time for the inevitable, is it?" Cronin said. Dennis was relieved to see that he had left his tam-o'-shanter in his room, but he still had his blackthorn stick.

"Between us, lad," he said as they made their way through the crowded lobby, "I fear we'll rue this day. But let's put on our bravest smiles nonetheless."

"Why should we rue it?" Dennis asked.

"Wait till you hear the oath he takes before the Papal Throne. This year they've added a vow of silence as total as that taken by any Carthusian monk."

Cronin dropped the subject when they reached the car and began telling funny stories about his days as a seminarian in the Irish College. Traffic forced them to detour down some side streets off the Campo dei Fiori market. One street seemed dedicated to junk: beakless vases, unattached telephones, staggering numbers of rusty keys, lifeless watches, abandoned medals. On the walls of the houses were scrawled numerous political messages, which Dennis asked Monsignor Tonti to translate. "It is Communist propaganda," he said. "Calls for demonstrations against the war in Vietnam. This is a very Communist district."

"And there," said Father Cronin, pointing to a plaque on the corner building, "is where Pope Alexander VI tore down enough buildings to open this street. It gave him quicker access to his beloved Vanozza, who ran an inn called the Cow—named after her no doubt—out on the Campo."

A small boy, not more than ten, raced out of an alley to shout something at their limousine. He ran along beside them, repeating it for almost a block. "What's he saying?" Dennis asked.

"He's making fun of our license plates," Monsignor Tonti said, casually pointing out the window to the limousine behind them. "SCV. It stands for Stato Cittal del Vaticano. But the Romans say it should mean: *Se Cristo vedesse*. If Christ could only see this."

Finally they arrived at the apostolic chancery, or *cancelleria*, on the Corso Vittorio Emanuele. Around them in the courtyard rose forty-four superb granite columns, supposedly taken from the ruins of Pompeii. The facade of the building, which occupied one whole side of the piazza, was unbelievably delicate. "I remember some English writer," said Bishop Cronin, "who said it reminded him of an ancient casket of mellowed ivory."

"It was built, you know, by Raffaele Riario, nephew of Sixtus IV," said Monsignor Tonti, "with money he won in a single night—sixty thousand scudi, I think—from the nephew of another pope. These Romans! And they sneer at us Neapolitans."

"Does it look familiar, Dennis?" Matthew Mahan asked. "The chancery office in New York is a copy."

"Another bad omen," muttered Bishop Cronin.

"What's in here now?"

"The chancery for the diocese of Rome. And the Sacred Rota," Monsignor Tonti said.

Inwardly Matthew Mahan twisted away from the answer to Dennis's question. Somehow he had managed not to think about the fact that he was receiving his official nomination as a Cardinal in the building where Mary Shea had sought in vain the annulment of her marriage.

Inside they were led down crowded corridors to a large hall which was even more crowded. It was known as the Hall of a Hundred Days, Monsignor Tonti explained, because it took the painter Vasari and two assistants only that long to paint the rather garish frescoes on the walls and ceiling. "Vasari boasted about his speed to Michelangelo, who said: '*Si vede*—it shows.'"

There were cheers and claps from some of their pilgrims as they pushed their way to the far end of the hall, where the other new Cardinals were waiting. Matthew Mahan exchanged handshakes with his four fellow Americans, Cooke of New York, Dearden of Detroit, Carberry of St. Louis, and Wright of Pittsburgh. Standing a few feet away were eight more Cardinals-to-be from other parts of the world. Cronin ticked off their names for him. Hoffner of Cologne. Tarancon of Toledo, Spain. Marty, Archbishop of Paris. McKeefry of Wellington, New Zealand. And an impressive-looking black man, Rakotomalala, Archbishop of Tananarive, Madagascar. "And old Derrieux of no place in particular," Cronin concluded.

It was the first foreign name that meant anything to Dennis. "Jean Derrieux, the Jesuit theologian?"

"In or out of the order, you're still part of the club," said Cronin sardonically.

"Which one is he?"

"Standing next to Cooke. There, the boss is discovering him now. He's a great fan of his. Fussed over him like he was the Holy Spirit incarnate during the council. They met in Paris during the war."

"A little professional jealousy in those remarks?" Dennis asked, as Matthew Mahan began talking jovially to Derrieux.

"No, no. No, no. I acknowledge his superiority," said Cronin. "He's got a mind of pure crystal, while mine is nothing more than Irish peat. But he's a cold cod, too cold for my taste."

Dennis nodded, studying Derrieux. The face was almost classically intellectual, deep-socketed eyes, a thin, bloodless mouth, a rather weak chin, and a sharp, somewhat feminine nose. He was smiling at Matthew Mahan now. But the smile was empty, formal, compared to Mahan's warm grin. Derrieux's name still stirred Dennis's mind. He had been one of the lonely intellectual heroes of the fifties, calling again and again for more freedom in the Church.

Bishop Cronin began telling him how he and several other Americans had persuaded Derrieux to join them in a scorching attack on Vatican II's schema on the communications media. "They had a clause in there that Joe Stalin himself would have applauded. I can still remember it. 'The civil authority has the duty of seeing to it in a just and vigilant manner that serious danger to public morals and social progress do not result from a perverted use of the media.' It was nothing less than the sign of the cross over state censorship. In spite of all we could do, they passed it by three to one. But we decided not to quit. We got Matt into the act, and the next thing you know, we had a circular signed by twenty-five Eminences and Excellencies from fourteen countries. Matt himself stood on the steps of St. Peter's handing it out.

"Along came that big ox Pericle Felici, the secretary-general. Believe it or not, he tried to grab the circulars away from Matt. It looked for a minute like there'd be a wrestling match right there in St. Peter's Square. Matt would have taken him two falls out of three, I'm sure. I was about to make a fortune selling tickets when up rushed Derrieux to play the peacemaker. He talked Matt into giving up the circulars and spent a lot more time assuring old Felici that no offense against the authority of the council was intended. I took a dislike to the fellow from that moment."

The hall of the chancellery was not very well ventilated. In fact, no one even seemed to have bothered to open the narrow fifteenth-century windows. More and more people continued to arrive, adding to the humidity and diminishing the supply of oxygen. Dennis felt claustrophobia stirring in his chest and began urgently wishing for the papal messenger to arrive.

In the Sistine Chapel, Pope Paul was meeting in a secret consistory with the present Cardinals. To get his mind off his breathing difficulties, Dennis asked Bishop Cronin what happened at that ceremony.

"Nothing much," said Cronin. "The Great Man sits on his throne and reads out the names of the *neo porporati*. The assembled yes-men in red raise their zucchettos and give him a little bow of assent. Then the messengers take the official letters—the *biglietti*—and head for us here and wherever else the new boys are gathered. Il Papa also often uses the occasion to announce some new appointments. Some of the old guard at the Irish College tell me that there's a new Secretary of State in the wind. Not even pusillanimous Paolo can put up with Cicognani any longer. He's only eighty-six, and it's a shame to retire him."

"Who's in the wind?"

"Villot, so they say. He's a mere lad, sixty-three. But let us thank God for small favors. At least he isn't Italian."

Suddenly Dennis thought he saw a face in the crowd that could not be here. A hallucination. You are still high on antihistamine. There it was again. Disembodied, peering over the shoulders of short monsignors and around the elbows of tall laymen: Helen, Sister Helen Reed. She was wearing her gray and black modernized nun's habit, with the small silver cross dangling between her breasts. Her gamin face had that solemn, earnest little-girl look that had stirred his soul (or was it just those great legs?) the first time he saw her. There was something childlike, something irreducibly innocent about her. But here? She was four thousand miles away, turning moderates into militants in the scabby side streets of St. Sebastian's parish. Then his staring eyes caught hers and her mouth became a radiant smile. She was real. He edged away from Bishop Cronin and squirmed and elbowed past the several hundred loyal followers pressing around the waiting Cardinals-to-be to end his disbelief once and for all by taking her hand.

"What are you doing here?"

"I talked Sister Agnes Marie into it. Somebody had to be over here to defend our position against your friend with the red hat."

Dennis laughed. "You've come a long way and spent a lot of money for nothing. I don't know what happened to him, but he told me yesterday he was dropping the idea. In fact, he turned down a lunch invitation from Cardinal Antoniutti."

Helen was clearly astonished that Dennis McLaughlin, the great intellectual revolutionary, could be so naïve. "You're sure he isn't lying?" Then she turned conspiratorial. "Maybe he's found out your—arrangement with Leo."

Dennis looked nervously around them. In the semicircle of Cardinals, Matthew Mahan was chatting amiably with John Dearden. "I don't think so," he said.

People continued to pour into the room and edge their way into the crowd around the Cardinals. The spectators were soon jammed together like passengers in a crowded bus or subway. Dennis could feel Helen's right breast against his arm. The temperature rose, and the oxygen supply continued to fall. Panic and anger mingled in Dennis's chest. It was impossible. He was always being pushed this way or shoved that way, frozen into one position or another, forced to feel when he did not want to feel.

"I've got an appointment at the Congregation for the Religious this afternoon," Helen said.

It was absurd, a charade, his entire life was a charade. He thought of his father silent beneath the white cross in the spring sunshine at Nettuno.

"I'm staying at the Pensione Christina, Largo Antonio Sarti

Eight. It's run by two Austrians. There's a beautiful terrace overlooking the Tiber."

The choice his father had made, the simple act of bravery, life like an arrow's trajectory from the happiness of home, the happiness of marriage, to the hero's grave. Wasn't that better than this comic stumble, this daily travesty that eventually drove everyone to his knees?

"Sister Agnes says I mustn't miss the Church of the Quattro Santi Coronati. You go through two courtyards to get to it, and you ring a bell. A nun comes out and shows you around a tiny cloister full of flowers and not a sound except the noise of a fountain. Have you been there?"

He shook his head. Matthew Mahan was not beaten to his knees. None of these relaxed, composed men, these Princes of the Church, showed the slightest sigh of inner anguish. What was their secret? Was it simply being born at the right time? Was the answer that simple?

"Hello, Dennis," whispered a rather sexy feminine voice into his right ear. He turned and found himself practically embracing Madeline McAvoy. She was wearing a stylish blue and white suit and startling oversized green sunglasses. "Jim's down with one of those Roman viruses. I need someone to tell me what's happening here."

"I'm afraid I don't know much more than the average spectator," Dennis said. "Bishop Cronin is the one with all the inside gossip."

Madeline laughed lightly. "Jim told me *not* to talk to him. An order which I have no intention of obeying."

Dennis tried to take a deep breath and inhaled nothing but Mrs. McAvoy's perfume. Where had he read that perfume testers, noses, as they were called in the trade, all died of cirrhosis of the liver? Another deep breath, and he would be on his way to a similar fate.

"Who's she?" Helen whispered jealously in his other ear, as Madeline McAvoy looked past Dennis in search of Cronin.

"Don't worry," Dennis whispered out of the corner of his mouth, "she's well married. Six kids."

From somewhere behind them a voice began calling orders in Italian. Since there were very few Italians in the hall, nothing happened. Then an American voice, which Dennis recognized as

Terry Malone, began bawling, "Make way, make way. Please make an aisle here."

Monsignor Malone and two equally large American monsignors brusquely elbowed and shouldered their way through the crowd. In their wake came a small, solemn-faced man in the red robes of a Cardinal with a sheaf of parchment-like papers in his hand.

"Who's he?" asked Madeline McAvoy.

"I don't know," Dennis said, "but he's carrying the *biglietti*, the official letters from the Pope, making them Cardinals."

Standing in the center of the semicircle, the Italian Cardinal read the official notification from the Pope and then summoned each man forward to receive his individual *biglietto*. He started with the non-American Cardinals at the left end of the line. As they walked forward one by one to receive their letters, Dennis found himself thinking about his high school and college days, when he and the other bright boys paraded to the platform at every convocation to get their first honor cards and other scholastic prizes.

Matthew Mahan was the last prelate to receive his letter. "Oh my God," said a deep feminine voice a few feet away from Dennis, "he's the thirteenth."

He turned his head and saw it was Mrs. Dwight Slocum speaking.

"Do you really think that's bad luck?" Madeline McAvoy asked the city's reigning WASP.

"I once gave a dinner party for thirteen people. The thirteenth guest died within a week. Is there better proof than that?"

"As usual," Dennis whispered in Madeline McAvoy's ear, "the Protestants argue from religious experience."

Cardinal Derrieux stepped forward to reply to the Vatican messenger. He spoke in Latin and Dennis could only pick up a few scattered phrases. Words such as *honoris* and *sancto pater* gave him the drift of the speech. It was a flowery tribute to the Holy Father for conferring this great honor on him, who was thoroughly unworthy of it, as well as on his fellow Cardinals, who were much more deserving. Studying Derrieux as he spoke, Dennis found himself sharing some of Cronin's dislike. Aside from the thickness of the compliments, there was a primness around his mouth as he spoke, coupled with a nervous intensity, a humorlessness that struck a jarring note at this happy occasion. The new Cardinal looked haggard, as if he had stayed up all night memorizing his speech. Dennis wondered if he was on the edge of the classic Jesuit syndrome of late middle age, a nervous breakdown.

"What's he saying?" asked Madeline McAvoy.

"He's announcing that all Catholic mothers with six or more children are going to get hand-illuminated copies of *Humanae Vitae*."

"You're terrible," Mrs. McAvoy said. But she obviously loved it.

"He's burying Pope Paul in compliments."

"Do you think it will work?"

Cardinal Derrieux finished his speech and stepped back into the ranks. Now the photographers took over. They burst from the crowd like a bunch of chorus boys and began snapping pictures from all angles. One even stretched out on the floor, hoping, perhaps, to make the American Cardinals resemble the faces on Mount Rushmore.

Next came the radio reporters with their tape recorders, thrusting their microphones into the faces of some new Cardinals and ignoring others. In the American contingent, Dearden and Cooke got most of the attention. Only one microphone accosted Matthew Mahan, and he spoke politely into it for a few minutes. The man seemed to cut him off in mid-sentence and hustled down the line to interview Derrieux.

"Is it all over?" asked Mrs. McAvoy, with evident dismay.

"No," said Dennis, "the next two ceremonies take place in St. Peter's. On Wednesday evening they get their red birettas from the Pope. On Thursday they concelebrate mass in St. Peter's and get their rings."

"Oh good," said Mrs. McAvoy. "Jim ought to be back on his feet by then."

"This afternoon they have *ad calorem* visits from other Cardinals, diplomats, officials, friends."

Mrs. McAvoy looked puzzled but was too proud to ask for a translation. "*Calorem* refers to the warmth of the visit," Dennis explained.

"I thought they were going to get their red hats right here," said Mrs. Slocum.

Madeline McAvoy turned to her and began explaining the routine. Dennis seized Helen's hand and edged away from them

254

into the stream of people who were moving toward the door. Many were obviously baffled and a little annoyed by the undramatic ceremony. Dennis heard snatches of conversation swirling around him.

"Couldn't they send it to his hotel?"

"It's an old Roman custom, I hear."

"In those days each Cardinal had his own palace."

On one of the eddies of the crowd, Andy Goggin turned up beside Dennis. He smiled down at them and said, "Doesn't it remind you of first-century Christianity down to the last little detail?"

"Absolutely," said Dennis. "The only thing I missed was a Christian or two coated with pitch and turned into a human torch."

"They do that tomorrow at the Vatican."

Dennis introduced him to Sister Helen, and she made a great fuss over him. "I've heard Dennis talk *so much* about you, the great biblical scholar."

Goggin gave him a suspicious look, and Dennis could only shrug wryly and murmur about his weakness for hero worship.

The next event on the schedule was a luncheon at the North American College for the five American Cardinals. The rector, perhaps the Cardinals themselves, would orate. "It makes me lose my appetite, just thinking about it," said Goggin. "I'm sure we could write out every cliché in advance."

"Do you have to go?" Sister Helen asked Dennis.

"Of course," he said. "If the Cardinal forgets a line, I've got to be on hand to whisper it to him."

Helen smiled. This was the Dennis she knew and loved. You will do anything, literally anything, to get laid, won't you? mocked his ironic angel. Goggin, obviously scenting blood, declared it was a point of honor for a Jesuit to avoid the portals of the North American College. Members of the order had been known to disappear into its labyrinthine politics, never to be heard from again. Sister Helen suggested lunch at her pensione. Goggin instantly accepted for both of them. Less than a half hour later, they were enjoying an aperitif on the terrace above the Tiber.

As Dennis stared across the river at St. Peter's dome, something stirred in his mind, an idea or the premonition of an idea that carried him back to the beach at Nettuno. Instinctively his hand went into his pocket, and he found himself fingering his moon shell souvenir. Was a dome the same as a spiral? A dome pretended to infinity but only achieved immensity, dwarfing the human. It was not a natural, it was even an unnatural symbol.

While he brooded, Helen was interrogating Goggin. He refused to take her seriously and fielded questions about biblical studies and his work on the Vatican Radio with deft irony. A little puzzled, she began asking him if he agreed with the revolutionary vision of the once and future church, as foretold by Dennis McLaughlin.

"I stopped smoking that stuff about a year ago," Goggin said. "I thought he did, too."

He leered deliberately at Dennis, who could only squirm and smile. With humiliating, almost maternal approval, Helen began telling Goggin what Dennis was doing to betray the inner secrets of Matthew Mahan's regime. Their food arrived. Like good young clerics they had chosen the cheapest thing on the menu, spaghetti. Dennis found his portion practically inedible, but he suspected it was not the cook's fault. The more Helen talked, the more his appetite dwindled. The whole thing sounded so incredibly childish, compared to the reality of Matthew Mahan, the memories that he now possessed, unavoidably, indelibly. The weary bedside watcher at 5 A.M. with the oxygen mask in his hand, the calm comforter among the white crosses at Nettuno.

With almost diabolical directness, Goggin proceeded to insert a verbal needle in this exposed nerve. "All this destruction that your friend Dennis talks about. Don't you think it breaks the first law of Christianity, love one another?"

"I think—" Helen looked hopefully toward Dennis for help and saw that none was forthcoming. "I think we're mainly interested in destroying phony titles. Misused, abused power."

"What if you can't destroy an idea without destroying the man who believes it? Titles, power, are equally difficult to separate from the human beings who possess them."

"A certain amount of suffering is inevitable," said Sister Helen. "Jesus said he came to spread fire on the earth."

"Jesus said a great many things, about half of which contradict the other half, or mean nothing. He was a rabbi, you know, trained in the art of finding verbal solutions to any problem. Render unto Caesar the things that are Caesar's and to God the things that are God's, for instance. Stop and think about that one for a moment. Are you any closer to a solution, after you hear it? Does it tell you anything you didn't know before you asked the question?"

"What's wrong with him?" Sister Helen asked Dennis.

"I told you he was unique," he said. "Uniquely intelligent and uniquely perverse."

As espresso was poured, the sunny sky began to grow murky. An April shower was on its way. Sister Helen glanced at her watch and hurriedly drained her small cup. "I have a date at the Vatican," she said. She jumped up and gave Dennis an anxious look. "Do what you can to change this great man's mind, please," she said.

She strode away from them through the fading sunshine, those lovely scissoring legs tormenting Dennis's eyes. The quintessential American girl, exuding health, vitality, self-confidence. Goggin stirred some sugar into his espresso. Dennis emptied his cup in a single swallow and poured another one.

"Do you take her seriously?" Goggin asked.

"To answer that question would involve me in a one-hour disquisition on the nature of love."

Goggin's laugh was a little forced. "Really, I wasn't trying to undo the romance. I was only talking to hear myself."

"You can be so damn cruel, do you know that? We both have a talent for it. So far we haven't used it on each other."

Goggin leaned forward and put his elbows on the table. He cradled his face in his hands and said. "Do you want me to say I'm in love with you, not queerly but sacredly? Do I have to spill my guts, too? I'm in love with you as a priest and, finally, with the idea of the Church. With Mother Church eventually creating the mystical body of Christ that embraces the entire human race. A body, an organism, with a hierarchy of powers that fulfills the hierarchy of human needs. That's what I'm in love with. That's what I thought you were in love with. But I begin to think that you're really in love with your cock."

Goggin strode out of the restaurant, leaving Dennis alone at the table. He sat there for a long time staring at the vile-looking Tiber. It was ocher-colored, a river of foul sludge. If you threw a match in it, Dennis wondered, would it catch fire like the Cayahuga or the Volga? Was thinking such thoughts a way of avoiding his loneliness?

He sighed, finished his coffee, and signaled the waitress for the bill. She smiled politely and told him that his American sister had already paid for it.

XX

"Your Eminences—if you'd just stand over here so that we get St. Peter's in the background."

The five new American Cardinals were in the garden of the North American College on Janiculum Hill. The luncheon and the speeches were over. The physical man and the spiritual man had been well fed, but the photographers remained insatiable. Matthew Mahan felt exhausted. A new kind of pain, less alarming but more depressing, throbbed in his stomach. He had eaten practically nothing at lunch, causing Cardinal Dearden to ask him in his genial way if he knew that Lent was over. He and Dearden had chatted amiably about priests' synods and parish councils, which Dearden, as the president of the National Council of Bishops, had done his best to urge on every diocese. So far, only about half had responded. Listening to him, Matthew Mahan wondered why and how Dearden got the nickname "Iron John." He was an essentially shy man, who rarely looked you in the eye when he spoke.

"When I told my suffragan bishops to start parish councils, old Eddie O'Neil stopped me in my tracks," Matthew Mahan said. "He said to me, 'I'm just too damn old to get mixed up in that stuff, Matt.'" This led to a discussion of aging pastors. Matthew Mahan topped everyone with the case of Monsignor Aloysius Dunn, who had ruled St. Malachy's with a harsh Irish hand for fifty-one years. Wright amused them with some stories about Cardinal Cushing. His favorite was one about a priest who came to Cushing and told him he had lost his faith. Cushing replied, "Don't talk nonsense, Father. Neither you nor I have brains enough to do that."

Cardinal Carberry of St. Louis, the oldest of the five—he was sixty-four—murmured as they lined up for the photographer that he was beginning to feel like the victim of a firing squad that couldn't shoot straight.

Cardinal Krol of Philadelphia now appeared in the garden with another photographer. He and Cardinal Wright shook hands and beamed into each other's faces, doing their best to scotch rumors of jealousy between the Archbishop of Philadelphia and his suffragan. It was very unusual for a suffragan bishop to be made a Cardinal, and everyone knew it meant that Wright could not return to Pittsburgh. Numerous reporters kept asking Wright where he was going, and the bulky Bishop of Pittsburgh kept insisting he didn't know. "I have no address. I am among the unemployed," he said. But at the luncheon they had discussed the virtual certainty that Pope Paul would appoint Jean Cardinal Villot of France the new Secretary of State. Since he had been prefect of the Sacred Congregation of the Clergy, it was almost equally certain that Wright would take this job, which would make him supervisor of 280,000 priests around the world. The mere thought of the headaches involved made Matthew Mahan shudder. There was something to be said for being an outsider.

Watching Cardinal Krol, who he knew would probably be the next president of the Bishops' Conference, Matthew Mahan suddenly felt uneasy. Krol was the kind of man the Vatican wanted to see running things in America and everywhere else in the world. He was an outspoken theological conservative, who hailed the birth control encyclical with trumpet blasts of rhetoric about the sacredness of human life. But at the same time he was a genial man, essentially likable. Was the Pauline line veering toward public relations to sell its bad judgment and worse theology? Stop, Matthew Mahan reproached himself. That was more than disloyal; it was almost heretical.

Riding back to the Apostolic Chancellery after lunch, Matthew Mahan told his driver to stop at a newsstand, and he bought several newspapers, including the Communist daily, L'Unita. All of them had extensive coverage of the consistory with profiles of the neo porporati and many paragraphs of speculation about the promotion of Villot, a moderate progressive, to the key post of Secretary of State. L'Unita doubted that it signaled any substantial change in the Vatican's direction, pointing out that conservative Archbishop Giovanni Benelli remained Substitute Secretary of State, and he was far more influential with the Pope.

Summing it all up, *L'Unita* dismissed the Villot appointment as another piece of Vatican window dressing, a sop thrown to the liberals.

At the consistory Pope Paul had appointed a theological commission, a recommendation that had been made by the first synod of bishops in 1967. The bishops' suggestion had been aimed at getting better representation for all schools of theological thought in Rome. Matthew Mahan winced to see how Paul had twisted it into a negative framework. The commission would, the Pope said, "set a limit to theological speculation," and define where speculation ended and heresy began. Three days ago, Matthew Mahan mused, he might have agreed with this approach. But now he heard only too clearly the harsh ring of the judicial gavel. But he did not want to go any further with that kind of thinking now. No, he sensed danger in it.

At the chancellery, the afternoon passed in a blur of faces and handshakes with dozens of diplomats, Cardinals, monsignors. Most were strangers to him; all were ill at ease in his presence. He was clearly a supernumerary. It was Wright and Cooke and Dearden that they came to see. Each of them had power, actually or potentially; it amounted to the same thing. He was an oddity, the accidental American friend of John. Matthew Mahan could readily imagine the whispered exchanges as they approached him. He could see the puzzlement in their eyes as they shook hands and extended suave congratulations. For a while, he found himself wishing Davey Cronin was with him, to give them his outrageous explanation of why Mahan was here.

The visits of Cardinal Jean Villot and Archbishop Giovanni Benelli were the only ones that caused Matthew Mahan to grow tense. Villot was now the second most powerful official in the Vatican. If Davey Cronin was right, and Romanita was the answer to his elevation to the cardinalate, here was the man who might tell him. But there was not even a hint of such a possibility in Villot's smooth very Gallic conversation. His thin face seemed animated by nothing but good humor as he talked of their mutual friendship with *neo porporato* Jean Derrieux. Benelli, a stocky intense man of medium height, had the same job Pope Paul had held under Pius XII. By reputation he was a tough operator, who often served as Paul's hatchet man. Today he had left his executive style in the Vatican. They joked about how well Cardinals

Mahan and Wright spoke Italian. If the habit spread among American bishops, Italy would be accused of cultural imperialism, Benelli said. Again there was not the tiniest hint of politics. But Romanita included the art of making the political remark at precisely the right moment. Perhaps this was not considered the time or the place.

Not until the end of the afternoon did Matthew Mahan see a face that he recognized as a friend. "Giorgio," he exclaimed when he saw the small, shy man in the doorway. It was Giorgio Bartoli, Pope John's valet. They shook hands enthusiastically, and Matthew Mahan inquired eagerly about his present status. "Oh, I'm well taken care of," he replied.

What was the name of John's secretary? He groped for a moment and found it. "How is Monsignor Capovilla? I hope they have taken good care of him, too."

"Oh yes. He is Archbishop of Chieti now."

"Chieti. I don't even know where that is."

"It is directly east from Rome, a few miles from the Adriatic coast."

"Is it what we call in America the sticks, the boondocks? An obscure place?"

"Very obscure," said Bartoli. "But that is what they want. All of us must be obscure. There is great fear of a cult, you know."

"Really?"

"Oh yes. I was warned that under no account must I sell any article of clothes, or religious goods, a Bible, a rosary, that sort of thing, that were given to me by the Holy Father. If I did, it would mean my head," he said, drawing his fingers across his throat. "You heard, of course, about the dedication of the doors?"

Matthew Mahan shook his head.

"The Manzu doors at St. Peter's, the bronze doors by the great sculptor. They were dedicated at sunset one day. No one was there but Manzu and his family and the Pope and a few monsignori. No one else. I was not invited, Monsignor Capovilla was not invited. The Holy Father's nephew, Monsignor Roncalli, was not invited. It was as if they wanted to keep the doors a secret."

Bartoli sighed and shook his head. "Some popes are as jealous as women. Do you know what Pope John said to Manzu? 'Let me know when your doors are finished and we will have a *festa*. We will invite everybody to come to St. Peter's to look at them.'"

Bartoli sighed again. "It is a poor way to do things. It has nothing to do with God, do you think, Eminence?"

"No," Matthew Mahan said. "No. Only with men. Popes are human, don't forget, my friend."

Bartoli nodded and stood up. They really had nothing more to say to each other. They were bound only by the name he had just spoken in Italian, *Papa Giovanni*. It was amazing how much better it sounded that way.

Matthew Mahan rode back to his hotel through the Roman dusk. It took a half hour to travel thirty or forty blocks in the appalling traffic. His stomach continued to ache dully. In the hotel lobby he saw Bill Reed sitting in a chair. Matthew Mahan was tempted for a moment to sneak past him. But he looked so forlorn, it would have been a sin against charity to even attempt it.

"Hello, Bill," he said. "Giving your feet a rest?"

"More or less," he said, good humor returning to his face. "Do you think maybe an atheist's feet get tired quicker than a Christian's feet tramping around all these churches?"

"I'll have to check that one out with the theologians at the Vatican."

One of the desk clerks touched Matthew Mahan on the elbow. "Eminence," he said, "this cable arrived for you an hour ago."

Matthew Mahan nodded his thanks and ripped it open. It was from Sister Agnes Marie at Mount St. Monica's College.

I THOUGHT YOU SHOULD KNOW THAT WE HAVE SENT SISTER HELEN REED TO ROME TO DEFEND OUR POINT OF VIEW AT THE SACRED CONGREGATION FOR THE RELIGIOUS. IF YOU WISH TO CONFER WITH HER, SHE WILL BE STAYING AT THE PENSIONE CHRISTINA.

"Look at this," Matthew Mahan said, handing the cable to Bill Reed. "That spitfire of a daughter of yours is here in Rome."

"Really," said Bill in a stricken voice. He stared dully at the telegram, and the forlorn look crept across his face again. "Well, I'm the last person she'd get in touch with."

"Now, that's absolutely absurd," said Matthew Mahan. "Let's get in a cab and go see her."

Bill shook his head. "No, Matt, I don't want to waste your time. In fact, as your doctor, I'm inclined to tell you to go upstairs and go to bed. You look exhausted."

"Baloney," he scoffed. "I'm operating on sanctifying grace."

"Sanctifying grace won't heal that ulcer," Bill said. "Only rest and quiet will do that. You've gotten damn little of either since we arrived."

Bill shook his head as Cardinal Mahan started to argue again. "It'll only be an unpleasant scene. And I'm not in the mood for one. Shelagh and I came here on our honeymoon, you know. I've been thinking about her ever since we arrived. I'm afraid it's got me down."

"All the more reason to see Helen. You used to say she was a carbon copy of her mother."

"Well—I would like to see her. But I don't want to hear—what I'll hear."

"Let's take a chance," said Matthew Mahan, deciding Bill was just depressed. What could a daughter, especially a daughter who was a nun, say to her father that would be so terrible?

Bill let himself be hoisted out of his chair and led to a taxi. It was another half hour of inching and horn blowing and cursing before they reached the Pensione Christina. The affable lady at the desk assured them that the American sister was in her room on the second floor. They went up the stairs.

"Who's that?" asked a young voice in response to Matthew Mahan's knock.

"A surprise," said Matthew Mahan.

Sister Helen opened the door. She was wearing a dark blue bathrobe and had her head encased in a towel. She had apparently just washed her hair. It made her face look stark and almost cruel in the shadowy hall light. Quickly, Matthew Mahan explained why they were here. "I thought you might want to have dinner tonight with me and this fellow," he said, nodding to Bill Reed.

His good cheer produced no response. "I'm sorry," Sister Helen said. "I already have a dinner date. With a friend of mine who left the order and is living here in Rome."

"Do you have time for an aperitif?"

"Not really. I'm getting dressed, as you can see. I have nothing to say to him," she said, staring stonily at her father. "Or to you, for that matter."

"Sister, this is no place for me to give you a lecture. But common politeness, not to mention Christian charity—"

"—has nothing to do with it," she said. "Neither of them. You must think you can work miracles with a wave of your episcopal hand. The difference between him and me is fundamental. It goes back to the Gospel. Didn't Christ say he would turn son against father and daughter against mother and so forth? That's what's happened here."

She stepped back and slammed the door in their faces. Bill Reed shook his head and took a deep breath. When he exhaled, it was almost a groan. "I told you, Matt. I told you."

As they rode back to their hotel in the taxi, Bill Reed looked moodily out the window at the Roman facades and said, "The one thing I can't figure out, Matt, is the way she quotes the Gospel at me. To be honest, I always thought that raising a daughter in the Catholic Church was the safest route I could take. The only thing I ever worried about was the possibility that she'd be too repressed."

"It isn't the same Catholic Church anymore, Bill," Matthew Mahan said mournfully.

"It looks the same and sounds the same to me—except when I start talking to Helen."

"Tell me something, Bill. Why haven't you married again? With a wife—"

"Yes, she wouldn't be able to hurt me quite so much. I know." He sighed, and still looking out the window, said, "I haven't got the guts, Matt. I couldn't go through—that pain again. Maybe it's because I'm a doctor. But it was a special kind of defeat for me to have my own wife die of cancer. To realize that I was hearing the symptoms at the breakfast table—and not paying any attention to them."

"Bill—that could happen to anyone. Any doctor."

"Sure. But it happened to me and I can't forgive myself."

"God forgives you, Bill."

"Yes, I suppose so. But I can't talk to him. So I'm stuck with doing the job for myself. We atheists, agnostics—whatever you want to call us, Matt—it all comes down to the same thing—have to play a double role, sinner and judge. We're pretty hard on ourselves."

"Can't you let a friend get into the act?" Matthew Mahan asked softly. "How about letting me masquerade as God for about sixty seconds? I'll put on all my regalia, miter, cape, the whole works.

No, better yet, we'll go up to my room and strip down to our undershirts and sit around drinking beer the way we used to in the aid station when there was a lull in the fighting. And when you're in the middle of telling me one of those dirty stories you loved to shock me with, I'll put my hand on your arm"—Matthew Mahan reached out as he spoke and made the gesture—"and say, 'Your sins are forgiven thee.'"

"Thanks, Matt," Bill Reed said in a choked voice. "But it wouldn't do any good. I'm a coward about pain, you see. I guess that's why I became a doctor. I don't have the guts to risk any more pain."

"Bill, that's bunk. You became a doctor because you love helping people. Do you think you ever fooled me for five seconds? Underneath that cynical mask you wear there's a man who cares— yes, even weeps the same way I do—for the children of men. That sounds like a sermon, but there isn't any better way to say it."

"You get tired of weeping, Matt, you just get tired, I guess."

They were in front of the hotel. Matthew Mahan stuffed some lire into the driver's hand and walked back into the lobby with Bill Reed. He was deeply worried about his old friend now. "My stomach would feel a hundred per cent better, Bill, if I made you a convert. Not necessarily a convert to Catholicism. A convert to—to the presence of God, to the awareness of someone who— who can lift the burdens off your back."

"But not off your stomach," Bill said mischievously. "Matt, it's enough for me to know I stir so much concern in you. It makes me believe that somehow, in spite of all the evidence to the contrary, I am doing something important."

Upstairs, Matthew Mahan sat down at the desk in his room and wrote a letter.

Dear Agnes,

I hesitate to write this letter to you. I am afraid I have always been a little in awe of you, since I sat beside you in old St. Patrick's and became convinced in a month or two that you already knew more than I could ever learn. Since that time I have heard even more awesome stories of your progress in the spiritual life, another field in which I fear I am only a dull normal at best. But a few hours ago here in Rome I encountered something so spiritually saddening, and at the same time so terrible, in one of your young sisters that I feel I must speak to you about it. I don't know whether you are even aware that Sister Helen Reed is bitterly alienated from her father. He is an introverted lonely man, a widower so deeply wounded by his wife's death, he has never attempted to achieve a comparable relationship with another person. This evening, with my usual overconfidence, I thought I could be the instrument of reconciliation. Instead, I made a fool of myself. I had to stand there and hear her say things to her father that only worsened his loneliness. I don't know where this great revolution which is wracking the Church will take us, but I am reminded tonight of a saying attributed to the liberator of Ireland, Daniel O'Connell, that no political revolution in the world was worth the loss of a single life. I believe that the greatest imaginable revolution in the Church is not worth the loss of a single soul. Tonight I saw a soul in torment, in grave danger of being lost. I should add that Dr. Reed is not a Catholic. But other sheep I have which are not of this fold.

Sincerely yours in Christ,
Matthew Mahan

P.S.: I've decided not to see Cardinals Confalonieri and Antoniutti. If we can't settle our differences among ourselves, we don't deserve to be called Christians. In next year's budget, your sisters will have $25,000 from the Archdiocese to help pay their expenses downtown. I will also try to keep St. Clare's Hospital open.

Letter in hand, Matthew Mahan knocked on Dennis McLaughlin's door. He found his secretary, his Jesuit friend Andy Goggin, and Davey Cronin poring over a road map. They were driving up to Florence tomorrow to visit the suburb of Isolotto, which was apparently involved in a nasty clash with the Vatican. Matthew Mahan shook his head. "Don't you ever quit looking for ammunition?"

"Now, Matt, you can't deny this isn't rare stuff," said Cronin. "A revolution practically in Il Papa's backyard. You might be glad to know a bit about it yourself the next time you get one of those nasty stop-everything billet-doux from some Curia Cardinal. You can fire back a comment about the beam in his own eye."

Matthew Mahan yawned and gave Dennis the letter to mail. "I'm going to bed. If anybody is looking for me, tell them I'm having my tiara fitted at Castel Gondolfo."

"Oh, I almost forgot," Dennis said as he was going out the door. "There was a priest named Mirante looking for you here at the hotel about a half hour ago."

"He's an old friend. I meant to tell you that I wanted to see him, no matter when or where."

"Here's his telephone number," said Dennis, handing him a slip of paper. "He seemed awfully anxious to hear from you."

Matthew Mahan sighed. All he wanted to do was sleep. But he went next door and asked the hotel operator to place the call for him. A half hour later, Father Mirante was in the sitting room of his suite, fingering a glass of Cinzano and talking about their mutual friend, Mary Shea.

"She is depressed, poor lady," Mirante said. "It is almost an epidemic these days in Rome among a certain sect. We might call them the Johannines."

"Is it—serious?"

"I have sent her to the best psychiatrist in Rome. One who understands—and even occasionally believes in—the reality of the religious factor. The situation as he explains it is really quite simple. She is celibate, like us. She, too, has invested most of her emotional capital in, shall we say, Vatican futures. And finds herself in a declining market."

"Is it really that bad, Guilio?"

Mirante's downcast mouth drooped to a Pagliacci smile. "You are asking a prejudiced observer."

"You're in trouble. Mary told me. Why?"

"You have perhaps heard of Isolotto?"

"Oh yes, the parish up in Florence. They seem to be having some sort of brawl with the local bishop. My secretary and my auxiliary bishop are going up there tomorrow to take a look."

"Eminence," Mirante said, "I am the last person in the world who should give anyone advice, but do you think that's wise? Are you prepared to inject yourself into the controversy?"

"Of course not," said Matthew Mahan, the pain in his stomach leaping into contrapuntal life. "I can't see any harm in them visiting the parish—"

"It is much more than a dispute between the parish and the

bishop. It has become a test of Roman authority. That is why I am no longer a member of the Jesuit order."

Swiftly he sketched the background of the case. Some militants had occupied Parma Cathedral to protest the links between diocesan authorities and local banks. The parishioners of the parish of Isolotto wrote a letter announcing their solidarity with the protesters. The parish priest, Don Inzo Mazzi, signed the letter. Pope Paul condemned the protesters, and the Cardinal Archbishop of Florence, Ermene Gildo Florit, immediately called on Mazzi to retract his signature or resign. It was the climax of a fifteen-year-old feud between Florit and Mazzi. The Cardinal had already made it clear that he disapproved of the pastor's attacks on the war in Vietnam and his fondness for letting laymen speak from the pulpit.

Mazzi turned the Cardinal's ultimatum over to the parish community. They stood squarely behind the pastor. Florit suspended Mazzi and closed the church. Months of guerrilla warfare followed. There were marches on the Archbishop's palace with placards saying, "Call off your fascist watchdogs," police arrests of demonstrators, packed rallies in the Isolotto church, and a meeting of parish representatives with Archbishop Benelli, the Substitute Secretary of State. When a neighboring priest, Don Sergio Gomiti, expressed sympathy for Don Mazzi, he, too, was fired and had his church closed. Currently, about three hundred people held a Bible service each Sunday in front of the still locked Isolotto church. Perhaps fifty people attended the official parish mass celebrated in a small chapel by a priest sent by Cardinal Florit.

"They sent me up to mediate. The cool intellectual who would see both sides of the question. I am an intellectual, but I am also a priest. And that part of my being was totally converted to the parishioners' side. These people are asking nothing more than the holy freedom proclaimed for the Church by John. They are good Catholics—better Catholics, in fact, than ninety-five per cent of the population in Cardinal Florit's diocese. I decided they needed support, not discipline, and I made a statement on their behalf. What followed was a nightmare. I was ordered to return to Rome immediately. When I arrived, I was told to say nothing more on the case, under the pain of excommunication. A week later, I was expelled from the Jesuit order and told to leave my quarters in the Borgo Santo Spirito within twenty-four hours.

"All my papers, my books, were confiscated, my orphanage taken away from me, and I was told to report to the Archbishop of Reggio Di Calabria, if I wished to continue to serve God as a priest. For the last week I have been living with friends in Rome. But this cannot continue. I must either go to Calabria or—"

He opened his hands in a gesture of helplessness.

"I'm appalled," Matthew Mahan said. "That's all I can say. Appalled. But what—what else can I say—or do?"

"Would Your Eminence consider allowing me to return to America with you? I would be happy to serve you—in any capacity. You have, as I recall, several parishes with a heavy percentage of Italians. I am not afraid of becoming a parish priest. Perhaps it is the very thing I should become. But to be sentenced to it, to go to a part of Italy where all my Roman instincts will revolt at the mere sound of their Italian. I think I could train an ape to speak our language better than a Calabrian."

"You won't hear any classic Italian in my downtown parishes, Guilio. The people are mostly from Sicily."

"But they are Americans. That is what I want to experience. To speak, to work with people who have freedom, or a hope of freedom in their blood."

"Don't romanticize that word 'freedom,' Guilio. It's a reality. It means something. But—"

"I will do my best to learn by your example. I can never forget that you—"

He stopped in mid-sentence. Did he see on Matthew Mahan's face the refutation of what he was about to say? This was too painful to believe. Softly, tautly, he finished the sentence for Mirante. "—were consecrated by John. But don't—for God's sake don't expect to see a saint like him in these shoes."

"I know, I know," Mirante said. "And tomorrow you will take an oath of obedience, of fealty to the new Pope." He drained his drink. "You see I can't even pronounce his name. For me he is—a usurper. A traitor. Yes, even a heretic!"

"Now, that is ridiculous, Guilio."

Mirante slumped back in his seat, setting his glass down with a clunk on the table beside it. "You're right," he said. "You're absolutely right. He's the Pope of Agony. But for me, his agony is obscene. He knows but he cannot act. When he acts, he tries not to know. The Pope of Agony, yes. But also Punchinello." He laughed bitterly. "Every night when I go to sleep, those lines from Giuseppe Giusti's fantasy come into my head. Do you know what I mean?"

Matthew Mahan shook his head. "I've never read him."

Mirante nodded. "There is no reason why you should. He was a minor poet, basically a satirist, who died in 1850. Most of his writing had to be printed outside Italy and circulated here surreptitiously. Those were the days when the Pope ruled the papal states, you know. At any rate, Giusti wrote this poem about Father Pero, a happy, simple priest who had been elected pope. The mere possibility of him practicing Christianity on the papal throne threw everyone in a panic."

Rapidly he recited in Italian.

> . . . questo papa spiritato
> che vuol far l'apostolo,
> ripescare in pro' del Cielo
> colle reti del Vangelo
> pesci che ci scappino.
> Questo e' un papa in buona fede,
> e' un papaccio che ci crede,
> diamogli l'arsenico!

Matthew Mahan translated it for himself, losing the poetry but getting the meaning easily enough.

> Here's a pope who's trying to be an Apostle
> Casting gospel nets
> For the fish that get away.
> Here's a pope who has real faith,
> A fool of a pope
> Who believes what he says
> Let's poison him today.

"That's very good, Guilio," Matthew Mahan said, smiling in the hope of restoring Mirante's sanity, "but I hope you're not suggesting—"

"No, no. I am in an extreme mood, but not that extreme." He even came close to smiling, but it faded away with the last word.

What should he do with this unhappy man? There was an air of

270

innocence about him that was touching. It reminded him of Dennis McLaughlin. Innocence and bitterness, with Mirante's bitterness more extruded, more Italian. "Excuse me a moment," Matthew Mahan said.

He went into the bedroom and returned with his checkbook. "The first thing you need is some money. Here's five hundred dollars. It ought to keep body and soul together for a month or so. Write to the Archbishop of Calabria and tell him you've decided, with his permission, to go to America. When you arrive, I'll have something lined up for you. Maybe at the university. Maybe in a parish. Our Italian-Americans are awfully conservative. I'm not sure how you'd get along with them."

"I see what you are thinking," said Mirante. "This fellow has proved himself a fool once. What happens if he does it again in my archdiocese and embarrasses me? Let me assure you, Eminence, the loyalty of the beggar is to the man who lifts him from the gutter. So it will be with this beggar, I swear it."

"I'm sure it will, I'm sure it will," Matthew Mahan said, too embarrassed to deny what he was thinking. "I just want to make sure you don't see me as another John. I'm not. I have no pretensions to that kind of holiness. A bishop—at least an American bishop—has to run his diocese with the greater good of the greater number in mind."

He stopped, somewhat appalled at the implications of what he had just said. But wasn't it true? Did all the emotion of the last two days wither in the cold rational light of this premise? No, somehow both realities must be sustained.

"That interests me greatly," Mirante was saying. "Is it because the great majority of American Catholics actively practice the faith? You are not faced with the dilemma of empty churches as we here in Italy?"

"Yes, that's partly true."

"I am told they are literalists. They take the folk religion and practice all of its precepts. But not the latest, on contraception. Why is that?"

"Because it makes no sense to them. Even the folk religion, as you call it, has to be in touch with the heart. With their experience. Well"—Matthew Mahan stood up—"I'm afraid I'm too tired to make much sense on this subject. Let me know your plans as soon as you complete them, and we'll do our best to make you useful. For the time being, I wouldn't say a word about this to anyone."

"Of course not, of course not." Tears suddenly filled Mirante's eyes. "I can't tell you how grateful—" He knelt and tried to kiss Matthew Mahan's ring.

"Oh no, please, Guilio, it isn't necessary." He helped the fragile, sad-faced man to his feet and threw his right arm around him. Where have you seen someone else do that? In a movie or— As he closed the door, he suddenly remembered. It was John. The way John had greeted him in the Vatican on his first visit.

XXI

Driving through Rome. Darkened streets, then squares flashing with lights from every century. Neon twentieth. Renaissance candle glow. Beside him, Bishop Cronin was strangely silent. Above Cronin's head, which only reached the Cardinal's shoulder, Dennis could see Matthew Mahan's somber profile in flashes, as the lights alternately filled and fled the gliding limousine. You would almost think we were going to a funeral, Dennis mused. What was it Cronin had said three days ago? Wait till you hear the oath they take.

The old boy probably knew what he was talking about. A Cardinal was the Pope's man. It was a special relationship. Old Davey did not want to see Matthew Mahan become anybody's man. Because he wanted him for himself? No, nothing quite so cheap or obvious. There was something mysterious between them, a common understanding that they shared about the Church.

It was visible when the Cardinal came into their room last night and told them to forget about their trip to Isolotto. He and Goggin had been outraged, but Cronin was amazingly mild about it. *I couldn't agree with you more, Matt,* he had said. *No point in stirring up the animals.* If they wanted to find out more about Isolotto, Mahan had suggested they call the Jesuit, Father Mirante, whom he had just seen. An ex-Jesuit, actually. But Matthew Mahan had wryly observed that he considered such a being a metaphysical impossibility. Once a Jesuit, always a Jesuit. "What do you think, Dennis?"

They had kidded for a few moments. Then Mahan had become serious, almost sad, and had urged him to go see Sister Helen Reed. "Talk to her about her father. I've never seen anything so cruel—" He told them about his impromptu visit to Helen's pensione with her father in tow.

Go see Sister Helen Reed. An episcopal command, no less. Why had he tried to make excuses, while Goggin eyed him mordantly? Was he afraid of what might happen? Did fornication in the shadow of St. Peter's dome guarantee damnation? Childish, mocking questions, along with buffets of intense anxiety. Torn between sex and your priesthood. When there was no conflict, no reason for a conflict in the new order, in the Church of tomorrow, where every act of love would be equally valued. Dennis squirmed in his seat, as if hands were seizing, caressing his flesh. He did not believe it. Too much history in his head. The mind, that unique analytical tool, mocked hope as well as faith.

But he had gone to see Sister Helen while Goggin and Cronin were seeing Father Mirante, the living contradiction. Another lunch on the terrace overlooking the brown polluted Tiber. Helen was furious. There were only two women—two—employed in the entire Vatican. It was enough to make her consider becoming a Buddhist. She had not even come close to seeing Cardinal Antoniutti. A polite monsignor listened to her tale for an hour and a half, took copious notes, and assured her that it would be brought to the Cardinal's attention. As for an answer before she left Rome—impossible, my dear Sister. The Cardinal's duties— the week of ceremonies for the new Cardinals.

Dennis tried to joke her into a better humor. He told her why Matthew Mahan had sent him. With enough money to buy the most expensive lunch on the menu. They would start with champagne. Then discuss the solution to their parent problems. He had a mother, she had a father. Match them up, and let them haunt each other. But seriously, her father was a charming man. Why—?

Yes, through all the mockery, the oblique intentions, there was a priest's concern. What was it, exactly? Perhaps you are about to discover something essential. You are the enemy of cruelty, of hate, the apostle of compassion, forgiveness. Marvelous. So is Mother.

So is Pious Paolo. What if that's all there was to it? No matter who else was for it or against it. To find out the precise tone your own soul struck. That would be something above mere knowledge, or beneath it. Beyond words, those razors that always cut flesh to clarify.

Then there were her hands. Leading you up the stairs to the blue-walled bedroom, the smoky Tiber flowing, sunlight on the quilted rose bedspread. Today what would it be? More half love, celibate caressing? No, no, no. Passion as the trembling hands shed clothes like leaves. Feet, legs, like roots deep in the ancient earth of Rome. No. Hands angry on the small snub breasts. Today would be the love of the man for the woman. Absolute, absolute, absolute sunlight and darkness there between her legs, dark hair, precious earth where seeds were summoned by nature's blind will. What does God have to do with any of it? God is clarity, light, light, light. Why at the very climax was there a desire to weep? Poor old Goggin, a dry wind whistling through the Dead Sea Scrolls.

Suddenly tears, a trembling woman in your arms. *Hold me hold me hold me please hold me. I'm afraid it's sinful to make love that way. Hold me hold me hold me. Dennis can we really love each other?*

For the first time the appalling truth of her woundedness. For the first time a glimpse of what loss of love, mother love, then father love, had done to her. Then strength, amazing compassionate strength flowing from you into her, strength of touch, of paradoxical tenderness, and strength of word, of promise. *Yes, yes,* had been the sure loving answer. Where had this strength come from? A mystery. Or was the answer sitting beside you in this car, the big bulky man in red looking mournfully out the other window?

"Is there a reception after this?" Matthew Mahan asked. "I've forgotten."

"Yes, but only a brief one, our monsignor says. No drinks."

"Good. My stomach is killing me. Did you get anywhere with Sister Helen?"

Dennis's chest tightened. For a minute he thought he was strangling. "No. She is—obstinately convinced that her father is the personification of racist reaction."

"God help us. What damn nonsense. Where do people her age get these ideas?"

From the newspapers. But you will not say it, Dennis. No, the apostle of universal love will be silent.

A half hour later, Matthew Mahan sat in the Hall of Benedictions directly above the entrance to St. Peter's Basilica. There were about two thousand people in the huge room, and at least a thousand of them were Americans. Their language predominated in the murmur of general conversation. The thirty-four new Cardinals sat on the right, the hundred or so senior Cardinals on the left. All were dressed in their red robes and ceremonial red capes and white lace rochets. Before them, on a platform about two feet above the floor level, sat Paul VI in white robes and a red cape fringed with ermine. Matthew Mahan had seen dozens of pictures of the Pope. Like almost every other Catholic American, he had followed on television his historic visit to the United Nations in 1965. But television images were no substitute for the living man. The television camera lied, just like every other camera. More important those earlier images in his mind were faded with age. Now, at this moment in time, he wanted to know what he thought and felt about this man.

The huge armchair in which Paul sat made him look almost ludicrously small. His feet rested upon two raised steps on the platform. The Pope began speaking in Latin. Matthew Mahan was dismayed. He had hoped that the speech would be in Italian. His Latin was a patchwork job, propped up largely by his knowledge of Italian. During the Vatican Council he had joined Cardinal Cushing of Boston and many other American prelates who had pleaded with the Pope for a simultaneous translation system, so that they could follow the debates and perhaps contribute to them in their own languages. The request had gone unheeded, and Cushing, who had no backup Italian to help him, had finally gone home in disgust. The Pope was talking about the place of Cardinals in the structure of the Church. He declared them to be of great importance. The task, he said, was to build up the Church. He called on them to serve, to witness, to sacrifice for the truth. Above all, he depended on them for their unswerving support of the Prince of the Apostles. He hoped he would always be able to say, "You continued with me in my trials."

As he had done in the previous consistory in 1967, Paul was reiterating his conviction that the College of Cardinals was no anachronism, as many leading churchmen of the liberal wing had been saying. Cardinal Suenens of Belgium had recently suggested that an annual synod of bishops or an assembly of the heads of the bishops' conference in each country should replace the Cardinals as the electors of the Pope. Paul was giving this idea the back of his hand.

It was easy enough to explain. Whether the explanation was sweet or sour depended on your point of view. Sour: The Curia had no intention of surrendering control of the Church to a bunch of unknowns. As long as they handpicked the Cardinals, they were almost certain to have one of their own in the Chair of Peter. True, the system wasn't perfect. A secret saint like John XXIII might slip by them once in a century. But the odds were heavily in favor of keeping all heads turned to Rome. In line with this, Paul was obviously working on the principle, the more Cardinals, the more Romans in the Church. Sweet: When you have inherited a system that has worked smoothly for four hundred years, you are not inclined to surrender it to critics who seem more than a little unstable emotionally and intellectually. Critics were hardly a novelty in the long history of the Church. Mater Ecclesia endures forever, the critics disappear.

On his throne Pope Paul was comparing the synod of bishops and the College of Cardinals. He said both offices were consultative. Neither one interfered in the least with the Pope's prerogative of personal universal and direct government. Basically the Cardinals assisted him in this responsibility.

There it was, the note that had been sounded with ever more insistence in the closing sessions of Vatican II. The Chair of Peter had no intention of abandoning its claim to absolute authority over the entire Church. Wasn't it, from Paul's point of view, the only possible decision? The responsibility for abandoning authority might be more agonizing than the results of wielding it. As a wielder of authority in his own small world, Matthew Mahan knew that much. Was there a dimension between these two alternatives, was that where Michelangelo's Moses was looking with that eternal spiritual hunger on his graven face? Was that where John XXIII lived? Why couldn't Cardinal Mahan and the men around him—above all, the tiny figure on the huge throne—enter this Promised Land? *O Lord tell us, tell us what we are doing wrong,* Matthew Mahan prayed.

Now the Pope asked each of them to take their traditional vow of fidelity to Christ and obedience to the Chair of Peter. There was, he explained, an additional passage added to the oath, in order to insure his access to the advice and counsel of all the Cardinals.

The priest standing to the right of the papal throne began to read the vow and the Cardinals repeated it after him, inserting their individual names in the first line.

I, MATTHEW MAHAN, CARDINAL OF THE HOLY ROMAN CHURCH, PROMISE AND SWEAR THAT FROM THIS HOUR ON, FOR AS LONG AS I LIVE, I SHALL BE FIRMLY FAITHFUL TO CHRIST AND HIS GOSPEL AND OBEDIENT TO ST. PETER AND THE HOLY APOSTOLIC ROMAN CHURCH AND TO THE SUPREME PONTIFF PAUL VI AND HIS SUCCESSORS LAWFULLY AND CANONICALLY ELECTED: FURTHERMORE THAT I SHALL NEVER DIVULGE TO ANYONE THE DELIBERATIONS ENTRUSTED TO ME BY THEM EITHER DIRECTLY OR INDIRECTLY TO THEIR DAMAGE OR DISHONOR UNLESS WITH THE CONSENT OF THE APOSTOLIC SEE.

MAY THE ALL-POWERFUL GOD SO HELP ME.

Matthew Mahan kept his eyes on the Pope's face while he repeated these words. Again he felt an intense desire to locate this man in his own soul. The words he had just spoken had enormous weight. He had vowed his personal loyalty, his personal obedience, to this man. It was a huge step beyond the loyalty and obedience he owed him as the head of the Church, and he was prepared, he truly was prepared, to say these words. But not the words of the added passage. The vow of silence traduced the first vows. A worm of nasty distrust entered with them. Why, why? Matthew Mahan knew what old Davey Cronin would say. The hallmark of authoritarianism. It always goes too far because it thinks in terms of power first and people second.

But Matthew Mahan did not see any of this on Paul's face. He saw only sadness there, a film of sadness through which the personal man spoke and acted. Was it the sadness of defeat or the sadness of the ultimately lonely?

One by one now, as each Cardinal's name was called, he mounted the platform and knelt before the papal throne. Solemnly Paul placed the red biretta on his head, repeating in Latin the ancient formula. "For the praise of the omnipotent God and for the honor of the Apostolic See, receive the red hat, symbol of the great dignity of the Cardinal, which means that you must show yourself to be fearless, even to the shedding of blood, for the exaltation of the Holy Faith, for the peace and tranquillity of the Christian people, and for the liberty and expansion of the Holy Roman Church."

Predictably, Cardinal Cooke got the biggest round of applause. At least five hundred of the thousand Americans in the hall were from New York. Finally, Matthew Mahan heard his own name and he rose to walk up the red-carpeted aisle. As he knelt before the Pope, he looked up at him and their eyes met. The tiniest hint of a smile appeared on Paul's lips. "*Frater noster taciturnus*," he whispered. Taking the red biretta from the monsignor, he placed it on Matthew Mahan's head, reciting the Latin exhortation once more.

Our silent brother. Back in his seat, Matthew Mahan fingered the hat on his head and pondered the words, which now seemed to have a voice of their own, repeating themselves again and again in his mind. *Frater noster taciturnus, our silent brother*.

He knew precisely what they meant. Old Davey was right. They were aware of his silence on the birth control encyclical, the great issue of Paul's pontificate. Yet he did not feel that the words were a rebuke. No, it was typical of the man at the moment of conferring the greatest honor in his power to bestow. All he could do was whisper these heartbreaking words. Not a rebuke, but a plea, a sad somber plea.

Then that insidious word *Romanita* flowered in his mind. The moment, the most precisely, cruelly effective moment, had been selected to deliver the essential message. What was the message? This honor that we are bestowing on you, Cardinal Mahan, has nothing whatsoever to do with your three decades of labor on behalf of Holy Mother Church and even less with what slim pretensions you might have to spiritual stature.

You have been bought up, Cardinal Mahan, as part of a worldwide, astutely managed political campaign. When we dangled the bait, you snapped at it on the first pass and now we are pulling on the hook.

No, Matthew Mahan told himself desperately, no. He refused to believe that appallingly cynical explanation. There was no proof, no proof whatsoever, that anyone, above all the sad-eyed man on the papal throne in front of him, was party to such a demeaning, dehumanizing, demoralizing plot. *Frater noster taciturnus.* It was perfectly natural for Paul to think of him as a silent brother. Yet he had placed the red hat on his brother's head. Couldn't that be interpreted as proof of his generosity, his willingness to tolerate reasonable dissent, loyal freedom within the Church? Yes, yes, Matthew Mahan told himself, he would not, he could not, allow his mind to accept the cynical explanation. *Romanita.* The word quivered down his nerves like fingers scratching a blackboard.

Cardinal Yu Pin, the Archbishop of Nanking, China, was now replying on behalf of the new Cardinals, expressing their gratitude to Paul and vowing their fidelity to him. He was not, in Matthew Mahan's opinion, the best choice to represent them. According to stories he had heard from several Italian friends, Pius XII had berated Pin for fleeing to Taiwan with Chiang Kai-shek when the Communists took over China. But the speech was only a formality, and Pin had probably been chosen for the color of his skin. It was Vatican policy to emphasize the Church's international composition these days.

After thanking Pin, Pope Paul announced a major change in his cabinet. Cardinal Jean Villot was to become Secretary of State, replacing Cardinal Amleto Cicognani. He summoned the eighty-six-year-old Cicognani to the platform beside him and asked Villot to join them. He praised both men for their devotion to the Church and their tireless efforts on her behalf, and particularly on behalf of the Chair of St. Peter. There was applause from the audience. Villot looked tough, and Cicognani's lumpy old-man's face was sour. In his twenty-five years as apostolic delegate to the United States, Cicognani had shown himself to be a blundering authoritarian, repeatedly sticking his nose into American church affairs and throwing his Roman weight around. Yet John XXIII had appointed him Secretary of State, the second most powerful man in the Vatican after the Pope. It was a tragic commentary on John's helplessness. Except for his epochal break-through, the council, he had been a prisoner of the Curia.

The consistory was over. Paul went down the aisle and vanished through the curtains at the back of the hall. Laymen and priests swarmed around their Cardinals for another round of congratulations. Matthew Mahan smiled, nodded into familiar faces, shook dozens of hands, while the words echoed in his mind. *Frater noster taciturnus*. A sullen ache crept across his stomach.

They drove directly to the Hotel Excelsior, where all of the Mahanites, as Dennis McLaughlin occasionally called them, were giving a dinner for their favorite Cardinal. It was a pleasant evening but a little embarrassing. Speaker after speaker heaped praise on him until he began to wonder if they were talking about somebody else. He heard himself extolled as a war hero, the finest chaplain in the U. S. Army, a friend of the blacks, the Jews, the Italians, the Irish, even the Protestants.

He stood up finally, to cries of "Speech, speech," and good-humoredly denied it all. "I just happen to be a very lucky fellow," he said. "I've been in the right place at the right time again and again." Informally, without the slightest pretense to having a prepared talk, he rambled from memory to memory, speaking to individuals in the audience. He asked George Petrie if he remembered the time the schedules got scrambled and the girls' basketball team from Holy Angels found themselves pitted against the downtown mugs of St. Sebastian's parish. He asked Madeline McAvoy if she remembered the dedication of Our Lady of the Angels Catholic Home for the Aged, when he inadvertently became the straight man for an eighty-year-old Irish lady. She asked him, " 'How old do you think I am?'

"I flattered her and said seventy. Then I asked her how old she thought I was. She took me seriously and guessed forty. I told her she was off by ten years and she didn't bat an eye. 'Well, glory be to God, Bishop,' she said, 'you never worked a day in your life.' "

Dennis McLaughlin sat in the back of the hall listening to the adulatory laughter. Beside him, Bishop Cronin was laughing as heartily as anyone in the audience, as the Cardinal reminisced now about his failings as a seminarian. "I am morally certain," he was saying, "that I am the only Cardinal in the history of the Church who got zero in a theology examination. I wasn't totally ignorant, but the teacher, a fellow named Cronin, only asked one question on the examination. If you didn't know a lot about that one subject, you were in deep trouble. That year, he asked us to discuss in depth the influence of the Council of Ephesus on the development of Christian theology. I got Ephesus mixed up with Chalcedon and a half-dozen other towns in the Middle East. I wrote pages and pages of absolute baloney, but I thought they were worth something. When I got a zero, I went to see this fellow Cronin and asked him why. He answered, 'Because there was no lower mark I could give you, Mahan.'"

What is the reason for your nonlaughter, Dennis? Was it the memory of this afternoon's lovemaking—an idiotic word, but somehow descriptive—in the Pensione Christina that made you unable to tolerate this sentimentality? Who knows, who knows. Jesus said no man can serve two masters. Loving one, hating another was inevitable. Or was it? Didn't the mind, the sovereign intellect, as someone called it, have something to say about such decisions? Or was democracy also a psychobiological phenomenon?

Was there a voice of the cells, the genes, that was summoning him now to reject once and for all this big bulky man in the red cape and incongruous lace skirt smiling at him from the head table? Why in the steady motionless light cast by electricity did shafts of sunlight repeatedly break across his eyes? Why did those rows of smiling faces turn without warning into white crosses? Why was there a hand on his arm, a heavy father's hand and a father's voice speaking, not the harsh words of contempt, condemnation (no, you spoke those—how merciless we will be to ourselves if we finally do get rid of God), but gentle forgiving words? Jesus, Jesus, Jesus.

He stood up. The Cardinal was still talking. There was only the slightest break as their eyes met. "I don't want you to think of me as Cardinal Mahan. I hope I'll always be Father Matt to every one of you. There's only one way in which I want to be a Cardinal. In Latin the word means hinge. I want to play that part in our city. I want to be a man who opens doors for everyone, doors to hope in the future, doors to faith in God, doors to love for every person in the city, no matter what his religion or his color may be."

Tremendous applause. Dennis McLaughlin turned his back on those noble words and rushed to the door. He tripped over someone's foot and almost fell on his face. His hand groped for the gold doorknob, cold beneath his sweaty fingers. Out in the hall then, gulping antihistamines, his chest expanding only to a point where pain awoke, like the thrust of a dagger. No, no, no. It was freedom that he was fighting to preserve. His precious birthright, stolen from him by Holy Mother Church. Yes, freedom.

He was breathing again. Freedom from Wholly Mother.

Did those ironies mean anything now? Weren't you really running away from that sentimental man at the speaker's table? That complex man who combined roars and smiles, power and guile, fear and love. Summed up in one unbearable word. Father.

XXII

Matthew Mahan's miter pressed painfully on his throbbing temples as the procession of white-and-gold-robed Cardinals left the Chapel of the Pietà and began the long walk to St. Peter's main altar. As they entered the immense nave, through the open front doors they could hear the distant sound of bands playing and crowds cheering. It was May 1, and Rome's Communists were filling the city's streets with pageantry and protest. Out there, some might say, was the voice of the future. Here they were about to pay obeisance to the past, to re-enact a ceremony that was two thousand years old.

Rome's streets had echoed to the march of many men, Caesar's legions, Napoleon's chasseurs, Hilter's troopers. It was easy to say that the Communists were another false faith, another easy answer to man's perpetual search for worldly happiness. While here within these sacred walls was the true answer, a faith that said life was not merely a puzzle to be solved. But recent years had made Matthew Mahan wary about this glib use of resounding truths. The hostility of the young had sharpened his eyes and quickened his ears to incongruous details like those distant Communist bands. Ahead of him marched thirty-three men like himself, Princes of the Church, dressed in white and gold. Should a church created by a man who said, "Blessed are the poor in spirit," have princes? His eyes rested for a moment on the chapel of Pius X where he knew the bronze relief of John XXIII reached out to the pleading faces behind bars. A moment later he stared at the white marble monument of tiared Gregory XIII, sitting on his coffin. Two statues symbolizing science and religion gazed in awe at his great achievement, dramatized on the side of the sarcophagus, the reform of the calendar. The Church had power in those days, unquestionably. But according to old Davey Cronin, Gregory had a natural son and used to spend most of his time during mass gossiping with his Cardinals. His chief interest was building the chapel named after him, the Capella Gregoriana. When he died, he was buried like a pharaoh, his body drenched in balsam and aromatic herbs, wearing full pontifical robes and a golden miter. What did monuments to these egotistical Renaissance princes have to do with Christianity, with the simple men in dusty robes who trudged the roads of Palestine? *The foxes have holes, and the birds of the air nests; but the Son of Man hath not where to lay his head.*

Who was sending him these thoughts? Was it the voice of John XXIII speaking to him? His mind drifted back to last night. The party had ended in his suite, with Mike Furia, Mary Shea, the McAvoys, Bill Reed, his sister in law Eileen, Monsignor Frank Falconer, and a half-dozen other members of his seminary class killing off some very good champagne. That was why his head was aching and his stomach twinging, and maybe it also explained his wayward mind. They had spent the last half hour discussing the difference between Popes John and Paul. He had surprised himself by rather strenuously defending Paul. He needed time. Turning the Church in a new direction was an immense responsibility; it had to be done slowly.

But inevitably, so it seemed, he soon found himself talking more about John. *When the editor of* Osservatore Romano *came to see him, it was the first time he'd been inside the papal apartment in thirteen years. Pacelli kept him at arm's length. The old guy proceeded to start interviewing John, on his knees. That was the way he talked to Pacelli. John told him if he didn't sit down, the interview was over.*

They call Montini the poor man's Pacelli, Mary Shea had said.

He loved to walk. The first time I met him, in Paris, we had lunch and then he suggested a stroll over to the Left Bank. He walked my legs off. And I was a chaplain in an infantry regiment.

So was he, come to think of it. Anyway, Pacelli told him to stop walking around Paris. It was undignified for a papal nuncio.

I never could figure out what we had in common. He was really an intellectual, you know. He used to call me his American education. He must have asked me a couple of hundred questions about America, that first day. We were the future, he said. Later, he called me his American son. It sounds better in Italian. More playful. Mio figlio americano.

Somewhere behind Matthew Mahan a roar of acclaim filled the cathedral. The crowd was greeting Pope Paul. On a raised platform to the right of the high altar, Dennis McLaughlin and Bishop Cronin sat next to a woman who obviously had no ticket to these select seats. She was Italian, as far as Dennis could gather from the prayers she murmured. She wore a red and black kerchief around her head, and a coat that was several decades old. In a bundle at her feet there seemed to be almost everything from cheese and bread on which she dined to handkerchiefs, books, a veritable portmanteau. With her was a small thin boy of about ten who knelt beside his mother and prayed with equal intensity.

When Pope Paul came in view, walking at the rear of the procession, his hand raised in blessing, the woman went berserk. "*Evviva il Papa, Evviva il Papa,*" she screeched, almost fracturing Dennis's eardrum. To anyone even a few feet away, her howl was swallowed in the general applause. Tears were streaming down the woman's face now. With surprising strength she raised her son high so he could see the Pope, too. She murmured to him in Italian, and the little boy began to cry.

Dennis pondered the paradox that the woman presented. Back at the university they had all agreed like good intellectuals that the Church must return to simple first-century Christianity if it was to serve the poor. Away with gold miters and bejeweled chalices, immense cathedrals with their stained-glass windows and overwhelming statuary. But what if the poor didn't want first-century Christianity? What if they *wanted* splendor, solemnity, mystery?

At a table on the high altar, the Pope and the thirty-four new Cardinals began concelebrating mass. They looked like a flock of exotic birds, Yeats' golden birds from fabled Byzantium, perhaps, except that these birds were flesh and blood, living anachronisms, Dennis thought.

On the altar, standing between Cardinals Cooke and Carberry, Matthew Mahan raised his eyes above the blaze of light that engulfed them and glimpsed familiar faces in the stands. It was a little like dying, he thought, watching the circle of loving faces recede from flesh to wavery vapor. There was Mary Shea and Mike Furia and Bill Reed, all looking very solemn. And his sister-in-law, Eileen, and Timmy. He had paid very little attention to them since he arrived. Timmy was probably sneering that he only had time for the big givers. But their pastor, Monsignor Frank Falconer, was taking good care of them, Eileen had told him at the dinner last night. Matthew Mahan said a prayer of gratitude for the good solid steady priests like Frank Falconer who refused to permit the current turmoil to distract them from the fundamentals of their job—an abiding concern for their people that showed itself in a thousand ways.

In gaps between the masses of spectators winked the red eyes of the television cameras. The old and the new. The Church was trying, trying so desperately, to come to terms with the transformed world. Somberly now, his eyes sought the face of Pope Paul, whose hands were outstretched, reading in Latin the prayer of the mass, asking God for the grace to follow the example and intercession of St. Joseph. Next he read the Epistle from St. Paul's letter to the Colossians, which began, "Brethren: Have charity which is the bond of perfection." How difficult it was to live those simple Gospel words.

Paul bowed his head and they joined him in the Gospel prayer which he recited in heavily accented English. To Matthew Mahan it would always sound better in Latin. *Munda cor meum ac labia mea omnipotens Deus. Cleanse my heart and my lips, O Almighty God, Who cleansed the lips of the Prophet Isaiah with a burning coal. In Your gracious mercy, deign so to purify me that I may worthily proclaim Your Holy Gospel.*

The Gospel was from St. Matthew and told the story of Jesus' failure in the synagogue of his native Nazareth. "How did this man come by this wisdom and these miracles? Is not this the carpenter's son?" the people asked. Mournfully, Jesus said to them, "A prophet is not without honor except in his own country, and in his own house."

Matthew Mahan thought of Pope John. To these Romans he had been the peasant from Bergamo, and now they were doing their best to keep him in the grave by calling him Good Pope John, the people's Pope. Good for an illustration on a holy card, but it would take a hundred years to repair the damage he had done to the Church. Whose voice was that? Not the voice of the Church, the people of God. It was the voice of the realist, the administrator, the man who wielded power.

Was this the voice that had whispered *Frater noster taciturnus* to him yesterday? The modern power broker, coolly rounding up the lost sheep by tempting him with trinkets of red and gold? No, he still refused to believe it. The sadness, the sadness with which the voice spoke, this was proof of the other meaning, of the man's innocence.

The Gospel was over. The concelebrating Cardinals descended from the altar and sat in seats reserved for them there. Pope Paul walked to a gold lectern and began to speak. He opened the sermon in Latin, then went to Italian, then to French, German, English, Spanish, and ended with Latin again. He talked about the Christian dignity of work and said it was something that should bring men together, not separate them. He lamented the "painful inequities" that existed between the various classes and urged his audience to bring the Church's social teaching to a world that desperately needed it. The end of the class struggle must be achieved not with violence, but with the meekness of the Gospel. Yet it must be done with the moral force of justice and with the explosive force of love. Finally, he urged the Cardinals to become more faithful disciples of the poverty of Christ.

After the sermon, Pope Paul descended to a simple chair at the foot of the altar. One by one, the names of the new Cardinals were read out, and each advanced to kneel before the Pope while he placed a plain gold ring on the fourth finger of his right hand. Solemnly, Paul repeated in Latin the formula: *"Receive the ring from the hand of Peter and may the love of the Prince of the Apostles strengthen ever more your love of the Church."*

Again Matthew Mahan was one of the last names called. He knelt before the Pope and their eyes met and he found himself searching desperately for the truth he was seeking on Paul's face. For a moment he thought he found it in the remarkable mixture of concern and sadness, gentleness and resignation. The stark contrast between this man's delicate, almost feminine personality and John's earthy reality overwhelmed him. He almost heard himself saying to this visibly suffering man John's unforgettable greeting at the opening session of Vatican II—*I am Joseph, your brother*. It would have the double meaning that it had in the Old Testament, when Joseph, sold into slavery in Egypt by his brothers, forgave them from his heart when they appeared before him as starving supplicants. What was the full quotation? *I am Joseph, your brother, whom you sold into Egypt. Do not be distressed or angry with yourselves because you sold me here; for God sent me before you to preserve life*. Yes, Matthew Mahan thought, those words not only would proclaim his fraternity but would also declare his forgiveness of this man, who had betrayed him into bondage. As the Pope slipped the plain gold ring onto his finger, Matthew Mahan found himself compressing his lips, as if he feared he might actually say the words.

To his dismay, with those almost spoken words came a surge of unexpected anguish—the very opposite of the peaceful humility he had hoped to achieve in this ceremony. To him this Pope suddenly personified the fragility and weariness of the old world, struggling to come to terms with the new world that was being born all around it. As an American, a man of the new world, he could cope with this birth agony. It was his continent and his country, America, with its vision of freedom as a new human dimension, an absolute spiritual necessity, that was creating this travail. *Trust us*, he wanted to whisper, *trust us. Have faith in us and we will make you free*.

He walked back to his seat in a daze, catastrophic voices shouting inside him. Who do you think you are, Mahan? The accidental Archbishop lecturing the successor of St. Peter. Perhaps you should have said it, perhaps you should have whispered the first sentence at least, whispered it in Latin. *Ego sum Joseph, frater vester* (I am Joseph, your brother.) Wouldn't that have been interpreted as insolence? Almost a sacrilege? Mahan, you are a fool. By now he did not know where he was. Cardinal Dearden had to reach out a hand as he passed him and gently guide him to his seat, preventing him from blundering into the audience.

As he sat down, his entire body was shaken by a fantastic throb of pain. It was a new dimension, a shift from primitive weapons to some kind of futuristic death ray. Or flamethrower, he thought as it happened again. A twentieth-century weapon. No need to reach for extravagant metaphors to describe this agony. He had learned to live with the first primitive visitor, why couldn't he convert this one into an old acquaintance, if not a friend? Was this his burning coal, that would enable him to worthily proclaim the Gospel?

Again and again it returned, a whoosh of pain that soared up through his body. Unbelievable. Was he going to faint, make a complete fool of himself? Slowly, carefully, he took a deep breath. The pain seemed to subside slightly. He was taming it, yes, he would make a friend out of it yet. What did John call death? Oh, yes, his sister. Sister Death meet Brother Pain.

The rest of the mass was a blur. Somehow he managed to return to the altar with his fellow celebrants. At the Agnus Dei the Pope gave the kiss of peace to Cardinal Yu Pin as a gesture of brotherhood, and it traveled around the altar. Matthew Mahan saw the black Cardinal who was standing next to him (what was his name?—unpronounceable, Rakotomalala from Madagascar), felt those dark lips brush his cheek and found a strange, unexpected comfort from them. Was that all you wanted, really, to escape this torment, to be gathered into the arms of God like a weary child? No, there were still miles to go. Like a drowning swimmer, he turned and groped toward Cardinal Dearden, embraced him, leaned forward to kiss him. Dearden eyed him strangely. Did he think he was drunk? God knows what sort of rumors the Vatican circulated about the Pope's *frater taciturnus*.

Going down the aisle at the end of the mass, he could barely see the smiling faces calling congratulations to him and other Cardinals. When he smiled and nodded, his head seemed to float up and down on a rubber neck, like one of those giant inflated toys in a Thanksgiving Day parade. Suddenly, with amazing clarity, his eyes found Dennis McLaughlin, sitting with Davey Cronin in the corner of one of the raised stands beside an ugly woman with a small, thin boy on her lap. Dennis seemed to be glaring at him, his face frozen in that blend of anger and arrogance that was the standard expression of the young these days. For a moment an incoherent voice in him almost cried out the truth of his agony. *Not all glory, not all glory*, the voice wailed.

In the chapel he handed his robes over to an obsequious monsignor and dazedly shook hands and exchanged congratulations with the other American Cardinals. He edged his way to the door and was enormously pleased to find Dennis McLaughlin waiting just outside it. He would never have found his way through the Vatican labyrinth to the Belvedere Courtyard, where the limousines were parked.

Matthew Mahan turned as they entered the sun-filled courtyard in the rear of the cathedral and pointed to a nearby doorway. "The first day I came to see John," he said, "we parked here and went in that door, and took the elevator up to the library."

Beneath medieval arches dripping with overhead spikes they rode, passing orange, red, and blue uniformed Swiss Guards and then on the right a cemetery with tall black cypresses among the gray gravestones. Finally the streets, crowded with people, and the distant sound of marching bands, crowds cheering. The driver explained rapidly in Italian that he would have to take a detour because of the parades and demonstrations. They headed north, crossing the Tiber on the Ponte Matteotti and racing through the park of the Villa Borghese. Beside him Dennis McLaughlin was silent, almost morose, gazing out at the lush green grass and brilliant flowers of the villa's lawns. Bishop Cronin, he explained, had met an old compatriot who had persuaded him to risk lunch at the Irish seminary.

As Matthew Mahan got out of the car at the hotel, the driver bade him an extravagant good-bye. He stopped, leaned against the car, and pulled a thousand-lira note from his pocket. "Give that to him," he said to Dennis.

Slowly, carefully, he picked up one foot and then another and managed to reach the lobby without attracting any attention. He felt like he was walking under water now, a giant fish with a hook in his belly. Some sadistic fisherman on the top floor persisted in trying to reel him in. "Have you picked out your twelve apostles yet?" Dennis asked.

"What?" he asked dazedly as they stepped into the elevator.

"For the audience tomorrow at St. Peter's, remember? You're supposed to pick twelve people and bring them forward to speak to the Pope."

"No, I haven't," he said. "Whoever thought of that was no fund-raiser."

"I know. You said that the first time you heard it."

"Pick out about twenty for me. I'll eliminate nine tonight."

"Any priests?"

"Just Petrie and Malone. What's the rest of the schedule today?"

Dennis gave him a puzzled look and took a notebook out of his pocket. "Lunch at one P.M. with your seminary class."

"Oh yes. Yes. I should go but—"

A spasm hit him, the worst one yet. He crumpled against the wall of the elevator. "Dear Jesus—"

He stumbled into the hall and asked Dennis to help him. "Put your arm around me," he gasped, "before I make a fool of myself." They walked together down the hall like a three-legged man. He handed Dennis the key to his room, and they continued at the same gait to the bed. "I'm afraid—the ulcer's kicking up, Dennis," he said. He retched and suddenly his mouth was full of muddy, mucky blood. He stumbled to the bathroom and spit it into the toilet.

Coming back to the bed, wiping his mouth, "You'll have to go down and apologize to them, Dennis. Say I've got a virus. I've had it for a couple of days. Worn out."

Dennis nodded obediently and departed. Matthew Mahan lay in bed, shuddering with anticipation before every spasm and almost crying out in agony when it hit. *Here is pain with interest for all those wounds you never got, my heroic chaplain,* whispered a crazy voice within him. *Here is the real teacher of humility, my dear Prince of the Church.*

Should he call Bill Reed? Or some other doctor? No, he knew what was wrong, and he knew it was his own fault. He had brought all this on himself by ignoring his diet. He had no desire to be lectured like a naughty boy, especially when he was guilty. He would suffer through, somehow.

Downstairs, Dennis McLaughlin listened to the class of '39 uninhibitedly recalling their seminary days. To hear them tell it, they were a bunch of rowdies, mugs from the city streets beyond all hope of reform in the opinion of their professors. Monsignor Eddie McGuire, pale and wasted from a recent operation for cancer of the prostate, asked if anyone remembered the time they had heated the bowling ball.

Cries of joy, gasps of laughter. "That was Matt's idea."

"Yeah, to get rid of that damn Benedictine."

Eddie explained to Dennis that the Benedictine had taught them plain chant. He insisted on them memorizing dozens of hymns, when all they needed to learn was how to sing Kyrie Eleison. He was also the monitor of the fourth floor of the dormitory and enforced every letter of the regulations. So they had stolen a bowling ball from the seminary's lone alley, heated it in a fireplace on the second floor, and hoisted it to the fourth floor in a bucket. There, Big Matt had balanced it delicately on a shovel, stepped into the hall, and sent it hurtling to the monk's end of the building. He had rushed out of his room and seen this engine of destruction rumbling toward him. Naturally, he bent to stop it before it put a hole in the wall. Only then did he discover that it was very, very hot.

"Back to the monastery for him," said Eddie McGuire, laughing so hard he almost swallowed his cigar, "after he got out of the infirmary."

Dennis sat there letting his eyes rove around the square of laughing faces in the private dining room. Nineteen had been ordained that year. Two were dead; one, Fogarty, was a failed priest, a drunk. The other fifteen were sitting here paying homage to the man who had been their leader "from the first day inside the wall," said Eddie McGuire, making "first" sound like "foist," which in turn made it sound like he was reminiscing about a reform school, not a seminary. Next to Eddie the Mug sat George Petrie, of the cultured voice and elegant phrase. Next to him sat slight reticent prison chaplain Peter Foley, the only man who did not have a parish.

"Remember the sermons we used to get about the younger generation?" asked Monsignor Harry Hall, another suave one. He was pastor of Christ the King parish in suburban Hollisport. He clipped the ends of his cigars with a set of gold nippers before he smoked them. But he was a hardworking thoroughly modern priest who had taken courses in psychology and marriage counseling on his own time and had, according to Matthew Mahan, saved several dozen marriages in his own and nearby parishes.

"Oh yeah," said Eddie McGuire, laughing in anticipation, "and the imitations Matt used to give of what's his name. The Wheezer."

"Father Dermot McNulty," George Petrie said.

"Yeah, yeah," gasped Eddie McGuire. "He had emphysema, I guess. He smoked about three packs a day. He worshiped Father Coughlin. We thought he was an asshole. In fact we thought they were both assholes. Anyway, Matt used to give this fantastic imitation of 'im. You know, a wheeze after every word."

"But his imitation of the Old Man was better," said portly square-jawed Monsignor Frank Falconer.

"It's a toss-up," said Eddie McGuire. "Old Hogan spoke in an absolute monotone. Not the slightest inflection. Not even when he got to a period."

From the doorway on the right came a droning voice: "I want all you young men to know how lucky you are to be here at Rosewood."

The room exploded into shouts of joy. "It's the Big Cheese himself," rasped Eddie McGuire.

Matthew Mahan stood in the doorway, smiling. He looked terrible. His face had a deathly pallor. In spite of the Cardinal's protests, Dennis vacated his seat at the table and sat down in another chair against the wall. A waiter came in, and Matthew Mahan spoke to him in fluent Italian.

"That's why he's wearing the royal red, fellas," shouted Eddie McGuire, "while we're all still pulling away at the oars. It's a ginny conspiracy."

"You didn't say that when I used to take you home and feed you the best spaghetti in the state, you two-faced mick," Matthew Mahan said.

"I know, Matt. But who ever heard of getting a red hat for slipping the recipe to Il Papa?"

"No, no, I got made Archbishop for that. To get here this time I had to come through with the one for ravioli."

Roars of laughter. While Dennis, the observer, smiles his outsider's smirk.

"You should have given it to the maître d'here," said Monsignor Falconer.

Matthew Mahan frowned as the waiter handed him a glass of milk. "Seriously, Frank, was it a bad lunch? Because if it was, we'll have another one tomorrow free of charge."

"Has Fastidious Frank liked anything that wasn't haute cuisine straight from the Champs Ulysses?" demanded Eddie McGuire. "I remember he used to complain on steak night."

"Because it only came once a year, you clod."

"Ah, tell it to your French chef, Frank," said Eddie, taking a large draft of his well-filled brandy glass. "You're a traitor to your own kind. On the level, Matt, how do you let him get away with it? Is there another rectory in the archdiocese, in the country, with a resident French chef?"

"Lest that young fellow be scandalized," said Frank with rumbling gravity, pointing to Dennis, "the chef is a French woman."

Hoots, whistles, cries of ooh-la-la. "She does the cancan between courses," Eddie McGuire bellowed.

"Sixty-five years old. Just an ordinary French cook. Which means that the food on my table is a hundred and fifty per cent better than anything these barbarians ever see, even when they eat in restaurants in our fair city."

"I'll vouch for that, Frank," said Matthew Mahan. "I had my best meal in a year the last time I visited St. Damian's."

Cries of bribery, conflict of interest. George Petrie suggested that Madam Proudhomme was Satan in disguise and was planning to force Frank to sell his soul for a perfect soufflé.

"Do I get to taste it before I make up my mind?" asked Frank.

"Come on, Matt, give us an imitation of the Wheezer," Eddie McGuire begged.

The Cardinal only had to gasp out a line or two, and they were all in convulsions.

"And Coyne. Give us Coyne, Matt," Eddie McGuire choked, laughing already.

Coyne had a high-pitched voice and a very feminine speech pattern. "Honestly, you fellows are *awful*. If you think I'm going to stand up here and discuss the liturgy while some joker blows soap bubbles around the room. Mahan, it's you again, isn't it? Admit it."

"No, Father, it's Foley."

More roars of laughter while Peter Foley grinned good-naturedly.

"Foley!" Matthew Mahan said, his voice contralto once more. "If there's one person in this room who's well behaved, it's Peter Foley. The only one, I might add."

They were boys again, Dennis thought, listening to the guffaws, watching them pound their fists on the table with glee. Maybe they were always boys. Maybe they never became men. Maybe manhood always eluded them; they were condemned forever to cavort in the boys' playground behind chastity's barbed-wire fence.

Was that really true? Were they acting any differently from any other random group of alumni, thirty years out? Probably not. If anything, they were remarkably normal for a group of celibates.

No matter how hard you try to disapprove of their humor and style, no matter how excluded you feel by the generation gap, there is a link between you and these men. No, more than a link. That word suggests chains, bondage. What held you was living, a sense of something shared. During lunch they had accepted him as one of their own, kidded him about being a runaway Jesuit, wanted to know how he survived working for the "Eminent Slave Driver." It had been a new experience, at first strange and then exhilarating. But the bond? What they shared— he suddenly realized—was this big smiling man, sitting in the seat of honor.

They were talking baseball now. It had been a major topic during lunch. They had lamented like obsessive Jeremiahs the city's perpetually losing professional team. Now he gathered that their class had been the seminary champions six years' running, thanks largely to Matthew Mahan on the pitcher's mound. "Tell the truth now, Matt, once and for all," croaked Eddie McGuire, swirling his almost empty brandy snifter, "didn't you use a spitter?"

"Eddie. I only had two pitches and you know it. The curve and the fast ball."

"What did you throw when you brained Osterhouse?"

"That was a fast ball. I was dusting him off because he knocked you down three times the inning before."

"Go on," said Eddie. "I was playin' center field. I could see what that ball was doin'. It curved in, out, up, down. Osterhouse dodged six different ways and still it hit him. You coulda made it in the majors, Matt. It musta broke your old man's heart when you went for the sem."

Suddenly Matthew Mahan saw for the first time the stricken look on his father's face when they shook hands that first seminary day. Bart Mahan had stepped back and watched while his wife embraced their son. He had said so little to his father, really. During the previous spring, when he had been leading the local college league in strikeouts, there had been that abortive conversation about inviting an old friend who was a scout for the New York Giants to see him pitch.

But I'm going in the seminary, Pop, didn't Mom tell you?

The seminary? No, no, she didn't.

"Ah, I wasn't that good, Eddie. If the old ump felt that way, he knew he was wearing rose-colored glasses."

"That ain't true," said Eddie. "My old man tended bar for him, remember, at the Hawthorne Avenue place? All he talked about was his son the pitcher."

A wave of weakness, of inner trembling, swept over Matthew Mahan. The truth, how often it comes hurtling at us unexpectedly, the truth on the lips of poor old Eddie McGuire, the class joker, with the pallor of death on his face. *Father, forgive me for I knew not what . . .* For a moment he almost wept. But he commanded himself to smile. "No kidding," he said. "Well, I'm glad he didn't talk to me. My head was big enough in those days. Where would I be now?"

"Now? You'd probably be in the Hall of Fame and be simultaneously managin' St. Louis. You're one of them guys, Matt, who can fall in a cesspool and come up with a diamond ring."

"Oh, is that what explains this?" He held up his Cardinal's ring.

Roars of laughter. "I move that the metaphor be accepted," said Peter Foley.

"Hey, listen to the jailbird," said Eddie McGuire.

Matthew Mahan finished his milk. Two dishes of cream of wheat and a dozen or so Titrilac tablets had dampened the pain, but the inside of his body felt raw, scalded. It was time to go home, he thought gloomily, time and past time. He needed to think about what was happening inside him, physically and spiritually.

Eddie McGuire was on his feet now, making a speech. He vowed that they had debated for weeks over what to give their new Cardinal to commemorate his elevation. They had no money, he said. "You take it away from us as fast as we rake it in." They thought about giving him Madam Proudhomme, but Frank Falconer wouldn't part with her. He didn't need a trip anywhere. Every time they called him at the chancery office, the switchboard operator informed them that the Archbishop was in Rio or Santiago or Las Vegas. They thought about renting a nun to do his thinking for him, but they found out that nuns were the only thing that Hertz didn't rent. They tried prying one of the doors off St. Peter's, but the Swiss Guards caught them at it. So they decided to give him something personal. A certificate proving that he really was a Cardinal written by George Petrie, the best Latinist in the class, and surrounded by their pictures, which proved they weren't fictitious witnesses.

"But then when we got here," Eddie continued, as the legal-looking document was handed up the table to Matthew Mahan, "we found ourselves with all these lire in our pockets and we went slightly nuts. We thought we had some real money. So we decided to get you a real present, one that would really serve a purpose." Bending while he talked, Eddie fished from under the table a sleek-looking multiband radio in a walnut case. "The guy we bought it from guaranteed us that you can get the Vatican on it. We couldn't think of anything a Cardinal needed more these days."

For an appalling moment, Matthew Mahan did not know whether he was going to laugh or weep or snarl. *I am Joseph, your brother.* The infinite sadness in Pope Paul's eyes. Did they *know*? Did they suspect? Were they mocking him, too, this little circle, the old reliables, the ones he never had to worry about? Michelangelo's Moses. Mary Shea's fragile fingers touching his hand in the lamplight. Mike Furia's bitter face. *I solemnly swear that I shall not divulge . . . I am Joseph, your brother.*

It was too much, too much to bear.

What should he, what could he, say to these old friends? Could he share with them his appalling sense of failure—and thereby ruin this happy occasion? Weren't they a mirror image of what had gone wrong? They were confusing themselves with the Church, confusing the affection, yes, even the love, they felt for each other with the extension, the multiplication, the agonies, the failures, the triumphs of love which was their mission. Hadn't all of them—or almost all of them—settled for something much safer, more dependable: doing the job?

No, that was unfair, Matthew Mahan told himself, desperately trying to regain his emotional balance. It is unfair, unjust, to pastors like Frank Falconer and Harry Hall and a half-dozen others around the table, men who rose unhesitatingly in the middle of the night to bring the sacraments to the dying, who rode and walked around their parishes tirelessly visiting the old, the sick, the widowed, who counseled unhappy wives and angry husbands and rebellious teen-agers, and tirelessly made small talk with mass-goers outside church every Sunday, who simultaneously struggled to balance books and lead souls to grace and worry about their own souls. Don't, the new Cardinal told himself, let your own sense of personal failure ruin your appreciation of these good men, or even worse, infect them with your malaise.

But it *was* true of others, not just those sitting here at this friendly table, but too many others among the 672 pastors and 1,982 curates of the archdiocese. Too many of them were satisfied with doing the job. And it was his fault, he was guiltier than all of them together, because he had failed to lead them in the right direction. He had been too busy doing his job, keeping the lid on the archdiocese, trying to balance liberals and conservatives, young and old, pastors and curates, optimists and pessimists.

But the gang, the class, sitting there in front of him, their faces wreathed in smiles, what better place to start changing this complacent mediocrity than here, with them? A beginning, Matthew Mahan felt desperately, a beginning had to be made.

"Matt—are you okay?"

Eddie McGuire's familiar croak returned him to reality. "What—? Sure I'm all right, Eddie. I'm just a little stunned by so much thoughtfulness from you lugs. In one sense—it's almost out of character—but underneath all those insults we dish out to each other, I know there's a lot of love. And believe me—it's reciprocated.

"But it's not enough for us to reciprocate it. I would like to see us share more of it. Share it with the people that we serve. Sitting here just now I couldn't help thinking—there isn't a man in this room who isn't doing a good job. And that includes me. But is that good enough for us—?"

Smiles were fading fast from every face. He was losing them. The last thing they expected or wanted now was a pep talk. But this wasn't a pep talk. This wasn't a summons to the old class, team spirit. This was from his soul to their souls. How could he make them see it? Only by sharing his failures with them.

"The other night I met a woman here in Rome, a woman from our diocese. I sent her here fifteen years ago to get an annulment. But that wasn't the real reason I sent her. I sent her because I didn't have the spiritual strength to cope with her agony. She's spent fifteen years here. She still hasn't gotten her annulment. She knew she could never get it. She came here to spare me, yes, even to save me from my guilt, my failure. We're all doing our jobs. But too often our jobs don't seem to include reaching out, going out, searching for these people. The lost sheep. Yet we know how important our Lord thought they were. When I get home, I'm going to dedicate myself, and if possible our archdiocese, to this mission. I'm depending on you for support."

The smiles had faded into bafflement now. George Petrie's had declined to obvious dismay. They didn't even know what he was talking about. As far as they could see, Big Matt was losing his marbles.

His eyes blurred with tears. One way or another, God seemed determined to make a fool out of him. He picked up his certificate and his Vatican radio and walked dazedly away from them, his head down. In the silence he heard Peter Foley say softly, "God bless you, Matt."

Eddie McGuire began to roar out "Auld Lang Syne," and in a moment everyone was singing it, changing the last words to "Good old thirty-nine," as they often did at their annual reunions. Matthew Mahan stood in the doorway smiling at them for a moment and then walked unsteadily down the hall toward the elevator. He did not realize Dennis McLaughlin was beside him until he heard him murmur anxiously, "Are you all right?"

He nodded. They stepped onto the elevator. Alone with Dennis in the wood-lined capsule, he slumped against a burnished wall. "They didn't know what I was talking about."

"Some of them did. I did."

Dennis's voice trembled slightly. For a moment the memories, the burdens, the pain, vanished from Matthew Mahan's body and mind. There had been a beginning, a new beginning after all.

XXIII

A full moon filled the Roman sky with golden light. Cardinal Mahan sat on the terrace of Mary Shea's penthouse sipping the sweet dessert wine known as Lacrimae Christi. Mary sat a few feet away from him, the moonlight glistening on her silver hair and white dress.

"I'm so glad you could give me this last night, Matt."

"You would have had it anyway. I'm glad I was able to give you—the rest of it, Mary. What we said."

"What *you* said."

They had eaten alone in her apartment. Soft, savory fettucini, a delicately herbed roast lamb, cool red Valpolicella wine, endive salad. Most of it was off his diet, but two days of living on mush had soothed his stomach, he hoped. It was not his stomach that worried him anyway; it was his spirit, and in some profound, mysterious way it was linked with this woman's spirit. To heal himself he must heal her.

So he had reached out, clumsily but urgently opening himself, confessing everything, beginning with his physical wound, the ulcer, then sharing what he had seen and felt on their first night in Rome in the Church of Saint Peter in Chains. He had told her everything, concealed nothing, not even the Pope's tormenting words, *Frater noster taciturnus*, Paul's sadness, the insane temptation to reassure him, the agonizing attack of pain in St. Peter's, but above all the desolating sense of failure, of guilt, of remorse, that involved her and the Church and his priesthood.

Mary had listened, deeply moved, at times almost weeping. When he began to tell her about his floundering speech to his seminary classmates, she cried out, "Oh, Matt, don't be so hard on yourself, don't." But she had let him silence her with a wave of his hand. She knew, she was too intelligent, too sensitive, not to know what he was doing. He was stripping away the Roman collar, the black uniform, the sacerdotal robes; he was coming down from the altar in a nakedness that was more real, more meaningful, than flesh.

Were they two in one spirit now, truly one? Otherwise what he was about to say would be rejected with scorn, rage, perhaps with despair. "You know what grieves me most, Mary? I've been afraid to say it to you, afraid for—all the reasons you can imagine. I think you should marry again. I think you should have married again four or five years ago."

"Why, Matt?"

"Because you're a loving person, Mary, and you have no one to love."

"I have my son. You. The Church—"

"Your son doesn't need your love anymore. I can't return your love in the way—the only way—it deserves to be returned. And the Church—you can't love the Church, Mary, the way you're trying to love it, without being wounded."

"You're speaking from experience?"

"Yes, I suppose I am. But I can bear it, Mary. I hope I can, because it's my choice."

"I made some choices, too, Matt, fifteen years ago."

"They were inflicted on you. You were born to love a man, Mary, to make him happy with your hands, your body."

"Oh, Matt, stop it, please. I can't bear it."

"Yes, you can. We can both bear it. You're only forty-four years old, Mary. You can love someone else, if you open your mind, your heart, to the possibility."

"Are you telling me to walk out of the Church?"

"No. I'm telling you that if you marry and come home, you have nothing to worry about. I'll receive you into the Church. I'll even give you my blessing. I'm going to begin a program in the diocese, Mary, for people who have divorced and remarried in good conscience. It's within my power as a bishop to do this; there are bishops doing it already. I didn't have the courage to do it before. I thought of what the conservatives would say. I thought of the people like yourself who had spent fifteen, twenty desolate years. I didn't know how I could face you. But now— I'm facing you."

"I don't know whether I can ever love anyone but you, Matt. And tonight makes the possibility even more dubious."

"That saddens me, Mary, saddens me terribly. Promise me this much. You'll try. You'll at least consider some offers."

"Now you sound like a marriage broker. What are you going to do, raffle me off to the highest bidder?"

"If I could, it would solve my fund-raising problems overnight."

"Don't. I don't want to joke about it."

"Why not? We celibates live paradoxically. We laugh and cry at the same time."

Mary said nothing. He sensed she was looking past him into the darkness. He turned his head and saw Saint Peter's dome riding on the gloom in the floodlights' glow.

"Have they approved this program, Matt?"

"No. That's another reason why I hesitated."

"What if they say no?"

For the first time all night, his stomach throbbed ominously. "Let's face it when—and if—it happens."

"I'm not worrying about myself, Matt, it's you."

"I know."

XXIV

The big jet poised at the head of the long sun-baked runway, like a sprinter waiting for the gun. They were off, racing down the concrete for a nerve-twisting sixty or seventy seconds, and into a forty-degree climb. At three thousand feet the pilot leveled off and said: "Thanks to His Eminence, Cardinal Mahan, we have been cleared to give you a last look at Rome. We're going to circle the city so you can say good-bye to St. Peter's, the Via Veneto, the Forum, the Colosseum, and all the other fabulous places you've visited during the past week."

The plane resounded with unbuckling seat belts. Heads twisted, necks craned toward the windows. Cries, groans, of appreciation and excitement.

Matthew Mahan stretched out his legs and thought about the last three days. The anticipation of his evening with Mary had given him a curious feeling of freedom, a euphoria that had carried him through the concluding round of ceremonies. On the day after the mass in St. Peter's, Pope Paul had held a special audience in the cathedral for the friends and families of the new Cardinals. The next day Cardinal Mahan had taken possession of his titular church in Rome's suburbs.

The papal audience had been pleasant but perfunctory. Pope Paul had nothing in particular to say to the twelve apostles (as Dennis kept calling them) whom Matthew Mahan had selected for the thrill of kissing the papal ring. They included his sister-in-law Eileen, Monsignors Malone and Petrie, a nun, a student, and four or five big givers such as the McAvoys. When he introduced George Petrie, Matthew Mahan added: "Here's the man I would like to have as auxiliary bishop, Your Holiness."

George had almost lost his vaunted composure, as Paul nodded and smiled.

The Pope had obviously selected in advance something nice to say about each new Cardinal. He called Matthew Mahan the "master builder," and for an irreverent moment he had almost replied, *Yes, they used to call me the patron saint of the contractors.* Instead, he disavowed the compliment. Looking at Mike Furia, Jim McAvoy, and the rest of his moneyed circle, he said that these dedicated people had made possible the miraculous multiplication of gymnasiums, parish houses, rectories, and parochial schools. He would have liked to add that they were now going broke trying to keep them all running. But it was neither the time nor the place to launch a discussion of American church policy.

The titular church was in a new Roman suburb, and was named for America's first saint, Mother Cabrini. The church had been donated by a wealthy Italian-American from San Francisco. It was one of those supersonic jobs with a roof that swooped upward to a knife edge, two wings that also swooped, and a great triangular stained-glass eye in the center of the facade to complete the resemblance to an exotic bird in flight. Cardinal Mahan had taken possession of it at the head of a procession of his own clergy and had warmed the president's chair during a mass that he had insisted on concelebrating, not with his fellow Americans, but with the Italian pastor. The congregation was mostly American, but he gave a brief sermon in both English and Italian, stressing, he said, the universality of the Church which knows no language barriers or geographical frontiers.

He had been unbothered by being given a church in the suburbs, instead of one of the more historic Roman churches, such as Saints John and Paul, which Cardinal Cooke had received as an inheritance from the late Cardinal Spellman. On the way out to the ceremony he had remarked to Terry Malone, "Maybe we can get out of this little rigamarole without spending a cent." He recalled that Spellman had spent a million on Peter and Paul. Cushing told him that when he received Santa Susanna as his titular church he had had to cough up fifty thousand dollars immediately to prevent the roof from falling in.

But Matthew Mahan's financial hopes had swiftly withered in the gale of sighs from the pastor of Mother Cabrini parish.

It was a working-class district, he explained, pointing to shiny white high-rise apartments which did not look very lower class. Mothers as well as fathers worked. The parish desperately needed another building which could serve as a nursery school in the morning and a recreation center for older children in the afternoons and evenings. Of course, there was no money. He had petitioned and pleaded at the *cancelleria* in vain.

Matthew Mahan had glumly reached for his checkbook as the pastor's Italian hands turned palms upward in a mute appeal to heaven. How much would the building cost? The pastor had no idea. Matthew Mahan declined to hand him a blank check. Instead, he gave him five thousand dollars now for an architect's fee. The balance would come when he saw the plans.

Turning away from the pudgy, balding pastor, Matthew Mahan's eyes had encountered Terry Malone's financial frown. He could practically read the dollar signs in the thick glasses and hear the lecture that would soon emanate from that disapproving iron jaw. It would cost them two hundred thousand dollars before they were out of it, if they were ever out of it, Matthew Mahan admitted to himself. But American Cardinals were supposed to be rich. How could they disappoint their adopted parishioners?

So much for the great event, the culmination of his clerical career, as one of the speakers at the North American College had called the cardinalate. Matthew Mahan felt the precise opposite. Not culmination but collapse. The more he thought about returning home, the more uneasy he became. Resuming the old way of life—playing the smoothie—was out of the question now. But an alternative remained a mystery to him.

It was simpler to think about some of the specific problems confronting him. At the top of the list was the diocesan deficit. What was the answer? A direct levy on each parish, scaled to its ability to pay? A special fund-raising drive later in the year? Tuition for the parochial schools, particularly the high schools? Already, some suburban pastors were charging modest amounts of money for their parish schools, or warning parents that if they did not appear prominently on the list of Sunday givers, they would be asked to withdraw their children from the school.

During visitations around the archdiocese, he had seen how deeply this troubled many pastors. They sweated mightily to exclude the poor from such prohibitions. But how did you deal with the almost poor or with the middle-class salaried man, overwhelmed by the cost of seven or eight children?

Mike Furia was sitting beside him reading *Business Week*. They had had very little to say to each other since their unpleasant exchange at the private dinner party. "Are we still friends?" Matthew Mahan asked as the pilot ended their circuit of Rome and began climbing toward their cruising altitude.

"I hope so," Mike said, holding out his hand.

A crunching handshake, and they were almost the same. Matthew Mahan knew they could never again achieve their old camaraderie. That had been based on his complacent assumptions, his bland acceptance of appearances. They began discussing the deficit. He spread the alternative solutions in front of Mike and asked his opinion.

"They all stink," Mike said. "Have you ever thought of the obvious solution?"

"What's *that*?"

"Get those parochial schools off your back."

"It's been suggested to me." He gave him a brief summary of his acrimonious exchanges with Mayor O'Connor on the subject.

"That's a good example of what I mean. Would O'Connor have it in for you if he didn't go to Catholic schools? Look at me. My old man wouldn't let me within a mile of a Catholic school. So I meet you and I think you're a great guy, and we're friends for life. Would I have felt that way if I'd had a couple of dozen nuns and priests yakking at me when I was a kid? I doubt it."

Matthew Mahan shook his head. He was not buying this idea. But Mike was undeterred. "I've been thinking about saying this to you for a couple of years, Matt, but I didn't have the nerve. From a business point of view, you're like a company that's putting out too many products. You're into too many things. Education. Hospitals. Old age care. Marriage counseling. Housing. When a corporation realizes this, it cuts back. Sells off subsidiaries. Concentrates on what it does best. Now, this may make you mad as hell, but you don't do education best. Yet you're spending ninety per cent of your income on it. That just doesn't make sense from a business point of view."

Matthew Mahan suddenly remembered Steve Murchison's wry

Methodist voice on the telephone, warning him: *You Romans are too visible, you've got too many things for people to criticize.* But he still stubbornly shook his head. Mike was asking him to turn his back on a part of himself, Matthew the Master Builder, the very achievement for which the Pope had saluted him. Those were *his* schools, so many of them. And wasn't that, asked another voice, precisely why you should be wary about clinging to them? Haven't you said good-bye to the heroic chaplain? Why not to the Master Builder also? But he still kept shaking his head. "There are too many people involved, Mike. Too many people who've made sacrifices—"

"I'm not telling you to junk everything overnight. You couldn't do that without throwing the city into chaos. But start phasing them out. . . ."

Another shake of his head, and the conversation ended. Matthew Mahan waited a diplomatic minute or two and shifted from the public to the personal. "Mike," he said, "would you consider taking some advice from me—even if I won't take any from you?"

"Try me," he said.

"Get a divorce. And get married again."

Furia drew back in mock surprise. "I can't believe it. After the way you worked on me—to make it a separation."

"We were both being men of the world, Mike. I wanted to keep you around as a fund-raiser. You wanted to keep on building schools and hospitals for me."

Mike nodded almost imperceptibly. The truth was being exchanged for the first time. "When we get back, I'm starting a new program—for divorced Catholics. Receiving them back into the church if their divorce is in good conscience. I know that won't mean anything to you, Mike. But it could mean a lot to your new wife."

Mike stared down at his hands. "Funny you should tell me this. I was—I thought of getting married again—just the other night. That disaster with Betty—it hurt me more than I admitted to anyone—even myself."

"To prove to you—and to myself—that I mean this for your sake—and only for your sake—I'm accepting your resignation as chairman of the Cardinal's Fund."

"Go to hell," Mike growled. "You're not getting it."

"I want it."

Mike shook his head and managed a smile. "You just missed a punch in the mouth the last time, Your Eminence."

Matthew Mahan met his smile. "That's a risk us brainless clerics take every so often."

He left Mike alone to do some thinking and wandered through the plane chatting with various people. He apologized to those who had taken the one-day trip to Pompeii without him. He had begged off that ordeal, at the strong urging of Dennis McLaughlin. It had been almost touching, the vehemence with which Dennis had pointed out that the excursion involved about nine hours on the bus. "Listen, it's just as well you didn't come," said Jim McAvoy. "With you along they never would have let us in that room with all the dirty paintings."

"They wouldn't let me in," said his wife. "Men only. I'm still mad!"

"Just think of all the time he'll have to spend in Purgatory, Madeline," Matthew Mahan said.

Many of the pilgrims were dozing. It made him feel better to discover that they were all as weary as he felt. Dennis McLaughlin and Davey Cronin were sitting side by side fast asleep. Matthew Mahan felt a rush of affection for both of them. "It looks like they'll stay out of trouble for the rest of the trip," he said to Bill Reed who was sitting in the aisle seat next to them.

Davey opened one eye and said, "The hell we will. I was just dreaming that you were crowned Pope."

"That's not a dream, that's a nightmare," Matthew Mahan said.

"Ah! Pope of the Reformed Catholic Church. Rome, you see, was destroyed by a natural catclysm. Buried under tons of spaghetti with clam sauce—"

"Another word and you'll be anathema."

"I've been that for years. You ought to try it, Your Eminence. It's a grand feeling."

Back in his seat, Matthew Mahan read his breviary and then slept until the stewardesses began serving supper. He groaned inwardly when he saw that the main course was veal parmigiana. He had forgotten to notify the airline about his special diet. A moment later, a stewardess was beaming down at him, saying,

"We'll have your chicken ready in just another minute, Your Eminence."

"How did you know I wanted it?"

"Oh, someone in your party—Father McLaughlin, I think— notified us about your diet."

He dared a little wine with the chicken, and his stomach seemed to accept it peaceably. When the stewardess removed the tray, he took from his briefcase the Pope's latest statement on the liturgy, Number 21, which was the final revision of the Roman missal. It was in Latin. English translations would come later. But he had enough skill with Latin to read it without difficulty.

Almost immediately, he found a phrase that made him grind his teeth. "We wish to give the force of law to all that we have set forth concerning the new Roman missal," Pope Paul wrote. Why, Matthew Mahan asked himself, why that obnoxious phrase, *the force of law,* to something associated with worship, an experience that had value only when it was free? He sighed and told himself to stop thinking revolutionary thoughts. He had taken a vow of fidelity and obedience to this man that he was criticizing.

Skimming rapidly through the rest of the Constitution, he saw that hardly any part of the mass remained as it was a decade ago. The Pope said that he hoped that this new mass meant the end of experimentation, while obeying the order of the Second Vatican Council to leave room for "legitimate variations and adaptations." However, all variations and adaptations must be submitted by local episcopal conferences to the Holy See for approval.

Again, Matthew Mahan found his jaw clenching. Why? After telling his fellow bishops repeatedly that they were his brothers, Paul was treating them like children again. Roman law, Roman legalism, couldn't they see how much damage it had already done to the Church? Didn't they realize, as old Davey was fond of pointing out, that the ancient Romans had gone out of their way to allow as much local autonomy as possible in their conquered territories? These new Romans were the heirs of Justinian, the Byzantine relic of the original Empire, centralized into a frozen defensive against a hostile world. It was not the way to run a church that only a few years before had gathered her bishops from all corners of the world to proclaim themselves in favor of holy freedom. Cronin was right. Brick by brick, the Curia was building a mausoleum around the Vatican Council II, entombing it in traditional architecture that proclaimed business as usual.

Matthew Mahan snapped his briefcase shut and thrust it under his seat. Forget it, forget it, he told himself. You are Cardinal Mahan now. Aside from your recent vow, where did you get this grandiose vision of yourself as the reformer of the Church? If some series of miracles put you on the papal throne, perhaps you could begin to take your ideas seriously. Perhaps you might reasonably assume that God was sending them to you for a purpose.

Back in the economy-class cabin, Dennis McLaughlin and Bishop Cronin were looking rapidly through a diary that their now mutual friend Goggin had smuggled out of the Vatican Library, photocopied, and returned. It was the private journal of Cardinal Antonelli, the Secretary of State during Vatican Council I. He had opposed the council and deplored the idea of infallibility, but had had to swallow his objections under the imperious commands of Pio Nono. In revenge, Antonelli kept a scrupulous record of the Pope's constant efforts to control the council. Cronin was wildly excited by the material. But the more Dennis read, the more uneasy he became.

What were they really proving? Old Davey hated Pio Nono with such a passion, anything he could find to blacken his character was automatically wonderful. But did the evidence prove what Cronin was hoping to prove? Just because Pio Nono was an SOB who wanted his own way—that is, infallibility at all costs—did that really invalidate Vatican Council I? There was not as much freedom as there should have been at Vatican I. But there was still a lot of it. The opponents of infallibility had fought ferociously against the declaration. There seemed to have been as much freedom of debate of the council as there was in the U. S. Congress.

If infallibility was to be denied on scholarly grounds, the challenge had to come from another direction. It had to include the history of Vatican I—and go beyond it. It had to stress the too often ignored fact that Vatican I was an incompleted council, disrupted by the outbreak of war between France and Prussia, and finally dispersed by the capitulation of Rome to Italian armies that had invaded the papal states to make Italy a nation at last. Thus the first Vatican Council had never really had a chance to address itself to the relationship between the bishops and the infallible Pope, and Vatican II, as Matthew Mahan had recently told him, was repeatedly frustrated by curial and papal maneuvers in its attempts to tackle this fundamental problem. Perhaps the council fathers of Vatican I had never intended infallibility to enhance the administrative and canonical powers of the papacy. The fathers of Vatican II had clearly demonstrated their hostility to these powers.

Dennis turned to discuss this insight with Cronin. The old man's head nodded toward his chest. For a moment Dennis was amused. Rome had worn Davey out. An odd droop at the corner of his mouth suddenly troubled Dennis. "Bishop, are you all right?" he asked.

Instead of answering, Cronin fell forward, scattering papers off the tray in front of him. He was sliding toward the floor when Dennis seized him by the arm and shoulder and lifted him back into the seat. He was shocked by how little the old man weighed. "Bishop," he said, frightened now.

"It feels like some blackguard angel friend of Pio Nono— clubbed me from behind. Wouldn't you know—"

"Dr. Reed—"

Dennis looked frantically around the plane. No sign of Bill Reed in the rear. He bolted into the forward compartment and found him sitting on the arm of the first row aisle seat chatting with Matthew Mahan. "Bishop Cronin—he's fainted," Dennis whispered. The two men rushed into the economy class ahead of him. Cronin was slumped in his seat, his head turned toward the window, his breath coming in noisy gasps. Mr. and Mrs. McAvoy hovered over him with exclamations of dismay on their lips.

"By God," Cronin gasped as Reed pushed the McAvoys aside and ripped away the white collar at his throat, "I sound—worse than you, Dennis. Maybe it's one of your pills I need."

"Take it easy. Take it easy," said Bill Reed in a voice that struck Dennis as surprisingly gentle. While he spoke, he was taking Cronin's pulse.

"If 'twas easy," said Cronin, "it wouldn't be—so hard."

His head flopped to one side, and his eyes rolled weirdly back until only their whites were visible.

"Cerebral thrombosis," muttered Bill Reed. "Get the stewardess. Pull up the arms of these seats."

The stewardess was already standing beside Dennis. She quickly pulled up the arms, turning the three seats into a narrow bed. Blankets and pillows were snatched from the overhead compartments. Bill Reed knelt beside the old man, his fingers still on his wrist.

"Is there anything you can do, Bill?" Matthew Mahan asked in a choked voice.

Reed shook his head. "You'd better pray."

Matthew Mahan stood in the doorway between the two compartments and said, "Bishop Cronin, our old and dear friend, seems to have had a stroke. He's gravely ill. Please join me in prayers for him."

Dennis stared numbly at the rosary in the Cardinal's big hand. It occurred to him that he did not even own a rosary. But he could not think of a better way to pray for Bishop Cronin.

"Our Father," Matthew Mahan began.

"Give us this day our daily bread—" responded the voices of the pilgrims, Dennis's among them.

"Hail Mary," said the Cardinal, and once more came the low mournful response from over a hundred voices, "Holy Mary, Mother of God, pray for us sinners now and at the hour of our death, Amen."

"Hail Mary, full of grace," said Matthew Mahan again, his voice faltering ever so slightly.

Once more the response. In the tiny interval between Matthew Mahan's part of the prayer and the reply, Dennis heard the harsh, painful sound of Cronin's breathing.

Five more times the Hail Mary was said. More than halfway through the first decade of the rosary. Dennis McLaughlin stared at the black beads, the dangling silver crucifix at the end of them. Bill Reed stood up and said, "You'd better give him the last rites, Matt."

"Get my briefcase, Dennis."

Numbly he obeyed. By the time he returned they had finished another Hail Mary. Matthew Mahan handed him the rosary, took the briefcase, and said, "Father McLaughlin will continue the rosary. I am going to give Bishop Cronin the last rites."

Slowly, in the silence that was not really a silence, that was filled as it had been from the beginning by the jet engines' pervasive throb, Matthew Mahan removed Cronin's shoes and socks. There was a hole in the sole of the right sock. Dennis's eyes blurred when he saw it. He fingered the rosary dazedly for a moment, then counted seven smaller beads of the first decade, pressed his thumb and forefinger on the seventh bead, and began, "Hail Mary . . ."

Mournfully the pilgrims responded with the same plea, to be remembered at the hour of their deaths. Matthew Mahan had the holy oil out now, olive oil in a small silver vial. Solemnly he anointed Bishop Cronin's eyes, ears, nose, mouth, hands, and feet, saying each time he placed his thumb on the old man's body, "By this holy anointing and His most loving mercy, may the Lord pardon you for any sins you have committed." Dennis could not hear him say the words. He only saw his lips moving. As the Cardinal finished anointing the feet, Dennis saw Cronin's eyes flutter. The rest of the plane responded to the tenth and final Hail Mary of the decade. Dennis paused and he heard Cronin whisper hoarsely, "The Church, Matt, the Church. The poor dear suffering Church. You must speak out—you must save it from them—"

Matthew Mahan's response was so extraordinary, Dennis's lips froze on the word "Our" as he began the second decade of the rosary. The big man bent his head low and without a trace of hesitation or embarrassment lifted the small frail old man into his arms. Dennis had no idea how long he held him close. Time seemed to stop. As the Cardinal slowly lowered his friend back on the seats, Dennis managed to continue the rosary. "— Father who art in heaven, hallowed be Thy name, Thy kingdom come, Thy will be done—"

Matthew Mahan stood up and asked Bill Reed a question. The doctor imperceptibly shook his head. Cronin was watching them. He saw and understood. Only then did Dennis see that he had a cross in his hand—the Cardinal's pectoral cross. With both hands Cronin raised it to his lips and then rested it on his chest, his eyes closed.

For the next hour, Dennis continued to recite the rosary,

while Matthew Mahan knelt beside his old friend. The shadows deepened inside the jet as the sun outran them and dwindled unseen below the western horizon. They were scheduled to land at eight o'clock U.S. time. For a while, death and darkness seemed synonymous. The whole world seemed to be dying. Everyone in the plane seemed about to be swallowed by death's immense dwindling draining emptiness. Only the plane, the thing of metal and wire that felt nothing, seemed alive. The Cardinal was still kneeling upright, his head bowed. He was holding Cronin's right hand now. The bishop's other hand still clutched the gold pectoral cross.

As Dennis reached the final Hail Mary of the seventh or eighth decade of the rosary, the Cardinal stood up and signaled him to stop. "I think he's gone, Bill," he said.

Dr. Reed bent low over the shrouded body, illuminated only by the single ray of the overhead reading light. He pressed his fingertips against Father Cronin's throat, held his wrist for a moment, and nodded. He began to cover his face with the blanket. Matthew Mahan stopped him. "No, please don't cover him, Bill. Somehow that makes death seem shameful—"

"I'm sorry, but he has to be covered. We have the other passengers to consider. This could create hysteria."

It was the stewardess speaking. For the first time, Dennis saw her. She was a baby-faced blonde with hair puffed out in curls on both sides of her head. Cardinal Mahan did not explode, as Dennis feared. "Of course, of course," he said, patting her shoulder. "But first we'd like to say a few prayers. There's nothing against that in the regulations, is there?"

"No—of course not, Your Eminence. I guess—I'm more upset than anyone. I've never had this happen before." She looked past him at Cronin and then turned her face away. "I've never seen anyone die before."

Matthew Mahan took both her hands in his. "It's all right, it's all right. Sit down now and let me say a few words."

He stationed himself in the doorway between the two cabins once more. "What has been until this moment a joyous experience has become a time of sorrow, and for no one more than me. I have lost one of my best, my oldest, friends. But even in this sorrow I hope you can join me in finding a different kind of joy. David Cronin lived and died a priest. His thoughts were forever turned to others, forever offering them advice, help, love. Everyone who knew him came away richer in spirit. He brought the same self-sacrificing love to the Church. He never stopped thinking of ways to make it more holy, more responsive to the needs and the hopes and the sorrows of men and women everywhere. God grant us all the grace to follow his example.

"In a way, we have all been privileged to be present at his death. He met God's summons with a faith that abolished fear. I would like you to come from your seats one or two at a time and kneel beside him with me, and say a personal prayer."

One by one they came and knelt beside Matthew Mahan. Many of the women and some of the men wept, although, as far as Dennis knew, they did not know Bishop Cronin well. Death itself was enough to make them weep.

By the time the last one—Mike Furia—knelt beside the Cardinal and whispered, "I know how you feel, Matt," it was totally dark outside. Matthew Mahan remained on his knees, gazing sorrowfully down at the silent shadowed face until the pilot announced that they were beginning their descent.

XXV

They landed smoothly. As they taxied to the terminal, Dennis saw an ambulance waiting for them, its red dome light flashing. Bill Reed joined two airport policemen, who took Bishop Cronin's body off the plane.

In the terminal the pilgrims clustered around Matthew Mahan for a subdued farewell. Photographers and reporters swirled around them, snapping pictures and luring individuals and couples away from the group for swift interviews.

Jack Murphy invited the Cardinal to a V.I.P. lounge where TV cameras were set up. As they walked toward that destination, the newspaper reporters swooped around Matthew Mahan, firing questions. Did he discuss the state of the Church with Pope Paul? Was the Pope critical of the American role in the Vietnam War? Was there any hint that Rome might abolish clerical celibacy? The Cardinal parried these queries lightly. Then

313

red-haired Tom Sweeney of the *Garden Square Journal* asked him: "Do you have any comment on the recent revelations about your finances and personal life?"

"What are you talking about?"

"There was a series of articles published during the past week in the Hard Times *Herald*—the underground newspaper."

"About me?"

"Yes. Quoting a lot of confidential information leaked by someone in the chancery office."

Already dazed by the intense emotions of Bishop Cronin's death, Dennis McLaughlin now found himself numb. Leo, his brother Leo, had not waited to find out the truth. He had not waited. The truth was not important.

A black reporter was asking the Cardinal what he thought about the reparations issue.

"Reparations? I don't know what you're talking about."

"A fellow named Forman, a black man, walked into Riverside Church in New York today and demanded five hundred thousand dollars in reparations for the injustices blacks have suffered in America. Father Vincent Disalvo's Council for Peace and Freedom has backed the idea one hundred per cent. They're demanding fifty thousand dollars from you."

"Are you kidding me?" Matthew Mahan asked.

"Straight dope, Your Eminence, so help me. Father Disalvo says that in the light of the revelations about your personal finances it should be a million."

Matthew Mahan laughed wryly. "If he can find fifty thousand lying around in my bank account, he's welcome to it."

Don't say that. The words spoke themselves in Dennis McLaughlin's mind. But he could not say them aloud.

"Can we quote you on that, Your Eminence?"

"Of course."

"Does this mean you endorse the principle of reparations?"

"No. Of course not."

"What do you think of the idea?"

"Now wait a minute. You people know where I stand as far as black Americans are concerned. I am behind their aspirations. I have tried to do everything in my power to help them move ahead. But this tactic is bad judgment and bad history."

"Then you won't consider the idea under any circumstances?"

314

By now they were only voices. Dennis had lost track of who was asking the questions. The joy in their eyes was blatantly sadistic. They did not care in the least that they were dealing with an exhausted, emotionally battered man.

As they entered the V.I.P. lounge, Dennis saw his brother Leo slumped in a chair just beyond the glare of the television lights. He was wearing his usual revolutionary outfit, a pair of muddy hiking boots, blue jeans, and a khaki jacket. Something about his smile disturbed Dennis. It was so brainlessly mocking. Almost immediately he saw himself arguing in a new, more serious way with Leo. Something had happened to him in Rome, something very important.

Before the battery of microphones, Cardinal Mahan was telling Jack Murphy, who was serving as pool reporter for the city's TV and radio stations, how glad he was to be home. They discussed the sadness of Bishop Cronin's untimely death. The Cardinal said that Bishop Cronin's last words to him had been full of concern for the Church. It was another reason why he had come home with renewed dedication to the people of the archdiocese. After a few more sentences in the same vein, Murphy introduced Mayor O'Connor, who welcomed the Cardinal home and said some effusive, totally insincere things about his importance to the "spiritual progress" of the city. The Cardinal replied warmly, and the ceremony was over. Dennis found himself almost ridiculously grateful for televison's superficial approach to news.

"What the devil are they talking about?" the Cardinal asked as the limousine rolled toward the city. "These articles about my finances?"

Confess? Dennis asked himself. Confess now? No, it would only make the Cardinal look foolish. Mike Furia was sitting beside him in the car. The McAvoys were sitting on the jump seats. Bill Reed was sitting in the front with Eddie Johnson. Why embarrass him when you can admit the truth in private and disappear quietly. No need to tell the world, even the friendly world, that His Eminence had naïvely employed a betrayer in his own office.

In the episcopal residence Dennis McLaughlin was distressed to see Matthew Mahan head for the office the moment that he put down his bags. "Call Joe Cohane," he said, looking at the carpet of mail about a foot thick on his desk. "Ask him what he knows about this series attacking me."

"You don't have to do that," Dennis said in a leaden voice. "I can tell you. My brother wrote it. Here are the clips. He gave them to me at the airport."

Matthew Mahan sat down in the familiar leather chair behind his desk and began to read them. The author's by-line, Leo the Great, made him almost smile. But that was the last kind thought he was able to summon for Leo the Great. The columns were sneering attacks on the way he ran the archdiocese. When it came to money, wrote Leo, Cardinal Mahan "behaved remarkably like a Renaissance prince or a Borgia pope." Leo described the "outrageous sums" he gave to "favorites" who were working as missionaries—really colonialist emissaries of American power—in Brazil. Other columns dilated upon His Eminence's personal finances which were described as "a smelly mystery." No accounting was ever made of them. But the cost of running the episcopal residence came to $32,567.80 last year and "travel expenses" for His Eminence came to $26,896.50. Equally "staggering sums" were funneled to his seven nieces and nephews who had charge accounts at all the city's department stores paid by the chancery office. In fact, tongues often wagged in the chancery about the Cardinal's long and frequent visits to his widowed sister-in-law who was "an attractive matron in her forties." Then there was the svelte divorcee, Mary Shea, whom the Cardinal visited regularly in Rome. As for Matthew Mahan's pastoral rating, Leo the Great found it almost as low as his finances and his personal morals. He was pictured as a conscienceless careerist, in secret disagreement with the Pope on birth control, but greedy enough to sell his convictions for the price of a red hat. At heart he was an authoritarian of the worst kind—interested only in maintaining his personal power.

Complicated things began happening in Matthew Mahan's mind and body. One part of himself, no, something more total, one version of himself, a man he had come to accept rather complacently and even to cherish until he went to Rome ten days ago, filled the room with roaring rage. Another self, a vision not yet real, faced Leo McLaughlin with tears on his cheeks and asked him why he inflicted these wounds. Both the version and the vision were useless, images out of chaos. He looked up at Dennis McLaughlin's stricken face. Echoes of the anguish that had erupted when he knelt before Pope Paul to accept his ring vibrated in his flesh. "Dennis," he asked, "do many people know who Leo the Great is?"

Dennis nodded and said, "Can I sit down?"

He slumped into one of the armchairs in front of the desk. "I—I want to confess something that will—probably end our relationship. Those columns are my fault. I knew how he felt about you. I—may have encouraged it. May have even caused it. I mean—I was the older brother. I was the one who filled him with bitterness about the Church, America, everything."

Matthew Mahan saw pain, essential pain, on Dennis McLaughlin's face. "Maybe I was changing when I came here. Or it started here. I don't know. I didn't really know what I felt about you until —until Rome. I had visions of this happening—with an exchange of mutual insults. And now—" Dennis shook his head, his eyes wet. "All I can say is I'm sorry."

"Wait a minute. Visions of what happening?"

"Of your firing me."

"I'm not firing you." Matthew Mahan was pleased by the sound of his own voice. It was sad, calm, perhaps even gentle. Maybe that roaring rager, that primary self, could be conquered yet. "You and your brother are not one and the same person, Dennis. No matter how much you love him, don't start thinking of him that way. I went through absolute hell with my brother because I let him maneuver me into that frame of mind. A man is not condemned for what his brother or his friend does or says. He shouldn't condemn himself either."

Should he tell him the whole truth? Dennis McLaughlin asked himself miserably. No, whispered a voice that was probably the instinct for self-preservation, but it utilized some very effective higher arguments. Tell him everything, and you have destroyed your chance to prove to yourself and to this man that you love him.

The truth, Dennis, time for the whole truth, murmured an opposing voice lancing deftly through the usual ironic smoke screen to the quivering self.

"It's worse than that," Dennis said. "I gave him things. From your files. I wrote him letters suggesting—things."

Too late, thought Matthew Mahan, too late. You had sensed a chasm between you. But was it really too late? There was still the knowledge, the memory of what had happened at the cemetery in Nettuno, the moment in the elevator after lunch with the class of '39. *They didn't understand. I did.* Matthew Mahan lit a cigarette. The match trembled slightly as it approached the white paper tube. Dennis McLaughlin found it easier to watch the trembling flame than to look the Cardinal in the face.

"Give me ten minutes to think this over," Matthew Mahan said.

Dennis nodded and silently departed. Matthew Mahan sat in his swivel chair for a moment, staring down at the smoking cigarette between his fingers. He started to stub it out in the ashtray, then suddenly crumpled it into a ripped, broken little pile of tobacco and paper. Rage came storming up through his body into his arms, his hands. He raised his big clenched fists and brought them down on his antique table desk with a tremendous crash.

Call him back, flay him alive, whispered a voice.

Desperately he prayed. *Lord, give me wisdom, give me the grace.*

For another five minutes he paced up and down the office, struggling for self-control. Slowly the rage ebbed from his body. Finally, he was able to light another cigarette, sit down at the desk, and call Dennis back into the room.

"I think what hurts me the most about these," he said, picking up the sheaf of columns and letting it flop back on his desk like a dead snake, "is the stuff about me giving money to my sister-in-law. It can't be more than three or four thousand a year. When old Hogan went to the Bahamas each year, he always stopped off in Palm Beach on the way back. He only had one relative, a niece, a single girl who had a very good job as an executive secretary. But the old fool would spend ten or fifteen thousand dollars on her. He'd buy her a whole new wardrobe, the latest styles. One year for Christmas he gave her a mink coat that was worth ten thousand all by itself. Year in, year out, he spent at least thirty thousand on her. And she didn't need it!" Matthew Mahan sighed and shook his head. He was sounding silly. He was too hurt, too tired, to think straight. "I guess it's an old story. You tell yourself you're doing better, a lot better than the previous regime. You never stop to think about how you look to the next generation. Until the day they cut off his head, Louis XVI probably thought he was doing a better job than old Louis

XV, right? Poor old Paul probably tells himself he's doing better than John in some ways—and Pacelli in other ways—"

He tried to smile, and failed. Dennis McLaughlin shuddered inwardly. The man was suffering so visibly, simply witnessing it was a punishment.

"Cohane will want to fire Leo for these," Matthew Mahan said, fingering the tattered columns.

"He's already quit. As far as that goes, I'm glad he's out of it. He's too involved with the Church. It's almost—sick."

"For a layman, you mean," Matthew Mahan said with a tired smile. "It's interesting that an apostle of the younger generation like yourself should reach that conclusion. I've had the same feeling myself about other people. Then I hear a voice reminding me that we're always begging laymen to get more involved. But ultimately I'm afraid there's a limit. I think it has something to do with priesthood. A layman can't understand that idea, really, not the depths of it. No matter how much we try to get in step and join the twentieth century, we're still men apart. There's a terrible loneliness in that truth, Dennis, but maybe there's a little glory, too. Our kind of glory."

Matthew Mahan took a deep drag on the cigarette and stubbed it out. "How are you feeling?"

"Terrible."

"I mean physically. Why don't we do a little work before we go to bed? At least organize this mess. We'll use the triage system. Disasters we can't do anything about go at that end." He pointed at the right. "The trivia at this end." He pointed to the left. "And the crises in the middle."

For a moment Dennis thought sure he was going to weep. He was being forgiven—without even the humiliation of hearing the words spoken.

"I'm ready whenever you are," he said.

XXVI

Although Matthew Mahan found himself able to control his rage over Leo McLaughlin's vicious attack on him, he soon found it was far more difficult to deal with its impact. Everywhere he looked throughout the archdiocese the exposé seemed to leer at him. On the previous Sunday at Holy Angels parish, Father Novak had announced from the pulpit that he was leaving the priesthood. He had denounced reactionary pastors and stand-pat Archbishops who, he said, played the Vatican game and were rewarded with red hats. If they thought he was making up this accusation, Father Novak urged his listeners to read a series of articles in the underground newspaper, the Hard Times *Herald*.

Father Vincent Disalvo had replied to Matthew Mahan's repudiation of black reparations by calling him a hypocrite and a reactionary. He now demanded a hundred thousand dollars from the archdiocese in the name of the black community for his Council for Peace and Freedom. "Black people," he said, "are at least as important as Cardinal Mahan's relatives, clerical favorites, and great and good friends, who are reportedly devouring twice this figure each year from the chancery trough."

Even Monsignor O'Reilly managed to make an oblique reference to Leo the Great's articles when he told his parishioners that they were lucky to be rid of Father Novak. He was a fraud masquerading as a priest, trying to tell people it was easy to get to heaven when it was very, very difficult. Every age had its special challenge. For the early Christians it was the threat of martyrdom. For the Christians of the Middle Ages it was the Crusades, the fight against the infidel. For our time it was the liars inside and outside the Church who twisted the word of God into meanings that were the opposite of what God had taught in the Bible. Fortunately, they had a great pope who was fearlessly preaching the truth about birth control even when many of his bishops, Archbishops, and Cardinals had lapsed into heresy on the subject.

Three days later Matthew Mahan still writhed as he read the story in vivid detail in the diocesan paper. It filled the lower third of the first page, beneath the headlines reporting his elevation in Rome. On the inside page it ran for another two columns, facing the page on which he knelt before Pope Paul to accept his red biretta. The care with which Joe Cohane quoted Monsignor O'Reilly left no doubt that his once liberal editor had become a crypto-conservative. But that worry was minor compared to the pain Novak caused. Several priests—and even an auxiliary bishop—had departed this way in other dioceses. But this was his first public defection.

He was slightly consoled to find that his primary reaction was not anger but sadness. It was not simply Emil Novak's failure—it was his failure, too. He telephoned Vicar-General George Petrie and told him to find Novak and ask him to come in for a personal talk. "Tell him I only want to do what I can to help," he said.

"Matt," Petrie said dubiously. "Do you think that's wise? After the way he attacked you. On top of Disalvo?"

Matthew Mahan tried to explain to his vicar-general that he was more concerned about Emil Novak's soul than he was about any damage Father Novak might have done to his already battered reputation. George Petrie found nothing humorous whatsoever in his halfhearted self-deprecation. The vicar-general hung up promising to contact Novak but expressing grave doubts.

Matthew Mahan soon discovered that the gravity of his vicar-general's doubts about the state of his reputation extended far beyond his policy toward Father Novak. Even in the chancery office, Leo the Great's obnoxious slander was doing its deadly work, like insidious, inescapable poison gas. On Thursday morning Chancellor Terry Malone called and asked for "an hour alone" as soon as possible. "You make it sound like we usually meet in the lobby of the Garden Square Hotel," Matthew Mahan replied. "Of course we'll be alone."

"I mean without Father McLaughlin around," the chancellor said. He sounded so absurdly conspiratorial, Matthew Mahan almost laughed. "The vicar-general will be with me," Malone added.

"All we have to do is close the door to Dennis's office, Terry. We'll be alone."

The burly chancellor and the suave vicar-general arrived at 4 P.M. on Friday. They looked pointedly toward Dennis McLaughlin's office to make sure the door was closed. Both were solemn as men on the way to a grave. It soon became clear that they hoped they were digging one. Vicar-General Petrie let Chancellor Malone do the talking. "Your Eminence—at the risk of upsetting you—it is our considered advice that you should discharge Father McLaughlin as your secretary immediately."

"Why?"

"I'm sure you've read those articles his brother wrote. Frankly, Your Eminence, so has every priest in the archdiocese. Are you going to issue a denial?"

"I think silence is the best answer."

"Joe Cohane says you could sue for libel and run Leo the Great and that hippie rag out of the state."

"I know. I still prefer silence, Terry."

"Then you have no alternative but to get rid of Father McLaughlin."

"*Why?*"

The chancellor glanced over his shoulder at Dennis's closed door. "For one thing, we strongly suspect he leaked a lot of that information to his brother. A thorough investigation—by me personally—exonerates the chancery office. Who else could have done it?"

Matthew Mahan told himself to be calm. At the same time came a warning: *You are not dealing with stupid men.* "Now Terry," he said, "those articles were such a mess of wild exaggerations, scandalous rumors, absurd charges. The fellow worked for the paper. He could easily have picked up most of his ideas just talking to priests who have no great love for me."

"There were facts in those articles that could only have come from our files. Financial facts that will upset a lot of younger priests."

"I have absolute confidence in Father McLaughlin's integrity—and loyalty to me," Matthew Mahan said.

"All right," said the chancellor, yielding so readily that it was clear he never expected to win this part of the argument. "But we still think you should discharge him—for your own good and the good of the archdiocese."

That was almost diabolical, Matthew Mahan thought mordantly. Using his own best argument against him. "Why?" he asked, sparring for time.

"He has a bad reputation. I've been checking up on him. When he was at Yale, he was a supporter of every radical cause you could find. That novel he wrote—it makes fun of everything—radicals and conservatives—the Church itself. If anything he's a nihilist."

"Do you think he's a nihilist, George?" Matthew Mahan asked his vicar-general. He knew George Petrie was too intelligent to wrap his case around the outmoded philosophic terms so dear to Terry Malone. For a moment the Cardinal felt almost light-hearted. Once he got his two chief lieutenants to disagree, it would be easy to dismiss the idea.

"Let me put it this way, Matt," Petrie said smoothly. "Even if he's innocent—and I am inclined to share Terry's doubts on that score—I think at this point you have to make a show of cleaning house. Even a gesture of authority is important at this point. Those articles were terribly clever. They were aimed at making you look not only corrupt but ridiculous. To keep the brother of the man who wrote them on your staff—in the most intimate of all jobs—he goes everywhere with you—not only reminds everyone who sees him of the wretched things but suggests you may really be as foolish as they make you sound. I can't think of a better way to demolish your authority."

That will teach you to ask smart questions, Cardinal Mahan, whispered a mocking voice as the vicar-general finished. He was right, crushingly right, and the voice in which he spoke—whose voice was it but Old Smoothie Mahan?—the very advice he would have given to himself if he had never gone to the Church of St. Peter in Chains in Rome, never visited a cemetery in Nettuno, never walked a Mediterranean beach discoursing on moon shells and dynamic spirals and Pope John XXIII with a young priest who suddenly seemed to share his feelings about these things.

Terry Malone cleared his throat. Outside the world of business, he was not terribly bright. But he was a veteran of a thousand encounters with Archbishops and knew when to press an advantage. "George is speaking mainly of the impact on your priests. I can assure you that keeping him around will have the same effect—maybe even a worse one—on the laity. The big givers. You know how conservative they are."

Yes, I know. Haven't I sold them carefully calibrated sections of my soul for the past twenty years? That was what Matthew Mahan wanted to say. But it was better to be silent, even at the risk of sounding like a fool.

"This is good advice—sound advice," he murmured. "I'll certainly give it careful thought. But there are—other considerations. I mean—spiritual ones."

The look of incomprehension on George Petrie's suave face and the frown of disapproval on Chancellor Malone's crusty forehead brought him to a dead stop. How could he explain to these men? How could he take them into his personal life? For ten years they had lived and worked together—but he had never had a personal conversation with them. Occasionally, he would reminisce with Petrie or exchange gossip about the class of '39. But most of the time it had been strictly business—doing the job. Worrying about Father So-and-So who ran wild with his Diner's Club card. Monsignor What's His Name who boiled curates for breakfast.

"He's—he's fighting for his vocation, you see. I think I can—help."

It was hopeless. He was contradicting the arguments he had used for the last year to hold the diocese together. The good of the majority was more important than the troubled minority, the individual. *The peace of the diocese, that was the paramount thing.* He could suddenly see Emil Novak's skeptical face on the third floor of Holy Angels' rectory. Now it was replaced by more obvious skepticism on George Petrie's face.

Somehow, Matthew Mahan got them out of the office with more promises to think the matter over very carefully. On Monday morning Terry Malone was back with a face like a gargoyle to hear the Cardinal tell him he wanted to find a million dollars to keep St. Clare's Hospital open and also give $25,000 to fund pilot projects for inner-city nuns. The Cardinal had to listen to forty-five minutes of objections and protests. The chancellor left assuring him that Monsignor Jeremiah O'Callahan, head of Catholic Charities, would be even more upset by these decisions. He was right, of course. With a master's degree in social work to bolster him, Jerry O'Callahan did not like amateurs like the Cardinal—or the nuns—invading his bailiwick.

The Cardinal decided to wrestle with O'Callahan some other day and spent the rest of the morning in conference with lean intense Monsignor Tom Barker, head of his diocesan Rota. Monsignor Barker, who had a doctorate in canon law from Rome, was aghast at the Cardinal's idea to receive good-conscience divorced Catholics back into the Church. Matthew Mahan nodded solemnly into the teeth of his warning that the Sacred Congregation for the Doctrine of the Faith, the Sacred Congregation for the Discipline of the Sacraments, the Sacred Roman Rota, and a half-dozen other Vatican departments were sure to disapprove it. He told Barker that he would take complete responsibility. Only then did the anxious canonist agree to write to the diocesan Rotas of Portland, Oregon, and Baton Rouge, Louisiana, where similar programs were already operating.

After a long-faced Barker departed, Matthew Mahan dictated a circular letter to all his pastors, urging them to seek out divorced Catholics in their parishes and advise them to petition the marriage tribunal for permission to receive the sacraments once more. Next he dictated personal letters to the bishops of Portland and Baton Rouge, asking their confidential opinion of how well their programs were working—and whether they had aroused any controversy in their dioceses or criticism from Rome.

At three-thirty the next day ex-Father Emil Novak appeared without warning in response to the message Matthew Mahan had sent to him earlier in the week. A very tired Cardinal, who had resisted Dennis McLaughlin's urging to take a nap after lunch and now regretted it, lit his sixth cigarette of the day and offered the last one in the pack to Father Novak, who primly shook his head.

It was an omen. There was nothing to discuss. Father Novak said that he was here only because he respected Matthew Mahan as a person. He no longer had any respect for his office nor for that matter for any other office in the so-called teaching church. Leo the Great's articles had confirmed all his suspicions and liberated him from his lingering illusions. He had meant every word of the sermon he had preached last Sunday morning. The teaching church was a monster, offering men scorpions instead of eggs, stones instead of bread. With Leo McLaughlin's help he was writing a book that would make all this very clear. He was also getting married next week—to an ex-nun who had taught the first grade at Holy Angels until she left the convent earlier this year. He said this with a note of triumph in his voice that made Matthew Mahan wince inwardly. He was a little boy finally doing the forbidden thing. He was not here out of any personal respect for him. He was here to tell off Big Daddy, the boss, face to face.

Again, Matthew Mahan sensed lurking in the shadows the man of angry power he once preferred. Not roaring rage, but cold, savage contempt was what he wanted to shower on this callow, half-formed young man. He could very possibly destroy him and his childish pretensions; at the very least it would be satisfying to try. But this version of his old self was now as unwelcome as the roaring rager.

"Emil," he said, lighting another cigarette and mentally reprimanding himself for doing it, "would you do me one favor? In your book, would you avoid personalities? I'm not pleading for myself here, I'm speaking for everyone you've met who has held an opinion you dislike. Criticize the opinion, but don't abuse the man. Give him credit for sincerity. I'm thinking particularly of Monsignor O'Reilly. He's not a likable man. Did it ever occur to you that he may know it, but be unable to do anything about it?"

"He doesn't give a damn about anyone enough to do anything—" Novak's voice choked with hatred.

Matthew Mahan sighed. Instead of Father Novak's shifty eyes and weak mouth, he saw Sister Helen Reed's innocent gamin face, illuminated by the same angry righteousness. "How do you *know?*" he asked. "Very, very few of us ever have the privilege of knowing what goes on in another man's soul."

Father Novak stared at him for a moment and then laughed shrilly. "That's the most asinine statement I ever heard in my life. I know exactly what's going on in Monsignor O'Reilly's soul. I have confronted that man's malignant soul every night for a year."

"No, you haven't. You saw a man consumed by envy. By frustrated hopes, unfulfilled expectations. I know much more about Monsignor O'Reilly than you. But I also know this. He was a young priest once like yourself, with a heart full of love. For God, for his fellowmen. No one becomes a priest without feeling those things. I have no intention of trying to explain to you why he's become a bitter old man. I only want to warn you that there are many, many roads to bitterness. They all have one thing in common. Arrogance."

For just a moment, Father Novak's bravado faltered. Perhaps he was facing his highly uncertain future for the first time.

"What are you going to do—what sort of work?"

"I don't know. I'm not going to think about it until I finish my book. Martha—my—wife—is teaching in Lincoln Township."

"Is she in complete agreement—about your leaving this way— not waiting to be laicized?"

"Of course."

"And the children—will they be Catholic?"

"They'll be people of God."

"Well. That means they'll be good people. We can't ask for more than that. God bless you, Emil."

Novak stood up. "Thank you," he said. "I—I didn't want it to end this way but—"

But, but, but. Matthew Mahan let the word toll in his brain as he watched Novak vanish through the doorway. Life was full of buts and ifs. If Monsignor Paul O'Reilly had not confused his ability to manipulate the tired, bored old man who had the power in this diocese with the power itself, he might still be vicar-general. But he went out of his way to be obnoxious to Monsignor Matthew Mahan, fund-raiser extraordinary. If Matthew Mahan had not tried to solve the problem of Monsignor O'Reilly's hatred diplomatically, by giving him one of the best parishes at his disposal, Emil Novak might still be a priest. Yes, Matthew Mahan told himself mournfully, that was where the failure lay—in his assumption that politics was the answer, when a bishop, a real bishop, would have had the courage to confront the man and say: *Your hatred of me will destroy your priesthood.* But smoothies didn't work that way. So now, ten years later, a priesthood has been destroyed, perhaps two.

Matthew Mahan picked up the microphone of his Stenorette and began dictating.

"Dear Monsignor O'Reilly, colon."

He stopped. What he wanted to say could only be handwritten. Official business could be dictated and typed. But this was not official business. He picked up one of his pens.

Dear Monsignor O'Reilly,

I hope you can read my atrocious handwriting. I just saw Father Novak. I wonder if we should both get down on our knees and ask ourselves what we have done. For many, many years I knew that you hated me. For almost as many years I returned the hate—which of course we both called dislike—with interest. I confess that more than once I enjoyed the thought of you sitting in your rectory, trying to understand how a lug like me could be presiding at the Archbishop's house. I should have gone to you a long time ago and said, "I need your help."

I cannot speak for you. I don't know what you could or should have done to prevent or resolve our failure. But I do know that you should never have allowed your hatred to spill over into the life of another priest. Torment me all you want, I probably deserve it. In fact, I am sure like most enemies we deserve each other. But why in the name of God did we destroy that young man's priesthood? I dread having to answer that question someday. I hope you do, too.

This is not simply a reproach or a confession. I am writing out of deep concern for the other young priest in your house, Father Cannon. Please give me your assurance without delay that you will exercise restraint and charity in any disagreement that arises between you and him.

Sincerely yours in Christ,
Matthew Mahan

He put the letter in an envelope, addressed it to Monsignor O'Reilly, sealed it, and put it in his out box. For a moment he debated asking Dennis to read it. Was the smoothie, in his blundering and much too late lunge for sainthood, making a fool of himself? It was impossible to know. Showing a letter like that to anyone could only look like grandstanding. That was one vice that his father, God bless his surly old soul, eradicated early.

Matthew Mahan could still see, feel, the day. A scorcher in July. He was in the seventh or eighth grade, pitching for the neighborhood sandlot team. After striking out nine in a row in the sixth, seventh, and eighth innings, he had called in the outfield and struck out the last three batters on ten pitches. As they trudged up the steps to the railroad bridge above the field where they played, he saw his father leaning on the sooty iron fence, watching them. That night at dinner, he had learned about grandstanding. *What are you saying when you pull a stunt like that? You don't need the other eight guys. Just leave it to Mighty Matthew. It's bad enough that the guys you beat that way will hate your guts. But your own guys wind up feeling the same way.*

The next day, the vicar-general reported that the Archdiocesan Association of Priests would almost certainly pass a resolution calling for a full and complete report on the archdiocese's finances at their meeting this weekend. There was even talk by some more militant members of a motion to demand the Cardinal's appearance to give them an explanation of his policies in person. In other words, to defend himself against the accusations of Leo the Great. Vicar-General Petrie thought there was not much chance of this resolution passing. "But anything is possible these days," he added with a sigh.

In the past, Cardinal Mahan would have testily told his vicar to make sure neither motion passed. The extralegal Association of Priests and the archdiocese's Priest's Senate had been handily controlled by groups of loyalists, with whom George Petrie kept in constant close contact. But the Cardinal could sense in the vicar's helplessness a certain satisfaction, an implied whisper of *I told you so.*

This news led to another wrestle with an even more recalcitrant Chancellor Malone. Matthew Mahan decided the best possible response to the priests was the prompt publication of a full honest financial report. The chancellor was appalled, dubious, sullen, as the Cardinal parried, evaded, and finally dismissed with regret his contrary arguments. "When can I get it, Terry?" Matthew Mahan asked.

"I have no idea," said the chancellor. "It's certainly not something we should rush into. I'll have to talk it over with our accountants. I'll check with the people in New York to see what they're issuing this year."

Matthew Mahan's hopes drooped. "There's no possibility of getting something out in a week or ten days?"

"Not unless you want to put us in jail."

When Matthew Mahan tried to reduce this exaggeration to reality, he got buried in an hour of technical terms. There were, it seems, thirty-two different "generally accepted accounting principles"—all of them so general that they often contradicted each other. Should they use "flow through" or "comprehensive" procedures? The Accounting Principles Board of the American Institute of Certified Public Accountants recently frowned on flow through, but the archdiocese's accountants still favored it. Then there was the new "costing" approach recently developed by a Big Eight accounting firm that had enabled one university to increase its government grants by 20 per cent. Should they use that to state the costs of their parochial schools? If the state legislature passed the private school aid bill, it might make the difference between millions gained and lost. But stating the costs at their ultimate might panic pastors and parents, if no state aid was forthcoming. Then there were a number of bequests recently received by the archdiocese. Among these were stock in a chain of nightclubs, a herd of beef cattle, and a half-dozen oil wells in Oklahoma. They were all in the process of being sold, as canon law required. But stating their value before the sale was a complex matter. There was a question about the widsom of selling the oil wells too hastily. The new federal tax law might permit some very juicy deductions from their income if they were held for a year, a latitude certainly permitted by canon law.

There was the hint of a grim smile on the chancellor's lips as he finally departed, promising the Cardinal that a report would be prepared with "all reasonable speed." By now Matthew Mahan realized he would be lucky to see a first draft in September.

The next day the vicar-general was back with news of two young curates who were asking for laicization. Almost too casually he remarked that they had said Leo the Great's articles were part of the reason for their making this negative decision. Petrie also reported that Monsignor O'Reilly was attempting to organize the older suburban pastors, to force a vote at the next meeting of their deanery, asking the Cardinal to repudiate Leo's allegations about his birth control beliefs with a ringing affirmation of *Humanae Vitae*. "I wouldn't be surprised if they form one of those conservative pressure groups, like that Midwest outfit, Te Deum," the vicar-general said.

Later that day came Mike Furia and Chancellor Malone to hold a wake for the fund drive. An interim report now estimated they would fall short of their goal by $2,500,000. It was especially disappointing to find out that contributions had declined during the past week, in spite of the extensive news coverage of His Eminence's triumphs in Rome.

"That hurts the old ego," Matthew Mahan said, silently adding: *What you needed, what you needed.*

"I don't think it has anything to do with a decline in your personal popularity, Matt," said Mike Furia soothingly. "Terry here's been telling us the day of personal fund-raising by amateurs is just about over. It looks like he's right. You'll have to rely on professionals, or tested techniques, from now on."

"Maybe the answer is really psychological," Matthew Mahan

mused. "What does the average guy think when he sees his Arch-bishop deplaning from his personal jet, being toasted and dinnered at the best hotels in Rome, marching up St. Peter's aisle in gold vestments? Maybe he thinks about the trouble he has meeting his mortgage and decides we can get along without his hundred dollars this year."

Terry Malone grumbled something about the importance of keeping up appearances. He obviously thought that the Cardinal was losing his grip. Morosely, he pointed out that their poverty solved at least one problem. There was no longer any need to de-bate building three new churches and three new parochial schools in the suburbs. That idea was kaput indefinitely.

"At least I can look like a statesman to the National Associa-tion of Laymen," Matthew Mahan said. "Who knows, I may even get a few lines of praise in the *National Catholic Reporter*."

"I hope not," growled the chancellor.

"Do me a favor, will you, Terry? Run a financial study of what the parochial schools will be costing us by 1976? Based on reasonable estimates of rising teachers' salaries, costs, that sort of thing."

The chancellor gave him a very suspicious look, but he glumly promised to get to work on it. "I bet it will knock your head off," Mike Furia said.

Mike lingered for a few minutes after Terry Malone departed. He wanted to tell Matthew Mahan that he was leaving for a six-to-eight-week trip around the world to check out his overseas companies. Mike had not resigned as chairman of the Cardinal's Fund, but this trip, while the fund was sagging so badly, was the nearest thing to it. Although Matthew Mahan had asked for his resignation, he still felt like his old friend was deserting him. *Get used to it,* a voice whispered to him.

But Mike was absorbed in his own problems. "I thought you'd like to know—I'm getting a divorce. My wife can't believe it. The Animal is finally standing on his hind legs and fighting back."

The bitterness in these words pained Matthew Mahan. "Mike," he said, "try to bring some charity, some understanding—"

"Charity I'm trying. I'm giving her five million bucks in com-pany stock."

"I mean charity—from the heart, Mike."

"I haven't got it, Matt. Not for her."

"All right. All right. We all have to do the best we can. At least you're not looking for revenge. I hope you get married again—soon."

"As a matter of fact, I've got someone in mind."

"Do I know her?"

"Yeah. But since I haven't asked her, I'm not going to tell you her name. It's probably a pipe dream anyway. By the time I get back from this trip she'll have forgotten my name—like my wife used to do."

"I hope not, Mike. I mean it. Have a good trip. I'll be praying for you whether you like it or not."

No comment, only a brief smile from Mike. They shook hands and he was gone.

A call from Father Philip Reagan, president of St. Francis Xavier University. "Your Eminence, I feel I should tell you this personally. We've been forced to discontinue your nephew's scholarship."

"Why?"

"Well—the Student Council demanded an explanation of why he had one. These articles on the archdiocese's finances in that underground newspaper—all the kids have read them, Your Eminence. It was common knowledge—although I only heard about it this morning—that Timmy's marks were atrocious and half the time he's on drugs. There's no—adequate explanation for him having a scholarship."

"I trust he can finish the term."

"Yes—of course. As for him returning next fall, I don't think he can do it without repeating a number of courses this summer."

"Why was this situation allowed to develop without anyone even bothering to tell me about it? I'm not talking about the scholarship now. I'm the nearest thing the boy has to a father; you knew that as well as anyone. Do you people *run* schools anymore? Lately I get the impression that they're running you."

"We're doing the best we can," Father Reagan said in a strangled voice. "I think Your Eminence should know that Timmy is not exactly one of your admirers. Rather the contrary. He supplied a lot of material for those vicious articles on you."

"I hope you have evidence for that statement."

"I can't produce witnesses, Your Eminence, but we do have a rather effective intelligence system set up out here to help us anticipate crises. Some of the people working for us know Timmy very well. I could arrange to have you talk with the priest who's running it."

"No. I'll take your word for it," Matthew Mahan said, hearing and hating the defeat in his voice.

He called his sister-in-law to tell her the bad news. Predictably, she began to weep. He murmured soothing phrases into the phone until she calmed down. Then he told her more bad news. He was being forced to cancel her charge accounts. Perhaps she had heard about the series of articles accusing him—? No, of course not. She had heard nothing, the whole thing was incomprehensible to her. He told her not to panic. He would ask Mike Furia to raise her salary. But she would have to learn to manage money better. Cash would have to stop slipping through her fingers. "I'll try, Matt, I'll try," she promised. "But I just think it's terrible that anyone should attack you. . . ."

He agreed, no question about it, it was terrible that anyone should attack such a paragon of sanctity as Matthew Mahan. He hung up and stared out the window at the vanishing sunlight. It was almost six o'clock. Except for twenty minutes at lunch, he had been behind this desk all day. Dennis McLaughlin appeared in the doorway to his office. "Why don't you take a nap before dinner, Your Eminence?" he said.

"What's this Eminence stuff from you? Didn't I tell you to call me Father?"

"I'm sorry—everyone else—"

"I can't do anything about the rest of them. But I've got you right under my thumb. It's Father or else."

"Or else you won't take a nap?" Dennis said with a smile.

For a few moments Matthew Mahan felt almost good. A month ago, even a week ago, he and Dennis couldn't have talked this way. Dennis would have retreated, hurt, confused, by the apparent rebuke. Did it mean anything? Was it worth it? Worth the loss of respect and loyalty it might cost him—in fact was already costing him—in his chancery office, worth the possible wreck of his authority as bishop? *Yes*, he thought. *Let the ninety-nine stay on the hills.*

"All right. All right. I'll take a nap. For a man who's supposed to be an authoritarian, I spend an awful lot of my time around here taking orders."

XXVII

Two weeks later, Matthew Mahan awoke at 3 A.M. He braced himself for a bout of pain, but his stomach was remarkably tranquil. Bill Reed had hauled him into his office a week ago and given him a very hard time about obeying his doctor's orders, staying on his diet, getting more rest, etc., etc. It was the worst tongue-lashing he'd received since the last time old Hogan summoned him to his sanctum to teach him humility. He had humbly confessed his faults and adhered scrupulously to his diet. So Brother Pain was keeping his distance. That was not why you were awake, Your Eminence, he told himself. No, he knew exactly why he was staring into the darkness, now. That call from Colin McGuiness, the episcopal vicar of the inner city, warning him that tomorrow's meeting of the inner-city deanery was going to be anything but pleasant.

The archdiocese was divided into a half-dozen deaneries, each governed by an episcopal vicar. Presiding at their meetings, held twice a year, had always been one of Matthew Mahan's more pleasant chores. Many Archbishops sent auxiliary bishops to represent them, but he felt the meetings were an excellent opportunity to keep in touch with his priests. He had always tried hard to find an interesting speaker, sometimes a priest, sometimes a layman, for each meeting, and attendance was usually good.

Father McGuiness had begun by remarking wryly that the attendance at tomorrow's meeting was likely to be almost too good. Many young inner-city priests had been deeply disturbed by Leo McLaughlin's articles. Father Vincent Disalvo was exploiting this disturbance with vengeful skill. There was almost certain to be a demand for the publication of an archdiocesan financial report. There might be even more ugly questions about His Eminence's personal finances. Vicar McGuiness's voice had trembled as he transmitted this warning. He obviously expected a blast of preliminary episcopal wrath. Matthew Mahan could almost hear Colin's relief when he simply thanked him for the call and told him not to lose any sleep about it.

It was 5 A.M. before he took his own advice, and even then he only slipped into a kind of waking doze full of disconnected, vaguely threatening images—Mary Shea weeping in Rome, Davey Cronin's anguished face crying out wordlessly—until his alarm went off at six. He felt half drugged with weariness as he and Dennis plodded through the morning mail.

"I'm a little worried about this meeting," he confided to Dennis as they left the residence to walk through the May sunshine to the waiting limousine. He told him about Colin McGuiness's call.

Dennis nodded grimly and got in the car feeling like a man on the way to his own execution. He had heard the same things from his brother in far more vivid terms. Ninety per cent of the younger priests in the diocese had read the series, Leo boasted, and their respect for the great man was gone forever.

To compound their difficulties, the deanery was meeting in the gymnasium of St. Sebastian's Church. That made Father Vincent Disalvo the host, and he was obviously enjoying it. When they arrived, his black militant and white student followers were eagerly serving coffee to the sixty or seventy priests sitting on the steel folding chairs on the floor of the gymnasium. The only consolation in sight was the refusal of the archdiocese's four black priests to go along with Disalvo. They obviously resented his grab for leadership and sat as far away from him as possible.

Vicar McGuiness shook hands with Matthew Mahan at the head of the steps leading to the stage. "Hello, boss," he said. "How are things?"

"Snafu, as usual," Matthew Mahan said. He was startled to note that Colin was almost bald and on his way to a middle-age paunch. The years went by so quickly. Colin had been his secretary for the first two years of his episcopacy.

"I'm afraid things aren't much better down here," he said. "I know you expect me to do something to head off this kind of thing but—"

"I know you're not a magician, Colin. Let's see how the situation develops."

He looked down at the audience and was startled to see eight or ten nuns sitting in the center of the priests on the right-hand side of the aisle. "Who invited them?" he asked Colin.

"The Ad Hoc Committee."

"What's *that?*"

"The Ad Hoc Committee for a More Relevant Deanery."

"That doesn't tell me anything. What is it? Who's on it?"

"I don't know. I only heard about it yesterday." Colin tried to smile, but the result was a sick smirk. "It's not exactly a vote of confidence in my vicariate."

"Who's on it?"

"Who else? Vinny Disalvo, Vinny Disalvo, and Vinny Disalvo, plus four or five more yes-men."

This time Matthew Mahan had to force a smile. He remembered rather mournfully that he had enjoyed Colin McGuiness's jocular sarcasm when he was his secretary. He also saw in the contrast between his bland mediocre face and Dennis McLaughlin's cool intelligence the distance he had traveled in the last ten years.

"Who's the speaker, Colin?" he asked.

As a step toward autonomy, he had entrusted the task of finding speakers to the local vicars. It had not been a particularly successful experiment. Lacking Matthew Mahan's prestige, they were unable to attract first-rate people. "I've invited this fellow from New York, Monsignor Joe Snow. He's the Associate Vicar for Religious. An old pal of mine from Rome. His mother is living in St. Patrick's parish with a married sister." Colin glanced nervously at his watch. "He should be here any minute."

George Petrie arrived, cool and debonair as ever. The vicar-general usually acted as the chairman at deanery meetings. "Good morning, Chairman George," Colin McGuiness said, mock Chinese style. "Whatever you do, do not declare one of those nuns out of order."

"That won't be necessary. It's obvious that they are out of order."

"I can't take those kind of puns at ten A.M.," Matthew Mahan said.

Monsignor Snow arrived. Tall, ruggedly built, with a hawk nose and a complexion that at first looked swarthy and was actually pale. One of those heavy-bearded men who always looked like he needed a shave. He proceeded to give a speech that Matthew Mahan could only consider a disaster. Delivered in a rasping voice, it might have come from a man of eighty.

"There is a cliché which religious bandy about these days and it sounds specious. It is the phrase The spirit is moving. I ask what spirit? Whose spirit? I submit that the spirit of God cannot be

336

at the heart of any movement that refuses to recognize the divinity of the Church. For some religious the word 'structure' is a dirty word. But any intelligent mind recognizes the need for some form of structure for the stability of any organization.

"The spirit of God cannot be at the heart of any movement that refuses to recognize the teaching authority of the vicar of Christ on earth.

"The spirit of God cannot be at the heart of any movement that accepts as infallible the fuzzy opinions of pseudo-theologians (and their number is legion) and rejects out of hand the teaching magisterium of the Church.

"The spirit of God cannot be at the heart of any movement which indulges in the contestation of religious authority."

Monsignor Snow declared that under the cloak of renewal and adaptation, many tragedies are taking place and have taken place. "Change most certainly was needed in religious life but not destruction nor revolution. Everything that is old is not bad and everything that is new is not good. The ideal is to hold onto the best of the old and to accept the best of the new. Change for change's sake is utterly ridiculous."

Applause was light. A priest sitting next to Vincent Disalvo—his name slipped through Matthew Mahan's tired brain—stood up and said, "As a member of the Ad Hoc Committee for a More Relevant Deanery, I would like to suggest to the vicar that from now on the members of the deanery should be consulted on the choice of speakers."

"The chair has not recognized you, Father," said Monsignor Petrie. "You are out of order in the first place. And in the second place as well. Your comment is grossly impolite to our distinguished guest."

"We don't have time for politeness," called a voice several rows behind Father Forgotten-Name.

"I don't agree. We have time for politeness. And for order," said Monsignor Petrie. "You all know the rules of these meetings. They are in force. They will remain in force. If anyone has a question or disagreement with the speaker, I trust it will be substantive."

Total silence. *Roma locuta est,* thought Matthew Mahan wryly. If only it were *finita.*

Monsignor Snow leaned over and murmured in Colin McGuiness's ear. He in turn murmured in George Petrie's ear, and he in turn explained to the audience, "Monsignor Snow's mother is ill. He only has a few hours in the city and he'd like to spend as much time with her as possible. If you have no questions, he'd like to be excused."

Monsignor Snow thrust his rolled-up speech into his inner jacket pocket, banged down the wooden steps beside the stage, and stalked out of the gymnasium. "If that's what they're preaching in New York," Matthew Mahan murmured to George Petrie, "perhaps we ought to declare them a mission territory."

"He's probably going back to suggest that Cookie do the same thing for us," the vicar-general replied. "Who do you think has more clout?"

"Oh well, I've always wanted to be a missionary bishop."

Studying the rows of faces before him, Matthew Mahan tried to judge their mood. The young ones all looked saturnine. The pastors, almost all of them sitting in a clump in the first few rows on the right, looked depressed.

"Before we go on to business from the floor," George Petrie said, "Cardinal Mahan would like to say a few words to you."

In the first row, Monsignor Paul Scanlon, massive as ever, with a senatorial head of gray hair, raised his hand. Another good pastor who had presided over St. Luke's parish for twenty years, watching it change from Irish to Spanish. Unfazed, he had spent a summer in Puerto Rico and came home speaking the language fluently. He was getting a little old, but he was still an effective, impressive priest. "May I presume to inject a bit of business first, Mr. Chairman?"

"I suppose so, Monsignor."

Scanlon rose and sonorously presented a resolution, offering the unanimous congratulations of the deanery to Cardinal Mahan on his elevation.

"That isn't business," said George Petrie, "that's a pleasure. May I hear the ayes in favor?"

There was a rumble of assent. "Any nays?" asked George with a jovial smile.

About ten or fifteen voices from various parts of the audience responded. Some were clear, some were murky, but they were definitely saying nay.

George Petrie lost his aplomb. "I can't believe what I just

heard. Do the nays have the courage to identify themselves and give us an explanation for this gratuitous insult?"

Matthew Mahan leaned back in his chair. He was aware of a faint smile frozen on his face. In search of a casual gesture, he lit a cigarette. He could hear Bill Reed rasping at him, *You must cut out smoking.* For an insane moment he wondered if those young nay-saying voices knew that there was no reason to congratulate His Eminence. What if he told them? Told them the whole story about *frater taciturnus?*

There was no response to Vicar-General Petrie's challenge. "George, may I," Matthew Mahan said, and slid the microphone down the table in front of him. "I think we're being rather childish," he said. "I think Monsignor Scanlon has gotten a clear majority for his resolution. I thank him for it, from the heart. I know many of us would like to see it unanimously approved. But maybe we can't expect unanimity in these confusing times."

The silence was stony. What do you expect, a round of applause for your benevolence? Matthew Mahan asked himself.

He stubbed out his cigarette and moved the microphone closer to him.

"Now I'd like to talk to you for a few minutes about St. Clare's Hospital. I know there has been considerable opposition to my plan to close it. I've reconsidered that plan and have decided to try to keep the hospital open on a new basis—operating largely as an outpatient clinic. I've acquired the services of one of the best doctors in the city, William Reed, to plan and direct this change. It isn't a perfect answer, I know. But to keep the entire hospital going would require the investment of millions to practically rebuild the whole plant from the ground up. It's still going to cost us almost a million dollars on an outpatient basis. We're going to triple or quadruple the present emergency room facilities, and we're also going to provide a lot more psychiatric counseling. I hope I will have your support for this decision. And I hope you will do your best to win the community's support."

The priest sitting next to Father Disalvo raised his hand and was recognized by George Petrie. "As vice-chairman of the Ad Hoc Committee, I would like to request a recess so we can ˙ᴘᴏ˙ ˙ to what His Eminence has just told us."

˙ᴠ ıl five minutes be enough?"

Five minutes would be enough. The Ad Hoc Committee members rose and filed out of the gymnasium. There were sixteen or seventeen of them, all young. Eddie McGuire rose from the ranks of the pastors and walked to the stage. He looked dreadful. He must have lost fifty pounds in the last six months. "Matt," he said, "you've got to get tough with those young punks. You can't let them walk all over you."

"Now, Eddie, don't get carried away," Matthew Mahan said. "Nobody's laid a foot on me yet."

Eddie looked dubious, and Matthew Mahan asked him how he was feeling. "Lousy," he said. "I thought I had this thing licked, but now they tell me I've got to start cobalt treatments."

Matthew Mahan promised to remember Eddie in his masses. They discussed other ailing members of the class. Eddie seemed to have a list in his head. The return of the Ad Hoc Committee rescued Matthew Mahan from depression. Their vice-chairman reported that the chairman, Father Vincent Disalvo, would like to say a few words.

Father Disalvo rose to his feet, smiling. He gave Matthew Mahan a respectful salutation and then began demolishing the Cardinal's plan for St. Clare's. First of all, the community would never accept Bill Reed, an uptown rich-folks doctor. The new head of the hospital should be black, and from the downtown section.

As for psychiatric services—were the psychiatrists going to be white? If so, the black community wanted nothing to do with them. A white psychiatrist was incapable of treating a black man or woman because he had no conception of the black experience.

The whole idea of turning the hospital into a clinic was unsatisfactory. How did His Eminence have the temerity to plead poverty in the light of recent revelations about the archdiocese's finances—and his personal finances? The hospital should be kept open on a full-time basis, and the millions needed to rebuild and modernize it be committed to the task immediately. Let us have an end to hoarding the Church's money and above all an end to personal indulgence in spending it. The money belonged to the Christian community, not to one man.

In the back of the hall, Dennis McLaughlin writhed inwardly as Matthew Mahan tensely tried to answer these charges. He called on his black priests to comment on the psychiatric problem. Bulky George Rollins, the leader of the group, soberly declared that a white psychiatrist who worked with black people for a reasonable length of time should have no difficulty understanding their special experience, if he had two functioning ears.

"We're not interested in what the Oreos think," Father Disalvo sneered.

To Matthew Mahan's dismay, George Petrie made no attempt to tell Disalvo he was out of order. Instead the vicar-general turned to Matthew Mahan and asked him sotto voce what an Oreo was. *Black on the outside, white on the inside*, Matthew Mahan scribbled on a pad in front of them, while Rollins and Disalvo exchanged more insults. After letting epithets reverberate through the hall for several minutes, the vicar-general reluctantly (so it seemed to Matthew Mahan) gaveled them into silence.

Matthew Mahan tried to regain a civilized tone as he defended Bill Reed's undeniable whiteness. He was a personal friend and was contributing his services free of charge. He had the experience. Matthew Mahan had seen him organize and run one of the most efficient and effective field hospitals in Europe during World War II. He guaranteed Dr. Reed's competence, his dedication. Moreover, as a former head of the county medical society, he was in a position to persuade many other doctors to donate their services to St. Clare's. Once the reorganization was completed, Dr. Reed would no doubt be happy to turn the job over to a black man.

Emotion thickened Matthew Mahan's voice as he took up the last charges—that the archdiocese was hoarding money and he himself was spending it for his own selfish purposes. Neither accusation was true—

The young priest who was Disalvo's alter ego leaped to his feet. "The members of the Ad Hoc Committee would like to know why you have failed to issue a financial report again this year."

"I had a conference with Chancellor Malone two weeks ago, and we decided to go ahead and issue one, even though it might be wiser to wait—and profit from the experience of other dioceses. I hope we can get it out before the end of the year."

"I hope it will include a thorough statement of your personal finances, Your Eminence."

"What do you mean?"

"A number of priests were deeply concerned by the evidence

brought to light by a columnist of the Hard Times *Herald*. We are even more concerned that you have made no attempt to deny any of these charges. All you've done is fire the man who wrote the articles from his job on the diocesan paper."

"I did not fire Leo the Great McLaughlin; he quit his job before I returned from Rome. As for answering the charges, I prefer to let my life and character speak for themselves."

A mistake. A lance of pain shot across his body. But what else could he say?

"Some of the evidence has been sustained by an independent investigation by this committee. St. Francis Xavier University has admitted that they gave your nephew a full scholarship at your request."

Out of the corner of his eye, Matthew Mahan could see *I told you so* on George Petrie's face. The words the Cardinal had spoken to Eddie McGuire a few minutes earlier mocked him. They are laying several dozen feet on you now, Your Eminence, they are walking up and down your torso and pivoting on your face, while your loyal followers watch with mounting horror and dismay. Doesn't the old smoothie owe them something? How far do you carry this would-be-saint business? Into a new kind of loneliness, wholly unexplored by the pseudo-saint, utterly unsuspected by the smoothie?

"Father, what are you trying to achieve? What is the purpose of this inquisition?"

The words had spoken themselves. Involuntary, a force inside him, using his own trembling voice.

"I guess you might say we're trying to start a Project Equality inside the Church."

For a moment rage stormed in his chest. He thought he would collapse, choking with fury, right there on the platform. With an agonizing effort he controlled himself. "Father," he said in the same trembling voice, "the Church is not a debating society. It is not a city council, a state legislature. We are witnesses to a truth, bearers of a responsibility that goes beyond limited political realities. Speaking before God, I am prepared to say that I have administered the affairs of this archdiocese with honesty and good faith."

Wrong, wrong, wrong, cried another voice inside him, while a jagged lightning bolt of pain cut through the center of his body.

"Then I take it, Your Eminence, that you consider yourself above questioning, above petty details like ten or twenty thousand dollars of the people's money handed over to your relations. I suppose the same principle applies to all other aspects of your administration. Well, at least we know where we stand."

Father Forgotten-Name sat down. Matthew Mahan stared at him, unable to think, much less speak. He saw Father Disalvo reach across his own lap and shake Father Forgotten-Name's hand. This was not what he intended, not what he deserved. *I am Joseph, your brother.* Why couldn't he say that? Why couldn't he find words that communicated this cry? Because the dismay in George Petrie's eyes, the grim expectation on the lined, solemn faces of Eddie McGuire and his fellow pastors would not permit him. He was trapped between the old and the new, between power and grace.

"I will not say anything about disrespect, about the moral aspect of publicly accusing—judging—a man in direct contradiction to the spirit of the Gospels. I merely want to say—I merely want to say—"

What? *I am Joseph, your brother.* Not permitted. The iron faces of the past, the old men in the first rows, glared up at him like weapons, forbidding his wish to move past them, to offer a cigarette to Father Forgotten-Name, to shake Father Disalvo's hand, to assure them that they were one in the spirit. Only details, petty details from the past, separated them. But it was both too early and too late.

A shifting among the pastors, a visible, audible uneasiness that flowed back from them to the rest of the deanery. They were waiting for him to finish his sentence.

"—I am very sorry to see this visible hardening of our hearts toward one another. For me, this is the real tragedy that is happening here. I dismiss—I disregard my own personal—humiliation. I want to prevent this other thing—this other terrible thing—from growing worse. I will go anywhere, meet with anyone, discuss any proposal to prevent it."

"Will you permit our committee to examine the books?"

"I'm willing to discuss it. But let me point out that it is not a practical idea. To make it worthwhile, you would have to understand accounting procedures. You would have to understand why we do a great many things in ways that are not—financially orthodox. But I'm willing to discuss it."

Father Disalvo rose to his feet. "Your Eminence, we are sick of discussing things with you. We are sick of being talked to—talked down to like children. You're like all the rest of our so-called leaders. All you want to do is talk while babies fry in napalm in Vietnam, and die of rat bites on the next block. I move that we respond to this offer with a vote of no confidence."

"As chairman, I must rule that question out of order," said George Petrie crisply. "Votes are only taken on specific issues, where the advice and counsel of the deanery can be of value to His Eminence."

"I think the results of this vote would be of great value to His Eminence," Disalvo shouted.

"The question is out of order. The meeting is adjourned." George Petrie brought his gavel down on the walnut table. For Matthew Mahan it had the thud of an executioner's ax. A silly metaphor. You have never heard an executioner's ax fall, except in the movies. The death of Thomas More. *A Man for All Seasons.* Once you had comfortably considered yourself a worthy candidate for that title. Alas, alas, on what sad days has the old smoothie fallen.

Usually at the end of one of these meetings the pastors and often the curates clustered around him to exchange a few words. Today they all hurried away, heads bowed, defeat on the faces of the majority. His defeat, which they charitably tried to avoid showing him. It did not help. He could see it in the angle of their heads, the droop of their shoulders. He and George Petrie and Colin McGuiness remained behind their table on the platform until the gymnasium was empty, except for Dennis McLaughlin sitting forlornly in the last row. "Can I give you a lift home, George?" he asked.

"No," said his vicar-general, avoiding his eyes. "I drove down."

"I hope there are still four wheels on the car when you get outside," Colin McGuiness said.

A fleeting smile from George Petrie. For a moment Matthew Mahan felt Colin McGuiness's eyes on him. Was he going to beg his pardon, plead for forgiveness, pretend that the whole debacle was his fault? *Be quiet, please,* Matthew Mahan prayed. Silence was easier.

It was also inevitable. There was nothing Colin McGuiness could say to his fallen hero. They walked down the gymnasium. A sad-faced Dennis McLaughlin joined them as they went out the door into the sunlit blacktop school yard. A burst of laughter greeted them. The Ad Hoc Committee was caucusing on the steps of the rectory, just beyond the iron fence on the other side of the yard. Heads down, like the rear guard of a defeated army, Matthew Mahan and his aides trudged out of the school yard to the littered street and their waiting cars.

XXVIII

Dennis McLaughlin stared gloomily at the letter on his desk from Monsignor Thomas Barker, head of the diocesan marriage tribunal, sometimes called the Rota. It was the fourth or fifth letter in the past two months from Monsignor Barker. He was constantly seeking advice, worrying or complaining about Cardinal Mahan's program for receiving good-conscience divorced Catholics back into the Church. This time he wanted the Cardinal to know that he had just returned from a regional conference with other canon lawyers, and they all agreed that Matthew Mahan was breaking sharply with tradition in permitting people to return to the sacraments based on their "individual subjective" consciences. "It was pointed out that the Church has never acted in this way in the past," Monsignor Barker wrote. "It was agreed that any decision to undertake this practice should be a decision of the whole Church and not of one bishop or a group of bishops."

Attached to the letter was a column by Daniel Lyons, the super-reactionary priest columnist of the *National Catholic Registry*. Lyons denounced in scorching terms the trend toward easy annulment and the acceptance of divorce in the Church. It was "such a scandal that the Vatican will have to rule against it," he intoned.

Dennis was tempted to throw both the clipping and the letter in the wastebasket. He knew that Monsignor Barker might use a nonanswer as an excuse to bring the good-conscience program to a dead stop. Yet he hated to put the letter on the desk of the weary man in the next room. It meant another hour of his time consumed cajoling, persuading, soothing Monsignor Barker from overt hostility to sullen docility again. These days, Matthew Mahan seemed to be spending most of his time on this sort of thing with almost everyone in the chancery office. Was there a single one of them who hadn't double-crossed him in one way or another in the last few months?

The telephone rang. "Hello." Helen Reed said, "Are you busy?"

"No more than the usual."

"Oh good. Why don't you come over for dinner tonight? Dad's meeting with the hospital's trustees. I'm eating alone."

The word tolled like an ominous bell in Dennis's mind. He knew—and certainly Helen knew—what had happened the last time they had spent an evening alone. First a kiss, then a caress, then half-guilty, half-defiant love, leaving him more muddled, more discouraged, than ever. Wasn't Helen saying with ever clearer boldness that it was time to stop feeling guilty, time for a decision?

"I'd—love to come. I really would. But there's a possibility that the Cardinal may need me. He had another bad night. Vomiting blood again."

"If he'd do what his doctor tells him—"

"I know, I know. Look, I'll call you back. I'll ask him."

"All right. But call me by five. So I can cook something *decent*."

Dennis hung up and sat there for a long moment, moodily contemplating his mess of a life. A little therapy was in order, he told himself. Ventilation. A letter to Goggin.

September 31, 1969

Dear Gog,

How are things in ye anciente tymes? Found any secret gospels lately? Or better a secret diary of Pio Nono confessing that he really didn't believe in infallibility, the whole thing was just a political ploy? The simplicities of the past become more and more appealing to me, as I grapple with the incredible intricacies of the present.

I told you in my midsummer communication the horrible

impact of the series of articles that my brother with my unholy help wrote on the Cardinal. The explosion of disaffection and disloyalty in the chancery office staff, right up to the chancellor and vicar-general. The outrageous scenes at the deanery meetings, with the vicar-general (now also our Most Reverend Auxiliary Bishop) entertaining every kind of insulting motion from conservatives and liberals like a Republican presiding at a Democratic caucus, practically encouraging them to tear each other and the Cardinal apart. It only proved, I know, just how fragile the whole situation was in the first place. How much discontent and rage and rebellion were seething beneath the surface. The Cardinal dismisses Leo's articles as the cause of the chaos. But I know (and it does not help my morale) that this is not true. Those articles have inflicted a near-fatal wound on his authority, particularly among the younger priests. I don't think people realize (at least I didn't) how much, even in a hierarchical, not to say authoritarian organization such as the Catholic Church, the man at the top can be incredibly harassed and frustrated if he loses the respect of those in the lower levels—the troops, as the Cardinal would call them.

The Cardinal's reaction to the situation has driven me even closer to distraction. He absolutely refuses to fight, much less suppress the various outbreaks of chaos, defiance, hysteria, and sheer brainlessness which keep erupting all around us. Six months ago he would have taken on all these birdbrains (I have grown a *little* partisan) and eaten them alive, feathers and all. A few bellows, a few twisted arms, a few transfers, and maybe a few secret flourishes of the checkbook, and peace would have been restored. Yet he has deliberately, consciously, refused to do any of these things. He is trying to be a different kind of bishop—one that really practices Pope John's holy freedom. The tragedy is, my brother's devious slanders have shrouded the effort in a miasma of meanness and distrust. And the liberals and the conservatives, who are creating most of the chaos, are so blinded by their own obsessions, they can't see what's happening in the first place.

Yet it's all perfectly visible. How can they be so blind? His Em. has sold off all those beautiful antiques which filled our residence, and replaced them with Grand Rapids traditional junk. Even our baroque chapel has gone to the auctioneers, and the money to the archdiocese. He also traded in his Cadillac for a Ford and sold his shell collection for a whopping two hundred and fifty thousand dollars. All without a peep of publicity, in spite of my pleas not to pass up a chance to look good for a change.

He was speaking last week at the annual reunion of the 113th Division. I wrote an absolute masterpiece of a speech. I talked out of both sides of the mouth, as only we intellectuals can. I supported the war in Vietnam in a major key and criticized it in a minor key. I added a scherzo on Korea and a pastoral hymn for World War II. It was symphonic, it was hypnotic. By the time he ended, the audience was guaranteed to have no idea what the point of it all was, beyond the need for personal courage. Then without warning, His Eminence departed from my text. With tears in his voice, he said, "But let us never, we who lived through it, let us never glorify war—above all this war. Let us listen not only to the voices of the living, but the voices of our dead. They have a claim not only on our devotion, but on our consciences. They speak to me often in the small hours of the morning. I kneel beside them again and hear their tears, their cries of pain, their death rattles."

It tipped the whole speech in a dangerous (politically speaking) direction. Afterward, the reporters swarmed all over him, asking him if he was planning to denounce the war. He pretended to be (or perhaps really was) baffled by their reaction. This enabled the New Lefties to put him down in their books as something worse than a convinced conservative—a cowardly liberal.

Cowardice or weakness has become the standard explanation for everything he does. When he refused to endorse a resolution of the Archdiocesan Association of Priests, condemning the Vietnam War as intrinsically immoral, he "yielded to conservative pressure." When he decided to keep St. Clare's Hospital open at the cost of a million dollars, he "yielded to liberal pressure." When he appointed a black pastor to St. Peter and Paul, and revamped the policy on the neighborhood use of church facilities downtown, he "yielded to black pressure." I suppose, when he refused to comment on the only true statement in Leo's diatribe, the gifts of money to his sister-in-law, they said he "yielded to family pressure."

The personal money thing is complicated by the reality of the diocese's financial structure. Unlike the Êpiscos and other Protestant churches where the laity are the legal owners, our bishops own it all. They have no board of laymen to whom they must present an audited report each year. An R.C. bishop is the corporation sole—with absolute control of all the diocesan cash—and of all the property, too, if he chooses to exercise it. When you own it all, there's not much point in paying yourself a salary. If Mahan did get a salary in line with his responsibilities, he could probably afford to give his sister-in-law twice what he has been giving her. But all this is impossible to explain in public. In a very ironic way he is a victim of the system.

Anyway the Cardinal would never try to explain it because it would only embarrass his sister-in-law. He also has much bigger money worries. The conservatives (read rich) have departed in droves, to give their money to the John Birch Society or some other institutional idiocy. The religiosos among them have formed a claque called St. Urban's League. I think it's in honor of Urban II, who proclaimed the first Crusade and tried to heal the Eastern schism. But it might equally be in honor of Urban VI, who was certifiably insane and created the great schism of the West by establishing an Italian majority in the College of Cardinals. The liberals don't have a patron saint (naturally); instead they have lawyers, and I think more than anything else they worship the Supreme Court. Currently they are suing the Cardinal to force him to make a complete revelation of the archdiocese's finances. He issued a financial report which was as thorough as anything you can get from a U.S. corporation, and much more comprehensible than any accounting I have ever seen from a city, state, or federal government. But the libs, led by my brother and our would-be Savonarola, Vinny Disalvo, will not be content until they have the Cardinal legally bound to ask their permission every time he writes a check.

I have tried to do some missionary work among the liberals. I met with Father Disalvo and my brother Leo, who is busy radicalizing the local chapter of the National Association of Laymen. The meeting was a waste of time. As long as I continued to work for Mahan, I was de facto despicable. Everything I said about the Cardinal's attempt to change his style was greeted with hoots and sneers.

The effect of all this on me—? My hours have improved considerably. The Cardinal no longer hurtles about the archdiocese like a berserk rocket. He turns down most invitations to speak; in fact, he has almost become a recluse. I have had time to plow through most of the mass of documentary evidence Bishop Cronin compiled against Vatican I. This has only confirmed my fear that the old boy was reaching for the unreachable star, trying to knock out the whole council with his lack of freedom argument. But it has whetted my appetite to write a serious history of the Church from a new point of view. Unfortunately I haven't found this necessary needle in my historical haystack yet.

At this point I'll shock you by snarling—the hell with me intellectually. I am a lot more concerned about the state of my soul—which is rotten. I find myself yearning for a scourging. In a way, I am in the process of getting one, sometimes on a physical level, and more often on the spiritual plane. You know what was happening between me and Helen Reed. It stopped when I got back from Rome. Maybe, thanks to your offensive malediction at lunch beside the Tiber, I became determined to prove I was not in love with my cock. I like to think it had more to do with Helen's reaction when we made love for the first time as a man and a woman and not a pair of separate spiritual freaks. I also know it has something to do with the Cardinal—my new respect for him.

Stopping didn't mean—and doesn't mean—that I stopped loving Helen. In fact, throughout the last three agonizing months I can honestly say there was never a day or a night when I did not want her in my arms. To make my torment more exquisite, I have been seeing her constantly.

Among the Cardinal's first moves when he got back to the city was a conference with Bill Reed. He asked him to reorganize and expand the outpatient services at St. Clare's Hospital. He warned him that this would involve working with his difficult daughter, who had been sent back to the hospital as head of nursing services by her Mother Superior, Sister Agnes Marie. Reed succumbed to His Em.'s reminiscences of their army days, when he had displayed organizational genius, etc., etc. I was told to work on Helen, to make sure that she cooperated.

Ironically, I was already making efforts in that direction. The Cardinal had described his attempt to reconcile father and daughter in Rome. I was outraged, yes, genuinely outraged (a remarkable fact in itself for someone so proud of usually feeling nothing). Was I angry because she was so unkind to Mahan? Or was I simply feeling sorry for her father, a pathetic man? Or was I genuinely concerned for her, as a priest rather than as a lover? You may marvel, but I prefer the third explanation.

I found myself with an unexpected ally. Her Mother Superior, Sister Agnes Marie, had apparently received a letter from the Cardinal telling her about the incident. Sister Agnes is a formidable character with a gentle but amazingly direct manner. Helen is in awe of her. She is one of those deceptively simple types who make holiness seem easy. Then she scares the bejesus out of you by telling you how hard it is. She knows St. John of the Cross like you know the *Code Sinaiticus* or one of the other original Gospel manuscripts. At any rate, once she went to work on Helen, my pastoral ministrations receded to a walk-on. I suspect there was also something hierophantic and intensely feminine involved, but I am weary of my search for explanations for everything. If the tree bears good fruit, let us praise it and go on to other things.

Dr. Reed also deserves a lot of credit. He threw himself into working at St. Clare's at the rate of ten and twelve hours a day. Watching him deal with patients and staff, Helen realized he was neither the Protestant ogre that the nuns of her youth had portrayed nor the militant reactionary that her New Left friends painted. In a month she went from raging antagonism to guilty adoration. Soon she was talking about leaving the convent to become a doctor. She is currently on leave from the order, living at home with her father. Dr. Reed is naturally ecstatic and is inundating her with biology and chemistry books.

To soothe my frustration, Helen has constructed a fantasy future for us. She gets her M.D., and I get a quiet country parish from my friend the Cardinal. By this time marriage will be a licit option for us diocesan padres. I will minister to my small congregation and write history, novels, poetry, while she practices medicine, dividing her time between our parishioners, whom she will treat for nominal fees, and the poor of the inner city. A lovely dream in which I consistently point out one large flaw. The chances of my becoming one of the first generation of married clergy in the last thousand years of the Roman Church are very slim. Do you hear anything sotto voce in the Vatican corridors that would alter this dour prophecy? If so, for God's sake rush the news to me. Because the more involved I get with Helen, the more burdensome my priesthood becomes to me. If it wasn't for the Cardinal, I am sure I would have walked out weeks ago. But I couldn't do that to him now.

Best,
Mag

Dennis quickly addressed an envelope to the Villa Stritch in Rome and scanned the letter before sealing it. From a literary point of view, it was interesting to note the decline of irony between the first paragraph and the last paragraph.

In the distance thunder rumbled. After a record September heat wave, a storm was moving across the city. A flash of lightning glinted on his small window. Suddenly Dennis could feel Helen's trembling body in his arms in the Pensione Christina. *Hold me, hold me, please hold me,* she had said. *Yes,* you had said, *yes, we can really love each other.* Last week, in the bedroom of her childhood, with her face smiling at you from a half-dozen pictures, in her white First Communion dress, her blue graduation gown, her postulant's white robes, you had felt the joy of entering not only her body but her self, her life.

But this other love, somehow more real, more terrible, stood between them, his love for this bulky man whose task was the orchestration of love, the movement of love beyond the personal toward some unspoken but promised immensity. Was it possible? Was he pursuing a chimera and sacrificing a love that existed outside power, intellect, theology, a love that inhabited the one surety for a man of thirty, the pulsing, wanting flesh?

Dennis went downstairs to mail his letter. He made it to the corner mailbox and back to the residence just as the first huge raindrops began to fall. On the second floor he heard a squawk of static. The Cardinal was listening to the Vatican radio again. It had become almost an obsession. Dennis walked through his own small office and peered into the inner sanctum. Matthew Mahan was getting nothing but barks and whistles. "Those crazy Italians really sound worked up today," Dennis said.

A weary smile came and went on Matthew Mahan's face. It was almost impossible to make the man laugh anymore. "I just had a phone call," he said.

"Who?"

"Father—or ex-Father—Novak."

"Really? What did he want?"

"He wanted to find out if there was any chance in the reasonably near future of him returning to work."

"What happened to the book he was writing?"

"He read a half-dozen books by ex-priests and realized that most of what he wanted to say had already been said."

Matthew Mahan dropped his wry tone and apologized for it. "It's sad, really. The poor fellow is having money troubles. His wife has become pregnant and her teaching job has evaporated. He's working for the local Office of Economic Opportunity, part-time. He paid me the compliment of saying that he'd keep the job, such as it was, and stay in the city if there was any hope of him getting permission from Rome."

"What did you tell him?"

"What else could I tell him? No."

"You don't think there's the faintest possibility?"

Matthew Mahan gave him a curious look. "Why so intense?"

"I think everybody my age lives in hopes," Dennis said evasively.

"I know," Matthew Mahan said. "I just got some confidential material from the Catholic Conference Office in Washington, D.C. They've made a secret survey which concluded that something like seventy-five per cent of the priests thirty-five and under expect to marry someday. Nobody in the hierarchy seems to realize it—or at least nobody is doing anything about it—but we're sitting on a land mine."

Could he tell him, should he tell him, what he had just written to Goggin? No, he could not add another burden to this man's weary shoulders. In the lamplight the Cardinal looked appallingly ill. His once well-padded cheeks were slack and hollow. Vitality had vanished from his eyes. Except for moments when he clearly summoned himself to make an effort, he spoke and moved like a man of seventy.

Yet there was also the need to be honest with this man. The Cardinal knew there was no longer any compelling need for him to see ex-Sister Helen Reed. He would have to construct one of those disgusting transparent lies—the old college friend in town for the night. No, it was time to speak the truth.

"Your Eminence—I mean, Father—could you spare me another five minutes?"

"You've got the rest of the afternoon if you need it."

Dennis sat down in one of the two mundane leather armchairs that had replaced the French antiques. "There's—there's a very good reason why I'm intense on this subject. I think you should know—about it. I'm in love with Helen Reed. I want to marry her. But I don't want to leave the priesthood. It's—an awful conflict. The two things are sort of—balanced in my mind. But I can't—I can't let Helen go on thinking—it only gets worse, for both of us. Do you think there's *any* chance of a married priesthood? Not this year or next year—but even in—five years?"

Matthew Mahan sat behind his desk like a statue. Not a man of marble, but of wax. Dull, mushy cheap wax. Another of his failures was confronting him. Another humiliation. He heard himself telling Terry Malone and George Petrie that he was prepared to risk his prestige, his authority, for the sake of this young priest. *Let the ninety-nine stay on the hills.*

But wait, wait. What is he really asking? What is he really saying? Isn't he trying to tell you how much he cares about his priesthood? Remember the cold-voiced young man in the car a few months ago: *Who knows where I'll be twenty years from now.* What a difference between him and this open, troubled young face.

"Dennis, you've read those drafts of the committee that's studying the subject for the National Conference of Bishops. You can see the direction they're taking."

"But those statistics you mentioned. Seventy-five per cent of the priests under thirty-five expect the rule to be changed."

"That won't change many bishops' minds, Dennis."

"If you spoke out on the subject now. That could—that could start a trend, a swing in the opposite direction."

"Dennis, don't you think I'm in enough trouble already?"

Disappointment stained the earnest young face. "I'm sorry. I didn't mean to put any pressure on you. I just wanted—you to know. Helen—invited me to supper tonight. Do you need me?"

"No. No, of course not."

In his own office Dennis found his hand shaking as he dialed Helen's number to tell her that he was free. The mockery in those last words temporarily overwhelmed him. Avoiding them, he sounded like a schoolboy. "I—can come. It's okay. When do you—?"

He was going to say *want me*. Every word, every phrase, was a land mine. "About six-thirty," Helen said cheerfully. "Would you pick up a bottle of wine at Sweeney's Package Store on Western Avenue? It'll be charged to our account."

"All right."

He hung up, telling himself: *Tonight you will be faithful, you will be faithful to your vow. For the sake of that man in there.*

For the first time since he had come to work for Matthew Mahan, Dennis McLaughlin visited the chapel. As he entered the now drab room and knelt before the tabernacle, he realized how regularly he had avoided this room after saying his obligatory morning mass. Only a single votive candle glowed before the tabernacle. Above it the crucifix looked like it had been bought in Woolworth's. *Lord, I am not worthy, I am not worthy of him. Say but the word and my soul shall be healed.*

XXIX

Matthew Mahan was standing beside a slimy ocher-colored river with Mary Shea beside him. But it was not the woman he had seen in Rome, not the silver-haired matron struggling bravely

355

against depression. No, this was the dark-haired smiling girl he had met in the chancery office on that sunny day in June of 1949, the girl who mingled hope and resignation and a wordless plea on her lovely face. And Monsignor Mahan, the firm but kindly cleric, had smashed them all into a grief-stricken mess with a crunching denial. *There is very little possibility of your marriage being annulled, Mrs. Shea.*

What is she doing here, this young lost face beside you, the hulking, middle-aged Cardinal? She keeps pointing across the river, as if she is acting a part in a childish pantomime. His yearning eyes run down the supple curve of that young arm until he sees in the distance a dome. There is only one dome that looms like that above its city, above the world. Suddenly, Lostmary, Youngmary, begins walking on the water, apparently oblivious to the oily, greasy surface. "O ye of little faith," she says playfully.

It is all a game, a childish, heartbreaking game. But the river was forbidding, or somehow forbidden for him to cross. How could he walk on water in these heavy robes, the chasuble, the cope on his back, the miter on his head, the crosier in his hand? "O ye of little faith," mocked Mary, strolling cheerfully back and forth about a dozen feet from shore. Then she suddenly grew serious. "How can we get there," she asked, pointing to the dome in the distance, "if you won't come with me?"

"We need time, Mary, time to build a bridge. I can afford it." Magically, instead of his crosier he was brandishing his checkbook.

Mary grew cross, like a petulant little girl. "There isn't time. There isn't time," she said.

Suddenly, she was no longer walking on the water, she was floundering in the slimy current. The checkbook fell from his trembling fingers. He stretched out his arm to her. She was beyond his reach. He began to tear off his robes. "I'm coming, I'm coming," he cried. But it was too late. The river was full of corrosive acid. How clever the enemy was. Mary was dissolving in front of his eyes. Her face drifted on the surface now like a one-dimensional photograph. He knelt on the shore weeping futile tears.

Bong, bong, bong. Three A.M. Pain gnawed in Cardinal Mahan's stomach. It was the fifth or sixth time he had had the river dream. Sometimes it was full of sharks, piranhas, crocodiles. Sometimes the other shore bristled with pillboxes and barbed

356

wire. Always he was afraid to cross. Always when Mary was in the dream, she died horribly, tragically.

With a sigh the Cardinal heaved his legs over the side of his bed and let his feet fumble for his slippers. There would be no sleep from now until dawn. He listened for a moment to the chilly November wind moaning past his window. A draft of cold air filtered through his sweat-soaked cotton pajamas. The temperature of the room must be sixty, and he was sleeping beneath a sheet. But he regularly awoke, his mouth dry, his whole body burning as if he were running a fever. The dry heat of desolation.

He trudged down the darkened stairs to the chapel and knelt on the prie-dieu before the altar. The anguished baroque Christ, the center of the magnificent hand-carved altar, was gone. So was the surrounding purple glow from the stained-glass windows, the ecstatic saints on the soaring, mystical ceiling. Sold to a Texas museum for $250,000. Everything had been sold, every last piece of old Hogan's antiques, for something close to a million dollars. Now the Cardinal prayed before a simple tabernacle shrouded in white cloth surmounted by a gold cross with a trite, drooping Christ on it. The art of the people, Dennis McLaughlin had said rather grimly as he stood the crucifix behind the tabernacle on the plain oak table they had borrowed from the chancery office. Vanished, vanquished utterly, the episcopal splendor. Within the walls of their palace, the Cardinal and his secretary were trying to live like poor men. He even urged economy on Mrs. Norton, who responded with ever more atrocious stews, dishes of meat loaf and pasta, against which she committed high culinary crimes.

And the money, where was the money? Matthew Mahan asked the trite, drooping Christ. Spent, the money is always spent. Like yourself, Cardinal Mahan, spent. The fund drive had ended in catastrophe, three million dollars short of its goal. They were borrowing operating expenses from the banks for the first time in the ten years of Matthew Mahan's episcopacy.

For the thousandth time, Matthew Mahan asked that figure on the cheap gold cross if this was the humiliation he could not accept. If so, he accepted it. Let me accept it, Lord.

He almost laughed. There were so many other humiliations, so many other nights when he knelt here and prayed for the strength, the resignation, to accept one of the other failures. Perhaps a catalog is in order. Help me to accept the abuse I take from

Monsignor O'Reilly and his friends. Help me to accept the decision of my auxiliary bishop and vicar-general, George Petrie, to join them. Help me to accept the lawsuit that Father Disalvo and his Ad Hoc Committee have filed, accusing me of fraudulently manipulating the archdiocese's finances for my own benefit. Help me to accept the latest demand from the Catholic teachers union—parity with public school salaries. Help me to accept my pastors' appalling lack of cooperation with my program to bring divorced couples back into the Church. Help me to accept the letters I receive each day from the conservatives and the liberals denouncing me as a coward and a liar.

No use, no use, you could go on cataloging for the rest of the night. That is all you can do, my Lord Cardinal, catalog your woes, your sores, you cannot offer them up. You cannot raise them an inch above your dry withered heart and they travel about the same deplorable distance beyond your bloodless lips. Catalog and swallow them, catalog and swallow them, that is all you can do. No wonder your stomach is always aching. Catalogs are not on Dr. Reed's diet.

What tortured Matthew Mahan more than anything else was his new ineptitude. It was simply incredible how badly he handled the crises that he had once smiled—or growled—or bellowed—through. Why? The obvious answer, the one that tormented him most, was his inability to scour the old smoothie from his soul. He was still in love with the flattery, the bowing and scraping, the deference, all the little perquisites of power that came his way, and when he tried to avoid them, to explain that he no longer wanted them, the result was confusion. Of course, there was another, more terrible answer—the feeling that thrust through the very center of his body and soul at unexpected moments—that it was all a fraud, a charade. This endless repetition of the word "Eminence," these calls from *Newsweek* and *Time* reporters, royal red robes and watered silk skullcap—not only was he unworthy of these things, but if the truth of why, how he became Eminence was known, even cynics would pity him. He was a purchased man, a pawn on the chessboard of international power.

The memory of the inner-city deanery's last meeting rose before his eyes. He heard the young, strident voices, saw the dismay on the lined solemn faces of Eddie McGuire and his fellow pastors. Eddie McGuire was the most painful memory. Weeks later, dying of cancer, the sad suffering face looked up at him from the hospital bed to whisper: "You can't let them walk all over you Matt." How could you tell him that he was part of it? The haphazard way he ran his parish, the top three floors of his school closed, bars and wire mesh on all the windows of the rectory and parish hall, the church locked from dusk, like an island fortress in a hostile sea. Matthew Mahan remembered sadly his halfhearted efforts to persuade Eddie to change his style, to welcome the black community—and his shock at discovering how deep and intense Eddie's prejudice was. You had failed to face that challenge then. What could you do now but nod sadly and ask him to offer up some of his pain for you?

That, of course, was only the beginning of your spiritual Joba-rama, Your Eminence. In the beginning was the ineptitude, then the catalogs, dry pages that you swallowed day and night. Then, one by one the prayers dwindled away, too. Now you cannot levitate the simplest cry. *My Jesus, mercy*. There it goes, spinning to the ground like a malformed toy airplane or a dead bug. Yes, your prayers have become more and more like insects, weightless insects that crawl up and down your body day and night, savagely stinging their creator for the crudity of his spiritual biology. Prayers without wings. Don't you know anything, Your Eminence?

Would a hair shirt help? Some apocalyptic penance seemed in order. Fasting was forbidden for the ulcer patient. Some desperate scourge was needed to batter the enemy, the smoothie, from his soul.

Patience, tolled the three-thirty bell. Oh yes, Patience, good old Patience. A friend of Common Sense. Associate of Reasonable Explanation. His Eminence had been consulting with those three physicians since the trouble started. At first, they seemed to be all the help he needed. It was inevitable, after so many decades of living under literal obedience, which Cardinal Mahan had softened to firm leadership. What was inevitable? These upheavals, these defiances, these challenges, to authority, these personal attacks. They would pass. In time the sensible majority would come to realize and revere what you are doing. They would use their holy freedom creatively. Thank you very much, gentlemen, that is just what I wanted to hear. It is amazing how precisely you always tell me what I wanted to hear.

As if it mattered. As if any of the things that were happening really mattered. That was the Death Valley of desolation, the Dead Sea with irreducible Masada looming above it. Not mattering. Mary Shea not mattering. Mike Furia not mattering. Bill Reed not mattering. Davey Cronin not mattering. Even Dennis McLaughlin not mattering. The final horror, the ultimate fear that you will pay any price, go any distance to defeat. Yet you are motionless, Your Eminence. You kneel here, tears streaming down your face, while the beast, whatever it is, that shapeless thing in the dark, moves closer to you every night.

My Jesus, mercy. Another toy plane on the floor and Sister Stella Dolores looming above you. Matthew Mahan playing with planes again. They're not even good toy planes. Hold out your hand. *Whop, whop, whop.*

Ah, Sister, with your childish seventh-grade tortures, if only you were here to scourge me until the blood flowed. If only you could give me the strength to stand beside my beloved Savior, equally torn, equally bloody.

With the loss of prayer had come so many other losses. He began to read the speeches Dennis wrote for him with leaden automatism. The power to persuade, to control a single man or a small group of men in private talks, lapsed too. Gulfs constantly yawned between him and other people. There was always disagreement or bafflement on other faces. Once and for all the legislature buried the bill to aid parochial schools. Mayor O'Connor did not even bother to write him a pro forma apology. Old friends such as Jim McAvoy found it difficult to talk to him. He could no longer bear to reminisce about the war. It brought him too close to weeping in public.

And this dream, this constant dream of water to cross. Sometimes it was the river, sometimes it was a vast shrouded sea. Sometimes Mary Shea was with him, sometimes it was someone else he loved, old Davey, his father, Dennis. They were all urging him to take a journey. Again the Cardinal almost laughed, dry aimless mirth. He knew the kind of journey Dennis was asking him to take—a vacation. *You should get away, really you should,* the young, earnest face had pleaded with him yesterday. Nodded in agreement, had Cardinal Mahan. It was imperative for the Cardinal to get away from Mahan. To escape this dry, drifting hulk of a priest. But that was easier said than done.

But the love, the concern, on Dennis's face. *Can't I accept that, Lord?*

No, another wingless insect on the floor, because his love is for something that doesn't exist, this Cardinal cum saint that he imagines, this defier of Vatican decrees as if some kind of revenge were the answer to their dilemma. Didn't he understand that a man who was trying to be human, a man of flesh instead of unforgiving marble, could only add what they had done to his catalog?

On July 1 a letter had arrived from Cardinal Carlo Confalonieri, head of the Sacred Congregation of Bishops. July 28, 1969, wrote the Cardinal, would be the first anniversary of the encyclical *Humanae Vitae*. Nothing would make the Holy Father happier than to see or hear a statement from Matthew Mahan on that day supporting the Pope's stand. The Cardinal pointed out that Cardinal Mahan and Cardinal Cushing were the only rulers of America's ten largest archdioceses who had failed to support the Holy Father wholeheartedly. For Matthew Mahan it was, of course, only a confirmation of everything he had dreaded when he heard *frater noster taciturnus* from Paul's lips.

The Cardinal had not shared that secret with anyone, even Dennis. So it was almost amusing—and oddly comforting—to see Dennis sputter in indignation as he realized that the choice of Mahan for a red hat was part of a carefully calculated carrot-and-stick operation. "It's unbelievable. It's so totally contrary to the spirit of the Gospels," Dennis had cried. "They honor you, and then they turn the honor into a weapon. They make it meaningless."

I accept it, I accept it, Lord, as one more rebuke to my endlessly resourceful arrogance.

But your resigned smile was not enough to satisfy Dennis. He wanted a ferocious bellow of defiance from you. The following day he had laid a clipping on your desk. An interview with Cardinal Suenens, the primate of Belgium, on the failure of the reform movement in the Church.

Matthew Mahan arose from the prie-dieu and wandered back down the hall and up the stairs to his office. The clipping was still on his desk. Dennis had speared it on one of the pens.

"What is wanted is to liberate everyone, even the Holy Father himself, from the system—which has been the subject for complaint for several centuries, and yet we have not succeeded in loosening its grip or reshaping it. For while the Popes come and go, the Curia remains," Suenens had said. He called for the election of the Pope by "representatives of the Universal Church" including the laity. With special passion, Dennis had underlined the final portion of the interview, when he laid it on Matthew Mahan's desk. *"There are some who insist on the primacy of the Roman Pontiff to the extent that it resembles the absolute monarchism of the time before the French Revolution. We (the bishops) are not only under the Pope, but we exercise our power with him."*

"That's exactly what I think," Matthew Mahan had said when he read it. "Thank God someone important is saying it. This could have a real impact."

"Why don't you agree with him—in public?" Dennis has asked, his face alight with fiery hope.

"No, Dennis, I'm not important enough."

Hope had turned to anguish on the young face. "You must be kidding." He waved a clipping from the New York *Times*—five column-length biographies of the new American Cardinals. "Here you are right next to Cooke and Dearden in the world's most important newspaper."

Haltingly he had tried to explain how he felt about the oath of personal loyalty he had taken to Pope Paul. "Suenens," he pointed out, "is one of John's Cardinals."

"Aren't your convictions more important than that damn red biretta?"

Matthew Mahan almost smiled, recalling his reaction to that challenge. For a moment, the old smoothie had almost turned on his shouting act. It was frightening to discover how very much alive he still was in your soul.

"Dennis," Matthew Mahan had said, "my convictions aren't the point here. The question is—should I attack the man who made me a Cardinal four months after I come back from Rome."

"You're not attacking him."

"Dennis. Don't pretend to be naïve."

Matthew Mahan began fiddling with his shortwave multiband radio. At this hour of the morning he was able to pick up the Vatican broadcasts with remarkable clarity. A voice began speaking in sonorous Italian. Coincidence. Another attack on Cardinal

Suenens. The Belgium primate had given two more interviews in the course of the summer, each a ferocious assault on the papal monarchy. The Vatican had replied with its heaviest guns. Matthew Mahan's old friend and fellow *neo porporato*, Jean Derrieux, had castigated Suenens for undermining the papacy. From the propaganda point of view, the tactics were superb. Liberal attacked liberal. The current broadcast was pursuing the same shrewd policy. Cardinal Eugene Tisserant, dean of the Sacred College of Cardinals and Rome's leading Orientalist—which de facto made him considerably less than a knee-jerk supporter of papal supremacy—issued a statement calling Suenens's attack on the Curia really an attack on Pope Paul. Then came a quote from the Pope. His Holiness had remarked with sorrow that there seemed to be a lesser sense of doctrinal orthodoxy today—and a certain widespread distrust toward the exercise of the hierarchical ministry. Criticisms of the Curia, said the Pope, were not all exact and not all just nor always respectful and opportune—and he personally lamented such protests and deviations.

Matthew Mahan snapped off the speaker in mid-sentence. He must stop listening to Rome. Everything he heard on this radio depressed him. It was enough to give him a primitive fear of the thing, as if it were an invention of the devil. But it was like the old nonsense song "Close the doors, they're coming in the windows, close the windows, they're coming in the doors." Rome had a dozen ways of reaching him. Only yesterday, Dennis McLaughlin had laid on his desk an analysis of the Pope's statement on Vatican policy toward apostolic delegates. Ignoring the obvious desire of most of the world's bishops to get rid of these diplomatic intruders, Paul had firmly upheld the current policy. Acidly, Dennis had pointed out the numerous references to papal infallibility worked into the document, all purportedly quotes from Vatican II. But an investigation revealed that the quotes were all from footnotes which in turn were quotes from Vatican I.

They'll stoop to anything, won't they? Dennis had scrawled at the bottom of his report.

He was tireless. The spirit of old Davey had obviously infested his soul. It was so Irish, this assumption that freedom had to include defiance. The Cardinal, the Archbishop, the priest, you are trying to become has another answer. Freedom is silence. It should have humility's quiet, the simplicity of the poor in spirit. It sought guidance in unexpected places, in rebukes and failures. *Frater taciturnus*. Yes, somehow what you must become, what you are groping to find, is in those words.

While you waited, while you waited on the shore for the journey to begin, on this desert shore, was there any consolation? He picked up one of a dozen letters he had received from divorced couples whom the diocesan marriage tribunal had accepted as good-conscience cases.

Dear Cardinal Mahan,

I feel I must tell you from a heart that is bursting with joy how grateful my husband and I are for the way you have reached out to us and permitted me to return to the sacraments. My husband is not a Catholic. My first husband was a cold sadistic man whom I divorced after five horrible years of suffering. I love my second husband deeply—more deeply than I ever thought possible. He is one of those men of goodwill, of no particular religion, yet always full of charitable instincts, ready to help others, to work for good causes. I continue to raise the two children from my first marriage as Catholic. This inevitably began to cause strains as they grew older. I had to tell them why I could not receive Holy Communion with them. It was terribly confusing for them to think of their mother as a sinner. Yet a sinner who loved them, and who did her best to give them love. It was very upsetting to me, too, and I think if it had lasted much longer it might have affected my marriage. But now these worries have vanished. I feel so much at peace—with God—with the Church—and with my husband.

God bless you.

Sincerely,
Irene Tracy

P.S. My pastor, Monsignor O'Reilly at Holy Angels, has never mentioned this program from the pulpit or in the parish bulletin. I learned about it from a friend who worships at the cathedral.

Consolation? Yes, a drop of water on the parched tongue. But the diocesan tribunal had processed almost a hundred cases now. And they had only a dozen letters like this one. What were the others seeing, doing, thinking? Were they telling their friends and neighbors that the Church had abandoned its teaching on divorce? Were they giving hundreds, perhaps eventually thousands, of people the impression that Mahan the swinging Cardinal had capitulated to modern mores? *Next month a pornographic missal* had been among the more polite sneers from outraged conservatives. You have no answer to that, Your Eminence. You do not know why the majority of your lost sheep have not bothered to say thank you. But shouldn't you really rejoice? Didn't Jesus receive the same complacent treatment from the lepers he had healed?

Of course, if you want to meditate on real failure, there is always Monsignor O'Reilly's reply to your letter of peace and reconciliation. He picked up the typewritten note with the name scrawled hugely beneath it in red ink.

Insofar as I can decipher your scrawl, your letter only convinces me once more of your utter incapacity for the high position you hold. There is no need for you to lecture me upon my responsibility in regard to heretics like Father Novak. Father Cannon has thus far resisted the spiritual epidemic which is raging all around us unchecked—indeed encouraged —by your silence. As long as he does so, you may be assured that I will show him the fatherly concern every responsible pastor has for the young priests in his care.

What about your visit to Sister Agnes Marie? Surely consolation there. You had healed your differences. You had ratified their inner-city programs, doubled the financial support from the diocese, abandoned your prohibitions about counseling poor women on birth control. You had called her Agnes, and she had (shyly at first) called you Matthew. You had told her what you were doing in the inner city. When Eddie McGuire died, you had appointed your best black priest pastor of the parish and vicar-general of the inner-city deanery. With your approval he had directed all the downtown pastors to open their playgrounds, gymnasiums, bowling alleys, social halls, and auditoriums to the people of the neighborhood, no matter what their religion—or color.

Agnes had smiled impishly and said: "That should shut up Father Disalvo."

For a moment he had been hurt. "I didn't do it for that."

"I know," she said.

He sensed, as he rose to leave, that she wanted to say something else. He was halfway to the door when the words came. "Matthew. I know what you're going through. I went through it myself many years ago."

"You?" he said incredulously.

She nodded. "God hasn't abandoned you, Matthew. It's his way of purifying us. Once you take the risk, once you rely on nothing but him, he has to make us worthy—truly worthy—before he enters the heart."

"Do you really think that's happening to me? I didn't—I didn't *ask* for this."

Sister Agnes laughed briefly. "Who would? But somewhere you made a fundamental decision to—go beyond the place where you were. Most people stop at some safe point along the way. There are all sorts of places to stop. Preacher, politician, man for all seasons. You were a very good bishop for the other Church. The one that is passing away."

He nodded, forcing a smile. He did not want to hurt her feelings. But his case was much more complicated. Perhaps he had made some sort of decision. But what he could not accept was the loss of power, the loss of prestige, the loss of popularity, that it seemed to involve. If God was turning his face away, it was because he, Matthew Mahan, was such a colossal spiritual failure.

"I can only promise you what I know. Someday it will end. Then the joy begins. A joy, a sweetness, that is beyond words, beyond everything. Then perhaps you will want to go further, into the very darkest night, walking not toward joy but light. Pure light. I tried. I couldn't do it."

What sadness was in those words.

"I won't even try."

He came back to the desk and took her hand. He was shocked for a moment by how warm it was. Her utter calm was not cold. It was a banked fire. "Thank you, Agnes," he said and walked toward the door again.

"Perhaps it would help," she said, her voice rising almost imperceptibly, "perhaps it would help to know that you are part of my joy."

No, no, Your Eminence, your soul cannot be tricked into levitation that way. There are too many years of accumulated dross in it. You are tied inevitably to the earth. Perhaps you should try

Bill Fogarty's solution. He had written from the monastery in Kentucky a few weeks ago, thanking Cardinal Mahan for saving his soul and shyly explaining that he had decided not to return to the archdiocese. He was going to spend the rest of his life as a monk. Who was that Cardinal—Leger of Montreal—he had resigned and gone to work among the lepers in Africa. Remember at the time how you had scoffed at the decision, even told yourself that the man was a coward, running out on the real job. If you can't stand the heat, you had said, stay out of the kitchen. But you were not talking about the heat of the Death Valley—Dead Sea circuit, where the failures toil and the water ranges from brackish to brine.

A knock on the door. Dennis McLaughlin peering anxiously through the gloom beyond the fluorescent desk lamp. "I saw the light in the hall. I thought—you might be sick."

"Just the usual insomnia."

Dennis pointed to the radio. "Any news from Vatican Hill?"

He summed up what Cardinal Tisserant and Pope Paul had just said about Cardinal Suenens.

"That wraps it all up, doesn't it?" Dennis said. "If you open your mouth, you're a heretic, a rebel, and you're disrespectful and inopportune."

Matthew Mahan lit a cigarette. "And you were telling me that he wouldn't take Suenens's sort of criticism personally?"

"Don't you have to go another step, then, and ask yourself what comes first, personal relations or the good of the whole Church?"

"If there was a clear answer to that question," Matthew Mahan said, "I wouldn't hesitate to make the decision."

Dennis obviously thought about saying the situation seemed perfectly clear to him. Matthew Mahan headed off this little confrontation by asking, "Have you gotten through the saints' mail yet?"

Dennis looked morosely toward his office, where there were stacks of letters from irate followers of St. Christopher, St. Catherine, and the two hundred other saints Rome had recently eliminated from the Church's calendar without warning.

The Pope claimed he was following a directive of the Second Vatican Council's Constitution on the Liturgy, which called for encouraging official devotion only to saints with universal significance. Nowhere was there any call for two hundred eliminations.

"About halfway. But more keeps coming in. I'm afraid the followers of St. Pudentiana have not yet been heard from."

"That sounds slightly obscene. Was there a St. Pudentiana?"

"There was. There isn't anymore. It seems there was a church named after Pudens, the senator who greeted St. Peter when he came to Rome—that's his chair enshrined in Bernini's Cattedra. The church was called the Basilica Pudentiana. Some sixth-century monk thought it was a woman's name."

"Half the ones they left in the calendar are just as dubious as the ones they bounced," the Cardinal said. "Like St. George the Dragon Slayer. How many letters did we get about losing St. Christopher?"

"About twenty. My favorite is the guy who accused us of making millions selling St. Christopher medals one year and abolishing him the next year. He claims it's a plot to transfer the medal deal to another saint, so we can make another million."

"It's funny—but not so funny, too. He won't give me any money, if he really believes that."

"I thought the fund drive was over."

"They're still trying to collect pledges. I understand there's been several dozen cancellations because of the saints. They were probably looking for a good excuse."

"The whole thing is a Curia enterprise," Dennis fumed. "They saw it as one more chance to demonstrate their authority, wield their power. The more you wield it, the more powerful power becomes."

What was he supposed to say now? Matthew Mahan wondered. He knew what Dennis wanted to hear—a call to the spiritual barricades. For a fiery moment that was exactly what he himself wanted, too. The American Suenens summons his fellow bishops to join him in a call for the end of the papal monarchy. But that was only another version of the marble man, a Napoleonic variation, with the old smoothie standing in the background urging him on à la Cardinal Richelieu. "Try not to be so bitter, Dennis. Be sure and tell those people that they can go on praying to St. Christopher. Put in all that stuff about Rome saying he may have existed, they just don't have proof."

"I'd like to send a cable to the Vatican. *Roma locuta est causa finita non est.*"

Matthew Mahan tried to laugh. But it died in his chest. He sensed he had to say something, he had to reach out to Dennis, not simply for his sake but for the sake of his own soul.

"Dennis, I've been thinking—thinking a great deal about you and Helen Reed. Praying, too. I've decided to speak out. Not the way you probably want me to do it—in public. But on the floor when the bishops meet in Washington next month. I'm going to see what I can do to change their minds about that statement on celibacy they're planning to make."

Dennis nodded glumly, old familiar dissatisfaction on his face. *Didn't you hear what I said?* Matthew Mahan almost cried.

"I wish—I wish I understood what you are trying to do," Dennis said.

Now was the moment for the grandiose spiritual remark. *I'm trying to save my soul, Dennis. I'm trying to save the soul of this archdiocese.* He could almost hear his father's growl: *No grandstanding in this family.* "I'm doing the best I can, Dennis, the best I can."

XXX

The long parting kiss Helen Reed had given him last night was still on Dennis McLaughlin's lips as he came downstairs to begin his day's work. Not even the taste of the bread and wine, the words of the consecration at his morning mass, *This is my body, this is my blood,* had diminished (no, they had intensified) the sadness, the anguish, of that kiss. Even as he said good night, Dennis had felt the brief joy they had created with their bodies transmuting into muddled guilt.

Another failure to spew into the ear of his confessor, Dennis McLaughlin thought wearily as he sat down at his desk. He had quietly found a confessor for himself about a month ago. Monsignor Frank Falconer, one of Matthew Mahan's classmates, pastor of St. Damian's, the nearest parish to the cathedral. He had been amazingly gentle with Dennis for his falls from grace with Helen Reed. "You won't be the first priest who had this problem and you won't be the last," he said the first time he confessed it. It was his own inability to forgive himself that was depressing him, Dennis realized.

His mood was compounded by his encounter with the Cardinal last night when he had returned to the residence at 3 A.M. He was sure that guilt was written in giant letters across his forehead when Matthew Mahan had invited him to join him in the kitchen for an "insomniac's lunch." In the harsh overhead light the Cardinal looked ghastly. More weight had vanished from his cheeks. For the first time, flecks of gray were visible in his normally glistening black hair.

He told Dennis he had just listened to the Vatican radio for a half hour. Pope Paul had made another comment on priestly celibacy—his fourth or fifth in the last month. They were all stridently against any change in the rule. Dennis heard deep sadness in Matthew Mahan's voice, saw it on his face, as he told him this bad news. For a moment Dennis almost begged him to stop worrying about it. In a travesty of his prayer he wanted to cry, *I am not worthy*.

As Dennis often did when he brooded over the way things were going, he found himself fingering the moon shell on his desk —the souvenir of his walk along the Nettuno beach with Matthew Mahan. Each time he became aware of the shell in his hand, he was irritated by the memory of something larger—an idea, an insight, even a reality lurking in those delicate brown swirls.

This morning the same thing happened. With a grunt of irritation he flipped the shell back on his desk. A knock on the door. Rita McGuire, one of the tall sepulchral typists from the chancery office, delivered the mail with her usual simpering smile. Quickly Dennis looked through it, spotting with an inner groan at least a half-dozen more complainers about dismissed saints. Then he seized a dull stainless-steel letter opener and slit the obvious leading contender for attention. The papal seal and the Washington, D.C., return address signaled a communication from the apostolic delegate.

Well before he reached the last paragraph, he began cursing softly to himself.

Your Eminence:

It pains me to be under the necessity to write this letter. Communications have been received by the Holy See from priests in your archdiocese informing the Sacred Roman Rota and other officials of a highly unusual program which you have initiated in regard to divorced persons who have entered second canonically invalid marriages.

Similar programs in the diocese of Baton Rouge, Portland, Chicago, and one or two other dioceses have also been brought to the attention of the Holy See. Our Holy Father, His Holiness Pope Paul VI, has been extremely distressed to learn of these programs. He has directed me to order all the bishops and heads of diocesan marriage tribunals who are administering them to suspend them immediately. The value (or scandal—here I add a personal comment) of these programs will be weighed by the proper authorities in Rome and a decision issued on the practice, which will be binding for the universal Church. It seems inconceivable to me, personally, that these practices will ever be approved. They contradict a thousand years of canon law and threaten the very essence of the Church's teaching on marriage.

Please communicate to me as soon as possible your compliance with the Holy Father's order.

Sincerely yours in Christ,

Dennis McLaughlin shoved the rest of the mail aside and walked into the Cardinal's office. He was sitting at his desk, reading another draft of the study on priestly celibacy. "Excuse me," Dennis said. "I thought you should see this immediately."

Matthew Mahan looked up with the blank startled expression of an old man who had difficulty concentrating on more than one thing at a time. It was hard to believe he was the same man who had volleyed seven different orders on seven different subjects per minute before they went to Rome. A little of the old self reappeared in his face as he read the apostolic delegate's letter. For a moment Dennis expected a roar of rage. He would have welcomed it, even if it had been directed at him. But Matthew Mahan only shoved the letter aside as if it were another helping of Mrs. Norton's atrocious pasta. His face seemed to crumble. His head fell forward until his chin sagged on his chest.

Spiritually Matthew Mahan was no longer in the room. He was in Rome again, facing the anguished woman whose soul he had so confidently promised to save, confessing to her this final humiliation. What would Mary Shea do? What would she say when you turned your back on her now? What would you say to the others who were waiting for your episcopal permission? What? Trust in God but not in the Church. No, that was unthinkable, unsayable. If the Church was not God's voice, if her arms remained folded across her supposedly loving breasts, if there was no hope of opening them, your whole life was a sham, a charade, Your Eminence.

"Why, Dennis, why?" he murmured, looking up and seeing the concern on his secretary's face. "I don't know why."

"Do you want to—reply to this?" Dennis said, pointing to the apostolic delegate's letter.

Matthew Mahan nodded mournfully. "Write a brief acceptance. We're suspending the program. Then send it to Monsignor Barker over at the Rota with a memorandum telling him to process all the cases now on the docket. But don't accept any more. Tell him to see me about setting up some kind of a counseling program for those we turn away."

As if the last words inspired the movement, Matthew Mahan swiveled in his chair and stared out the window at the traffic moving meaninglessly up and down the Parkway. "There should be a story in the paper, too. Tell Cohane. Make it clear that I take full responsibility for the program. Say something about my being pleased that Rome has decided to give this matter serious attention. But make it clear, as I said, that it's my fault—that I regret raising the hopes of so many couples prematurely."

"I won't write that. I can't," Dennis said, almost in a shout.

"Dennis, please don't make it more difficult for me."

"Why don't you *fight* them?"

Matthew Mahan shook his head. "This may sound awfully maudlin to you, Dennis. But I love the Church more than I love your good opinion of me. And I love that and want it very much. If I can't have it"— A ghost of a smile strayed across his lips. "God seems determined to deprive me of everything I love."

"But it doesn't make *sense*."

"Yes, it does. The kind of sense that Papa Giovanni made. He spent thirty years in the desert, do you realize that? Thirty years playing diplomat, making small talk to Bulgarians and Turks. Obedience and peace. That was his motto. I'm hoping—

praying—that if I can live up to the first part, I may taste a little of the second—"

Dennis strode back to his cubicle and sat down, fuming. It didn't make—sense? Suddenly with the force of a physical blow he realized how utterly and totally he had lost contact with the spiritual life. A decade of Jesuit retreats suddenly engulfed him. Phrases from the spiritual exercises of St. Ignatius thundered in his brain. *To regulate his life so that he will not be influenced in his decisions by an inordinate attachment. . . . In the present meditation I shall ask for shame and confusion. . . . Working against their own sensuality and carnal and worldly love will make offerings of greater value and importance.* Numbly, as if someone else were directing his hand, he reached out for the moon shell. Abruptly he turned it over so that the narrow tip was pressing into his palm. He stared at the lines spiraling up wider and wider.

Stupid, stupid, he denounced himself. What are you seeing, O ye of little faith? The dynamic spiral—it was the image of the Church's growth. The idea that had tantalized him, that had lurked just beyond his mind's reach since they had left Italy. The holy spiral, wholly unpredictable, moving upward in ever more widening circles toward infinity, each spiral both a new beginning and a continuation of the past, changing color, sometimes even shape, the living edge like a great expanding wave, not repudiating, simply growing beyond the dead past.

He must write to Goggin, he must write to him immediately. Here was his needle in the historical haystack, the point of view that included a New Gospel and a new history of the Church, books that would proclaim and create a new beginning. The subject of the history would be nothing less than the struggle of the Christian community to achieve the freedom its founder had died to create—a struggle that was in essence a series of defeats, culminating in Pio Nono, the Pope who snarled, *Tradition— that's me.* But from that total defeat, the proclamation of absolute spiritual despotism, had come the seeds of a deeper more profound growth of freedom. Why was that surprising? Wasn't that the very essence of the Way, the Truth, the Life, the constant flowering of victory in defeat, joy from desolation, love from hatred and contempt?

Where could he find a better place to observe this drama than his present job? This man, this suffering Cardinal next door, who was trying to impossibly combine obedience and peace, he was intimately connected with this new beginning. He must become its spokesman in the land where its possibility, its very heart, a new confidence in human freedom, was born. He must become John's living voice, consecrated by John's own hands—

The phone was ringing. Dennis snatched it to his ear and heard Mike Furia's familiar ebullient rasp. "Is the boss around?"

The children of this world perpetually distract the children of light, Dennis thought as he asked the Cardinal if he would speak to his former fund-raising chairman.

Matthew Mahan picked up the phone with a sudden sense of dread. He was going to hear some bad news. "Hello, stranger, how's the world treating you?"

"Australia's treating me pretty good. Japan lousy. Italy very, very good. The rest of Europe stinko."

"How long have you been gone, eight weeks?"

"Closer to nine. I got in the day before yesterday. It's the first chance I've had to call you. From the cables I got, I gather our collection plate isn't doing much better than it was when I left."

"Unfortunately true. Maybe it'll be good for us in the long run."

"Did you ever get a report from the chancellor on the projected cost of your schools?"

"I got it last week. It indicates that we'll be in the red for ten million dollars by 1976."

"I told you it would knock your head off. What are you going to do about it?"

"I'm sending out a memorandum to all pastors, telling them to face up to the necessity of phasing out the parochial school system on the grammar school level."

"Really? Congratulations, Matt. That took guts. It must have been tough to write."

"The advice you gave me—helped me face up to it."

Only partially true, but it might help to restore their friendship, Matthew Mahan told himself.

"I'm glad. Listen, I've got something personal I want to talk to you about. Are you free for lunch or dinner?"

"Either one."

"Lunch would be better. I'll see you in the Men's Grill at the Athletic Club at twelve, okay?"

374

Riding downtown at eleven forty-five Matthew Mahan tried to divert himself by cheering up Eddie Johnson. Eddie was not the same man since the Cardinal had traded in his limousine for a Ford. The spring had vanished from Eddie's step, the spontaneity from his smile. Jim McAvoy, who had given Matthew Mahan a new limousine every year free of charge, was equally unhappy. But his wife, Madeline, who was much more in touch with contemporary spiritual problems, had calmed Jim down and they were still friends.

"Come on, Eddie, admit it, this car handles just as well as the Cadillac," the Cardinal said.

"Ain't going to ever get me to admit that, Your Eminence. Fact is, I think you take a serious risk drivin' around in this hunk a junk."

"But Eddie, if God isn't watching over me, who is he watching? I think we've got a built-in guarantee that's better than any dealer can give us."

"Yeah, but they was so polite when I took the car into McAvoy's garage. This new place, they don't even look at me. They just say stick it in the corner. As if I was drivin' some tinhorn lawyer or somethin'."

Matthew Mahan almost smiled. Eddie, too, was learning humility and not liking it.

In the lobby of the Athletic Club, Mike Furia crushed his hand and then refused to let it go. "Hey, what the hell's wrong with you? You look awful."

"Oh, the usual, Mike, working too hard. And not sleeping very well. You're looking great."

It was the truth. Mike had lost ten or fifteen pounds on his world tour. His face was tanned. He exuded energy and vitality. Or was he just extraordinarily nervous? At the table he fiddled with knives, spoons, forks. He gulped a scotch on the rocks and was into a second one before Matthew Mahan had taken more than two sips from his glass of milk. He had expected an interrogation over the milk and had decided in advance to stop trying to conceal his ulcer. But Mike was too self-absorbed to notice it. Finally, Matthew Mahan decided to relieve the suspense.

"What's this personal matter? I thought of picking up some

boxing gloves in the exercise room before I tried to give you any more advice."

Mike grinned. "Okay, here it comes. I finished my trip around the world in six weeks. For the last three weeks I've been persuading someone to marry me."

"That's great, Mike. Who's the lucky woman?"

Mike hesitated, his second scotch in midair. He took a sip and slowly put the glass down on the table, his eyes on Matthew Mahan's face. "Mary Shea," he said.

For a moment, Matthew Mahan could not see Mike Furia across the table. Blackness engulfed him. He thought he was fainting. Then Mike's worried face reappeared. A blurred version, like a picture taken with an unsteady camera.

"That's—that's the most wonderful news I've heard in a year, Mike."

"Really?"

Mike was very serious. That tough, square-jawed swarthy face was plainly worried that the Cardinal was lying to him.

"Really. Why don't you believe me?"

"She's told me everything, Matt. I know what she's been to you. I'm not sure you want to see her married to a lug like me."

"Don't be ridiculous." With an enormous effort Matthew Mahan stifled an urge to weep. "Tell me, tell me how it happened."

Mike smiled. "It started last May, during the week of your elevation. I remember looking at her at that small dinner party, asking myself why the hell I never had the brains or luck to find someone like her. We had dinner together one of our last nights in Rome that week. When I got home, I started telephoning her every other day."

"Where is she, where's Mary now?"

"Right here in the city."

"Why didn't you bring her along?"

"She's as nervous about what you'd think as I was."

"No," Matthew Mahan said, "no, Mike. I'm the one who's nervous. I'm the one who has something—shameful to tell you."

"What?" Mike was utterly baffled.

"You want me to receive you and Mary into the Church, don't you?"

376

"She wants you to do more than that. She wants you to marry us."

"I can't do either one, Mike."

He told him about the letter he had received from the apostolic delegate that morning. Mike's face twisted with an emotion that was hard to identify, a mixture of contempt and anger. "Matt, what I told you in Rome still goes. I've got my own arrangement with God, or whoever the hell is running this crazy world. But I don't know what this is going to do to Mary."

"I don't, either."

"There's nothing you can do? You can't pretend you didn't get this letter for a month or so? Once you give us permission, it can't be revoked, can it?"

"Another letter went to the head of our marriage tribunal, I'm sure. The apostolic delegate'll be on the phone to me if I don't answer him by return mail."

"What would it be worth to *him* to lose track of the problem for a while? It would be worth a hell of a lot to me."

"That would only get his back up."

Mike smiled wryly. "I should know better. You can't bribe a pope with five hundred million in liquid assets. What do we do?"

"We have our lunch and go straight from here to see Mary. Tell her the truth. And hope for the best."

Mike nodded and beckoned to the head waiter. It was an unpleasant lunch. Mike's mood was sour. He proceeded to tell Matthew Mahan every vicious negative story he had heard about the Vatican during his three weeks in Italy.

"That ex-Jesuit—what's his name, Father Mirante?—tracked us down and gave us an earful on the latest inside stinks."

"What happened to him? I gave him five hundred dollars and never heard another word from him."

"He sends you profuse apologies. He's got some sort of family troubles. Anyway, the big news he thought you should know is about celibacy. He's really bugged on that question. He says the Dutch bishops are going to maneuver Il Papa into a corner on it."

"Really," said Matthew Mahan, instinctively disliking the idea of a confrontation.

"Where do you stand on it, Matt?"

Was Mike being deliberately sarcastic? Matthew Mahan decided that it did not matter. "It's a question that should be left open for the whole Church to debate over the next decade. I'm more and more inclined for optional marriage myself."

"Good thing. According to Bill Reed, you may be hearing wedding bells in your residence before long."

"You mean Dennis and Bill's daughter?"

"Doc says they can barely keep their hands off each other."

Matthew Mahan nodded mournfully, pretending to know all about it, although the words suggested a more painful reality than Dennis had admitted to him. "Dennis told me."

"Il Papa sold his thirty per cent interest in Immobiliare to a French syndicate. I hear he got about thirty million for it. It's part of a new policy. He wants to reduce the Vatican's visibility in the business world. I met one of the guys who handled the final bargaining. Do you know who was right there at the table keeping track of the smallest decimals? Old Paolo himself."

Mike began discussing the men around Paul, his secretary, Macchi, the Substitute Secretary of State, Benelli, making each of them sound like crypto-Fascists who would welcome the resurrection of Mussolini. There was venom in every word, and Matthew Mahan began to wince at the thought of this man living with Mary, saying these things to Mary, destroying her faith day by relentless day. Was God a mad joker? How could he insult him this way? How could he permit this black comedy that starred him as the perpetrator of this marriage?

Going uptown in the Cardinal's Ford, they were silent. They got out at 2600 Parkway, the most expensive apartment building on the city's most expensive street, and went up in the elevator. Mary sat in the living room, conferring with Raymond Snodgrass, the city's leading decorator, a small, ugly man with loving-cup ears who cheerfuly never pretended to be anything but a homosexual. He had handled the sale of the episcopal antiques and greeted Matthew Mahan as an old friend. "It's such a *delight* to be working for Mrs. Shea again. I did her first apartment."

"Do you think he's a jinx?" Mary said, welcoming Matthew Mahan with her warmest smile.

"Oh no. Raymond's good luck. He's like one of those statues of the Little Flower. I bet he glows in the dark."

378

"Oh, that's mean, Your Eminence," Raymond said. He giggled. "I do."

They got rid of Raymond and sat down, Mike beside Mary on the couch, Matthew Mahan in an easy chair a few feet away. Did it hurt to see her kiss him on the mouth and entwine her fingers in his thick tanned hand? No, old losses, old wounds, no longer counted. He admired several paintings by a young pop artist named Fontanella whom Mary had recommended to Mike, and pretended to understand while they told him about visiting the artist's studio, where he showed them a whole series of paintings in abstract expressionist style.

After Mike put away the paintings and sat down beside Mary on the couch again, she abandoned any pretense of a casual visit. "Did you enjoy communing in your masculine sanctum sanctorum?" she asked.

"Listen," Mike said. "I picked the Athletic Club after you said you couldn't come, you had to commune with *Raymond*."

"You don't tell Raymond when to come. He tells you."

"Baloney. I think you're afraid of this guy." Mike gestured to Matthew Mahan. "A frown from him, and it's all over between you and me."

"Oh really?" Mary lifted her chin in mock disdain. "I didn't act that way in Rome—did I?"

They were talking to each other almost as if he were not in the room. Six months ago it would have been humiliating, enraging. Now it had a strange reverse affect. For the first time in months his heart stirred with a tremor of hope. They were in love. Intensely, physically in love. For a scarifying moment he saw them in each other's arms, exultantly delighting in the touch and taste of breasts, lips, loins, the dark parousia that he would never know. Did his own poor love shrivel in the white glare of that vision? Yes, yes, of course it did. But it was used to that, used to the glare of the desert sun. It sat mutely like a dumb suffering animal waiting for permission to speak.

"Wait till you hear what he's got to tell you about his good-conscience divorce program," Mike said.

"What?" said Mary expectantly.

He told her, humbly pleading behind the neutral words for a pardon he did not deserve and could not receive.

Mary sat in strangely composed silence for a moment. Was she fighting off the stricken haunted look that had tormented him in Rome? "Oh, Matt," she said, "I feel so awful—for you. I know how much this meant to you. But let me tell you something—that I know now. It isn't as terrible for the others or for me as you think, Matt, assuming that the others are as much in love as I am."

She untwined her fingers and slipped her arm around Mike's massive bicep. "I know it won't bother me, Matt. I know I'll be all right now. I needed someone to care for, someone to care for me. I tried to get it from you, Matt. I inflicted myself on you. It was so unfair, so awful what I did to you. All you could give me was a small part of yourself; the rest was parceled out to all those other people you have to care about. When I turned to the Church as a whole to find it—it was like trying to embrace a cloud. I needed a whole person—and I've found him."

How could he tell her that her words were like manna to the desert wanderer, like rain in Death Valley, stirring life in petrified, withered seeds, making the barren earth bloom? Then came a warning note, a sudden realization that Mary was talking too rapidly, with too much intensity in her voice. She was trying to reassure herself, as much as him. Even though everything she was saying was true, good, profound, it was failing to penetrate the deepest level of her self.

"Of course, I did want you to marry us, Matt. That would have made everything perfect. It would be more—more complete if I was at peace with the Church. But I guess we can't have everything in this world."

"You are at peace with the Church, Mary. As long as you know in your inner heart that you're doing the right thing. I have a definite feeling that God has played a part in this—this happiness."

"I do, too, Matt," Mary said. "Of course, this pseudo-atheist or agnostic, or whatever he is, scoffs at that kind of thinking. But I scoff right back at him."

She made a fist and pushed it against Mike's big chin.

Again, Matthew Mahan sensed a false note, gaiety concealing a conflict that could cause trouble. He tried to gloss it over by joining in the cheer.

"Well, children," he said, standing up, "even if I can't do much for you legally, there's nothing in the rules that prevents me from giving you my blessing, for whatever that's worth."

"It's worth a lot to me."

"And me, too," Mike Furia said.

"Don't kneel down. There's no need for any ceremony."

Quickly Matthew Mahan made the familiar cross in the air above them with his right hand and murmured the prayer. Mary looked up at him, her face solemn. Then she was standing beside him, full of frowning concern. "Matt, you look so tired. What have you been doing?"

"Oh—worries. Work. Old age. And problems. Lately even my problems have problems."

"Yes—but you—"

What was she going to say? You used to thrive on hard work and problems? How could he explain to her the overwhelming sense of failure that tormented him now? A failure so large, it was laughable. He had to step back, look at himself, and smile at the utter futility of his episcopate. The Good Shepherd—good for what?

"Bill Reed told me you should take a month off," Mike Furia said.

"I know. I know. Maybe I will, after Christmas."

"I was hoping you could marry us just before Christmas," Mary said with an ominous falling note in her voice. "We wanted to spend our honeymoon in Hawaii. Mike says it's marvelous at that time of the year."

"We'll still do it," Mike said. "Just because Il Papa's eliminated this guy—"

Wrong, Matthew Mahan thought, too abrasive, Mike. I'm not your enemy; I'm your friend here and everywhere else.

"When we get back," Mary said, ignoring Mike's nasty tone, "I'm going to make you take a vacation if I have to go down there and lock you out of your residence. I had a dream about you the other night. You were terribly sick in Rome. I kept crying and saying, 'The world won't be the same. The world won't be the same.'"

Matthew Mahan laughed. "You women are terrible creatures. If you don't get your way with flattery, you try threats and then witchcraft."

"Take care of yourself, please," Mary said and kissed him on the cheek.

Riding home in the back seat of his Ford, Matthew Mahan found himself thinking about Dennis McLaughlin. He suddenly remembered vividly the expression on Dennis's face when he had told him to extinguish all hope of a married priesthood. It was alarmingly similar to the sadness that he had glimpsed on Mary's face when he had given her his blessing. A patina of hopelessness as if each in his (her) own way was saying: *I am not worthy.* When all the time it was he, the blesser, the voice of authority, who was the unworthy one. *Take me, O Lord, do what you will with me, for their sake.*

XXXI

On December 21 Matthew Mahan opened the evening paper and read that Michael J. Furia and Mary Shea had been married at a private ceremony in the mayor's office, with the chief justice of the state's supreme court, an old friend of the bride's father, as the officiating magistrate. It was no surprise to the Cardinal. He had had dinner with the loving couple only a week earlier. Mary was defiantly gay, Mike exultant. But again Matthew Mahan had sensed a strain, a tension, an unreality in their manner.

While Mike was pouring after-dinner cordials, the Cardinal found Mary looking somberly at him as if she wanted desperately to say something but was forbidden to speak. He could only hope and pray that it would pass, that she would be sustained by Mike's obvious devotion to her. The danger he sensed was very Italian. Mike had a tendency to consider the man as the arbiter of all opinion in the family. He obviously assumed that Mary agreed with him when he unleashed another round of wisecracks on Vatican capitalists and the financial games they played around the world. He made a small speech on the Vatican's refusal to pay any tax to the Italian Government on its investment profits in Italy. Last May Mary had joined in this vitriol; it had been niccly attuned to her bitter feelings about the Church. But Mike seemed to have no awareness that he was also talking about the church of John XXIII, the institution that had re-awakened hope in her heart.

The next day he had called Mike at the office and tried to explain this to him. Mike thought he was trying to tell him what to think, or worse, indirectly influence Mary through him. "Listen, Padre," he said, "she's out of your hands now. I think the best thing you can do is stay away from her. Frankly, you're bad medicine. She was really sort of depressed this morning when we got up. I didn't want to see you again before the ceremony, but she insisted on it. I still think we can be friends—but on a strictly social level."

"All right, Mike. If that's the right thing to do, you can depend on me to do it. I'm only trying to help—"

"I know, I know," Mike said impatiently.

The happy couple, the paper informed its readers, left immediately for a one-month honeymoon in Hawaii.

Nothing more was heard from the Furias, not even a postcard. Matthew Mahan did his best to put them out of his mind. It was easy to do at Christmas. He had several dozen appearances to make at old-age homes, orphanages, hospitals, and other diocesan institutions. In his very limited spare time he worked on drafts of the American bishops' statement on priestly celibacy. With Dennis's help he did his utmost to urge on the other members of the task force an undogmatic point of view. But his letters and memorandums might as well have been fired into outer space. The final draft of the twenty-seven-page statement that arrived on his desk from the residence of the head of the committee, Archbishop Francis J. Furey of San Antonio, Texas, was an all-out defense of celibacy. It did have some sympathetic comments about those who were unable to live up to the hard calling. But it came down to an unwavering affirmation of the prevailing rule.

Ten days later, Matthew Mahan and Dennis McLaughlin rode to the airport for the trip to Washington, D.C., and the semiannual meeting of the American bishops. They did not say a word about Matthew Mahan's promise to speak out at this gathering. Was there any point to it now? he wondered, thinking about the disheartening evolution of the celibacy statement. Never had he been more aware of his outsider's role in the American hierarchy. The only Archbishop with whom he had felt an emotional and spiritual kinship, genial Paul Hallinan of Atlanta, Georgia, had died last year. Perhaps he should have written to the twenty or thirty bishops who attended that session with married priests at the Houston meeting. Recalling what he had heard there, the sadness and the anger in some of the statements of the married priests, renewed his determination to speak out.

At the flight gate Dennis somberly handed him his heavy briefcase, with a wry remark that he did not have to worry about something to read on the plane. The final draft of the celibacy statement was on top of the briefcase's load of papers. There was no sign that Dennis had even read it, Matthew Mahan thought gloomily, as he paged listlessly through it. Then he reached the last page and a scrawled note.

Did it ever occur to you that maybe we've got the whole sex thing backward? The more I think of it, the more I see the current policy as interference with the most essential human freedom—the freedom to love. The Pope's idiotic encyclical threatens this freedom within marriage itself. Archaic canon laws cripple those who attempt to recover from the failure of a first marriage. A meaningless celibacy prevents priests—supposedly men dedicated to love—from realizing it on the deepest level of their lives.

The passion in those words made Matthew Mahan wince. Dennis was obviously writing lines that he envisioned his Cardinal hurling at his fellow American bishops. Even subtracting the passion, Matthew Mahan mused, there was a lot of truth in Dennis's words. Except for abortion, everything about the Church's teaching on sex was against life, against joy, against forgiveness, against the young. How else could anyone explain the Furey statement—its total refusal even to consider the thinking of the priests of Dennis's generation?

Cardinal Mahan could have spent the evening strolling about the Statler Hilton lobby collecting congratulations on his elevation from other arriving bishops. He fended off a few of these as he checked in. But he had arranged a special after-hours admission to the National Museum. It had been years since he roamed their five-million shell collection, and he wanted to see some of his old favorites. Once more he gazed in loving admiration at *Sthenorytis pernobilis*, a tiny pure white shell with deep volutes in its spiral. Utterly unique, it came from the Barbados. Equally rare was the big brown and white *Pleurotomaria salmiana* from Japan, with its almost perfectly oval spirals. Only a half-dozen living specimens had been discovered. It was a link with immense blank eons of prehistoric time. Loveliest were the two glowing yellow valves of the *Lima dalli* from the Philippines. Was there better proof of God's infinite creativity than this awesome profusion of shapes and colors?

As he left the museum, he mused over the theory that Dennis had tried to explain to him the other night, about the dynamic spiral being an image of the Church's growth. Dennis seemed particularly excited by the difference between a spiral and a dome. One was open-ended, potentially infinite, the other rigid, encompassing. He saw what Dennis was trying to say, but it did not particularly stir him. Symbols were not his bag.

The next morning, the American bishops, three hundred men in sober black, gathered in the ballroom of the Statler Hilton to make decisions. The president, Cardinal John Dearden, began the meeting with an almost rhapsodic report on the recent Synod of Bishops in Rome. He heaped compliments on Pope Paul for his recognition of the rights of his brother bishops. Dearden quoted the Pope at length, with special emphasis on the "love which bishops must nourish between themselves." He closed with a call to his fellow American bishops to co-operate in attacking the nation's spiritual and social problems.

The applause was warm. It was hard to argue with such sentiments. They turned to the agenda of the meeting. A committee report recommending the establishment of a national office for Black Catholicism was overwhelmingly endorsed. The English translations for the new order of the mass were also approved with little discussion. Another committee reported that eighty-seven men had been enrolled to train as deacons at four national centers. Six dioceses were planning to begin diaconal programs in the coming year. Deacons could perform many parish duties. They could also marry. Was this the answer to celibacy? On numbers alone, Matthew Mahan thought, the answer would have to be no.

Finally came the discussion of the celibacy statement. Matthew Mahan opened it by declaring that he admired it as a comprehensive survey of the subject—but he could see no point in

America's bishops making a statement now. He had heard from friends in Europe that the Dutch bishops were going to raise the question soon as something that the entire Church should debate. Why not see what the response of the rest of the world's bishops was before making such a definitive statement?

One of Cardinal Krol's suffragan bishops whose name escaped Matthew Mahan took the floor and asked with heavy sarcasm if he was implying that a majority rule should be the determining factor in making such a decision.

"Of course not," said Matthew Mahan. "I am suggesting the possibility that new light may be shed on the subject by bishops from other countries and other rites."

"Didn't you just tell us that this was a remarkably comprehensive survey of the subject?" asked his opponent, a stocky middle-aged Irishman with a crewcut. "What has been omitted? Weren't you a member of the committee? If any aspect of the subject should be developed, why don't you enlighten us now?"

"I have no pretense to being an expert on the subject. Nor did I say the report was omniscient," Matthew Mahan said.

A California bishop—what was his name, Cassidy?—arose. The same type, stocky, beefy in the neck.

"It seems to me, Your Eminence, that you are missing the main point. We know where the Holy Father stands on this subject. He has asked us for our support."

"I would like to think he has asked us for advice," Matthew Mahan said.

A murmur of disapproval ran through the room. Shocked eyes confronted him wherever he looked.

"I think he has made it clear that this is an issue in which he does not want advice."

"He may need it, whether he wants it or not."

Bishop Cassidy glowered. "Last spring when you knelt before him, did you feel that way? Did you feel he was a man who needed advice?"

The sadness in Paul's eyes burned into Matthew Mahan's soul once more. Why were they forcing him to make these arrogant statements? "I felt—I felt he was a deeply troubled man."

More shock and dismay. "Gentlemen, please remember I am saying this to you in private. I would not dream of discussing this publicly. My feeling for the Holy Father, our feeling for him, is not the issue here. I am only suggesting a delay, not a repudiation of this statement. I don't know what your young priests are telling you. But the haste with which we are rushing to get this statement on record will strike the ones I know as disheartening. We seem to be more interested in supporting the Pope—who after all does not *need* support—than we are concerned for their priesthoods."

Another member of Krol's entourage—was it the bishop of Wilmington?—one of those early-middle-age balding types with steel-rimmed glasses and an acne-pitted face, arose to accuse Matthew Mahan of gross sentimentalism. What the younger clergy needed was leadership and not shilly-shallying. This was what Pope Paul was trying to give them on this difficult question, in spite of the slanders and obfuscations of those who, at bottom, were enemies of authority in the Church. Give way on this question, predicted the speaker in a voice that quivered with rage, and there will be a union of priests telling the bishops what to do; marriage, contraception, and abortion laws will be dissolved and the Catholic Church will become indistinguishable from the Unitarians.

Matthew Mahan looked around the ballroom. Was anyone on his side? *Thy will be done, Lord,* he prayed. Cardinal Dearden was recognizing someone on the far side of the room. It was a western bishop, a new man, not more than forty. In a Southwest twang he declared himself very much on Matthew Mahan's side. There was a great deal of false alarmism being broadcast in the room and in the Church. He did not think the domino theory applied to Catholic theology. Cardinal Mahan was giving them—and Pope Paul—good advice. A bishop from Minnesota rose to agree with the western spokesman. He assured his fellow bishops that the Catholics of Minnesota would not in the least be upset by a married clergy. Matthew Mahan was tempted to add a few more words of his own, summing up his argument. But the mere thought of getting to his feet and speaking sent a shudder of exhaustion through his body and turned the faces around him into a blur. Remember, he told himself wryly, you are the silent brother.

The opposition insisted on having the last word. From the rear of the room a voice with a New Jersey accent made a ferocious attack on the Dutch Church, and obliquely on Cardinal Mahan for suggesting that the American bishops should even consider the possibility of listening to anything that came out of Holland. Nowhere was the revolt against the Church's authority more blatant than among the Dutch. Perhaps Cardinal Mahan was misled by the difficulties he was having in his own diocese into imagining that there was a similar revolt against authority across the United States. It simply was not true. Most American bishops had the courage and the conviction to use the authority given them by the Holy Father to preserve a healthy respect for order and obedience in their dioceses.

Who would have thought six months ago, Matthew, that you would have been accused of incompetence, cowardice, and disloyalty before your fellow American bishops? It was logical, it was part of the path for which you seem fated, the way of humiliation and defeat. Yet the gall did not taste any sweeter, for knowing this. It still seared your heart and ravaged your stomach like liquid fire. He told himself he was not the first, nor would he be the last, man to endure such a beating. Two years ago he had watched a dying Paul Hallinan take even more brutal punishment as he led the fight for more liturgical freedom. Sneers about his loyalty to Rome and prophecies of chaos had been used to pound him into silence.

Cardinal Dearden called for a vote. Did the bishops approve the substance of the document? Only two no votes were recorded on this question. Should the document be released? A two-thirds majority was required. To Matthew Mahan's amazement, the vote on release was 145 in favor and 68 opposed. If three bishops had voted the other way, he would have won the debate he thought he had so humiliatingly lost. In agony he asked himself why he had not risen to reply to the final assault from New Jersey. As he stood up and felt his legs trembling under him, he knew the answer. He was simply too exhausted.

Up in his room he flung himself on the bed and wept. There were so many reasons for tears. There was no need to explain them to himself or to God. He wept for the death of that old self, the smoothie whom he still loved, in spite of all his attempts to evade him. He wept for Dennis. He wept for the Church. In his humiliation he ate dinner alone in his room, telling himself it was the best way to stay on his diet.

This sacrificial gesture did not seem to satisfy his ulcer. In the middle of the night, he awoke with Brother Pain clawing at him, followed by sudden nausea, which sent him rushing to the bathroom to vomit more blood. When it happened again at 5 A.M., he decided that even the mild tension of speaking before his fellow bishops was too much for him to handle in his exhausted state. He skipped the rest of the meeting and flew home.

Dennis met him at the airport. The celibacy statement had already been released. Dennis had heard a capsule version of it on the midnight news. "I tried to talk them out of it," Matthew Mahan said, and told him how close the vote on releasing it had been.

Dennis shrugged. "If you'd won, I'd start believing in miracles."

It had been sunny and warm in Washington. But the weather here was cloudy and the wind was raw. A sliver of icy air struck him in the throat and he asked Eddie Johnson to close his window. A second later, he was shaken by a terrible premonition of disaster. Whether it was personal or something to do with the Church or with the nation, he did not know. He tried to thrust the feeling away, telling himself it was easy enough to imagine doom was imminent, just from reading the newspapers. As he left Washington, the city had been preparing for a siege. They expected a quarter of a million antiwar demonstrators to rally around the Washington Monument tomorrow.

He mentioned this to Dennis and he barely nodded. It was obvious that he was thinking about more personal problems.

Two weeks later, Dennis handed him a letter from the vice-secretary of the Sacred Congregation of Bishops, a Monsignor Carlo Dotti. Cardinal Confalonieri, having been rejected on *Humanae Vitae*, was not risking his dignity with Cardinal Mahan again. The letter informed him that "confidential information" from the Netherlands had forced the Holy Father to reach the grievous conclusion that the Dutch Pastoral Council, which was to meet early this month, would urge the Dutch bishops to adopt optional celibacy for priests. The Holy Father planned to exhort the Dutch bishops to reject this demand. He hoped that bishops from other parts of the world would write their brothers in Holland and urge them to respond to the Pope's plea.

Matthew Mahan did not reply to the vice-secretary of the

Sacred Congregation of Bishops. "At the very least," he remarked to Dennis, "I think they ought to know that if they kick a fellow in the teeth, he doesn't rush to do them favors."

He and Dennis began listening to the Vatican on their multiband Italian radio almost every night. As predicted, the Dutch Pastoral Council, composed of both priests and laymen, voted overwhelmingly for optional celibacy. They called on their bishops to support them. The Pope in turn issued a statement exhorting the Dutch bishops to reject the council and defend celibacy with all the power and eloquence at their command. A month later, the Dutch bishops replied. They said that their country would be better off if there was optional celibacy, if married men could be ordained priests, and if priests who had married could return to the ministry. They affirmed that the Pastoral Council had "expressed the opinion of a substantial part of the Dutch community on celibacy and the priesthood." They asked their fellow bishops around the world to consult with them and with the Pope in order to reach "an understanding of this complicated situation." Meekly, they said they could do nothing "without consulting the Holy Father and the world Church."

"It's beautiful, too beautiful," Dennis said as Matthew Mahan turned off the radio. "They have old Paul up against the wall."

Matthew Mahan nodded mournfully. "If he meant what he said about cooperation with his brother bishops—"

"There should be a consultation."

Matthew Mahan felt guilty for a moment. In the dim study he suddenly saw Pope Paul's face as he knelt before him last May. The man's extraordinary sadness penetrated his heart once more. "I don't envy him."

"He deserves it," Dennis said.

The heartlessness of the young. But Davey Cronin would have said the same thing if he was sitting there. Perhaps the young and the old only *seem* pitiless. They tell the truth. For them reality is not fogged by the peculiar sympathy of middle age. We who have failed and cannot swallow our failure, who perpetually pray for an opportunity to regurgitate, we are the flinchers from the truth. But isn't charity another word for it?

At 2 A.M. Matthew Mahan was still awake, wrestling with these painful thoughts. The telephone rang. The night watchman at the chancery office was very apologetic. "Your Eminence, this fellow says he's a very close personal friend and he's got some very important personal news for you. His name is Furia."

"Put him through."

"Hello, Padre."

"Mike. Where are you?"

"San Francisco. Have you seen Mary?"

"No. Why should I? Isn't she with you?"

"I thought she might stop—she left me, Matt. She went back to Rome."

There was anguish in Mike's voice. "We got into an argument about the Church. I started giving her the usual line—that it was a crock. All of a sudden she burst into tears. I didn't know what was happening. The next morning—she left. She wrote a note—saying she loved me—but she didn't have the strength—to be worthy of me. Did you ever hear anything crazier than that? Her worthy of me? What the hell should I do, Matt?"

"The first thing you better do is cable Father Guilio Mirante. Tell him to find her and make sure she doesn't do something serious."

"Like what?"

"Like killing herself."

"You think that's possible?"

"From what Mirante told me, yes. The second thing—" He hesitated, unsure whether to say it. "This will make you sore, Mike."

"Tell me, the hell with that."

"Start taking the Church seriously. Whether you believe in it or not, take it seriously. Stop talking as if the Pope and the bishops were just another bunch of businessmen. Our business is caring for souls, Mike. Now maybe it's yours. Caring—for one soul."

"I get the message, Matt. Maybe you're right. Maybe I've let that Roman cynicism about the Church eat into my brain. Say a prayer for her—and me, will you, Matt? Because if I lose her—I think I'll get drunk for life."

"I'm praying right now, Mike."

Matthew Mahan went down to his private chapel and knelt there for the rest of the night. His knowledge of what else was happening added to his torment. Mary in Rome now—when Paul was about to commit another blunder. There was no doubt in his mind that the Pope was going to blunder on celibacy, as he had blundered on every other sexual problem in his papacy.

Surely this was a kind of climax, a moment of truth the whole world would recognize. Or was it only his personal moment, created by the peculiar dimensions of his fate?

The following morning, Dennis handed him a letter from the apostolic delegate. Why had he failed to answer the letter from the vice-secretary of the Sacred Congregation of Bishops? Surely Cardinal Mahan must know that the Holy Father had special reasons for depending upon him. Could he possibly fail to come to the support of the man who had raised him to the Sacred College of Cardinals and so forth and so forth? Matthew Mahan flipped the letter to the edge of his desk. He looked up and saw Dennis studying him. What was he searching for? A sign that there was something here beside an automaton, a greedy collector of clerical honors who had played the game all the way up to the red hat and now would pay his debt like a good little politician? What else will he see if you humbly capitulate?

Something had to be done, something had to be done, a voice drummed in his head. Pain began to gnaw in his stomach. A pulse throbbed in his forehead.

"Let's let him stew a little longer," Matthew Mahan said.

Dennis trudged back to his office. The slump of his shoulders, the droop of his head, wrenched Matthew Mahan's heart. He got up, fought off the by now familiar wave of weakness that assailed him almost every time he rose from a chair, and went downstairs to the chapel. Kneeling on his familiar prie-dieu, he contemplated the cheap crucifix above the tabernacle. When the choice is between love and obedience, what is the answer, Lord? he asked. Does the time come when the Shepherd's words are not enough, when he must risk himself to prove his love? Answer me, Lord, answer me.

Of course, there was no answer. Why should He look upon this caricature of a shepherd, this utterly worthless bishop, this pseudo-suffering servant whose service was so consistently lousy?

As he came out of the chapel, he almost collided with Dennis. "A cable from Rome. Just arrived," he said, handing him the yellow envelope.

He opened it. It was from Cardinal Confalonieri, head of the Sacred Congregation of Bishops.

WE WISH TO INFORM YOU THAT HIS HOLINESS PLANS TO RESPOND TO THE DEFIANT AND UNAUTHORIZED STATEMENT OF THE DUTCH BISHOPS ON CLERICAL CELIBACY ON OR ABOUT FEBRUARY FIRST. WE URGE YOU TO HAVE PREPARED FOR PUBLICATION IN YOUR DIO- CESE AN ENTHUSIASTIC STATEMENT SUPPORTING HIS HOLINESS. THE BISHOP OF ROME, THE HEIR OF PETER, INTENDS TO MAKE NO COMPROMISE ON THE GREAT PRINCIPLE AT STAKE. HE WILL MAKE IT CLEAR THAT THERE WILL BE NO CONSULTATION, NO DISCUSSION OF CELIBACY TOLERATED WITHIN HIS CHURCH. THE PRINCIPLE WILL BE AFFIRMED ONCE AND FOR ALL.

"My God," Dennis said, who was reading the words over his shoulder.

Something had to be done. Something had to be done. Anguish throbbed in Matthew Mahan's mind and body. Dennis's sad face dropped before him. In Rome he saw Mary's suffering mouth and leaden eyes beside that greasy river, in the ominous shadow of that huge inhuman dome. She and Dennis had to *know*, they had to *see*, that love existed for them, love unto the limits of risk. "Dennis," he said. "Make arrangements for us to go to Rome as soon as possible."

XXXII

Give me strength, give me strength, Matthew Mahan prayed as the jet thundered skyward. Whom was he talking to? Obscurely, he sensed it was Pope John. But would he approve of this trip? The man who chose as his episcopal motto "Obedience and Peace."

It was insane, this sudden assumption of the role of a latter-day Cardinal Gibbons. Wasn't it a kind of diseased reaction to Davey Cronin's bizarre lectures and months of patient brainwashing by Davey's spiritual heir, Dennis McLaughlin? Gibbons had been the leader of the American Church. He had behind him the solid support of almost every bishop and the vast majority of the laity when he had rushed to Rome to prevent Leo

XIII from denouncing trade unionism as a pact with the devil. Who is supporting you, Cardinal Mahan? Only the voiceless generation, Your Holiness, the younger priests and the voiceless legions of the divorced and the voiceless multitude of unwanted, unloved children and their mothers and fathers broken in health and spirit.

Wouldn't that be a lovely answer. He took out of his briefcase the letter he had written to the Pope and reread it for the twentieth or twenty-fifth time.

Your Holiness:

A brother bishop, a brother in Christ, writes to you out of the fullness of a heart that shares a shepherd's concern for the flock of the people of God. I must tell you, Your Holiness, speaking with a directness that I like to think is American, that the Church in my nation—and since we have within our borders the descendants of so many nations, that must mean the Church in many parts of the world—is in grave danger. Never before in the history of the Church, Your Holiness, have we, the shepherds, set ourselves against the great mass of the faithful. Even when we enforced what we believed to be the law of God with the utmost severity, with fire and sword, in the Middle Ages and the Renaissance, we were really chastizing only a few. But now, Your Holiness, we are alienating the many. Your encyclical on birth control has for the first time turned the women of the Church against us. This is truly new. Even in nations like Italy and Spain and France, where great numbers of men turned against the Church for political reasons, most of the women remained faithful. This is no longer true in America, because in their deepest hearts our women no longer feel that you have any right or power to tell them how many children they should have. As for the divorced, there is scarcely a family in America without at least one relative who has suffered this tragedy. What can they think of our Church, when we treat these unfortunate people like pariahs, while other Christian churches are glad to embrace them, when they come to them seeking forgiveness? Now you are threatening to lose your priests, by insisting that they adhere to a rule which no longer makes any sense to them. They have been taught to regard their fellow Christian ministers in other churches as brothers, equals. They see them supported and enriched by happy marriages. They see their congregations uplifted by the example of genuine love in their midst. Why, they ask, can we not have the same opportunity to experience love, and to shine it forth to others?

I come to you without a mandate from my fellow bishops, without a following among my fellow priests. I have spoken to no one about this letter, or about what I am seeking. I have remained true to the vow of secrecy I took when Your Holiness raised me to the cardinalate. I only wish a chance to sit down with you as I was privileged to sit with your beloved predecessor and open my heart to you, to give you advice that I do not believe you are hearing within the walls of the Vatican, to warn you that the Church that we both love, the vessel in which the spirit of God voyages among the children of men, is in danger of catastrophe. Hear me, I beg you, before you speak against the Dutch bishops. Do not become another Pius IX or, worse, Julius II, a name spoken with regret by those who speak with charity, and with execration by those who speak the truth.

Sincerely yours in Christ,
Matthew Cardinal Mahan

He had rewritten it a half-dozen times. It said too much, too much. He should have waited a day, until he was calmer. But it told the truth, the spiritual and the emotional truth. That was what he wanted to do, that was what he had to do from now on.

Beside Matthew Mahan, Dennis McLaughlin tried to make up his mind whether he was frightened or exultant. He exulted to see the vision of his challenge to the papal monarchy suddenly assuming such staggering reality. Events and the courage of the man beside him were catapulting him light-years beyond the world of books. There was no need to take notes, to cite authorities, to elaborate arguments. This was a living challenge.

Then his fright or his fear would take charge. It was not concerned with possible punishment, some unforeseen public humiliation. It revolved around Matthew Mahan as a human being, as a man he loved. From the moment he said those words about going to Rome, Dennis could literally see the torment that began tearing the man apart. It was not simply one conflict, it was several. The smoothie, the man who hated to rock the boat or have his boat rocked, was appalled by the utter unorthodoxy of the act. It was so easy for him to put himself in Paul's place, and ask himself: *What would I do, what would I think?*

The humble bishop, the disciple of Pope John that he had been struggling to become for the past eight months, was equally appalled. Wasn't this arrogance of the worst sort? Who was he, ex-infantry chaplain, ex-hotshot fund-raiser, the nonscholar who barely graduated from the seminary, who was he to come hurtling into Rome to lecture the Prince of the Apostles, surrounded by the world's best theologians? Then there was the loyalist, the man who shuddered at this implied threat to betray the man who had made him a Prince of the Church. Dennis's eyes strayed to the right, and he saw Matthew Mahan fiddling with his Cardinal's ring. The familiar symptom of inner disturbance. It had become acute in the last three days. He was tempted to say: *Why don't you take it off and put it in your pocket?* But it was better, much better, not to let on how much he knew. Perhaps it made his guilt easier to bear.

If Matthew Mahan had slept an hour in the last three nights, it would be remarkable, Dennis thought, eyeing him covertly. His face was ashen. Undoubtedly his stomach throbbed with pain. He watched the big hand with the mass of black hair sprouting from its back move slowly across his belt line. Now they were piling on top of this exhaustion the ultimate barbarity, a night flight to Europe.

"Why don't you take a pill and try and sleep?" Dennis said.

"I never sleep on planes, I'm afraid."

Five minutes later he was dozing. Dennis signaled the stewardess and she took a blanket from the overhead rack and spread it across the Cardinal's chest. Watching the big head as it nodded to one side, Dennis found himself praying. *Dear God, watch over him, please. Give him the strength, give him the strength.* He stared moodily out the window at the stars. What were their chances, really? Weren't you more interested in the attempt than in the possibility of success? He had poured out a lot of his guilt to Helen Reed last night. Calmly, she had told him to endure it.

He *was* guilty. It was marvelous, the way women accepted reality.

Dennis squirmed in his seat. He had been unable to tell her the next thought that had coruscated through his brain. If they failed, and he left the Church to marry her, would his book be worth writing? Wouldn't the author be dismissed instantly as one of those failed priests who was trying to justify his weakness? A gust of desire had shaken him as he kissed Helen last night. Now you are going back to Rome, back to where love and sunshine mingled above the Tiber for the first time. Would it also be where love died?

He fell asleep. He, too, had spent much of the previous three nights staring into the darkness. When he awoke, harsh slices of daylight were cutting through the drawn curtains. The overhead lights came aglow. The stewardesses began passing out orange juice and coffee. The pilot told them they would be landing in a half hour.

"Do you think the baggage handlers are still on strike?"

"I don't know. At least we won't have to worry about four hundred pieces of luggage," Matthew Mahan said.

He shook out some pills and swallowed them with his orange juice. "Hey, that isn't on your diet," Dennis said.

"I know. But I'm thirsty."

His smile was almost boyish. There was a reckless glint in his eyes. "Did you wire Father Mirante to meet us at the pensione?"

"Yes. I'm not sure that was a good idea. If they find out you're talking to him—"

"I know. But we have to talk to him. He knows where Mary Shea—Mary Furia—is."

They made an uneventful landing, passed swiftly through customs, and taxied to the Pensione Christina. Dennis had selected it because it was inexpensive—and the Cardinal could be anonymous there. Father Mirante was waiting for them in the lobby, an especially doleful expression on his sallow face. He went upstairs with them to the single room they had reserved and Matthew Mahan ordered a second breakfast, a glass of milk for him and coffee and rolls for Mirante and Dennis. While they waited, he showed Mirante his letter. He read it swiftly and said something in Italian. Matthew Mahan laughed. "He says I've been seized by a heroic inspiration. That's a polite way of saying I'm out of my mind."

Mirante smiled nervously. "No, no, Your Eminence," he said in English. "It makes me all the more certain that I will return to your archdiocese with you, with your permission."

"You have that already."

Mirante murmured something about personal matters delaying him. "Never mind, never mind," Matthew Mahan said. "What do you think our next move should be?"

"I would call Confalonieri or his deputy. I presume you sent him a copy of this letter?"

"Of course. It's his business, too."

"He's not a bad fellow. But he won't even begin to decide what to do about you."

"Is there a chance of getting to see His Holiness?"

"There's always a chance," Mirante said. "What will happen if you see him and he tells you to go home and keep your mouth shut?"

"I'll go home and keep my mouth shut."

"Are you sure? Or is it possible that your young friend here will persuade you to do something more daring?"

Suddenly Dennis did not trust Father Mirante.

Matthew Mahan asked him if he had located Mary Shea. Mirante nodded. "She is staying at a little convent to which she has contributed a great deal of money. It is on the outskirts of Rome."

"Take me there, now."

It was a long cab ride—almost a half hour down the Via Ostia, the road that Peter and Paul had taken when they first came to Rome. Mary met him in a small bare sitting room, a crucifix on the wall the only decoration. She looked ill. "I'm not sleeping," she said, with a wan smile. "I'm trying to make it this time on prayer. No pills."

He told her why he was here—the clerical reason, first, the letter to the Pope, the imminent declaration on celibacy. "But you're the real reason, Mary. I'm here to tell you something. Something I never thought I would have to tell you."

"What?"

"You've committed a sin. A serious sin."

She shook her head, wide-eyed. "How—?"

"A sin against the Christian ideal—the Church's ideal—of love, Mary. You can't do this to Mike. You can't let a man start to love you the way he loves you—and then turn your back on him."

"I thought it was better to do it now, Matt, than later."

"That's another sin, Mary. A sin against faith."

Her lovely face crumpled. Tears began to flow. He braced himself to endure them. "Matt—if you could have married us. If I felt I had your—your real blessing."

He seized her arms and gave her one fierce shake. "Mary! You have it." Behind those words, he was saying: *Receive ye the Holy Spirit.* "As a bishop of the Holy Roman Catholic Church, I absolve you of all stain of sin in the love of this man. I affirm before God that it is true, good, holy marriage." *Receive ye the Holy Spirit.*

"Oh, Matt."

She crumpled against him. He held her in his arms and prayed once more, *Receive ye the Holy Spirit.* He let go, totally, absolutely forever the wish to hold her, to love her in any other way. Suddenly in his soul there was a soaring joy, like light-filled water leaping from a fountain in a deserted square.

He felt guilty. He searched Mary's face for similar joy. It was not there. "Mary, I cabled Mike. He wants to come here. Come to you."

"Yes."

Her voice was calm. But there was no joy in it.

"Are you—all right, Mary?"

Those old familiar words. She smiled. "Yes, Matt, I'm all right. Are you?"

"Only if you are."

The convent bell tolled, summoning the nuns to chapel. They were surrounded by prayer. Matthew Mahan could only add his favorite plea: *Lord, say but the word and her soul shall be healed.*

Dennis McLaughlin spent the afternoon trudging and riding around Rome in search of his friend Goggin. He wandered through the Biblical Institute in the Piazza della Pilotta, near the Fountain of Trevi. No sign of Goggin there. He taxied to the Villa Stritch on the Via della Nocetta just off the Ancient Aurelian Way, west of the Tiber and the Vatican. He hurried across the villa's beautifully trimmed green lawn to learn from a fat smiling young Irishman from Chicago that "the Fifth Evangelist" was not at home. The Irishman, who said that he worked for Cardinal Wright in the Congregation for the Clergy, and who looked as if they were eating the same desserts, cheerfully hunted Goggin by telephone, and found him at work in the office of the Jesuit general in the Borgo Santa Spirito near the Vatican.

Goggin was naturally astonished to discover Dennis in Rome. "I'll meet you at the foot of the Spanish Steps in fifteen minutes."

In twenty minutes they were drinking *cafe doppios* in a marble-floored, old-fashioned restaurant on a street full of fashionable shops only a block or so from the Steps. Dennis told him what was happening, and Goggin's eyes widened with disbelief. "As the French general said at the charge of the Light Brigade, 'Magnificent, but it isn't war.'"

"I know," said Dennis, "but it may be something better than war. It may be peace."

"Old pal, don't get grandiose on me."

"All right. What do you know about Father Guilio Mirante, fellow ex-Jesuit or Jesuit, take your pick?"

"Nothing," said Goggin, "but I'll do my best to find out a few things."

Dennis told him that he suspected Mirante was working for the Vatican. "Leave it to ye old biblical scholar," Goggin said. "I'll give them my absentminded professor act."

"What else do you hear from your employer?"

"If this was 1570 instead of 1970, there would be a pall of smoke hanging over the Netherlands. The Sacred Inquisition would be buying up firewood all over Europe. It would have been a marvelous opportunity to see how bishops burn. As for *your* employer, he would be in a cell in the bottom tier of Castle St. Angelo, which the Tiber floods regularly."

"Paolo is not happy."

"Paolo and everyone around him are steaming. I spent the morning translating a little something for the radio that will probably be in *Osservatore Romano* tomorrow. It talks about the Church being prepared to use its coercive powers in order to insure the unity of the faith."

"Nice."

"Why don't you retreat to the first century with me while there's still time? We can spring our coup on them without warning. From now on your employer will be anathema. And they won't let you within a hundred miles of any library with archives worth looking at."

Dennis shook his head. "This is more important. This could make your book an official text, a sacred document, instead of an underground classic."

"But politics are so boring." Goggin finished his coffee, stood up, and saluted. "I am off to see the Jesuits."

Back at the hotel, Dennis found Matthew Mahan sitting on the edge of the bed, talking on the telephone. "I'm sorry to hear that Cardinal Confalonieri will be on retreat for the next two weeks. May I speak to Monsignor Draghi, the secretary of the Congregation?

"Oh? He's on retreat, too. Odd that they would go at the same time, isn't it? Well, you tell them that I called. I may still be here when they get back. I intend to stay in Rome until His Holiness gives me an appointment."

He hung up and nodded to Dennis with a grim half smile. "The freeze is on," he said. "Everybody's out of town."

"Including the Pope?"

"No. I haven't called him directly. But I tried calling Villot. I got Benelli, the Substitute Secretary of State. He pretended he didn't know what I was talking about. No, that could be unjust. Maybe he didn't know. Anyway, he said there was absolutely no hope of a break in His Holiness's schedule for at least a month. I asked him to see what he could do to change that, and he got a little unpleasant."

Dennis nodded. "I took a walk and bumped into my friend Goggin, the biblical scholar and part-time Vatican translator. He said they're breathing fire over there."

Matthew Mahan sighed and looked across the Tiber at St. Peter's dome. "Well, we knew it was probably a fool's errand. But let's just sit here for a day or two and see what happens."

Father Mirante returned that night after supper. The ex-Jesuit could not have been more negative. All his friends at the Vatican were appalled by what Cardinal Mahan was doing. No one had heard so much as a whisper about his arrival. Almost certainly, his letter had been routed to the office of the Secretary of State, where Archbishop Benelli, the chief administrator of the department, would take charge of it. He was a fierce combative man.

"How do we get around him?" Matthew Mahan asked.

"There is no way around him, Your Eminence," said Mirante. "He is a colossus. He bestrides the Vatican. No one speaks to His Holiness without his permission."

"Did you tell your friends how serious I was?"

"Of course."

"And their advice—"

"—is go home."

"These are people who are on our side?"

"Assuredly. Insofar as a man is capable of maintaining that position in the present atmosphere."

Mirante departed once more. Matthew Mahan paced restlessly up and down the room, growing gloomier and gloomier. A half hour later, Goggin called. "I've been told our friend is negotiating. He's a baddy. Went sour a year or two ago, started chasing girls. When his superiors tried to straighten him out, he trotted up to Isolotto and jumped on that little bandwagon. He misjudged the temper of the times, oh grievously. He didn't realize that the word was out to get tough. By now I'm sure he's ready to perform all sorts of services for the Prince of this world or anyone else."

"Thanks," said Dennis. "We'll be in touch."

He told Matthew Mahan what he had just heard. The Cardinal sat down slowly in a wing chair and began to nod mournfully. "It's really a little like war, isn't it?"

"Yes," said Dennis, ruefully recalling his overblown words about peace to Goggin earlier in the day.

That night Dennis awoke to find Matthew Mahan stumbling around the room. He turned on his bed lamp and the Cardinal said, "Dennis, I'm sorry. I got completely disoriented in the dark and couldn't find the bathroom. Look at the mess I just made."

Dennis walked around the bed and saw a three- or four-inch splotch of blood on the rug. "Are you—all right?"

"Yes, yes, of course. Nothing unusual. Let's clean this up."

They scrubbed with cold water and towels until there was only a faint stain.

Dennis turned out the light and lay awake in the darkness for a long time, listening to Matthew Mahan move restlessly around his twin bed. Once he took a deep breath and released it in a kind of sigh that made Dennis's heart skip. It must have been close to dawn when Dennis finally fell asleep. He awoke to find Matthew Mahan quietly saying mass on the top of the room's dresser. For a moment he wondered why and then groggily remembered that they had decided before they left to conduct themselves as anonymously as possible in Rome.

Outside the weather was foul. Rain drizzled miserably from the gray sky. People scurried along the street below the pensione, their coat collars turned up against a wolfish wind. "Sunny Italy," Dennis said, staring out the window at the viscous-looking Tiber.

"People have told me you can get pneumonia here in the winter quicker than you can in Chicago," Matthew Mahan said. "Now I believe them."

After lunch, having read *Osservatore Romano* and two or three other dailies, Matthew Mahan sent Dennis out to buy a copy of Pope John's autobiography, *Journal of a Soul*.

"Should I get an extra copy to send to the Vatican?" Dennis asked.

It was as cold and as miserably wet in the streets as it looked. In the lobby on his way back, he met Father Mirante. As they went up in the elevator, Dennis said, "What do you think you'll get if you talk him into going home? A professorship at the Gregorian, perhaps?"

Mirante glared at him as they stepped out of the elevator. "Your career, if it deserves such a term, is finished. You must know that," he said.

"I never had a career."

Dennis started to walk ahead of him down the hall. Mirante seized him by the shoulder and spun him around. "Would you believe me if I said that it is to his advantage as well as mine that he goes home? Do you think it's impossible for a man to act in his own interests and out of love and concern for a friend at the same time?"

The pain on the middle-aged face was exquisite. "I'm beginning to think anything is possible," Dennis said softly.

"He is a great soul. Why do you torment him? You are the evil genius here."

"Evil?" Dennis said. "Compared to you, Father Mirante, I don't think I even understand the meaning of the word."

They walked down the rest of the hall in silence. Dennis handed over the copy of Pope John's journals. Father Mirante launched a feverish monologue in Italian. Matthew Mahan listened somberly, then turned to Dennis. "He says they are preparing to disgrace me. There'll be an accusation that I've misused the finances of the archdiocese. Apparently Leo the Great's columns have traveled far."

"They wouldn't dare. They have more to lose than you in a mess like that."

"Yes. I think so, too," Matthew Mahan said. He looked out the window at the gloomy sky. St. Peter's dome looked forlornly gray. "I should have expected this. But it still hurts."

"They can be petty as well as stupendous," Father Mirante said. "Your Eminence, I see only the futility of this. The danger both to your reputation and your health."

"I know, I know, Guilio. But when it's something your soul summons you to do—"

"Isn't it we that summon the soul?"

"The souls of others. It's seldom—too seldom—that we let our own souls speak. Don't you think so?"

Tears suddenly streamed down Mirante's face. "Yes. Yes." He fell on his knees and clutched Matthew Mahan's right hand to kiss his ring. "Forgive me, forgive me," he said. "I am not worthy of your friendship. I am not worthy of anyone's friendship."

"I don't know what you're talking about, Guilio. But whatever it is, you're forgiven. Not by me. God's forgiveness is always yours for the asking, you know that."

Mirante shook his head. "What does his forgiveness matter when you cannot obtain it from yourself? For a wasted life, a ruined career?"

Matthew Mahan said nothing. He just stood there letting Mirante cling to his hand. On the other side of the room, Dennis McLaughlin thought: I must never forget this moment. The slight Italian, his lined, world-weary face wet with tears on his knees before the tall, somber American Cardinal.

Mirante lurched to his feet and stumbled to the door. "I will tell those bastards that I am on your side."

The door slammed. He was gone. Matthew Mahan looked at Dennis, and sat down to read Pope John. "I'm so glad you found this book," he said after about an hour. "It makes me feel close to him again. I think I told you how close I felt last May. But this time, I only felt his absence."

He sighed and began pacing the floor again. Each time he passed the window, he looked out at St. Peter's dome. "I'm getting mad," he said. "I'm an Archbishop of the Roman Catholic Church. I don't think I should be left sitting here like a pensioner." He paced for another ten minutes. "Paul is so sad. He breaks your heart. If I hadn't taken that vow—"

"Couldn't you argue that it was taken under duress?"

"Now, now. Don't use your Jesuit logic on me. Either we do this straight or it isn't worth doing."

They ate supper. Dennis noticed that the Cardinal barely touched his chicken. He drank his milk, ate a little bread and some canned fruit. "Are you planning a hunger strike?" Dennis said.

"No, I—I'm just not hungry. Actually I feel a little nauseous. Maybe I'm getting a virus."

The telephone rang. It was Mirante. "I am calling from a phone in the street. This is not the conspirator, this is the friend," he said. "Tonight you will be visited by Jean Cardinal Derrieux. Prevent him if possible, my young friend, prevent him from seeing your Cardinal."

"Why? They're friends. He's—"

"He *was* a great liberal. Now a week scarcely passes without him denouncing one of the Pope's enemies in *Osservatore Romano* or elsewhere. He sees Villot on the throne. A French pope. For that, he will do anything."

Dennis hung up. "Who was that?" Matthew Mahan asked.

Lie to him? No, this thing has to be done straight. "Mirante." He told him what the Italian ex-Jesuit had just said.

Matthew Mahan looked both pained and puzzled. "Derrieux? I can't believe it. If he comes, I'll certainly see him. I think Guilio's like a pendulum, swinging from one extreme to another."

At eight-thirty the phone rang again. A voice introduced himself as Monsignor Caspieri. He was Cardinal Derrieux's secretary. The Cardinal wished to see His Eminence, Cardinal Mahan, as soon as possible. Would 9 P.M. be convenient? Dennis passed on the question. Matthew Mahan nodded. "Give him the room number."

Precisely at 9 P.M. there was a knock on the door. Dennis

opened it and Jean Cardinal Derrieux stepped into the room. His face seemed starker than Dennis recalled it. The pinched cheeks, the small narrow mouth, the dominating high-crowned nose, and intense dark eyes had the impact of a knife blade. He wore a red cassock, and a jeweled pectoral cross glittered on his chest. He held out his hand, ring turned upward. Dennis bobbed his head toward it and brushed his lips against the thin, feminine fingers. He got a whiff of cologne. He stepped back and let Matthew Mahan shake hands. He was wearing his plain clerical black without a trace of red on it. "Jean," he said, "I'm glad to see you. If they had to send anyone, I'm glad—"

"I wish I could agree," said Derrieux in a voice with only the hint of a French accent.

They sat down in the room's two wing chairs. Dennis stood against the far wall. "I think it would be best if he left," Cardinal Derrieux said with a sideways nod of his head.

"I see no reason for that. Father McLaughlin is completely aware of why I am here."

"Too aware, from what I hear. Time is short, and we are talking about things too important for niceties. I am told from many who know you, many from your own archdiocese, that you are this young man's dupe."

"I've never heard anything sillier in my life," Matthew Mahan said. "I don't think I am any man's dupe."

Cardinal Derrieux reached inside his cassock and took out a single piece of paper. "I have been given this letter which you wrote to His Holiness. Cardinal Villot, the Secretary of State, gave it to me. He is, of course, horrified by it. So am I."

"Has His Holiness seen it?"

"His Holiness is an old man. Not a well man. It is our task to protect him from this sort of aberration."

There was pain on Matthew Mahan's face. Dennis felt it in his own body, along with anger. *Get mad, get mad. Tell him off,* he begged silently.

"Aberration?" Matthew Mahan said. "I can't believe that you— would say such a thing. One of the great spokesmen for freedom in the Church."

"So you have your freedom," Derrieux said with an almost animal bark, "this is what you do with it. You and your friends in Holland."

406

"I have very few friends in Holland."

"You are prepared to lie as well as threaten?"

"That's a very serious thing to say to me," Matthew Mahan said.

"I say it with the evidence in hand," Derrieux snarled, shaking the envelope in his face. "Do you take us for fools? The Dutch bishops betray the Pope one day, and you join the assault the next day. Without collusion, without any plan in advance?"

"I am prepared to swear on this cross to the truth of what I am saying," Matthew Mahan said, picking up his pectoral cross from the small table between them.

Derrieux gave no sign that he had even heard him. "You people have succumbed to the vilest of all beliefs, the end justifies the means. You will do anything, say anything, to destroy the papacy. You want to rip down in a night what two thousand years of sacrifice have created, the one voice through which God speaks to men clearly, infallibly."

"I am not a theologian. I would not dream of debating with a thinker of your reputation."

"But still you throw down the gauntlet," Derrieux shouted, shaking the letter again. "You presume to lecture the Holy Father."

"I presume to tell him what's in my heart and head."

"Nonsense, my friend, that is what is in your heart and head, vile nonsense. You are the captive of this young mountebank and his generation, who want to stand everyone on his head so they can proclaim the substitution of genitalia for thought."

"I will not allow you to insult Father McLaughlin," Matthew Mahan said in a voice that remained low but was now very tense. "He is a fellow priest, a dedicated fellow priest."

"We have evidence that suggests other conclusions. He has a carnal relationship with an ex-nun, a woman named Helen Reed. Moreover, he connived with his brother to disrupt your diocese. When your most intimate advisers, your chancellor and your vicar-general, urged you to dismiss him, you refused."

"Is that—is that true?" Dennis McLaughlin asked Matthew Mahan.

The Cardinal avoided his eyes. "Derrieux—my friend—" he said with a tremor in his voice, "this has nothing to do with my letter."

"It has everything to do with it. What else could produce this monstrosity but evil, a web of evil in which you have been trapped, my friend, with your tragic American innocence." He pointed his delicate index finger at Dennis. "I see it on his face. Hatred of the Church, of the priesthood. I see it in his eyes. The words are almost on his lips."

Just hatred of you, Your Eminence. With a mighty effort, Dennis did not say the words. He prayed that his face was expressionless.

"This is vicious," Matthew Mahan said.

"Evil, the kind of evil he represents deserves no mercy," Derrieux said.

"Please!" Matthew Mahan brought his fist down on the table. His pectoral cross bounced onto the floor. He picked it up. "Please let us discuss what is in that letter. Let us discuss what is happening to the Church. What will happen unless those warnings are taken seriously. While we sit here reviling each other, we are losing souls, Your Eminence. People are dying spiritually. Some of them sit at the gates of the Church begging while we walk past them, loaded with our spiritual riches. Priests are sitting in rectories watching their vocations dying day by day." He pointed to Dennis McLaughlin. "This young man is a priest. Deeply, profoundly a priest. If he falls away, anyone can fall away, anyone will."

No, no I am not worthy, Dennis thought. *Forget me, forget this absurd love that has happened between us.*

"Your infatuation with this heretic is truly alarming, Your Eminence. It suggests the most frightening thoughts to me. I pray to God for the sake of your soul that they are not true."

He stood up and flipped the letter onto the table top. "The Church, which you see as crumbling, dying, is undergoing a transformation that will carry it triumphantly into a new era of greatness."

He snatched up the copy of *Journal of a Soul.* "We are purging ourselves of the infection of this holy fool. I'm told that you are one of his disciples. Perhaps that is another explanation for this act of idiocy you have committed."

He let the book fall back onto the table with a thud. Dennis heard in its echo the sound of nightsticks hitting bodies, of gavels falling, of guillotines.

Derrieux walked to the door and turned with a royal sweep

of his cassock. "I am told by the Cardinal Secretary of State to give you the following order. Go home to your diocese and write another letter, asking the Holy Father's forgiveness. He will try to obtain it for you. But he guarantees nothing."

He opened the door and strode away down the hall without bothering to close it. Dennis kicked it shut and whirled to face Matthew Mahan. He was eager to explode, to ignite this man with his own anger. But what he saw strangled the hot words in his throat. Matthew Mahan sat in the wing chair like a beaten man. There were no scars or bruises on his face, but his head lolled back against the blue cushions, as if he had been battered by a hundred punches and kicks.

"He was my friend," he said in a small, sad voice. "We used to have coffee together once or twice a week during the council. I used to introduce him as my walking graduate school."

"He's a son of a bitch. A power-hungry son of a bitch," Dennis said.

The sadness in Matthew Mahan's eyes was almost unbearable. "Did you—did you refuse to fire me?" Dennis asked. Matthew Mahan hesitated. Dennis realized he already knew the answer. Blindly he stumbled in another direction. "I mean—how would he know about what the chancellor or the vicar-general said to you?"

"One—or both—have been writing to Rome," Matthew Mahan said wryly. "It's probably George Petrie. I'm sure by now he thinks he can do a better job than I'm doing—and he's probably right."

"No!" Dennis cried. "Remember what you said—about just doing the job. You've been doing so much more than that. Petrie's just too dumb—or too ambitious—to see it."

Matthew Mahan nodded, a sad unconvinced smile on his face. For a moment Dennis felt close to weeping; the next, he was struggling for breath. The room was charged with defeat, disaster.

"You're not going to let him discourage you, are you, that—that clerical De Gaulle?"

Matthew Mahan forced a smile. "No. No. I said we'd stay here until the Pope saw us. We will."

Conviction, strength, had vanished from his voice. "I'm sure the Pope hasn't even seen your letter," Dennis said. "Write a covering note and I'll take it back to the Vatican tomorrow. Hand-deliver it."

"He saw it," Matthew Mahan said. "Why else would I be told to ask his forgiveness?"

Dennis was silent. It was his turn to pace the floor. "That man would lie about anything. He talks about evil, infection. It's all over him like sores. The infection of power."

"Paul saw it, Dennis, he saw it. It had the ring of truth," Matthew Mahan sighed. "Let's go to bed. I feel terribly tired. We can talk in the morning."

By ten-thirty they had both showered and were in bed. Dennis turned out the light and lay there rigid. Sleep was out of the question. Matthew Mahan was apparently doing no better. The springs of his bed creaked every time his big body moved on it. Hours passed. Dennis dozed. Half in, half out of sleep, he heard bells tolling distantly. Then a voice, equally distant, calling: "Dennis. Dennis." It was a dream, of course. The voice was so faint it was unrecognizable. Who was it, his brother Leo? "Dennis—" The voice was half choked now. He woke up. The harsh unmistakable sound of a throat struggling for air filled his ears. "Den—" Gurgling.

He turned on the light and cried out with anguish. Matthew Mahan was slumped against the back of his bed. The shirt of his blue pajamas was soaked with blood. There was blood everywhere. On the pillow. On the sheets. On the floor beside the bed. As he stumbled to his feet, more blood gushed from Matthew Mahan's mouth.

"A hemorrhage," Matthew Mahan whispered. "Bill Reed warned me—" He choked and tried to hold back a mouthful. It burst through his fingers. "Get me to the bathroom—"

"No. Lie still," Dennis cried and snatched up the phone. A sleepy clerk answered after twenty rings. The pensione had no doctor. He was new to the city, a stranger from Bergamo. He knew nothing about doctors. All this in incredibly broken English.

"Call the police then. An ambulance."

"*Ambulanza?*" asked the clerk.

"*Ambulanza. Ambulanza,*" Dennis shouted. "*Presto. Subito.*"

"Get me a towel, Dennis. I'm making such a mess," Matthew Mahan said as he hung up.

He got him a towel. Within minutes it was soaked with blood. "Oh Jesus, where is that ambulance?" Dennis cried.

A knock on the door. The room clerk stood there wide-eyed. "Where's the ambulance?" Dennis screamed.

"*Dottore.*"

The fellow turned and ran down the hall. Dennis realized that he had not called the ambulance yet. He had decided to come upstairs and see if these crazy Americans were drunk or something.

Another towel slowly turning red in Matthew Mahan's clutching fists. Then it was over. No more blood. Over. "Thank God," Dennis prayed frantically.

"Let me get this off you," Dennis said, unbuttoning his soaked pajama shirt with trembling fingers. He stripped it away, threw it into the bathroom. "Can you move to my bed?"

Matthew Mahan nodded and tried to say something. Dennis draped his arm around his shoulder and pivoted his feet over the edge of the bed. His flesh was incredibly cold. When he stood up, his knees buckled. He was like a dead body, a dead man already. The two of them lunged forward and fell onto Dennis's bed. For a moment Dennis lay there crushed beneath his weight, pure terror swallowing him. He struggled free and with an enormous effort managed to straighten him out in the bed. Tenderly, tears streaming down his face, he wiped the blood from his lips and hands. As he drew the sheet up over him, swearing that the doctor had to come soon, Matthew Mahan smiled faintly and whispered, "Anoint me, Dennis."

"What—? No."

"Anoint me, please."

He found the silver vials in their special compartments in the briefcase. He took them in his hands and knelt beside the bed for a moment, struggling for self-control. Then he dipped his finger in the oil and made the sign of the cross on Matthew Mahan's eyes, ears, nose, mouth, hands, and feet, repeating the formula, "By this holy anointing and His most loving mercy, may the Lord pardon you for any sins you have committed—"

"Thank you, Dennis. I would like to go to confession and receive Communion."

No, I can't hear your confession. The guilty cannot forgive the innocent. Of course, he denied the words, took a stole from the

Cardinal's briefcase, draped it around his neck, and knelt beside the bed. "My deepest and most inveterate sin has been pride," Matthew Mahan said. "I struggled against it. But it has a thousand disguises. As soon as I thought I had expelled it from my soul, it was back again with a new voice, a new demand. I've also struggled, usually in vain, to forgive those who hurt or attacked me. I loved the power and the privileges of my office too much. I thank God for having made me aware of this—but it was almost too late. I ask his forgiveness for those earlier years of self-indulgence."

At first, when Dennis tried to speak the words of absolution, they froze in his throat. A wave of sobs racked his body. Then he heard a voice that did not belong to him but to his priesthood saying, "I absolve you from your sins, in the name of the Father and of the Son and of the Holy Spirit."

From a small watch-shaped silver pyx he took a white Host. He filled a glass with water and put it on the night table beside the bed and then placed the Host on the Cardinal's tongue. He tried to swallow it and began to choke. The water saved him.

"Thank you, Dennis," he whispered. "Now we have nothing to fear, nothing to worry about."

"Where is that ambulance?" Dennis cried.

The room clerk was back in the open door. He babbled in Italian. Dennis could not get a word, until he repeated three or four times *sciopero, sciopero, sciopero.*

"What does it mean?" Dennis asked Matthew Mahan.

"Strike," he whispered. "The ambulances are probably on strike."

"Call the Villa Stritch, Father Goggin," Dennis said.

He scribbled both names on the back of the title page of Pope John's book. The clerk fled once more.

"I don't think it matters, Dennis," Matthew Mahan said. "That's too much blood—even for a fat man like me—to lose."

"No. You're going to be all right. I know it."

"Dennis. Don't blame yourself. We came a long way—together. I knew the risk. I knew it all the time."

The phone rang. It was Goggin. Dennis frantically explained what was happening. "I'll get a taxi. I've never been sick here. But someone must know where a doctor—"

Dawn was turning the sky from glossy black to furtive gray. Traffic began roaring in the street below. Dennis thought of rushing to the window and screaming for help.

"Did I ever tell you what Pope John said to me, the day he consecrated me bishop?" Matthew Mahan said.

Dennis shook his head.

"He said—he said he would be the first to greet me in Heaven. Is there anything to worry about—when you have that kind of a promise?"

"The Church—the Church needs you. I need you."

"Don't be—too anxious about the Church, Dennis. Take your time. We have our Lord's promise. Tell them the truth in your book—but be patient if they don't hear you."

"The hell with the Church! No—I don't mean that." He struggled to control himself. "Are you in pain?"

"No. No pain at all."

For some reason those words struck Dennis like the tolling of a funeral bell. There was no hope, no hope at all. Incredibly—he would reproach himself bitterly for it a moment later—his mind leaped beyond this claustrophobic room where death was strangling his naïve vision of the future. He saw himself writing to Helen Reed, telling her with nausea in his throat that the choice, the brutal choice must be made, and he was choosing his priesthood instead of her. But he knew even as the amputation wracked him that he alone was the sufferer, that Helen no longer needed him, she had reached that inner circle of healing love. He had reached it, too, thanks to this dying man beside him.

Matthew Mahan had closed his eyes. Within the darkness he seemed to be voyaging across a vast sea. There was a sense of flowing, as if he walked or rode a current in its center that carried him toward a blurred horizon. At times the sea was turbulent. He was carried up toward an angry sky on great waves of regret. One after another, his failures surged up through his soul. His brother's wounds, which he had never healed. Monsignor O'Reilly's hate-filled soul, which he had tried too late to purge. The young priests to whom he was at best a fool and at worst a corrupt authoritarian. Father Disalvo with his hysterical rage. Timmy, his nephew, with his twisted heart still contorted with loss and hate. The divorced, the lonely, the poor in spirit, the lost sheep whom he had failed to seek strenuously, all the things he had never said to so many priests and friends, never warned George Petrie against the keenness of his ambition or Terry Malone against his opinionated anger or Dennis, yes, even Dennis, against his intellectual pride. So many failures. Why was there at the same time this incomprehensible peace?

He opened his eyes and saw Dennis McLaughlin's tear-stained face. Behind him, although he knew they were not there, he saw Mary Shea and Mike Furia and Jim McAvoy, dumb but brave. Who knows what would have become of Jim if he had not helped him discover his courage in France? And Bill Reed and his daughter Helen, the last two not sad at all, but smiling. Did they already know what he had never really understood—that love was so terribly difficult, it was almost a miracle to achieve it even with a single person. What an incredible challenge the Church had taken upon herself, to tell men and women that this unique achievement should be universal and that she, the Church, would discover and teach the secrets of the spirit that make it possible.

There were other faces beside the bed now. Dennis's friend Goggin looking frightened and a stocky swarthy man with a black bag. He heard their voices saying disconnected words. "Exsanguination—transfusions—ambulance." He felt the doctor's hand on his wrist. Then the metal disk of the stethoscope pressed to his chest.

"*Ambulanza. Subito. Subito.*" Goggin was telephoning private ambulance services.

"It's all right, Dennis, it's all right," Matthew Mahan whispered. "Just hold my hand."

He felt the smaller hand inside his fingers. He tried to close them, but there was no strength left. No strength, no pain. Behind his closed eyes, he saw a wide white beach, the kind he had walked with his father as a boy. The air seemed full of bells ringing out a song of praise. Whom could it be for? Then the beach vanished. One of those fogs that used to roll in unexpectedly between sunrise and mid-morning. It was ghostly, but he was unafraid. The air was still full of bells. He heard a soldier's voice calling, "Padre, hey padre," and an Irish brogue greeting him with : "Matthew me boy." Then the clipped harsh American accent of an umpire saying "Matty." Finally a voice that came to meet him in the mist: "*Mio figlio americano.*" My American son. With it came strong peasant hands that seized him, rough familiar arms that crushed him to an unseen chest, while unseen lips touched his cheek. He knew that he was safe in the land of his fathers.

XXXIII

"*Troppo tardi, troppo tardi,*" Dennis McLaughlin heard the doctor saying. He turned and saw two big men in the doorway, with a folded stretcher between them. Goggin had found a private ambulance service. Too late. The doctor was telling them. Too late.

It was 6 A.M. The bells of Rome were ringing. Through the gray dawn he could see the looming hump of St. Peter's dome. Dennis looked down at Matthew Mahan. Strangely, he felt no grief. They had been defeated, utterly, totally defeated. But he felt no grief. Why?

Dennis spent the day filling out the endless forms that governments require when shipping a dead man across borders, finding an undertaker to prepare the body for the trip, persuading the city officials to waive an autopsy, sending cables to the archdiocese, fending off reporters with the ritual "No comment," haggling bookings for himself and the Cardinal's coffin on the first available flight.

The grimmest task was telling Mary Furia. She cried out with pain when she heard it. "O God, it's my fault, my fault," she sobbed.

"No. It was mine," Dennis said. Then he spoke as a priest. "But really—neither one of us did it. He knew. He knew what he was doing."

It was mid-afternoon by the time he and Goggin returned to the pensione. On the corner, Dennis picked up a newspaper that had a large headline announcing something about "Il Papa." Goggin rapidly translated. Paul had refused to consult the Church on clerical celibacy, as the Dutch bishops had requested. Celibacy "cannot be abandoned or subjected to argument," the Pope said.

"The Emperor has spoken. But the case is not closed," Dennis said.

"Why doesn't somebody see that he has no clothes on?" Goggin said.

Upstairs, Matthew Mahan's body lay on the bed. Mary Furia knelt beside him. The undertaker had dressed him in his red cassock and cape. The brown metal coffin waited in the hall flanked by two burly assistant undertakers. "I trust you are satisfied, Father," said the undertaker, a short, fat man who sweated profusely.

"Yes," said Dennis.

"Shall I—?" the undertaker began.

"I feel the need for a ceremony," said Goggin.

"Make it short," said Dennis, still puzzling over why he felt no grief.

Goggin took from his pocket a small looseleaf book and paged rapidly through it. Dennis realized it was a draft of the New Gospel. Goggin stood at the foot of the bed. Mary Furia stood on the right. Dennis stood on the left. Matthew Mahan's face was empty. Death was truly a thief, Dennis thought. It robbed everything, even the personality.

Goggin began to read.

" 'What is this talk of being a shepherd?' the people asked Jesus. 'We are not sheep, to be led to the trough or to slaughter as you choose.'

" 'You are sheep in your needs,' said Jesus. 'In the hunger of your hearts for my peace. You are sheep in your blind worship of lust and money. You are sheep in your hatreds. You are sheep in your endless fears for tomorrow. You are sheep in your loneliness. This is why I say that I am the good shepherd, who sees that he must lay down his life to feed his sheep with the truth of his love. My father loves me because I lay down my life that you may take it up again more abundantly. No man takes my life away from me. I am laying it down of my own will, so you may have power to take it up again. This commandment I have received from my Father.'

"A dispute rose among the people over these words.

"Many of them said: 'He is possessed by the devil, he is mad. Why do you listen to him?' But others said: 'These are not the words of the devil. Can the devil open the eyes of the blind?' "

Dennis looked out the window at St. Peter's dome. In his pocket, his index finger slowly circled the outer spiral of his moon shell. "Amen," he said. "Amen."